D1162735

WITHDRAWN

Other books by Kim Heacox

BIOGRAPHY
Shackleton: The Antarctic Challenge
Visions of a Wild America

NATURAL HISTORY ESSAYS
AND PHOTOGRAPHY
Alaska Light
Alaska's Inside Passage
Antarctica: The Last Continent
In Denali
Iditarod Spirit

Caribou Crossing

A NOVEL

Kim Heacox

BALDWIN PUBLIC LIBRARY

Copyright © 2001 Kim Heacox
All rights reserved.

This novel is a work of fiction. The events described are
imaginary, and the characters are fictitious and not intended
to represent specific living persons. Any references to real events,
establishments, organizations, people, or locales are intended only
to give the fiction a sense of reality and authenticity. Other names,
characters, and incidents are either the product of the author's
imagination or are used fictitiously, as are those fictionalized
events and incidents that involve real persons.

Page 3, Bull caribou in Kobuk National Park, Alaska
Photograph by Kim Heacox

WINTER WREN BOOKS

An imprint of Companion Press
Santa Barbara, California
Jane Freeburg, Publisher/Editor

Printed in the United States of America
First Edition, 2001

ISBN 0-944197-70-1

Notes on Capitalization

The word arctic should be capitalized as a geo-
graphic region, yet in this book it appears in lower
case to distinguish it from the Arctic National Wildlife Refuge. Wilderness established by Congress (by
authority of the 1964 Wilderness Act) is capitalized to differentiate it from wilderness as a general
condition of an area.

LIST OF CHARACTERS

ANZA AMERICA
Alan Quail, Chief Executive Officer
John Sires III, Deputy CEO
Maya Donjek, lobbyist & linguist
Charles DeShay, geologist (early retirement)
Captain Carl Zarki, Chief of Security, Anchorage
William Alt, security guard, Anchorage

U.S. SENATE
Oliver Longstreet, Senator, Alaska (R)
Tyler Kyle, Chief of Staff
Jeff Meola, legislative aide

Sam Matlin, Senator, Alaska (R)
Jude Matlin, daughter & college student
Kelly Calvert, Chief of Staff
Harry Arnold, press secretary
Shannon DeShay, legislative aide
Denali Sisto, legislative aide

Bruce Janstadt, Senator, Minnesota (D)

U.S. HOUSE OF REPRESENTATIVES
Jack Worley, Representative, Alaska (R)

THE WASHINGTON POST
Gil Trebideaux, Editor-in-Chief
Lowell Hutchinson, Managing Editor
Mark Meadows, reporter
Tony Carzoli, reporter
Rollie Dawson, freelance photographer

FEDERAL BUREAU OF INVESTIGATION (FBI)
Liam Bristol, Deputy Director
Lincoln Crozier, Special Agent

PARKENDALE INVESTIGATIVE SERVICES
Johnny Parkendale Jr, President

"We thought, because we had power, we had wisdom."

–Stephen Vincent Benet
Litany for Dictatorships

KIM HEACOX

PROLOGUE

(nine years earlier)

She walks to the river with her boots unlaced and finds him sitting crosslegged on the hard earth, coffee cup on his knee, head tilted, squinting that squint of his. A rock hammer rests idle on his belt. Stratigraphic maps remain rolled and unused in his tent. The reluctant geologist, he nods at her, an almost imperceptible nod. Aching to be like him, she sits without a word and lets the river do the talking.

Tendrils of fog have advanced in the night and burdened the tundra with dew. No sign of the arctic sun in its long and languorous arc. This fog has tenacity and she welcomes it, as it keeps the ANZA helicopters away, those shrieking Cretaceous birds that descend into camp and steal his soul. The fog came from the north, off the Beaufort Sea, and knocked temperatures down twenty degrees. Still, she knows where the mountains are, the broken spines of rock, the open steppe and treeless tapestry, the constellations of wildflowers, all charted in the chambers of her heart.

She allows it to comfort her, this ancient river, always moving, always there. She was named for a river in Ireland she has never seen, a famous waterway lacquered with topsoil and tears and the bitter trials that brought *her father's father here. She believes that rivers are saints that care for the lost and wounded; that when mountains become hills and forests burn to the ground, rivers carry it all away, all that is lost and given to the sea. Only if the world were flat would rivers die.*

Nothing is flat here. The Brooks Range, the North Slope, the talus and scree and cutbanks and cliffs. If Ireland was ever like this, like the first day of creation, it was a long time ago.

The river has receded in the night and pulled back its shores. Of course night is a different beast here. It dominates in winter but hides in summer, six months of darkness followed by six months of light. He told her once that every spot on the earth receives the same number of hours of light in a year, it's just distributed differently. The equatorial regions settle for little seasonal variation while the arctic indulges and abstains. The June solstice sun rolls to the north and bridges dusk with dawn in an unbroken borealis of ambers and pastels, arctic light so compelling that after a couple days she stopped going to bed at a civilized hour, for civilization means nothing here. Instead she stayed up all night, drinking the light, falling asleep at hours she didn't record or count.

He sees something in an eddy at the river's edge; dips one hand in and pulls it out, cool water pouring through his fingers. Hundreds of gray hairs pattern his wet palm. She takes one and feels its coarseness between her thumb and forefinger. He looks upriver into the fog, back into his hand, back upriver.

—Musk oxen? she asks.

—No. Caribou.

Again he looks upriver to where the muted green tundra disappears into the fog. A quarter mile visibility.

—How many? she asks.

—A lot.

Ten minutes later they move fast. She is strong and can keep pace with him on the gravel river bar. But once they climb onto an alluvial terrace beset with ankle-twisting tussocks, she falls behind. He seems to glide along as she stumbles at half his speed. Up ahead, he stops and listens, tilts his head in that special way, moves on. When the fog threatens to separate them, he stops and looks back. She struggles on unseasoned legs, but he must conclude that she is not disheartened, as he turns and continues without her acknowledgment.

She joins him on a bluff half an hour later. He motions her to keep low.

Over the rise the river comes into view, a silver ribbon wreathed in fog. He smiles a deepness she didn't think possible. His face seems—what? What is happening?

—Do you see them? he asks.

—No. She searches through the fog. No, I don't.

—Close your eyes and listen, he says. Let them come to you.

She finds herself holding her breath, close to him, nearly touching, lost in stillness and magic. A distant rhythm moves the ground, one river crossing another, unbounded, unbroken, the last of its kind. After several minutes she looks at him and sees that his cheeks are wet with tears. It is the only time in fifteen years she has seen him cry.

—Dad, are you okay?

—No, Shannon. But I'm better than I was.

Winter

December

ONE

The first skyscraper in the last frontier climbed thirty stories above downtown Anchorage and made no apologies to antiquity. Framed in steel and gilded in glass, its windows rested at elegant angles to capture the Chugach Mountains to the east, Cook Inlet to the south, Mount Susitna to the west, and the Alaska Range to the north. Rare was the passerby who didn't turn to admire the building that had appeared on a dozen covers of architecture and business magazines. The Chamber of Commerce intended to make it as much an Alaskan icon as Mount McKinley.

Beyond the lobby, entrance was by invitation only.

On this snowy Saturday night the Fifth Avenue driveway bustled with arriving cars and parking attendants who met them with holiday cheer. Despite the weather, turnout for the annual ANZA Christmas party would be strong. Everyone who was anyone among the Anchorage cultural and political elite had been invited.

Outside, three flags fluttered on tall poles that flanked the ornate doors. From the middle pole flew the Stars and Stripes. To one side flew the state flag of Alaska. To the opposite side, equal in height with the others, flew a flag showing an elegant fossil leaf within the sun, the emblem of ANZA AMERICA, the largest oil conglomerate in the world. Floodlights illuminated the flags amid falling snow that faded skyward into a winter penumbra. A lavender sign between the building and the adjacent parking lot read: ANZA AMERICA: TO STRIVE, TO SEEK, TO FIND, AND NOT TO YIELD.

The parking attendants, all sons of ANZA executives, were high school boys who greeted each car, handed the driver a claim tag in exchange for the keys, and drove the car into the parking lot. As the traffic increased, the boys devised a game to see who among them could park a car and run back to the entrance the fastest.

No wonder that none of them noticed the building's northeast corner where a sheet of black plastic had been wrapped over a floodlight to dim the wall. The surrounding footprints would have been a giveaway, but no one noticed them either. And each passing minute lessened the odds as falling snow erased the tracks and their route from the floodlight through the terraced shrubs to the corner of the building where a dark figure, crouched like a cat, uncoiled a rope.

TWO

"C razy kids," William Alt mumbled to himself from behind his security desk. He watched the attendants out the window, running and slipping on the icy parking lot, pelting each other with snowballs. The window afforded him an incomplete view, but enough to see that one attendant, the responsible boy named Tom, stood aloof from the frolicking.

For the hundredth time William surveyed the ANZA lobby with his gray turbid eyes. He studied how the arriving guests came through the door in their expensive clothes and starched manners, how they admired the Christmas tree and the framed Stonington and Doolittle prints, how they walked across the lobby to the security desk. He offered a warm smile only to mirror their own warm smiles, and spoke only when spoken to. He recognized politicians, broadcast journalists, industrialists and educators from television and the newspapers, all accompanied by ANZA executives. He imagined these people as royalty, and wondered about the totems and taboos in their lives, who they loved and who they cheated. Never did he think he could have such a job as this, yet here he was the guardian of the gate, a graduate of the

ANZA Security Academy of Houston, Texas, second in his class, working his first swing shift on the most important night of the year.

After signing at the desk the visitors proceeded through an arched metal detector buttressed by shatterproof glass, and beyond that to elevators programmed to run continuously between the lobby and the penthouse, on the thirtieth floor. From his desk William controlled a Doyle-Ballard 90-SSA Netcom Security System that monitored every high security room via motion, heat and laser alarms. While the south and east lobby walls gave him partial views of Fifth Avenue and the parking lot, the north and west walls offered elegant designs of Italian marble and Indonesian black walnut. Often when alone on night shift he would run his fingers over the dark wood and wonder about its distant origin. He had served in Seoul with the U.S. Army and found a passion for woodcarving. When off duty he visited carving shops where little old men worked ankle-deep in teak and mahogany shavings and spoke in bird-like voices. Soon he began to carve there himself. The old masters apprenticed him, and laughed at his early attempts. But he learned quickly and started dating the granddaughter of one of the carving masters. A fragrant girl, she had skin like rose petals. Just touching her made him dizzy. Then one night everything ended when two drunkards attacked him on the street. The petal girl screamed and William broke a man's neck. The Army held a court-martial. ...*On the charge of murder, the members of this court find the accused, Corporal William Alt, not guilty*...

William snapped from his dark reverie when the lobby doors opened and Carl Zarki entered with a woman and another couple. Zarki was William's boss, chief of ANZA Security, mid-fifties and medium built. William considered him stern but fair, a private man not given to climbing social strata at pompous parties.

"How are things tonight, William?" Zarki asked.

"Fine sir."

"Is the day shift report finished?"

"Yes sir." William searched a shelf under the opposite end of the desk while Zarki signed in. The report was not where it should have been, and this flustered William, who couldn't get his mind off Korea. He finally found it and handed it to Zarki, who leafed through the pages while the other three signed.

William said nothing, his eyes watchful, separated by a broad, flat nose. He licked his dry lips.

Zarki perused the final page and handed it back. He noticed a dozen guests enter the lobby. "Good turnout for a snowy night," he said.

William nodded.

"Okay young man, keep up the good work."

"Yes sir. Enjoy the party."

The foursome proceeded through the metal detector and into the elevator. More guests arrived. The lobby filled with reunion and laughter, men shaking hands and women kissing cheek to cheek until a loud thud truncated the gaiety and everybody fell silent. William stood to see a man in tattered clothes pushing his way through the Fifth Avenue doors while two parking attendants restrained him by his legs outside. The man fell as the heavy doors closed against him like pincers and he yelled in a drunken slur, "Let me in, damn it. I'm cold."

A crowd of onlookers stared in mute disbelief.

"Damn it, let...me...in."

William secured his desk and radioed Jerry, his partner, thirty floors above, to tell him his plan. He locked down the elevators with a command key and walked across the lobby to the huge doors. "Everybody stay where you are," he said in a deep voice. "This will only take a minute."

Winter drunks often attempted to find warmth in the ANZA lobby. Throwing them out was more than routine for William, it was sport. Tonight he would need to curb his enthusiasm under the watchful gaze of ladies in red fox fur and gentlemen in Armanis. He regretted that his audience was without Carl Zarki, as he intended to make a good show of things.

William grabbed the drunk's hand and twisted at the wrist.

The drunk yelled in pain. "Out you go," William said as he raised him to his feet and wrenched his arm behind his back. He escorted him out the doors and shoved him down the steps, certain he would fall. But the drunk kept his balance and skidded feet first on the sidewalk below. William stared at him. He was difficult to age: forty-five, maybe forty. He wore Army surplus fatigues, an old torn and oil-stained parka, a loose wool hat, a destitute war vet look. That was the problem. It was a *look*. His face was flushed red but his eyes were clear. Was it whiskey or the cold or a good act that made him so ruddy? He began to climb the stairs as two more cars arrived. Twenty guests milled in the lobby, agitated by the delay.

William turned to the attendant named Tom, whom he knew as an eager apprentice in the ANZA Young Leaders League. "Do you remember the security procedure you learned in September?"

"Yeah," Tom said.

William tossed him the terminal command key. "Go sign the people in, check their names off the invitation roster and unlock the detector and elevator by inserting this key into the E-eight command. You comfortable with that?"

"No problem." Tom had worked at ANZA for two summers as a courier, then as a bright star in the AYLL, learning the security basics under Zarki's mentorship. He dashed inside as the drunk, halfway up the steps, turned and headed back down.

William collared him. "Not so fast, buddy. It's time we had a little chat."

"Whazzat?"

William held him at a distance and looked at the three other parking attendants. "You, you and you, get these guests inside. Now."

The attendants jumped to action as the drunk squirmed in William's grip and said, "C'mon man, give a guy a break."

William pinned him against the wall, a strange man who didn't grimace or resist or complain. He just wore a goofy grin. "Who are you?" William asked him.

"Uhhhhh…"

William smelled his breath, sweet but unrecognizable. And that grin. He pinned him harder. "What's so funny?"

"Nothin' man." And somehow everything. His eyes were too clear, his teeth too clean, his nerves too steady. A little voice told William that nothing would be the same after this night, like that other night in Korea. …*On the charge of conduct unbecoming a soldier in the U.S. Army, the members find the accused guilty as charged and recommend that he be dishonorably discharged.*

"Get lost," William said as he shoved the drunk down the stairs. This time he landed on his back but executed a perfect shoulder roll. *Who is this guy?*

He climbed to his feet and brushed himself off with absurd nonchalance, as if he were an Edwardian gentleman who'd spilled cigar ash on his best tweed suit. He began to walk away.

"Hold it," William shouted as he went down the steps after him. But in an instant the man broke into a run, his legs pumping like a locomotive as he disappeared into the darkness and falling snow.

The dark figure climbed quickly and quietly with the hardware of a mountaineer: carabiners, webbing, seat harness, chest harness and two jumars. Polypropylene liners protected the fingers. A balaclava covered the head, leaving only the eyes visible behind clear goggles. Layers of black Spandex and Polartec covered the torso, legs and arms. The first twenty feet were the most vulnerable, for although the north wall was solid and dark, the east wall was lobby glass that emitted enough light to brighten the outside terraces and street. A passing pedestrian would only have to stop and look skyward, blinking snowflakes from the eyes, to see the dark figure—more like the shadow of a human than a human itself—climbing a fool's errand up the concrete and steel corner of the tallest building in Alaska.

THREE

For as long as she could remember Shannon DeShay found solace in the snow.

Years ago she and Travis would play fox and geese in the front yard, running through trails four feet deep. Dad built castles of snow with tunnels and turrets and bright bandanas fashioned into flags that flew from the highest battlements. There among the colors stood Shannon, a wooden sword in her hand and a wool scarf around her neck, ready to vanquish infidels and barbarians. The snow fell unmindful of her fantasies now, nearly twenty years later. It still touched her that the darkest season should bring the whitest gift. But her past would need to fade before her future could take her to Washington. Snow mended things and slowed things down, but snow also melted.

She sat at her bedroom window and watched it fall, unconcerned about the minutes ticking by. A gust of wind threw the flakes into wild spirals. A deep drift formed along one side of a broad birch, a delicate patina along the other side. Her Eskimo friend Eddie Tagarook once told her that when you live with winter your entire life, you have many words for snow, twenty or thirty words with edges and icy consonants she once knew but could no longer remember.

Mom called from the kitchen in her thin, serrated voice.

Shannon grabbed her overcoat and breezed down the hall to her father's room. He lay motionless in a custom-built bed, his head propped up by pillows, his eyes fixed on the television. She touched him and felt her heart break as it always did seeing him like this. No number of months or years would change that. She squeezed his atrophied arm and stroked his scalp. He didn't laugh anymore, didn't tell stories or burst into song or play a sly game of cribbage. He just lay there, existing not living, his beard shaved off to keep spilled food out, his hair thinning and eyes far away, his head traumatized from the brutal impact of skull on steel. It was enough to deny Christ and God, as Shannon had done for awhile. But her Catholic heritage prevailed—Mexican mother, Irish father—and in time she accepted misery like salvation, a thin wafer on her rascal tongue. Among the oaths taught to her by sandal-footed Franciscan monks in Mexico, she harbored one of her own: never cry like your mother.

"Shannon, let's go. It's getting late."

Shannon whispered into his ear. "Mom and I are off to mingle with the ANZA royalty. Stay out of trouble, okay?" He blinked, and for a moment Shannon thought she saw him smile. But of course she knew such things were too easily imagined.

They backed down the driveway in silence, mother and daughter, Susan and Shannon DeShay, oil and water. Shannon drove as the snow fell in blinding curtains and the windshield wipers struggled to keep up.

"It's horrible out," Susan announced.

Shannon preferred weather to climate and reminded her mother that deep snow would founder moose and help wolves.

"You know I don't care about such things, Shannon."

"Dad does, or he did."

"Yes, well, let's not get into that."

Shannon pulled onto the Seward Highway at a crawl. Clouds

of snow billowed around them.

"Go slower," Susan said.

"I'm only going thirty, Mom."

They passed two accidents attended by police officers, with patrol lights flashing and flares burning. Susan turned the rearview mirror toward her to apply lipstick, lifting her chin as the headlights of an approaching car illuminated her. Shannon realized it was furtive, half-lit glances like this, not the shadowless reign of common hours, that unveiled her mother as Susannah Solorzano, the alluring debutante who nearly thirty years ago had titillated a young geologist named Charles DeShay on the parquet dance floors of Mexico City. Charles had come south to study volcanoes, and in Susannah he found one. Their courtship lasted a month. The day after they married, Susannah shortened her name and her temper. A year later Travis was born, Susan's perfect son, and three years after that, Shannon, her imperfect daughter.

Susan added yet more perfume under her ears, dabbing it on with her little finger. Shannon shook her head. *Good grief, Mom, it's one thing to wear perfume, it's another to marinate in it.*

"What?" Susan asked, seeing her daughter's reaction.

"Nothing."

Susan twisted her mouth. "I thought you were going to wear that Victoria's Secret dress I bought for you last year." She was anxious to see Shannon married and pregnant.

"It's a Christmas party, Mom, not a high school dance."

Susan fumed for a minute, then said, "I spoke with Sam Matlin today. He's found an apartment for you in Georgetown."

"I know."

"I suppose you'll share it with Jude."

"I suppose."

The former mayor of Anchorage, Sam Matlin had just been elected to the U.S. Senate, and had offered Shannon a position on his legislative staff. Jude was his daughter.

"Did Jude offer to guide you around the party tonight?" Susan asked.

"Yes."

"Don't stand in her shadow. She's a showboat."

"She's excited about moving to Washington."

"There's lots of crime in Washington."

Shannon opened her mouth to speak but Susan forestalled her with a raised hand. "I know, Sam's very persuasive."

"He's a politician."

"Yes, well, I've always liked him. He was good to Travis."

"He gave him his first guitar."

"Yes, his first guitar..."

Shannon drove past midtown and let her mother fall into her customary silence after any mention of Travis. Shannon finally said, "The storm is lightening up."

"What?"

"The snow. It's lightening up." She paused, then said, "I'd go to Washington even if you didn't want me to."

"I know. Maybe you'll find a nice man there."

Translation: find somebody rich. Shannon had heard this before when she traveled with her mother to Mexico City and suffered the smog and prattle of señoras and señoritas who folded towels and sipped tea and talked about titled men and marriage like characters in a Jane Austen novel. *Women who run with rabbits.*

"Shannon, do you see that stoplight?"

They skidded into the middle of the intersection. A lone car approached from the right and turned slowly past them.

"What's wrong with you?" Susan snapped. "I swear you don't belong to this world sometimes."

Shannon put the car in reverse and backed up.

Susan exhaled loudly and rubbed her temples. "I asked you to stay home all these years until your father got better, and it hasn't been easy, I know. I just thought he'd get better."

"So did I."

"You worked hard in Sam's office. He thinks a lot of you. His offer is a nice one." Susan paused, then added, "I've decided to put your father in the Mount Susitna Care Center."

Shannon nodded.

Her mother stared at her. "You knew?"

"It works both ways, Mom. You know what I'm up to and I know what you're up to. We're a family."

Susan responded in a hollow voice, "I suppose we are...just the two of us, a family."

Shannon turned onto Fifth Avenue and thought about her father wilting away in a nursing home with dozens of other sick people, slipping deeper into the half-life of the dying, a sad husk of the robust man who once knew rivers and caribou and tundra and bears.

Susan said. "Oh look, there's the ANZA Building. Isn't it beautiful?" Her soft Mexican accent cajoled the word into *buoyoootiful*.

Shannon shook her head, thinking, *Dad loathed that building. He called it a monument to money.*

~

William reviewed his desk. Twenty-five people had passed through security while Tom manned it. Everything seemed in order. But William knew he had erred. He told Tom to say nothing to Captain Zarki, and radioed Jerry with the same instructions.

The rush was over and the lobby clear when Susan and Shannon DeShay entered. *At last,* William thought.

Susan marched straight to the desk while Shannon studied the Bev Doolittle camouflage prints. The mother was heavier than William remembered, the kind of Latin woman who loses her beauty when she stops fighting the dessert table. What intrigued him about Shannon was how she looked like her brother.

Six years ago William had slipped into the cathedral during Travis' funeral, wanting to say something, to express any fraction of the greater whole of his secret debt to Travis. But words would only get in the way; *they always did.* He remembered Shannon as a lanky tomboy then, ill-suited to a woman's finery. How dashing she looked now with her black hair in a braid, her thin waist and sienna skin and Irish angles in the cheeks and jaw. He could see her confused eyes trying to register his stare as she signed in.

He watched her walk through the detection gate with her mother, then enter the elevator. As the doors closed Susan turned to Shannon, and William heard her ask, "Do you know that man?"

Jumars set. Carabiners checked. Harness adjusted. Fishing line affixed to a clever device two floors below. The dark figure took two deep breaths, hoisted the metal ball overhead until the line was taut, and heaved it outward into the physics of arc and acceleration. For a moment the wind stilled and the snow fell in elegant cascades, and the parking lot seemed miniscule below. The ball was not heavy, five pounds at most, but it followed its path as faithful as a moon and developed tremendous force as it accelerated toward triple-pane glass and the element of surprise.

FOUR

The elevator door opened and Shannon stepped into a glass-walled anteroom where a man wearing white gloves and a top hat took her coat. A second man handed her a glass of Dom Perignon. A third opened the French doors as she and Susan entered an evening of ANZA opulence. Susan knocked down her champagne in two quick gulps and grabbed another from a passing steward. Her words rang in Shannon's head: *Do you know that man?*

The security guard, brick-faced, military-cut, cloudy-eyed. *Who was he?*

Shannon quickly forgot him as she absorbed the scene before her: the penthouse—the entire floor—beneath a vaulted ceiling festooned with ribbons and lights; music drifting from a dance band, hundreds of voices in a merry din of chatter. She saw Sam Matlin at a distance, as he did her. They exchanged waves.

Years ago, before Dad's accident, when Sam was like an uncle to her, he would greet her with smothering bear hugs. But these were formal times and professional matters, and she expected nothing more than 50a warm handshake. A robust man with a

28

deep voice and a crop of rusty hair that receded across his ample brow, Sam was a so-called New Republican—fiscally conservative, socially moderate—who enjoyed wide popularity as a two-term mayor of Anchorage. Soon he would enter the national arena and take Shannon with him. "Things will be different in Washington," he had told her. What he exactly meant by that, she didn't know.

Jude appeared at Shannon's side, half in and half out of a tight-fitting teal-trimmed dress that left little to the imagination. Jude's mother had always believed her daughter was a prodigy, a prodigy of what she didn't know, so she had tried it all. Jude the baby pageant beauty queen, Jude the ballerina, Jude the concert pianist, Jude the actress. With her mother as producer and director, Jude had breezed through childhood never actually being a child, but rather a miniature adult besequinned in blue ribbons and trick pony outfits. Her only regular childhood friend had been Shannon. For years they read the same romance novels and listened to the same music. Shannon taught Jude to run through the woods and jump creeks and identify birds, while Jude taught Shannon about male anatomy and filterless cigarettes. Their paths diverged in high school when Shannon spent her summers in the arctic, and Jude hers in theater programs back east. They remained friends, yet each understood the other would chart the chasm between them with her own maps and compass.

"C'mon Shan," Jude said as she grabbed her arm, "I gotta show you around this place." Jude had been to many ANZA parties; for Shannon it was a first.

They navigated through chairs and sofas fronted by glass tables and perfectly potted poinsettias. Chandeliers sparkled overhead, Christmas ribbons crossed the ceiling, tinsel brightened the windows and floor. Along the walls stretched elegant buffets on white tablecloths with red candles, sprigs of cedar and endless platters of turkey, salmon, halibut, king crab, medallions of broiled caribou, cheeses and a vast selection of drinks.

The band played a Latin beat and Jude pretended to dance.

She had her father's rusty hair and full face, yet her mother's Mediterranean nose and small bones. She was shorter than Shannon and possessed little athleticism, but flaunted a womanhood that bordered on seductive when she drank. It occurred to Shannon that Jude was always center stage in a play nobody was watching. After all those years of grooming she was just another unprodigal daughter, a mediocrity. *Like me. Except in the arctic. Nothing is mediocre in the arctic.*

Jude grabbed a king crab leg, nibbled it, tossed it half-eaten into a Waterford crystal bowl, and escorted Shannon down the table.

"Is Oliver Longstreet here?" Shannon asked about Alaska's senior senator.

"No, but some of his staff are. I'll introduce you when the time is right. Oh look, there's Jack Worley and Pastor Rainey."

Alaska's only delegate in the U.S. House of Representatives, Jack Worley had been elected to a tenth term on a ticket of rewriting the Endangered Species Act to protect business more and wildlife less. People called him Kodiak Jack because he once guided bear hunters on Kodiak Island. Joshua Rainey, Anchorage's best-known televangelist, preached an anti-abortion, anti-gay, AIDS-as-the-wrath-of-God sweatfest every Sunday to his fundamentalist congregation. Dressed impeccably, with his hair combed back and slicked down, he reminded Shannon of the salesman who if he can't sell you salvation, would you be interested in a used car? She wondered if he would remember her or her father. She heard them discussing guns and bears as she and Jude approached. Jude said, "Congressman Worley, How are you?"

"Hello Jude. Nice to see you."

Jude introduced Shannon. Handshakes all around. Worley and Rainey congratulated Jude on her father's victory. The pastor turned to Shannon. "Aren't you Charles DeShay's daughter?"

"Yes, I am."

"How is he?"

Shannon said he was fine. Her father's accident had been front-page news six years ago. Jack Worley said, "I remember that accident. That was your father, the ANZA geologist?"

Shannon nodded. She didn't trust Worley. He had the accoutrements of civility—silver-rimmed glasses, a double-breasted blazer, hands washed of cigar stains and bear blood—but she knew him to be a pit bull.

"What you may not know, Jack," Pastor Rainey said to lighten the moment, "is that Charles DeShay attended one of my sermons once. It was an interdenominational Easter service at Kincaid Park. Were you there, Shannon?"

"Yes."

"Well, Father Benjamin had spoken and it was my turn, and I decided to speak on the prophets one by one, and I suppose I went on a little too long, over an hour or so, and I got to Isaiah and said, 'Isaiah, what shall we do with Isaiah?' And Charles stood up and said, 'He can have my seat, I've heard enough.'"

Worley threw his head back and roared with laughter, his teeth flashing gold. Pastor Rainey chuckled, and Shannon found herself admiring him for a deprecation she would have thought beyond him. Jude launched into a story to win back her thunder, but was interrupted when others arrived in the circle. With everyone distracted, Shannon slipped away, tired of playing Salieri to Jude's social Mozart.

Time for chocolate. She drifted about, pleased with her anonymity, nobody calling her name or probing her past. She walked through a cloud of cigar smoke that burned her eyes.

The wind shifts campfire smoke into her, the sharpness of burning willows. She takes a sudden short breath as years fall away. She opens her eyes on the tundra.

—Do you see them? he whispers on the bluff above the river.

—Yes.

It is a shaman's dream, a concert of caribou, tens of thousands of animals moving single file, braiding over the terrain as if they too, like the waters they approach, were a river. They come from the west, the source of all great Ameri-

31

can visions. *They move with ancient purpose, and seem not so much to cross the land as to emerge from it, born from the tundra itself. One minute she can see thousands, the next minute none. When they reappear they seem more of a mirage than the truth. At the river's edge the large bulls hesitate and shake their antlers.*

—Watch closely, he says.

The cows arrive with their calves gamboling on three-week-old legs. Ever watchful, they inventory the river, its rapids and false promises and subtle signatures. One cow plunges in, her calf right with her. Others follow. Dozens, hundreds, cows, calves, bulls.

—It's the mothers that lead, she says.

—That's right. They know where their calves can make it and where they can't.

The waters are swift and carry the caribou downstream. They swim boldly toward the shore below Shannon and her father, and struggle up the steep bank. They emerge through a tangle of willows and shake themselves dry, then with what Shannon can only describe as exuberance, they run upslope with their heads high and mouths open.

—They're drinking the wind, he tells her. Stay low. Don't move.

They charge by in a grand procession, thousands upon thousands of them, pounding the earth until time itself means nothing and Shannon feels herself sinking into the tundra, her heart beating with the primitive percussion of hooves.

—This is the way it used to be, he says, when bison and antelope and wolves and bears owned Kansas and Nebraska, the Dakotas, Montana, California.

Every day thereafter, whenever she closes her eyes, even with a blink, she sees caribou.

The cigar smoke tearing her eyes, Shannon grabbed a fork and plate and hovered over the dessert table: cherry and apple pies; vanilla, German chocolate and carrot cakes; dozens of kinds of cookies; nuts and fudge. While pondering where to begin, she became vaguely aware that somebody had sidled up next to her.

"Paralyzed by possibilities?" he asked.

She cocked her head at him; his thin frame and blond tousled

hair that needed a comb, better yet a cut; his w
slightly askew on a narrow, intelligent face that
tawny beard; his gray oversized suit with a pink
tie.

"So many choices," he said. "You look like yo
by possibilities." He had a pleasant, uncontrived
musical in its inflections.

"You're right." She eyed the German chocolate

"I'm partial to these little guys." He grabbed a
and popped it into his mouth.

She placed a piece of cake on her plate.

"German chocolate," he said, "a good choice."

Who is this guy? She turned his stare back onto hi
unabashedly and asked, "Do you work for ANZA?"

"My father did."

"Ah." He nodded.

Before he could ask another question, Shannon sa
for Mayor Matlin these last couple years while I fini
gree."

He seemed to weigh her words with eyes older
of him; eyes focused on some distant place. He rem
the uncomfortable conformist who would still marc
sing Bob Dylan songs, and stick flowers into the ends
Guard rifle barrels. "Your degree?" he said. "What in

"Geology and political science."

"Geology and political science? That's unusual."

So are you.

He chewed his cookie. "I've always thought there
thing as political science. Political analysis, but not p
ence."

"It's an oxymoron," Jude said as she joined them, as
stranger from head to toe as she tossed back her tarni

"An oxymoron," he said, "like mournful optimist."

"Jumbo shrimp," Jude shot back.

He grinned. "Pygmy mammoth."

"Pygmy mammoth?" Jude stammered. "There's no such thing."

"There was in the Pleistocene," Shannon said.

"The what?" Jude looked mildly befuddled.

"Hog futures," the man said with a grin.

"Progressive imperialism," Jude retorted, back on her feet.

Intimate strangers, Shannon thought of herself and her mom.

"Senate ethics," the man said.

Jude put her hands on her hips. "Senate ethics isn't an oxy-moron."

"Sure it is," he insisted.

"I disagree."

He shrugged. " 'I may not agree with what you say but I'll efend to the death your right to say it.' Voltaire said that. Or vas it Rousseau?" He looked at Shannon.

"Voltaire was French," Jude quipped.

"He was?" —that grin again— "I thought he was from Chi-ago."

"Studs Terkel was from Chicago," Shannon corrected him.

"Oh, that's right." The man grabbed another pecan sandy and oopped it down. A dusting of powdered sugar lingered on his lip. He attempted to look sheepish, but Shannon could see he was ull of mischief.

Jude blushed. "Who are you?"

"Mark Meadows." He offered a piece of fudge to Shannon. She accepted.

"Mark Meadows," Jude said in a searching voice, "the *Wash-ngton Post* reporter?"

"Guilty as charged. And you're Jude Matlin, the senator's daughter."

"That's right."

He turned to Shannon, "And who are you?"

"Shannon DeShay, political analyst and amateur geologist."

Jude stepped forward and was about to ask Mark to dance, and Mark about to ask Shannon, when the music stopped and a silver-haired man stepped on stage and walked to the microphone.

"Who's he?" Mark asked.

Jude said, "That's Alan Quail, CEO of ANZA, one of the most important businessmen in the world. I'm surprised you don't know that."

On cue from Shannon, Mark dabbed the sugar off his lip.

Quail raised his hands for silence. "Good evening ladies and gentlemen, families and friends of ANZA..." He spoke no longer than Lincoln at Gettysburg, and in that time summarized the value of every ANZA employee, the commitment to community, the excitement of exploration, the importance of national security and the future of Alaska. His voice pitched and fell with perfect magnetism as he swept the audience across the moral canvas of the American Dream. He reminded everyone that eighty-five percent of Alaska's state revenue comes from oil, most of it from ANZA's operations at Prudhoe Bay, where production was declining. But a new dawn awaited just one hundred miles east of Prudhoe Bay, in the 1002 Area of ANWR—he pronounced it "Anwahr," short for the Arctic National Wildlife Refuge—where a hidden elephant waited to power the engines of progress. That elephant being the most promising on-shore oil field in North America, perhaps as big as Prudhoe Bay. The 1002 Area, so much oil you could almost smell it. "ANZA appreciates your support and congratulates the winners in our recent elections, especially our new Senator Sam Matlin. God bless America. God bless you all."

The crowd erupted with applause, and a circle of admirers widened around Sam as he nodded and waved.

~

William stared at the flashing alarm on his security desk. Room 2622 had a window breach. Floor twenty-six was one of only two floors rated at maximum protection. The other was twenty-eight. He entered VISPROG 2622, and his monitors instantly showed images from two cameras mounted in the room.

"Guard, this is control," William called on his radio.

Jerry responded from the penthouse anteroom. "Guard here."

"We've got a live window alarm in room 2622, northeast corner. Visuals show a hole in the window. Motion sensors are negative."

"Okay," Jerry said. "Clear me on elevator three."

William decoded elevator three, which had been set to stop only at the lobby and thirtieth floor.

Jerry descended to the twenty-sixth floor and walked swiftly down the wide, lighted hall. Every door was locked, as required, since most of the offices belonged to senior executives and contained exploration results, leases, taxes, royalties and other ANZA cards held close to the corporate chest.

Jerry reached room 2622, paused outside and listened. Hearing nothing, he typed a ten-digit code on the keypad. The door unlocked and he entered. William watched on the monitors as Jerry made a sweep of the room and found a hole about one foot in diameter in the corner window, surrounded by dendritic cracks its full width and height. Jerry looked out and saw a blizzard of snow. Turning back, he spotted a black ball opposite him on the floor, smashed against a desk. He walked to it, crunching broken glass under his feet. He radioed William, "Control, this is guard."

"Go ahead."

"Looks like the damage was done by a metal ball of some sort. It's got aircraft markings on it, and fishing line."

Aircraft markings? Fishing line? William was about to respond when the console alarm signaled a window breach in room 2820, two floors above Jerry. *What the hell?* Motion sensors sounded, then temperature sensors. William activated his monitors, but they flashed back, DAMAGED.

"Shit." William quickly reversed the tapes for room 2820 and found forty seconds of a dark figure coming through the window, wearing a harness and moving cat-like to neutralize both cameras.

"Guard, this is control. Move like hell, Jerry. We've got an intruder in room 2820. Repeat, an intruder in room 2820, two floors straight above you, northeast corner. Probably armed."

"I'm on my way."

"Get up there and wait for back-up. I'm calling the APD."

William dialed 911. In thirty seconds the Anchorage Police Department had three patrol cars en route to the ANZA Building.

~

Jude bubbled, "I thought Alan Quail's speech was tremendous."

"I thought ANZA was more interested in getting into the Caspian fields in Baku, in Azerbaijan, than into the Arctic Refuge," Mark Meadows said.

"So did I," Shannon added.

Jude grabbed Mark's hand. "Let's dance."

Shannon watched them disappear onto the floor. She grabbed a third piece of fudge as the music stopped for another announcement, this one from a junior ANZA executive who invited everybody to view the ANWR 1002 Exploration Display at the far end of the room.

~

Jerry checked his .44 Magnum revolver as he exited the elevator on the twenty-eighth floor and moved rapidly to room 2820. The door had a small window. Glancing in, he saw the intruder. "Control, this is guard," he radioed softly, turning down the volume.

"Control here," William answered.

"I'm outside 2820. I can see the intruder. Looks like a small guy, dressed in black."

"Hold up, Jerry. The cops will be there in a few minutes."

"Shit, William, I can handle this guy. He's a twerp. He's kneeling in front of a vault with his back to me. Looks like he's monkeying with the laser alarm. I'd better get in there."

"Stay where you are," William commanded. But he wasn't in command. The two men held equal rank and authority in a situation like this. ANZA procedure called for Jerry to wait for the police. "Hold your position Jerry. Jerry, are you there? Jerry?"

Jerry turned off his radio, decoded the keypad and opened the door. He held his .44 revolver in his right hand, supported by his left, and aimed at the intruder. "Freeze."

The intruder remained kneeling, facing the vault, motionless, his back to Jerry, hands hidden. He appeared to be wearing a mask.

"Did you hear me?" Jerry said, his voice hard. "I want you to cross your wrists behind your…behind your…" Jerry felt a weird tickle in his throat that quickly turned into a dry burning. His eyes watered and his nose felt on fire as he struggled to focus. "I want you to cross your wrists…" He was overheating, claustrophobic. He couldn't concentrate or make sense or see anydamnthing. The fire inflamed his throat and eyes and ears as a strange orange gas surrounded him. "I want you to…What the hell…?"

Acrid air poured into his mouth. His watery peripheral vision caught somebody moving to his left. He swung to shoot but something hit his forearm; pain shot through his elbow and the gun sailed away. Jerry threw a left hook and fanned the air as a sharp blow landed to his solar plexus. He wheezed and stumbled. *I can handle this guy…I can handle this guy.*

Another blow hit him in the ribs. Wobbling, coughing, crying, he fanned the air again and felt a sharp, nauseating pain in the groin. He doubled over, knees together, arms crossed, still on his feet. *Shit, William…he's a twerp.*

A final powerful kick to the head and everything went black as Jerry Levy fell, unconscious before he hit the floor.

FIVE

O il is so abundant here," said an ANZA executive as he swept his hand over the 1002 Exploration Display, "that it naturally seeps to the surface of the tundra."

Dozens of guests gathered around as a caterer walked among them serving halibut and salmon. Another followed with refills of champagne.

The three-dimensional display stood waist high and was tilted five degrees for optimum viewing. Illuminated by overhead track lighting, it showed Prudhoe Bay to the west, the Brooks Range to the south, the U.S./Canada International Boundary to the east, and the Beaufort Sea—part of the Arctic Ocean—to the north. In the center was the 1002 Area, a strip of Coastal Plain roughly eighty miles long by forty miles wide. Oil Country.

Dressed in charcoal pin stripes and a red power tie, the executive explained that while most of the refuge was designated Wilderness and closed to development of any kind, the 1002 Area was not. The name 1002 came from the Alaska National Interest Lands Conservation Act of 1980, Section 1002, that specified the Area be exempted from Wilderness and studied for its promising petroleum potential. If Congress would pass a drill bill and the President sign it, the Area would be open for exploration and production.

Precisely how much oil was a mystery. A single test well drilled by ANZA ten years ago on a KANAK Native Corporation inholding within the 1002 Area remained the most closely guarded secret in the American petroleum industry. From surface and seismic data—not as reliable as a test drill—geologists had estimated eight billion barrels. A bonanza.

"Extracting that much oil will require a couple decades and will employ more than seven hundred thousand people," the executive said. "It will mitigate our nation's reliance on OPEC, and jump start our economy, and build a bright future for Alaska."

Shannon noticed that he used the active verb, *will*, not its past tense and weaker cousin, *would*, as if opening the 1002 Area to big oil was inevitable. She studied the display. It showed the Area painted in greens, whites and blues to depict tundra, ice and rivers. She recognized the Canning, Hulahula, Kitvik and Jago Rivers, braided, wild and northbound. More than geographical features, they were her friends; she'd rafted them all. The Canning and Hulahula emptied into Camden Bay, where loons built their nests in June's midnight light.

—Yellow-billed loons, her father says, the northernmost species. Common loons usually don't get this far north.

They sit together, cross-legged, cool air pooled in their laps.

Shannon says, I don't think any bird should be called common.

—Oh?

—Common makes the bird sound ordinary or unwelcome. I don't think there can be too many loons. Can there?

—No, Shannon, I suppose not.

—Loons aren't ordinary.

Neither are you, dear girl.

On those same boreal shores he teaches her the dialects of ptarmigan, sand-

piper and plover. In the foothills he finds a wolf den, and with Shannon approaches on hands and knees to watch the pups play. He falls asleep, wakes up hours later, and there she is, still watching, chin on her hands, baseball cap backward on her head, black hair spilling out, bandana tied to her beltloop. They climb ridges and camp in the rain and greet breaking storms. He rolls onto his back and drinks from the vast bowl of July sky.

—Listen, he says. Do you hear that?

—What?

—The arctic silence. It's so profound, so deep; it's more of a presence than an absence.

"...And now for the future," the ANZA executive was saying. "I would like everyone to pay careful attention as the sun sets on the 1002 Area of the Anwahr Coastal Plain."

Jude and Mark joined Shannon. Accompanied now by CEO Alan Quail, the executive rotated a dial that dimmed the lights above. Everybody leaned forward as night appeared to fall over the arctic. Then a single switch illuminated the display with a brilliant grid of lights. A collective gasp rippled through the crowd.

"Welcome to the future," Quail said. "Imagine flying into this region ten years from now. It's dusk and the lights below represent the culmination of decades of arctic technology, the Anwahr Coastal Plain full-leasing and drilling scenario."

"It's beautiful," somebody said.

"Incredible!"

"Better not let the environmentalists see this."

"On the contrary," Quail said. "We intend to let the entire world see it. We intend to march it into the full chambers of the House and Senate. Isn't that right, Jack?"

"That's right," Congressman Worley said from the crowd. He stood next to Pastor Rainey, holding a glass of champagne.

"We have nothing to hide," Quail continued. "All the technology perfected at Prudhoe Bay will be used here. This will be the most sophisticated and environmentally safe oil extraction operation in the world."

Shannon felt a knot in her stomach.

The illuminated display showed one hundred miles of road and three hundred miles of pipeline cutting across the Coastal Plain, fifty to sixty drill pads punctuating the tundra, each connected by pipeline and road to central production facilities; two major airstrips, two minor airstrips, two seaports and two seawater treatment plants, half of them in Camden Bay.

Somebody asked Quail, "What are the chances of getting Congress to approve this?"

The crowd quieted. Everybody knew that previous efforts to open the 1002 Area had failed in the wake of the Prince William Sound oil spill. A poorly focused national energy policy didn't help. Environmentalists would introduce their own bill to designate the area as Wilderness, closing it to oil exploration. It promised to be a nasty fight. By an outrageous twist of geography and fate, a remote slice of northern Alaska had become a focal point where two great forces, each convinced the other was morally bankrupt, were destined to clash in ways neither could fully predict. The 1002 Area had become an arctic grail.

"We've financed studies on the caribou and tundra ecology," Quail said. "It will all be protected and safeguarded for the future, and life as we know it will not end. It will be better."

People raised their champagne glasses in salute.

Shannon felt a hand gently touch her shoulder. She looked around to see Mark Meadows, his eyes periwinkle blue.

She stared back at the display. It depicted major topographic features and rekindled fond memories, but it failed, didn't it? She allowed herself the acknowledgment. *It fails to capture the spirit of the place, the honesty a landscape speaks when appreciated not for what it can become, but for what it is. Simply for what it is.* She realized the genius of the display, a clever ruse of colors and forms enhanced by bright lights to look as though ANZA's presence would actually *improve* the place.

"Yes," an ANZA executive was saying to a rapt group of listeners nearby—the large crowd had fractured into many smaller ones

— "every road and drill pad will be constructed on gravel beds to absorb the freeze-thaw effects of permafrost. As you know, the ground fluctuates with changes in the seasons."

"Where will you get the gravel?" a woman asked.

"From borrow pits along the rivers," the executive said.

"You intend to put it back?" Mark asked him.

"The gravel?"

"Yes. You said 'borrow pits.' Does that mean that when you're finished with it you'll put it back where you found it?" His hair was still tousled, his dinner jacket two sizes too large.

"Yes, we'll put it back."

Mark nodded.

The ANZA man said to the crowd, "Wildlife habitat will actually be diversified and improved by our construction, since the roads and drill pads will be elevated and will create dry spots for nesting ptarmigan and other birds. The pipelines will be raised in some places and buried in others to accommodate the caribou."

Mark said, "Once you take that much gravel from the beds of those arctic rivers—forty to fifty million cubic yards of gravel, if I'm not mistaken—you *really will* return it to where you got it? All those years later, after the oil is pumped out?"

Everybody stared at him.

Mark shrugged. "That's a lot of gravel."

The ANZA man casually straightened the cuff of his suit.

"My estimate might be too high," Mark added. "I've been told millions of times not to exaggerate."

More stares.

"Another thing," Mark said, "congressional rules of protocol will forbid you from showing this display in the full chambers of the House and Senate, and in committee rooms. It's too big."

"I don't think so," the ANZA man said.

"Check the rules book."

"Who are you?" asked another man, shifting the knot in his tie.

"He's a reporter with the *Washington Post*," Jude said.

There was a pause as everybody absorbed this.

A tall woman blinked through her heavy eyeliner and asked, "Are you aware that the United States imports more oil than it produces?"

"I am," Mark said.

"Don't you think that's dangerous?"

"I think it's more dangerous that five percent of the world's population uses thirty percent of the world's energy."

Shannon suppressed a smile. Jack Worley and Pastor Rainey stepped into the ring. Besotted with champagne, Worley appeared half a bubble off level.

"Merry Christmas, congressman," Mark said.

"Causing trouble on both sides of continent, Mr. Meadows?"

"Just in search of the truth."

Worley snickered, "Ah yes, the truth, the credo of every East Coast journalist who thinks he knows more about Alaska than Alaskans. And what exactly is the truth?"

Mark thought for a moment. Shannon was amazed by his serenity.

"I'll answer that," Alan Quail said as he cut through the crowd. "Truth is conformity to knowledge, fact, actuality or logic." He stared at Mark with deep, knowing eyes.

Mark said, "Truth is also the enemy of power."

"The enemy of power?" Quail responded contemplatively. "I like that."

"Sounds like Karl Marx," Worley added.

"Edward Abbey," Mark said, "from his last book of essays."

Worley rolled his eyes, slightly bloodshot.

"You disagree?" Mark asked him.

"The industrial footprint in the refuge will be very small," Worley said.

Mark stroked his tawny beard. "This term 'footprint' fascinates me. Robinson Crusoe lived alone on an island and was at peace until he found the footprint of another man—just one footprint—and his whole world changed."

"It changed for the better," Worley said.

"Maybe it did. But I wonder if solitude will someday be more valuable than gold."

Or oil, Shannon thought.

"You don't know all the facts," a man from the crowd told Mark.

"If he doesn't know all the facts," Worley said, "he can't get confused by them."

People chuckled, but not Alan Quail.

Mark studied him and said, "I thought you were more interested in developing oil ventures in Baku than in arctic Alaska."

"Don't read everything you believe," Quail told him.

"You mean don't believe everything you read."

"No, I meant what I said. It's valid both ways."

Mark offered a modest smile. "So it is."

"The trouble with people like you," Worley said to Mark, "is that you crave a past you wouldn't want to live in. How did you get here tonight? Not by car, because cars use gasoline. You must have ridden a bicycle."

"I rode a magic carpet."

Jude laughed—a cackle. She was the only one who did.

"A magic carpet?" Worley said. "So you floated into the lobby and up the elevator?"

"It was too crowded. I landed on the roof and came down the chimney."

Nobody laughed.

Pastor Rainey said, "I don't understand you journalists today. All that interests you is conflict. If you'd been around two thousand years ago, I think you would have covered the Crucifixion and missed Christianity."

Mark nodded. "You're probably right, pastor."

"Maybe it's time to reinvent the American press," somebody said from the crowd.

"How so?" Mark asked. He seemed to be enjoying this.

"Rewrite the First Amendment," Jude said. "It's an idea that shouldn't be tossed aside lightly."

"I agree," Mark said. "It should be heaved out with great force." Jude scowled.

"What the hell is wrong with you?" Worley barked at Mark, his face crimson. "Don't you understand..."

Shannon didn't hear his words, only his tone and anger and hot breath...

—*They died in battle, her father tells her, shaking his head at the knotted antlers.*

Shannon runs her fingers along the veined bone, tracing the antlers to the sharp tines. She tries to pull them apart, but cannot. Two sets of antlers, skulls still attached, bleached in the sun, locked together on the tundra, the remains of two bull caribou that jousted so viciously, so uncompromisingly, they couldn't undo the knot they tied, a knot made of hard antler and stubbornness. And so locked together, they died.

—They both lost, her father says; men are like that. The bitterness in his voice alarms her as he walks away.

"Bullshit," Worley barked at Mark, "There's no evidence of that."

"Easy Jack." Pastor Rainey restrained him. "Don't let him provoke you."

"He already has, dammit." Worley glared at Mark as he gulped his champagne and spilled half onto the floor. Shannon refocused on the argument.

Rainey intoned, "Remember, the meek shall inherit the earth."

"But the strong will get the mineral rights," Mark said.

"Damn you." Worley lunged at him and the crowd gasped.

Mark sidestepped the ponderous congressman as a matador would a bull. Worley slipped and fell hard to one knee and screamed with pain. "Whoa, Mr. Worley," Mark said, "I think my karma just ran over your dogma. Get hold of yourself, man."

The crowd froze with disbelief.

Alan Quail pushed through the crowd and said, "That's

enough, everyone. Let's break this up." He pulled Mark aside and said, "I don't remember seeing your name on the guest list. Were you invited to this?"

"No."

Carl Zarki suddenly appeared at Quail's side. "Then how'd you get in here?"

"I came in a rental car and parked it in the lot. Your corner floodlight is out, by the way, and I think you should credit Alfred Tennyson for the motto."

"What motto?" Quail asked with distracted irritation. The crowd lingered, listening to every word.

"The motto on your sign," Mark said. "'To strive, to seek, to find and not to yield.' It's from Tennyson."

"No, it's not."

"Yes, it is," Shannon said. "It's the last line in his poem about Ulysses."

Quail looked at her; everybody looked at her.

Caribou: the only species in the deer family where the females grow antlers.

"What the hell is all this bullshit?" Worley screamed from his sitting position on the floor. "Goddammit, somebody kick that journalist outta here. He screwed up my knee."

Zarki dispersed the crowd.

Five minutes later, Shannon found herself in the company of Sam Matlin, his avuncular voice soothing her, his arm around her shoulder. He had pulled her far from the fray and was introducing her to some people. She tried to focus. Oh yes, Jeff Meola, she knew Jeff from the University of Alaska. And Maya Donjek, and Harry Arnold... "Maya and Jeff work for Senator Longstreet, and Harry used to," Sam was saying, "but he's joining our team next month. Isn't that right, Harry?"

"That's right, senator." Harry was bald and clean-shaven except for a full black moustache.

Shannon embraced Jeff, her old friend, who was short and slight, like Harry, but didn't look well. His face was pale, his hands were cold, his posture rigid. Stomach flu, he said; the cramps had begun after dinner about an hour ago. As she watched him walk away to the men's room a voice from behind said, "It's a fine act, don't you think?"

Shannon turned to see the woman named Maya, her golden hair brushed back from a widow's peak above unblinking emerald eyes and a narrow nose. She wore a flowered dress open down her back. A feather of a woman, she seemed to be built of shafts and quills. "You have an interesting name," Shannon said, regretting the comment the instant she said it.

"It's Polish."

"What do you mean 'a fine act?'"

"Have you ever known Jeff Meola to be sick?"

"No."

"Neither have I." Maya's bejeweled eyes offered only facets that changed with each subtle turn of her head. The lines in her neck appeared as delicate as the ribs in a leaf. "Your father is Charles DeShay?"

"Yes. You know him?"

"Not really." Maya looked away, as if more through time than distance. Another turn of her head, another facet. When she looked back she appeared lost, and said vacantly, "Things aren't always the way they seem."

Shannon changed the subject. "Do you like working for Oliver Longstreet?"

"I did. I work for ANZA now." Maya offered no reciprocating inquiry, but instead seemed bored, as if this conversation had degenerated into prattle, a waste of her time.

Harry Arnold burst their bubble. "Champagne?" he asked as he extended a glass to each. They declined. He shrugged, chugged one full glass, then the other. Shannon wondered which of them he was trying to impress. The exotic Maya, no doubt. She detected an ionized energy between them, a language of valence and innuendo. She scanned the room for Mark Meadows.

Jude leaned over from a neighboring conversation and said, "What do you think the cops want?"

Shannon followed her gaze to the glass-walled anteroom where two police officers spoke with Alan Quail and Carl Zarki. Urgency filled their faces as they stepped into the elevator.

~

"He's okay?" Quail asked.

"We think so," an officer answered. "The paramedics said he's got a concussion and maybe a couple broken ribs, like he got beat up by the Karate Kid or something. He's down in the lobby now. We found him unconscious in the hall with a gas mask on his face."

"A gas mask?"

"The corner room is full of pepper gas. It'll knock you on your butt if you open the door."

"Corner room, twenty-eighth floor?" Quail asked.

"Yep."

Quail pursed his lips. "Let's have a look."

"Better not," the officer said. "You can't enter the floor without setting your eyes on fire."

"Stop at twenty-eight," Quail demanded. "This is my building. I have jurisdiction here."

Zarki said nothing. The officers shook their heads and covered their faces with handkerchiefs. A second later the elevator doors opened at twenty-eight and the four men erupted into coughing and gasping. "Close the doors," Quail yelled.

Half a minute later the doors reopened and the four men staggered into the ANZA lobby, coughing and gagging. "Shut down this elevator," Zarki sputtered at William Alt. "Open the lobby doors and keep them open. Flood the lobby with fresh air."

William turned a key to lock down elevator three. The parking attendants opened the lobby doors. A woman detective walked up to Quail and threw a glass of water in his face. Quail felt shock followed by immediate relief as his burning eyes cooled. She gave him a second glass to drink. Zarki received the same treatment.

"We're worried about this pepper spray invading the whole building," she said. "What's your ventilation system?"

"Central heating, central ventilation," Zarki said. "We've got to evacuate everybody as soon as possible."

"I agree. The fire department is en route."

"Who did this?" Quail asked.

"We don't know. Your security man's got the intruder on tape. Looks like he climbed up the outside of the building like Spiderman and busted through the window."

Karate Kid? Spiderman? What the hell? Quail shook his head and rubbed his eyes, still red from the pepper spray.

"So where is this Spiderman now?" Zarki asked.

"Probably still in the building. We've had it surrounded for ten minutes. There're no fresh tracks in the snow below his climbing rope outside. We've got six units here already, including a K-9. We'll need to secure the entire building."

Zarki walked over to William at the main desk and asked, "Did every guest sign in tonight by standard procedure?"

"Yes sir," William lied.

Zarki turned to Quail. "I recommend an immediate evacuation with everybody signing out as they signed in."

"The K-9 should sniff-search the guests as they leave," the woman detective said.

"No," Quail said. "Some of the most important people in Alaska are up there. I won't have them herded out like cattle and sniffed by a damn dog."

"You're willing to let the intruder slip away with everybody else?" Zarki asked.

Quail stared at the dog, a handsome German shepherd, and said, "Evacuate them, watch them for anything unusual, and do it graciously."

"And the dog?" the detective asked.

Quail shook his head. "No dog."

~

Shannon found her mother and told her they had to leave. Lines formed at the elevators as the crowd speculated about the problem. Quail announced that it was a ventilation mishap, a terrible inconvenience. Very sorry. He rubbed his eyes.

Shannon spotted Jude with Harry Arnold and Jeff Meola; Maya Donjek with the Matlins and a hobbling Jack Worley. All by himself, eating a pecan sandy, was Mark Meadows.

~

William Alt and Carl Zarki watched four hundred guests sign out and exit the building past the restrained police dog. Parking attendants retrieved cars as fresh air blew through the front doors and cooled the lobby to forty-five degrees. Zarki placed the videotape of the intruder in an evidence bag, sealed it and signed it. Two fire trucks arrived. Zarki decoded access to the stairwell and four firemen in full gear began the long climb to the twenty-eighth floor. Two more police units arrived as the guests watched and muttered to each other. Mark Meadows was detained for an extra five minutes, then released. In less than an hour every guest had departed the building, and Quail and Zarki had filed reports with the police. Zarki asked William if all the guests were accounted for? Yes. Did the signatures match? Yes.

Two officers then invited Zarki outside to where a sheet of black plastic had been tied around a floodlight. The men looked into the sky with snow falling into their eyes. Maybe the parking attendants knew something about this.

William watched from his desk as Zarki, the two officers and the four young attendants spoke on the steps outside the lobby doors. The attendants began to act out something. One fell halfway into the lobby and flailed his arms on the floor while two others held his legs. A feeling of dread tightened in William's throat as he saw Zarki kick a door in anger, then walk toward him, his eyes grim.

~

Thirty-three hundred miles away in suburban Maryland, just
north of Washington D.C., a small man sat in his small apartment and drowned the rain with Beethoven's Fifth Symphony,
Andante con moto bridging C minor to C major, cellos reaching
beyond their bass-line function, the music of madness and genius. The only light came from his computer screensaver, where
DIGITAL UNTOUCHABLE scrolled across the monitor, red on black.
He folded one milky hand over the other and closed his eyes
against the filth and decay of liberal America. The clock on his
desk read 3:30 a.m. The symphony ended. He opened the computer file, wrote for another hour, finished his six-page treatise
and e-mailed it to his colleagues in Idaho and Alberta. They would
understand. "End of privacy" meant the end of freedom; "global
village" meant world cultural homogeneity; and most important,
"collateral action" meant revenge.

He dozed for one hour, awoke at five, took the early Metro
to Capitol Hill and was in his office in the Hart Senate Office
Building ninety minutes before anybody else. Ample time to pre-
pare the day for Oliver Longstreet, senior senator from Alaska,
the instrument of his agenda.

January

SIX

Rollie Dawson slouched in the front seat of his rusted Subaru, feet on the dash, Country-Western on the tape deck, a six-pack of Diet Pepsi on the passenger seat, a bag of no fat, no salt, no taste tortilla chips on his lap. He was feeling sorry for himself and needed to lose thirty pounds and figured this was the best way to do it.

The singer on the tape said it all. "She took everything but the blame..."

Rollie sang along, thinking about Angie, another wife gone; walked out on him just like that, back to the casinos in Atlantic City where he'd met her only three months ago. She's waiting on tables while she's waiting for the tables to turn. Damn, wimmen were mysterious beings. Only Country seemed to sum it up, not the music, but the words. The Beatles, the Stones, the Grateful Dead, they sang lyrics, and that was fine. But when it's words you need, there's nothing like Waylon, Willie and Merle. *When the phone don't ring, you'll know it's me.*

Rollie cranked up the volume and sang along, "How can anything that sounds so good make me feel so bad?"

53

He was parked in a row of cars seventy yards from the tarmac at Clymmer Field in Leesburg, Virginia, convinced this was the airfield they would use. Just a hunch, but Rollie had always been good at hunches. That's why Mark had *hired* him. Well, not really hired him—more like a favor, with maybe a little money thrown in, now that he was a stringer with the *Post*, and not full time. *I thought I wanted a career, but all I really wanted was a paycheck.*

Sure enough, like a convoy, six long Mercedes arrived in a line and parked next to the small tower, under yellow glow of high-pressure sodium lights. Rollie bolted upright and turned down the music.

A minute later a Learjet landed and the drivers stepped out of their Mercedes and looked about. Rollie studied them through his Nikon 500-millimeter lens magnified by a 1.4x teleconverter. He had already loaded the camera with 36-exposure high-speed film, grainy but fast, good for low light. One driver, a big guy, scanned the parked cars and appeared to stare right at him.

Rollie slouched down. When he inched back up, the drivers had turned their attention to the plane as it taxied toward them. Rollie fired off a shot to test his motor drive.

The Lear stopped, a door opened, a ramp descended and six senators deplaned.

Rollie framed the senators with the ANZA emblem on the Lear's tail. They were exactly who Mark suspected they would be: each a Republican and a committee chairman, each a walking manifestation of power, privilege and indulgence. First among them was none other than Oliver Harding Longstreet. Rollie finished the roll. He removed the camera from the mounted lens and set it next to him. It dropped between the bucket seats. The bag of tortilla chips spilled on top of it. Rollie cursed his clumsiness—*When I'm alone I'm in bad company*—as he grabbed a second camera, already loaded, affixed it to the lens and shot another half roll before the last senator disappeared into a Mercedes.

"Damn, I'm good," Rollie said to himself. "Wimmen, who needs 'em?" *Don't want that floozy in my Jacuzzi.*

Longstreet slid into the back seat of the idling Mercedes where his chief of staff, Tyler Kyle, waited with one leg tucked behind the other, elbows on the armrests, his delicate white fingers tented beneath his nose, his eyes watchful behind tinted glasses.

"God, what a disaster," Longstreet said as he kicked off his shoes.

Kyle said nothing.

From a small cabinet the senator grabbed a bottle of Scotch whiskey, poured a glassful, dropped in two cubes of ice and drank it dry before it could chill. He poured another, his hands shaking, and sat back and allowed himself to exhale.

"Alan Quail was difficult?" Kyle asked.

Longstreet shook his head. "I thought he wanted oil in the 1002 Area more than oil in Baku."

"He wants both."

"Well, Christ, all he talked about was Baku. You'd think he'd show a little more patriotism."

Kyle made no comment, though a hundred things came to mind. He knew that Baku held an estimated two hundred billion barrels of crude, the largest reserves in the world, more than twenty times the estimate for the 1002 Area of the Arctic Refuge. He also knew the legendary story of Alan Quail, who had visited Baku when no other western oilman bothered for seventy years. The richest oil city in the world in the 1890s, Baku had been considered pumped dry by experts everywhere. But Quail wondered what new technologies could extract that old ones could not detect. Just as other oil powers began to realize their own blindness, ANZA signed the "Contract of the Century" with the Azeris to develop Baku's Caspian fields. It would be the biggest deal ever for ANZA, if the area remained stable—a big 'if.'

Sandwiched between Iran and Russia on the western shore of the Caspian Sea, Baku held great promise but also its own breed of uncertainty. Iran and Russia were, well, Iran and Russia. Political unrest and ethnic clashes were common. The Russian mafiyas had arrived. Contract law was a nightmare, corruption a way of life. "Quail wants a delegation of committee chairmen to go over there and secure his interests," Longstreet said with exasperation. "He even wants the President."

"He'll never get him," Kyle said. "He's too busy with flood victims and his Millennium Project."

Longstreet shook his head. "That bastard can cry with one eye."

"Was John Sires there?" Kyle asked about the deputy CEO of ANZA, Quail's strong right hand, a third generation oil man from the Permian Basin of East Texas.

"Oh yes, so we ended up playing golf. I swear the only thing that's important to that guy is golf and women and oil, and probably in that order." The senator crunched a piece of ice.

Kyle saw his eyelid twitch, a nervous disorder—a fasciculation—that worsened when he drank. The poor old man, he should have called it quits after his last term, but he was a dog with a bone, and Alaskans had re-elected him as always with a fifteen-percent margin over his nearest challenger. A former district attorney and professor of constitutional law, Longstreet was an expert on Madisonian doctrines who scoffed at the notion that Americans were pious towards their history in order to be cynical toward their government. Black bifocals rested on his bulbous nose, old horn-rims that seemed to impede rather than aid his sight. He was forever peering over them, raising and lowering his chin to assess a world that was either too mad to inherit or too precious to ignore. A terrible burden, America today, thanks in no small part to environmentalists. God, how he hated them and their deep ecology and their love for Henry David Thoreau, that bookish transcendentalist who escaped humanity at Walden Pond and in his own vainglory managed to be racist toward his own race.

Kyle had recommended that Longstreet not join this ANZA junket to Houston. It was too dangerous. If the liberal press ever got hold of it they would excoriate the Republican-controlled Senate as a "bought-and-paid-for" tool of big oil. That's what they liked to call it: "Big Oil," as if it were a cartel, like OPEC. But Longstreet had a draft bill to show to Quail and Sires, a bill written by Kyle himself, a marvelous piece of work.

Longstreet pounded the bundle of papers against his leg. "I told them that this is the most comprehensive energy bill ever written, one balanced between aggressive domestic exploration and responsible conservation, one with an inextricable 1002-drilling rider woven in so tight it will escape floor debate. I told them I could have forty cosponsors in a week."

"And?" Kyle asked.

Longstreet shook his head. "Quail was skeptical. You know what he said? 'Oliver,' he said, 'I'm sure you understand that I make money and you spend it. I'm a businessman; you're a senator. This bill might work, and it might not. To be honest—that's what he said: *To be honest*—I can't promise you a thing right now. I'll be in Baku in a few days, and I'll let you know if you have my endorsement after I return.' " Longstreet's red nose turned crimson. "Can you believe that? Who the hell does he think he is? I chair Appropriations. I've got thirteen subcommittees under my command. I tie people in fiscal knots and I set them free, and he has the gall to tell me that he makes money and I spend it." Longstreet took another drink.

"His daughter is ill," Kyle said softly.

"What?"

"Quail's daughter, Aliena, his only child, she's ill. That could have something to do with his attitude."

Longstreet stared at him. Before he could respond, Kyle said, "You should know that Maya is sleeping with John Sires."

The senator peered over his bifocals with an 'are-you-serious?' incredulity. Of course Kyle was serious. Humor and sarcasm were beyond him. If anybody on Capitol Hill had no funny bone, let alone no capacity for sarcasm or levity, it was Tyler Kyle. He did not smoke or drink, not even coffee or colas. He never attended parties, and never had an affair, at least none that anybody knew of. As far as Longstreet knew, Kyle was asexual, like a parthenogenic lizard living in a desert. Fine. It kept him beyond scandal and coercion. He might be a bit strange, his eyes darting behind tinted glasses, his copper-colored hair swept across a pallid brow. But he was smart and clever and cunning, and very personable when necessary, immeasurable attributes on the Hill. So he had risen fast, a supernova who kept to himself and ate cold cereal morning and night in his office, who listened to Beethoven, Schubert and Brahms, who read every opinion-shaping book, newspaper, magazine and journal pertinent to the senator's political ambitions. He never missed an opportunity and never guessed wrong, if he guessed at all. And nothing ever fell through the cracks.

"You never did like her, did you?" the senator asked.

"Maya? No, I didn't."

"And now she works for ANZA, and you're worried that she could tell them about our operations on the Hill?"

"Yes."

Longstreet clicked his teeth. "There's a term for that, isn't there? When people from the public sector go to work for the private sector, and take valuable secrets with them."

"Industry capture."

"Ah yes, industry capture. Well, we're not a regulatory agency like the EPA or the FDA, and Maya's not a whore. But if what you say is true, I agree, it's disturbing."

"It's true."

Of course. Longstreet poured another whiskey.

Kyle watched out the window as the Lear copilot retrieved the senator's suitcase and walked toward the Mercedes, pulling the case on rollers. The Mercedes driver, a boxcar of a man, accepted it and put it in the trunk. The driver motioned to Kyle, who glanced out the opposite window toward a row of parked cars seventy yards across the tarmac. He signaled the driver with a careful flip of his hand.

Longstreet saw none of this as he sank deeper into the soft seat and nursed his whiskey. "Any new developments on Janstadt's Wilderness bill?" he asked as he loosened his tie.

"Nothing significant." Janstadt had picked up six more co-sponsors, including two Republicans, but Kyle saw no advantage in telling Longstreet that now. Using tongs, he added a couple ice cubes to the senator's whiskey. Ice cubes from a separate bucket.

"Thank you, Tyler." Longstreet took another drink and asked, "You think he'll try to filibuster this energy bill? Janstadt, I mean. You think he'll try to knock the 1002 rider out of the air?"

"Probably not a filibuster, but he'll try something."

Senator Bruce Janstadt, the tall Minnesotan and former Lakers star, had a way of knocking things out of the air, primarily basketballs and Republican bills. He had fame, clout, prestige and most important, access to the President and Vice President. Environmental organizations loved him. Last year the Sierra Club gave him their highest accolade, the John Muir Award. Now he carried a new torch: his own bill to make the 1002 Area of the Arctic Refuge officially designated Wilderness. Like most environmentalists, he referred to it as the Arctic National Wildlife Refuge. Never ANWR, or Anwahr.

"There are ways to handle Janstadt," Kyle added cryptically.

Longstreet didn't seem to hear him. He spoke for a minute about what happened in Houston, then asked, "The staff believes I spent the long weekend at home, right?"

"Yes, senator. I told you not to worry about that. Did Quail say anything about last month's Anchorage break-in?"

"Only that Parkendale's on it." Parkendale Investigative Services.

Kyle frowned. "Johnny Parkendale's not the investigator his father was. I'm surprised Quail is using him."

"Habit," Longstreet said.

"A bad habit. We need to invite Caltex into your office and make overtures about Anwahr leases. Nothing worries one oil giant more than another oil giant." Caltex was ANZA's chief competitor in the United States.

"So we scare ANZA?" Longstreet peered over his glasses.

"Yes, but we don't say it that way."

They discussed the ANZA break-in and Alan Quail's secrecy. "Damn him," Longstreet said. "He drilled that test well in the 1002 Area ten years ago and he's never hinted at what he found there. He owes me some disclosure and he knows it. Whoever broke into his building last month was probably looking for that result. I hope he found it."

Kyle closed and opened his hands, slowly working his fingers in and out of alabaster fists. He asked, "Have you ever heard of the Locard Exchange Principle?"

The senator shook his head and yawned.

"It's a forensic term that states that any time a person goes into an environment, he leaves part of himself there and takes part of the environment with him. Whoever broke into ANZA last month was very good. He didn't leave a trace. No prints, no hairs, no skin cells, not even epithelial cells in the gas mask."

"Epithelial cells?"

"From the inside of the mouth, very fast regeneration time. They slough off constantly, even during sleep."

Longstreet yawned again.

Kyle said, "He climbed the building with jumars, mountaineering devices used to grip a rope, but these were customized to slide up vertical grooves in the concrete."

"Was Mark Meadows involved somehow?"

"I doubt it."

The senator yawned yet again. "Will Parkendale crack this whole thing?"

"I doubt it."

"I appreciate your honesty, Tyler, even when it hurts."

I doubt it.

The senator closed his eyes, slumped into the seat and nearly spilled his drink.

Kyle carefully lifted the glass from his hand. He signaled the driver to climb back inside and close the door quietly, then to wait until the other five Mercedes had departed. It was important that the senator remain asleep for the next ten minutes. Kyle suspected something like this might happen, just as he had carefully measured the amount of colorless, tasteless powder he applied onto the ice cubes that he dropped into the senator's whiskey.

One minute later, Oliver Harding Longstreet, Chairman of Senate Appropriations, one of the most powerful men on Capitol Hill, began to snore.

Kyle signaled the driver to go.

The first car made a wide turn, its lights momentarily washing over Rollie's Subaru. He slouched down and tried to discreetly remove his lens from the window mount, hands over his head. A second car went by, headlights flooding the darkness. A third went by, a fourth, a fifth...

The sixth and final car went by, but sounded as if it stopped. Rollie thought he heard a door open, then footsteps. *Shit.* He struggled with the window mount, trying to undo the lens clamp. A huge hand grabbed him by his arm and pulled him off the seat, jamming him through the window.

His head hit the car roof and he heard himself scream. The door opened and he was pulled out. A horrible force wrenched his arm down and back, a terrible pain, and from the distant recesses of his mind came the awful knowledge that this was just the beginning. *Damn.*

If today was a fish, I'd throw it back in.

SEVEN

S hannon had a boyfriend once who was a mechanic. He loved
Volkswagens and worked on them all the time, climbed under them, inside them, got greasy from head to toe. He never did
clean under his fingernails, which horrified Shannon's mother and
was part of her attraction to him. He said a good VW was like a
good friend. Get one running just right and you could measure
that rightness not by the quartet of cylinders or the percussion of
pistons, but by the exhaust; you could tune and cajole a VW
until it breathed an exhaust of perfect opacity, what he called
"pretty gray."

Shannon looked up from her pile of constituent mail, all addressed to The Honorable Sam Matlin, U.S. Senate, Washington, D.C., and stared out the far window, visible across the vast
clutter of boxes and papers. The Washington sky was not pretty
gray, but dirty somehow, sticky with urbanism. The naked trees
seemed more dead than dormant. She thought about the boreal
forest of white spruce and black spruce where the caribou would
be now, in their winter feeding grounds, the ecotone between

tundra and taiga, struggling against the cold and snow and wolves.
A forest of eyes.

—Have you found your four-legged shadow?

—What?

*—Your four-legged shadow? Your father tells me you been watchin' wolves.
I thought you might be runnin' with 'em by now.*

Shannon gives him a deprecating look, one she will regret.

—Hey, I jokes.

*He pours himself another cup of coffee, this Eddie Tagarook, smiles at
Charles through the gap in his front teeth, then at Shannon. She doesn't know
what to think of him. He unties his ponytail, lets his Eskimo hair fall down his
back. Walks with one stiff leg. The wind kicks up and he drives metal stakes
into the tundra to tie down the wings of his Piper Super Cub.*

*Shannon helps him. He teaches her new knots. She notices his hands, each
a terrible beauty, an allegory of the arctic.*

*He's a pilot out of Kaktovik; an old friend of her father who contracts with
ANZA off and on, more off than on. It's best that way, he says. He brings ice
cream—chocolate almond—and lands the little fabric-winged plane on tundra and river bar with impossible skill. Her father says he once landed on a
river bar that was too short, so he skimmed the tires on the water first, to slow
the plane down before touching the bar and stopping with one foot to spare.*

—How did you take off? Shannon asks him.

*—Like an albatross, Eddie says. Wait for a strong wind and lift into it.
Birds invented the wind, you know?*

—No, I didn't know that.

—Sure maybe, it's true.

Shannon thinks for a minute. Then who invented caribou?

—You know the answer to that, her father tells her.

—I do?

"You ready to go?" asked Audrey, the receptionist, as she stood
over her.

"Oh, sure." Shannon snapped from a northern latitude and
took a deep breath. She grabbed her coat and purse and joined

three women, all staffers for Senator Matlin who had a lunch date at a Thai restaurant. As they exited the office and walked a balcony above the atrium, one of the women, a sunny-faced blonde named Denali Sisto, told a story about an avocado farmer. Shannon liked Denali, and was humored that her friends called her Denial, as that's where she often seemed to be, in denial, her life a runaway train of never-ending absurdities. For instance, Denali was talking about this farmer, a nice man in Guatemala who had twelve sons, each of them virile, soft-spoken and stupid. Her Spanish was poor, and in trying to tell the Avocado Brigade that she was embarrassed, Denali apparently mis-conjugated a verb and said she wanted to get pregnant. She was only seventeen at the time, an exchange student, and she barely escaped with her virginity. Shannon and the others laughed until they saw a small man in an overcoat and a fedora shuffling toward them. Audrey held open the elevator doors.

"Hello Tyler," she said with mild surprise.

"Good morning ladies. Are we busy defending democracy today?"

"What's democracy?" Denali asked.

The women snickered.

"Sometimes I wonder that myself," Kyle said as he stood near the door with his back to the women. As the elevator descended, Shannon saw Audrey lift an eyebrow at the others. Denali smothered a giggle. The doors opened at ground level and Kyle exited without looking back or saying another word.

"Is that who I think it is?" Shannon asked as they watched him walk away.

"Tyler Kyle," Audrey said with admiration.

Outside, Kyle felt the weak sun on his face. He would have preferred a cold wind, the smell of wet sage, the atomizing elements of water and rock that freed him on a cliff so many years ago. He remembered it like yesterday. It had been raining...

The rain fell hard as Adam Kyle and his younger brother, Tyler, climbed a basalt cliff a thousand feet above the Snake River in Southwest Idaho. Soaking wet in jeans, tennis shoes, windbreakers and ball caps, they moved to stay warm, climbing into the clouds, their ungloved hands clasping shotguns for hunting chukars. The only thing they shared was their teenaged intolerance of each another, each satiating the dark worm of his own discontent.

For what seemed like the hundredth time Adam berated his brother for moving too slowly. He planned to hike him into the ground and let him find his own way back to the ranch. Moving higher, they gained the top of a fin-backed precipice where Tyler stopped and asked for food. Adam told him it was all gone. Tyler called him a liar, and there followed some sharp words that cut deep. A dozen years of persecution erupted inside Tyler as he thrust a lightning fist into his brother's chest, catching him off guard. Everything seemed in slow motion after that, or perhaps in fast forward: Adam stumbling back on a tabular rock that shifted under his weight, his left arm windmilling as he raised his shotgun with his right, pointing it at his brother. *Dear God...*

A gust of wind caught him, the gun fired. Tyler felt birdshot tousle his hair as the recoil knocked Adam over the cliff. Seconds later, maybe hours—time passed strangely then—Tyler heard the thump of soft flesh on boulders far below. He peered over the edge and saw a broken body, face up, motionless, dying. A warm sensation surged through him, as if a gravitational constant had changed and everything would go his way. He hadn't intended to kill his brother, only to push him, but now that it was done, it seemed right somehow. Destined.

In the genetic roulette of human reproduction and death, the odds that make saints and monsters, Tyler Kyle had found his brother too much like himself. It was reported as an accident. Ma Kyle died of cancer one year later, smoking her Marlboros to the end. Pa died not long after he lost a court battle with the federal government over grazing fees. Folks who knew him said that verdict hit him hard, maybe as hard as the death of his first son, the son who was most like him. The family ranch foreclosed, and Tyler, parentless and uprooted at fifteen, moved east to live with his Aunt Winniemae in a farmhouse in Maryland, near Chesapeake Bay, just in time to watch her and her husband Pete lose a fight with the National Audubon Society over pesticides.

It was madness, watching inventive, hard-working people suffer. The same people who made America strong had no merit in the backward ideology of environmentalists and their so-called green revolution. In the beginning Tyler's anger was raw and chafing. He joined militant xenophobes who chanted about the "end times" when America would be subsumed into a cultureless, nationless, one-world government. But those chants required a Goliath, and the chanters, not having a Nazi Germany or a Soviet Union, simply hammered at their own government and the "jack-booted thugs" at Waco and Ruby Ridge, the secret black UN helicopters that would one day fill the sky with Chinese mercenaries; the Internet and World Wide Web that was a totalitarian plot to homogenize and systematize *everything*. Such drivel. Tyler knew there had to be a better way.

He never protested in public or served jail time, and he assiduously avoided the press, those mousy men and women whose words and images became public record. He knew that one day he would play the game differently, with greater cunning and stakes and skill. He would go to the scene of the crime—Washington, D.C. —the birthplace of laws that were supposed to free people, not handcuff them.

He earned a law degree and moved to Alaska where paranoias have a way of magnifying to frontier proportions, yet Tyler kept his in check. By understatement, not overstatement, he would achieve his goals; by low profile, not high profile. In his favorite dream he saw a painting of the U.S. Senate with himself as a vanishing point, invisible yet influential, so influential that he determined the relative power of all those around him. This became his great ambition: *to be the ultimate puppeteer*. He made important friends and began working on the political campaign of one Oliver Harding Longstreet. That too, was a long time ago...

He rode the Metro Blue Line to Federal Triangle, then walked to a courtyard opposite the Old Post Office. He slipped on a pair of thin gloves, entered a phone booth, dialed a number in Idaho and deposited two dollars in quarters. Cellular phones were out of the question; too susceptible to scanners. He never called from the same pay booth twice in a month, but instead exercised what the FBI termed "disciplined randomness." He'd read their manuals.

A voice answered. Kyle spoke in code, hung up and walked to a booth across the courtyard. A minute later the phone rang and he picked it up.

"Hello, my friend. How's the sorcerer's apprentice?"

"Fine," Kyle said.

"How are things at the scene of the crime?" The voice was deep and raspy, the voice of his mentor, Merlin, code-named for the wizard of Arthurian legend. Kyle had never known his true name.

"Still criminal," Kyle replied.

Merlin laughed a loud belly laugh. "I've been reading Henry Kissinger. Listen to this: 'The conventional army loses if it doesn't win; the guerilla wins if he doesn't lose.'"

"I've heard it before."

"I'm not surprised. We researched Rollie Dawson. He did that photo exposé years ago on open pit mines leaking heavy metals into ground water."

"The one that hit Butte and Salt Lake City?"

"Yep. Got those make-believe cowboys all riled up, the gentrified Rockefellers and Rothschilds who said it was time to heal the earth. Fucking watermelons." *Green on the outside, red on the inside.* Like Kyle, Merlin was a cornucopian who believed the greatest resource on the face of the planet was people; the more self-actualized, resourceful people the better, people who could solve any problem that bureaucratic stupid people created. He further believed that the population bomb was a dud; that Custer's work must go on, that Dixie would rise again, that national parks, preserves, monuments, forests and wildlife refuges had no greater sanctity than the average man's garden and should thus be tilled. Farmers should go farm, fishermen go fish, miners go mine, loggers go log, drillers go drill, and environmentalists go to hell. "These New Age people," Merlin said, breathing hard. "I'll tell you what, I don't feel their pain or listen to their therapists or buy their gestalt. Have you been in a bookstore lately and seen all the self-help titles and other crap on the shelves? They aren't bookstores anymore, they're spas for narcissism."

Kyle imagined his huge belly like a bellows, his jowls like a bloodhound's, the phone receiver tiny in his hand. The first time he met Merlin, at a secret camp in Idaho more than twenty years ago, the big man wore a T-shirt that said I SHOT JFK.

"So what about Rollie Dawson?" Kyle asked as he looked out the phone booth at the cluster of gray federal buildings, mindful of everything around him.

"He studied journalism at Columbia. Guess who he roomed with?"

Kyle had an uneasy feeling. "Mark Meadows?"

"Yep. Your man got just one camera with one roll of film, nothing showing Oliver Longstreet deplaning an ANZA Lear."

Kyle groaned. "Okay, I'll get the rest of the film."

"And Dawson?"

"Right, him too."

"Good. What's the latest with Mr. Longstreet?" Merlin always referred to conservative, pro-development senators as mister, and their liberal opponents as mizzz, as in Ms.

Kyle told of his discussion with Longstreet in the Mercedes, the senator's frustrations with Alan Quail, and Quail's cold reception of the energy bill. They spoke about Baku, and Kyle said he thought Russia could destabilize soon and throw the Caspian region into chaos. Merlin disagreed, and reminded his protégé that Lenin's birthday was the same day as Earth Day. "Lenin is nothing new anymore," Merlin added, "other than the name of some discothèque in Siberia. And Bolshevik is a kind of biscuit. The Soviet Union is dead my friend, now and forever."

Kyle reported on Longstreet's poor health and twitching eye, adding that "Janstadt's Wilderness bill has him worried."

"How is Mizzz Janstadt?"

"I'm working on something from his scoutmaster days that could sink him. He volunteered with the Boy Scouts of America during the NBA off-season."

Merlin ripped into a hacking cough. Kyle held the receiver from his ear until it subsided, then asked, "Did we get a man into Parkendale? I need him to send me a copy of the ANZA guest list from the party that night."

"He's in, he'll send it." Merlin sucked down several deep breaths.

They speculated on who might have broken into the ANZA Building, and what Mark Meadows was doing there uninvited. Kyle mentioned Meadows' argument with Congressman Worley, and Merlin said, "Worley is a imbecile, letting a journalist provoke him like that." He paused and added, "Better have the boys visit Mark Meadows too."

"I was just about to recommend it."

"Great minds think alike, Tyler." Another wheezing breath. "Have you made that call to Anchorage?"

"The minute I hang up with you."

"Well then, I'll ask for a full accounting. Your limit is fifty thousand."

~

William picked up the phone on the first ring.

"William Alt?"

"Yeah."

"I have a job for you."

"Who is this?"

"That's not important right now."

William hung up. He didn't have time for pranks. He resumed pumping weights in the squalid Anchorage apartment he shared with Jerry Levy, who, like him, was still licking his wounds from that final night at ANZA. But while Jerry's poverty and cracked ribs didn't prevent him from slamdunking cheeseburgers at a local Spenard dive, William stayed home to study the classifieds. The phone rang again. "Yeah?"

"Twenty thousand dollars, Mr. Alt. Hang up on me again and it goes to somebody else." The same voice, a soft monotone, a whisper more distinctive than the words themselves.

William stopped pumping. "Who is this?"

"Let's say I'm a simple man working for a better America, someone who can help you as you can help me?"

William's mind pinwheeled. *Twenty thousand dollars.* "Is this job legal?"

He laughed in a quiet way. "A good question. Law serves to emulate justice, and sometimes achieves it. I suppose it will be for you to decide."

Justice? Emulate? "Are you a lawyer?"

"I used to be."

"Why should I do this?"

The voice didn't answer right away, as if to give William time to weigh the merits of his question. "Because I know where you come from. I know what happened to you, how you made something of yourself. You're a hero. You shot and killed two Koreans in self-defense and—"

"I should have never gotten a less than honorable discharge for that."

"I know. You should have been decorated."

"You...you think so?"

"I know so. So do you, but America-at-large doesn't know it. They don't see the dangers around us."

"I know, I know," William said excitedly. "Foreign investors and environmentalists are in bed with our own government."

"A government that regulates everything we think, touch and smell," Kyle added. "The America you inherited is not the one you deserve, William. You can take it back. That's my invitation to you. It's honorable work at good pay, one hundred percent voluntary."

William said nothing. He knew only one thing: *this was not a prank.*

"Interested?" the voice asked.

"Uh…yeah, I guess."

"Not good enough. Are you interested?"

"Yes."

"Good. Be at the Wise Use convention in the Sullivan Arena on the first Saturday of Anchorage's Fur Rondy. You'll be contacted. No word about this to anyone." The phone clicked off.

William Alt sat down, stunned.

EIGHT

Shannon studied the faces of people flooding with and against her on Connecticut Avenue, their eyes locked away at the end of the day, hands buried in their pockets, collars turned up against the winter wind. How many lives of compromise did they represent? How many broken dreams? How many tides come and go, and with them these hermit crabs tight in their shells? City people.

Mark Meadows walked beside her. Yes, he was odd and unkempt and sometimes brazen. The reasons to avoid him were numerous. But he had dropped a pebble in her pool that night in Anchorage and she wanted to see where the ripples ran.

They turned off Connecticut Avenue, followed a side street and entered a small Italian restaurant. Mark had reserved a corner table with a checkered cloth, a sprig of Alaskan yellow cedar and a rose-scented candle. The wine steward arrived and Mark asked Shannon, "White or red?"

Yesterday Greek food; this afternoon, Thai; this evening, Italian. I'm eating my way through Washington. "Red sounds nice."

~

From across the street two men watched Shannon and Mark through the window of their truck, then drove southwest across the Potomac River, bound for sabotage in Vienna, Virginia.

~

They shared their histories, or the margins of them. Mark said he was raised in Maine and Virginia, and when Shannon asked which one he preferred, he said he was equally homesick in both. "And your parents?" she asked.

"They're dead."

"Oh, I'm sorry." She told him about Mexico and her mother, Susannah, now Susan, the youngest daughter of Hector Solorzano, the deputy oil minister who was indicted on anti-trust violations and thrown into prison. The scandal broke one week after young Susannah met Charles DeShay, the Irish Catholic who would rescue her from disgrace and take her to a new life in the United States. Charles never wanted to work for ANZA. He wanted to be a professor. But professors make no money, Susan told him again and again. You need to work for an oil company. She could be very persistent.

Your mother wins every argument, Shannon. That's just the way it is. She always has the last word. Anything said after that is just the beginning of another argument.

"He didn't like his work?" Mark asked Shannon.

"No."

"And you blame your mother for that?"

"I guess I do." Shannon curled fettuccini around her fork, and seemed to travel far away and back again before she asked, "Does it ever snow here?"

Mark grinned. "Now and then. This is a southern city, south of the Mason-Dixon Line. We get a lot more rain than snow." He bypassed the margarine and lathered butter on his bread.

"You use butter instead of margarine?"

"I trust cows more than chemists."

Shannon chewed her parsley. "You enjoy being a radical, don't you?"

"Do you know that radical comes from the Latin, *radicalis*, meaning rooted?"

"I think the root of radical pertains to free radicals in chemistry."

Mark sipped his wine. "I'd rather be a free radical than an imprisoned one."

Shannon studied him.

"Go ahead, ask," he said.

"Ask what?"

"About the night at the ANZA party, my argument with Jack Worley. You're dying to know why I did it."

"Am I that transparent?"

"Afraid so."

"You provoked him. You didn't have to." She paused. "He was on crutches until a couple days ago."

"I know, I heard. A pity."

She offered Mark a rueful smile. "Honestly, I have no sympathy for him. He's gutted more acres of wild Alaska than anybody."

"Anybody except Oliver Longstreet."

"Yes." She leaned back. "Oliver Longstreet."

"That's quite a delegation you've got from Alaska. Right out of the nineteenth century."

Shannon took a deep breath. "I'm hoping Sam Matlin will change that."

Mark appeared ready to throw cold water on her idealism, but instead offered his appraisal of Washington and the age of poll-shaped opinions and politicians who didn't represent ordinary people anymore. "They're an aristocracy that afflicts the afflicted and comforts the comfortable." His eyes seemed dusted when he said this, almost sad.

Shannon asked him if he liked poetry.

"Oh yes." He brightened and said, "Mary Oliver is good, and Gary Snyder. But Emily Dickinson is still my favorite."

~

The two men arrived at the Virginia-Potomac Light & Power substation, set the plastic explosives and short-circuited a fifty-block-grid of southeast Vienna. They drove to Harcourt Street and entered the apartment with flashlights and guns.

~

Mark shook his head and became wistful again. "I've been at the Post for eleven years. I keep telling myself that I'll be gone in a year or two, that I'll move to a farm in New Hampshire and write a novel. But the power game keeps me here, the belief that I can make a difference somehow. It's the same for many people. They call it Potomac Fever."

Shannon nodded. She'd heard of this; it seemed a sad sickness to her. She said, "Parkendale agents called twice and asked me about what I saw that night at the ANZA party, how long I talked with you, and what time I first noticed you. They asked Jude the same thing."

Mark took a bite of bread. "Hey, this has sourdough in it."

"You hate ANZA, don't you?"

Mark drew back in a frosty reproach. "Is this an inquisition?"

Shannon held her ground, eyes unblinking.

He lowered his voice. "Hate is like taking poison and expecting somebody else to die. Let's say I have contempt for institutional greed. There's a difference."

"Because they're powerful?"

"Not exactly." He thought for a moment. "It's because they create their own science and logic and religion. The faster they grow, the faster they want to grow. They're insatiable."

"The people who work at ANZA aren't evil, Mark."

"You don't have to be evil to destroy, you just have to be

wrong."

She noticed his soft blue eyes and gossamer hair. *He has a way of making intelligence erotic. This is crazy.* "There are many good people who work for ANZA."

"Such as your father?"

"You know about him?"

"A little."

Shannon studied Mark's fine features, his golden beard surrounding a small mouth, his eyes with crow's-feet wrinkles at their corners, his perfect teeth, clean hands and thin fingers, his misfit clothes on a lanky frame, that Websterian vocabulary followed by a wry grin. *Is this the face of a caring friend or a sly journalist? A man of relationships, or affairs? Was it really ANZA that was insatiable, or Mark?*

—Wolves.

—Wolves created the caribou? She asks.

—That's right, Eddie says. Isn't that right, Charlie?

—Yes, her father says, that's right. He fashions a spoon from a willow branch with his whittling knife. Holds his head at that angle; has a youth and a peace about him, sitting on the ground, legs crossed, wood shavings in his lap. He hasn't touched his rock hammer or petrology data or seismic equipment in days. She understands now. This is his secret love: to eat and sleep in a roadless place that infuses the soul with its own contours and gives a man or a woman peaks and valleys of whatever dimension he or she desires. A topography of the heart.

Eddie and Shannon dust off the ice cream, half a gallon between them. Shannon feels the mountains embrace her, the river speaking. Always the river.

—You know, Eddie says, those wolves can break caribou bones with their teeth and jaws. They don't have thumbs. They don't need them. Just teeth and legs and tails.

—And ears, Shannon says.

—Damn straight, Eddie says. Good for you, girl. He slaps her on the back. Ears. Wolves talk with their ears.

—Then what do they listen with? She asks him.

—Their hearts, her father answers, still whittling. Wolves listen with their hearts.

His voice floated into her.

"What," Shannon asked.

"I heard him speak once," Mark said. "Your father, here in Washington. He gave a talk on the Arctic Refuge at the USGS."

"Oh?"

"Are you okay?"

"I'm fine." She looked away, thinking about the few times in her life she has cried. *Tears for the past are the waters of truth, her father once told her. The only reality is the earth, the wind, the land, the rivers, the places we came from long ago. Everything else is just smoke and mirrors.*

"He was a great public speaker," Mark said, his tone conciliatory.

"Yes," Shannon replied distantly, "before the accident."

Mark leaned toward her. "Actually, I have a theory about that."

"A theory? About the accident?"

"If you want to call it that."

"What do you mean?"

Mark searched her eyes.

"What?" Shannon said. "What's wrong?"

"I've been doing some research and I think the accident that crippled your father and killed your brother wasn't an accident at all. I think it was murder."

NINE

"You're crazy." Shannon pushed away from the table.

Mark didn't shrink under her glare. "Sometimes I wish I were."

Shannon's mind cascaded back to the June afternoon six and a half years ago when the Alaska State Troopers arrived at the door, hats in their hands, badges heavy on their chests. A raven's wing closed over her then, so soft yet black, a hole in the sky. Mom collapsed into her arms and screamed, *no, no, no,* while Shannon, only eighteen—one month out of high school—thanked the troopers in a voice that didn't seem her own.

"This isn't funny, Mark. I don't believe you."

He rubbed his hands across his face. "Neither would I if I were you."

"Then why tell me this?"

"Because I need your help."

Shannon's mouth was a tight line.

"You okay?" Mark asked.

"Considering what you've just told me, no. How could I be? I still don't believe you."

"Give me a chance."

"This is crazy. Why would somebody want to do such a thing?"

"Because your father was one of ten people who knew the result of the ANZA test well drilled in the 1002 Area a decade ago."

"So?"

"It's political dynamite. It's never been publicly revealed. Not even within ANZA or KANAK, the native corporation that owns the inholding where the drilling took place. It cost ANZA forty million bucks and they've kept the result locked away ever since. The 1002 might be another Prudhoe Bay. It might be dry. Nobody knows, except those ten people. And get this"—Mark lowered his voice— "five of them have died, four in questionable accidents."

"And you think they've been murdered?"

"Yes."

The waiter removed their plates and the candle burned low. Shannon composed herself. "So you're saying my brother Travis was in the wrong place at the wrong time?"

"I'm afraid so."

"Wait…there was another man in the car. He was killed too. His name was Richard Leavitt."

Mark nodded. "He was a contract consultant for ANZA. That's all I know about him."

"Maybe he was the intended victim. Maybe—"

"No, Shannon. It was your father because he knew the 1002 test result. I wish it weren't true, but from everything I've researched a strong pattern is there. Something very wrong is going on."

Shannon's pain graduated into intrigue. "How long have you been working on this?"

"Off and on for three years. More steadily the last six months."

"Why those four or five particular people?"

"Probably because they wanted to go public with what they knew. I can't prove any of this. That's why I need to talk with your father. He's the only one of the five who's still alive.

"He can't talk, Mark, he—"

"I know, I know, but can he hear? Can he understand? Can he signal somehow? Can he answer simple yes/no questions by blinking his eyes or moving his fingers?"

"Sometimes." A faraway fondness softened her. "In the arctic we used to signal each other with our hands and fingers when we watched wildlife. And for awhile after his accident he could signal by blinking his eyes. But now, I don't know. I feel guilty being here in Washington, but I had to get away. I never thought he would die like this." Her voice trailed off. "I guess I thought he would never die at all."

"Impermanence is a hard thing, isn't it?"

"What?"

"Impermanence. It's not easy to accept change in everything, yet impermanence itself is the only thing that's permanent, isn't it? It's the only thing we can really hold onto."

Shannon stared at him.

"Think about it. If you just let go and accept one thing passing into another, then you can let go of all your loss and suffering."

"Individual caribou live and die, but the herd survives. The river survives. The earth survives."

"But even it trembles now and then, doesn't it? To remind us that we can't take everything for granted."

"Earlier you said that your parents were dead, as if it didn't bother you. Most people would say 'deceased.'"

"I'm a Buddhist, Shannon. I believe that death is something to celebrate, not to mourn or fear."

"Even when it's untimely?"

"No, I agree, that's hard."

She looked away, lost in thought. He let a minute pass, then reached over and lightly touched the back of her hand. "Are you okay?" he asked. How sexy she seemed in her defiance, how tough yet somehow vulnerable. He studied her.

"What?" she asked.

"You know why we acquire a language as children? To tell the stories that are already in us."

She offered a small smile.

"You father has a story inside of him, Shannon. He's had it there for ten years and he needs to tell it. He could be aching to tell it. I've got all my research on hard drive and back-up disks, plus dozens of hospital, government, ANZA and KANAK documents. Once you see their significance, I think you'll be convinced."

She looked away to resurrect old ghosts: the death of Travis, the withering of Dad, the painful abandonment of her and her mother on the same lonely shore. But if Mark were right, if this were in fact a crime, maybe something could be done about it. She could right a wrong. *Find your four-legged shadow. Listen with your heart.* "Your research, where is it?" she asked him.

"In my apartment, in Vienna."

"I want to see it." She grabbed her coat.

"Really? Now? Tonight?"

"Yes, now, tonight." She pushed back her chair and looked at him with cold clarity. "Let's go."

"Would you like some ice cream for the road?"

She yielded another small smile. "Chocolate almond would be nice."

TEN

Beethoven's Seventh Symphony pulsed through the small, solemn apartment and the man, seated on the chair, who was equally small and solemn, his posture fastidious like his clothes, hands on his knees, eyes closed. The symphony teased in and out of crescendo, and Tyler Kyle stirred. He loved this music because it exercised influence, not power, and influence was his business. Influence was to gain consent, not just obedience; to attract adherents, not just an entourage; to have imitators, not just courtiers. His computer monitor illuminated his face with a red glow from the axiom: DISTRUST MORAL RELATIVISM. He told himself again and again, he must do better.

~

"You drive a Volkswagen?" Shannon said as Mark opened the door.

"I do. Is that okay?"

"It's fine." She climbed in.

He pulled out of the parking lot and said, "I hope I

haven't...you know, about your father..."

"I'm fine." Shannon stared at the mesmerizing torrent of headlights and taillights and said something about the pace of life in the city.

"It's insane," Mark observed as he accelerated in open traffic. "Everybody in such a hurry. One of my favorite philosophers said, 'Even if you win the rat race, you're still a rat.'"

"Yogi Berra?"

"No, Lily Tomlin. I read it on a tea bag. How's the ice cream?"

"Good, thank you."

They sat in silence as Mark drove from Leesburg Pike onto Chain Bridge Road. His apartment was ten miles ahead, on Harcourt Street. He glanced over at Shannon. "How are you doing?"

"I'm fine, Mark. You can stop worrying about me."

"Thinking about your dad?"

"Actually, no. My brother."

"Travis, a math major and a brilliant classical guitarist. Your mother took him to Mexico City every summer to study under the masters, while you and your father went to the Arctic Refuge."

"How do you know that?"

"Research, Shannon. It's my job."

"To research my family?"

"I'm not the CIA or the FBI or the IRS. I'm just an investigative reporter working on a theory."

Shannon set her empty ice cream cup on the VW floor. "At the ANZA party, you knew my name before you asked me, didn't you?"

"Yes."

"Is that why you were there? To meet me?"

"You're too perceptive."

"What else haven't you told me?"

"Nothing."

"Out with it, Mark."

"Nothing, I swear. I'm not the criminal here. If you want to get to the bottom of your father's and brother's fates, then help me investigate these bogus accidents."

Shannon confessed, "Travis and I never got along."

"Maybe you never got to know him."

She sighed. "He always fussed about his fingers, afraid that he would hurt them. He didn't like climbing trees or sleeping on the ground. How can a brother and a sister be so different?"

"Whoa, you'll have to find some old transcendental bearded guy sitting on a mountaintop to answer that one."

"Travis was Mom's favorite and I was Dad's, and look what we end up with, each other. Oil and water." *Pipelines and rivers.* Her voice was deep and bitter. She rolled down her window, lifted her face to the cold air and breathed it in like an elixir, let it sweep back her black hair.

Mark said nothing.

"Dad was supposed to get better," Shannon said, "but he hasn't. Sometimes I want to take him out to the tundra and leave him there and let him die like an old wolf."

"With dignity."

"I suppose, whatever that means."

Mark turned onto Harcourt Street and parked in a lot next to a five-story brownstone. "That's odd," he said. "My apartment window light is off. It should be on. It's on a timer."

"That's them," one man said, seated in the truck. He followed Mark and Shannon with binoculars as they walked to the apartment building. The other man adjusted knobs on a listening device.

Mark stared at the lobby door and the unresponsive small red security light next to it. He inserted his key card but nothing happened. Shannon pulled on the door and it opened. As they entered the lobby an elderly woman cracked open her first-floor apartment door and peeked out, her sour face dissected by a security chain.

"Hello Mrs. Luther," Mark said. "What's up with the security system?"

"We had a power outage," she cackled through her false teeth. "You know that. I heard you upstairs during the blackout."

"You heard somebody in my apartment?"

The old woman gave Shannon a skeptical stare. "Who's this girl with you?"

"She's a friend," Mark answered.

Shannon forced a smile.

Mrs. Luther's face softened. "It was a blackout. I lost Archbishop Michael on TV, but I had some candles, praise the Lord. The security system still isn't working. I think management has sent for a technician."

"When did you last hear the noise in my apartment?"

"Oh, dear me, it must have been an hour ago or so. I've been afraid to look out my door."

"Are you okay now?" Mark asked her. "Do you need anything?"

"I'm fine," the old lady said. "Thank you for asking."

Mark headed up the stairs with Shannon. They heard Mrs. Luther close and bolt her door.

"Interesting woman," Shannon said.

Mark shook his head. "A Catholic named Luther, can't be easy."

"Do you have much crime around here?"

"We'll know in a minute."

"Shouldn't we call the police?"

Mark reached the top of the stairs and was about to answer when he saw his apartment door open to the hall. "Nobody would still be in there and leave the door open like that," he said.

Shannon saw his shoulders sink as he flipped on the lights. The apartment looked like the aftermath of a tornado: drawers and files opened, papers scattered, furniture upended, Tibetan rugs shoved into the corners, bookshelves toppled. Mark walked through the chaos and said, "This wasn't vandalism. It was a search."

"For what?"

"My ANZA files, I'll bet." He booted up his computer, typed in a password and accessed files. "Everything seems to be here."

Shannon had a thought. "How could they get into your computer if there was a power outage?"

Mark pointed under his desk to a maze of boxes and wires. "It's plugged into a powerverter that runs off a deep-cell, twelve-volt marine battery that connects to a battery charger and plugs into the wall. I can lose power for eight hours and still operate."

Shannon admired a Michio Hoshino photograph on the wall, a freeze-frame of silhouetted bull caribou splashing through an arctic river, velvet streaming off their antlers, heads high, droplets of backlit water surrounding them like so many stars in the sky. Kinetic perfection. Drinking the wind. While most wildlife photographs captured animals, this one somehow freed them. The glass was cracked and the frame splintered. "Who would do this?" she asked.

Mark didn't answer as he inventoried his files.

After a minute she asked, "Are you on the Internet?"

"Yeah, but I don't use it like I use books. I prefer literary backroads to the information superhighway."

"What about back-up disks?"

"Shit." Mark jumped to his feet and went into the kitchen. He opened the refrigerator freezer and pulled out a small, clear package. He counted the contents and breathed a sigh of relief. "All present and accounted for. I keep my disks double-sealed in freezer-strength Ziploc bags. Even if this place burned down they'd survive. All my ANZA research is right here."

"You really think that's what they were looking for?" Shannon asked.

A third voice answered, "Maybe not."

Shannon's heart slammed against her chest as she spun around to see a forlorn figure standing in the doorway, his face drawn, his arm in a cast and a sling.

"I'll bet they were looking for this," he said through a bruised mouth. He opened a small cloth bag and pulled out a Nikon camera.

"Geez Rollie," Mark said. "It's not every day you scare two people half out of their skin. What happened to you?"

Rollie Dawson shrugged and told about getting roughed up on the tarmac at Clymmer Field, and how he spent most of last night in a hospital emergency room. He stepped over a spilled bookshelf, plopped into a chair, and said, "You got anything to eat? One meal of hospital food and I think I'm poisoned." *I don't know what it is, but I sure miss it when it's gone.*

Mark grabbed a jar of applesauce but Rollie shook his head and said, "How about a beer?"

Mark fetched him one and sat down heavily next to his friend. "Tell me what happened."

Tears came to Rollie's eyes.

Mark had suspected the senators were on a weekend ANZA junket, and had asked Rollie to stake out an airfield with his camera. "But I didn't think you'd get hurt," he said. "I really didn't."

Rollie quietly asked, "You got any tortilla chips? Nacho flavored?"

Shannon opened the refrigerator and found tortillas, cheese and salsa. "How about some quesadillas?" she asked.

For the first time Rollie seemed to acknowledge her. Of course she looked like Angie, but then he could find something in every woman that looked like Angie. He blushed. *I keep forgetting that I forgot about you.* "Quesadillas would be nice," he said as he glanced at Mark.

Mark told Shannon she would find everything she needed in the refrigerator.

Shannon got busy in the kitchen while Rollie told his story from Clymmer Field, how some goon beat him unconscious and broke his arm and got one roll of film from one camera. But not the other roll. "It's right in here," he said as he tapped the Nikon. "He must have missed it under a bag of spilled chips between the bucket seats in the car."

"Who were the senators?" Mark asked, leaning forward.

"Longstreet, Drummund, and Balznic for sure, I couldn't get an exact lock on the others."

Mark repeated the names, savoring each one.

"Yeah, and I know I got Longstreet," Rollie said, "'cause he was first off the plane, and this camera contains the first roll of film."

Shannon grated cheese and found a frying pan. She moved toward the apartment door to shut it, but it was already closed. No, that wasn't the door blocking the entrance, it was a huge, hulking man. She stepped back, caught her foot and fell over an end table and hit the floor.

ELEVEN

Aye...calm down, woman" said the man in the door, raising his hands in peace. "I'm not the boogieman. I just need me cab fare." His voice was Jamaican basso profundo, a tuba with soul.

Shannon caught her breath and examined him. Black skin, white eyes, forearms the size of her calves, upper arms like her thighs. A tattered coat hung on him like a shawl. He had no neck, just sloping shoulders. A Vienna Taxi ball cap crowned his melon-sized head. Faded blue jeans with holes in the knees hugged his pillared legs and descended to mismatched socks and an old pair of Nike Air Jordans. He easily stood six-foot-six.

Rollie said, "Sorry, Quinn. I got distracted up here talking. What'd you say I owe you?"

"Call it forty-five, man."

Rollie turned to Mark. "Have you got it? He drove me here. I'm outta cash."

Mark handed Quinn fifty dollars and told him to keep the change. Rollie offered him a beer.

"No thanks, man," Quinn said as he scanned the apartment.

"This place looks malo, don'tcha know?" He looked at Shannon with a face full of apology as she stood up and composed herself. "Sorry to put the frights in ya like that, pretty woman." He tipped his cap and left.

Shannon returned to the kitchen while Mark monkeyed with the bolt in the jammed door, trying to close it. "You okay?" he asked her.

"I'm fine." She began heating oil in the frying pan on the stove.

A minute later, maybe two, as she knelt to retrieve tortillas from the bottom of the refrigerator, she heard a loud thud.

She stood to see two men moving fast, each wearing a ski mask and gloves, one pointing a gun at Mark while the other grabbed the camera from Rollie and shoved him into a chair. The door was open, and it seemed to her that they had come from nowhere. *But that's what we tell ourselves, don't we, creating the myth that we cannot predict human behavior?*

Mark moved suddenly and the man hit him hard in the head with the butt of his gun. Mark fell, and Shannon felt the acid rising in her throat. The other man yanked a small microphone from the underside of Mark's desk, and Shannon understood: they had pillaged the apartment, bugged it and plotted their return as they listened from outside. *They must know everything.*

One man said to the other, "Get the woman and the bag of disks."

He came into the kitchen, grinning at Shannon through crooked yellow teeth, motioning with his gun. He looked like a shrew, and Shannon remembered her father telling her that if shrews were the size of bears, they would be the most frightening animals on earth. *Act, don't think.*

She flipped the skillet of hot oil at him.

He ducked, but the oil hit his neck and he screamed and dropped his gun. She hit him hard on the head with the frying pan, and he crumpled against the wall. She reached for his gun but a terrible pain shot through her as the other man grabbed her by the hair and yanked her down. He raised his gun to strike her, and that's when the black paw saved her. Quinn grabbed the gun and twisted, a finger cracked. The gun fell and Shannon reached for it. She could hear the burned man hyperventilating, and Quinn struggling with the other man, synapses screaming in her ears. She tried to focus as horrible sounds assailed her. She smelled the sweet odor of fear, the struggle of men fighting for their lives and pissing their pants. She blinked the wetness from her eyes and saw two shrews bolt out the door, hunched with pain, one pulling the other. Quinn turned to look at her, his lower lip and teeth scarlet with blood. Only then did she see her outstretched arm pointing at the open door where the two intruders had fled. And at the end of her arm was her hand, and in her hand a gun, her finger on the trigger; not a deer rifle or a shotgun, but a pistol, a handgun that fit too well.

—Squeeze, Eddie Tagarook whispers.

Shannon squeezes. The rifle explodes against her shoulder. Ten caribou scatter through the riverside willows while one remains, its blood and spirit ebbing away. Dear God, Shannon thinks as she, Eddie Tagarook and her father walk to it, what have I done?

It is a large bull with magnificent antlers recently shed of velvet, prepared for the rut it will never see. The pelage is meticulous auburn; the eyes open but sightless. The carotid artery severed. A clean shot. Eddie kneels beside the caribou and asks Shannon and Charles to join him. They each place a hand on the animal's warm flank. Shannon fights back tears as Eddie speaks in Inupiaq, then English: We feel no pride at this moment, great spirit. Only thankfulness. We will not boast of this, for that will bring dishonor to you and to us. This animal gave itself to us. We will not take our brothers lightly. Thank you for this gift. Today a girl becomes a woman.

Shannon knelt beside Mark. She wanted to go into the kitchen and get a washcloth for his wound, but her legs felt like iron.

Rollie vomited in the kitchen sink, apologized in a weak voice, and vomited again. He leaned on the counter and mumbled a prayer. "Drop kick me, Jesus, through the goal posts of life."

Shannon lowered her gun and began to shake, the weight of it suddenly heavy, the metal cold.

"Who are they?" Mark mumbled. He could barely comprehend what was happening.

"They're gone," Shannon told him. "We got the disks and the camera."

He raised his bloody head and tried to focus. "What happened?"

"Your ANZA research got discovered," Shannon said. "You're a wanted man."

~

Senator Longstreet departed his home in Alexandria at 5:30 a.m. and headed northeast on I-395 for Capitol Hill. He drove himself and listened to KGOP, the voice of reason. Even in winter's predawn blackness this was his favorite time of day, alone in his toreador-red Ford Explorer sport utility vehicle, sailing along at seventy miles an hour and fourteen miles to the gallon, free from the traffic that an hour later would cauterize the arteries of Washington. He had kissed his wife without waking her, downed a big breakfast of ham and eggs prepared by a maid, patted his two blue-eyed Siberian huskies goodbye and slipped out the door. At Fairlington he pulled off the freeway into a coffee shop parking lot. A minute later a Saab appeared from the darkness and parked alongside him. He rolled down his window. "Good morning, Maya."

"Good morning, senator."

Longstreet had invited her to call him Oliver after she left his staff, but she never did. Her green eyes and golden hair seemed to produce their own light.

"Alan Quail is on his way back to Baku," she said without preamble.

"I know. What's he saying about the 1002 Area?"

"Nothing."

Longstreet shook his head.

"Things are more promising overseas right now. He's interested in Alaska, but he wants assurances that ANZA will get exclusive leasing in the 1002 Area, among other things."

"He wants exclusivity? Fine, tell him to release the test result."

She gripped the steering wheel and locked her elbows. "I wouldn't put too much faith in that."

"That he'll release it?"

"No, that the result is what you think it is. I really shouldn't say anything more."

"Good God, Maya. I hope you didn't talk bullshit like this when you worked for me."

"This isn't bullshit."

"Then what? Tyler says the 1002 test result should be good. Is ANZA's prized new lobbyist telling me otherwise? They would shoot you if they heard you telling me this."

"My grandparents were shot and killed by Nazis. Nobody will ever shoot me. Ever."

The air seemed suddenly cold. Longstreet popped down his nitro and took a deep breath. *Helluva way to start a day.* The ham and eggs sat in his stomach like a rock.

Maya started her Saab. "I have to go. I'm part of Alan's entourage to Baku."

"What if the Russians mess things up between the Azeris and the Armenians?"

"Then we pray to Allah." She failed to mask her sarcasm as she shifted into gear.

"And Alan Quail will beg to get into the 1002 Area."

"I doubt it. CEOs never beg." She accelerated away and disappeared into the same darkness from which she had emerged.

TWELVE

On the balcony above the atrium in the Hart Senate Office Building, Senator Longstreet found Jeff Meola and Harry Arnold talking. "You're just the fellows I wanted to see," he told them. "Come into my office."

Jeff and Harry looked at each other with surprise.

"Sit down, sit down," Longstreet said as he swiveled into his leather chair behind his desk. "I've read your reports on the ANZA party last month. Have Parkendale agents called you?"

"They sure have," Harry said too eagerly as he brushed lint from his Italian-made suit.

"Tell me what you saw that night." Longstreet looked at Jeff.

Jeff spoke in staccato sentences, saying that he and Harry had arrived together. They heard Alan Quail's speech and saw the end of Jack Worley arguing with Mark Meadows.

"We didn't exactly arrive together," Harry corrected him.

"Yes, we did."

"How would you know, Jeff? You were sick."

"And Maya?" Longstreet asked them.

"Maya?"

"You saw her there?"

"Sure did," Harry said. "She wore a flowered dress."

"She arrived before us," Jeff added. "I remember she asked me about the drunk in the lobby."

"She arrived after us," Harry said.

Jeff glared at him. But the senator seemed to lose interest as he turned to look out the window where six pigeons strutted about and squirted guano on the sill. To Jeff and Harry, he seemed a thousand miles away. He suddenly stood up and walked them to the door, asking Harry as they departed, "How are things in Senator Matlin's office?"

"Not as organized as they are here, senator. I'll whip them into shape."

"I'm sure you will, Harry."

After they were gone, the senator asked his secretary about Tyler Kyle and was told that he had left a message saying he was doing research in the Library of Congress. Longstreet nodded, unaware, like his secretary, that the message was a lie. He closed his door, returned to his desk and fumed over Maya's caveats about ANZA and the 1002 Area test drill. *Inscrutable woman.*

He opened the window and the pigeons scattered. In his bottom desk drawer he found his Verminator slingshot and a box of birdshot. He loaded and waited as the pigeons returned. He wanted one in particular, the felonious one with the white body, mottled head, iridescent rainbow neck, peering eyes and ridiculous strut. He aimed and fired and saw an explosion of torn feathers. One less pigeon would henceforth defile the Hart Senate Office Building.

~

Tyler Kyle loved Aunt Winniemae's cooking and her country-style kitchen and Maryland farmhouse, and the embroidered aprons she wore. He loved how she served hot plates with her gnarled, arthritic hands, and how, as a retired nurse, she tended to the oil burns on Jimmy's neck, and Pyro's broken finger. And how, while doing all this, she spoke in a matronly way about Nietzsche and Kant and best of all Ambrose Bierce, author of *The Devil's Dictionary*, wherein liberty, she said, "is defined as one of imagination's most precious possessions."

From the way they shoveled down their meal, Kyle's associates enjoyed her cooking too. Winniemae made up beds for each of them. After saying how nice it was to have them in her home, she retired. The three men stayed up late and listened to the tape recording that Jimmy and Pyro had made from bugging Mark Meadows' apartment. The voices seemed to mock them as Mark, Shannon and Rollie discussed the incident at Clymmer Field, the roll of film still in Rollie's possession, the ANZA research disks still in Meadows' possession.

At midnight a truck rumbled up the driveway. A minute later Stephen opened the back kitchen door. He joined them at the table, where Kyle poured him some warm milk. He had satin eyes, black hair and a contemplative manner. As he listened to the tape, Jimmy and Pyro watched him with admiration, aware that he was Kyle's number one assassin, and that his name, like their own, was a ruse. None of them actually knew the true identity of the others. Jimmy, the old-growth logger put out of work by the Sierra Club Legal Defense Fund; Pyro, the nephew of a foreclosed cattle rancher who was caught poisoning wolves. Beyond that, identity didn't matter. Only their cause. They practiced a paramilitary protocol and knew not to interrupt Kyle and his prized killer. Kyle played the tape again and said to Stephen, "The woman is Shannon DeShay. Ring a bell?"

"Some relation to Charles DeShay?"

"His daughter."

Stephen stroked his chin with long, strong fingers, each a replica of his overall physique, his mind thinking back six years: *Shannon DeShay, sister of Travis DeShay, who died when I ran him and his troublesome father off the Seward Highway.* One of Stephen's favorite tactics was to approach a target vehicle head on in the night, lights on highbeam, and force it off the highway like James Dean in *Rebel Without a Cause*. It had worked every time except with Charles DeShay, who ended up severely disabled, which Kyle had assumed was enough.

Kyle said, "Meadows is a problem. He's sought out Shannon DeShay because he's researching ANZA and the 1002 Area test well."

"Does he know about the murders?"

"Probably."

Stephen drank his milk.

"You'll need to find him," Kyle told him. "Get those disks and the password."

"And Dawson's film?"

"That too. Find out what Shannon DeShay is doing in Washington, and how she might lead you to Meadows. Last I heard her father was unable to speak or communicate in any way. I thought he'd be dead by now. He knows too much."

"So we find Meadows and Dawson and DeShay and get the password and files," Stephen confirmed. "Then what?"

Kyle adjusted his tinted glasses. "Have you ever heard of the Locard Exchange Principle?"

That night the face came to him, rising up from the rocks, faster and faster like an oncoming train, a thing in flight, everything about it lifeless except the eyes that opened and asked, *Why?*

Kyle jolted awake and sat up in a cold sweat, panting.

THIRTEEN

Denali Sisto was in denial again. No, she said she never flipped a sea kayak in the middle of a pod of orcas in Glacier Bay. She just lost her paddle and drifted into Icy Strait where a fishing boat picked her up. Didn't the skipper ask you to marry him? somebody asked. No, Denali said, he just offered me his bunk, with him in it. Everybody laughed, nobody less than Denali, her full moon face sprinkled with freckles and framed by unruly blonde hair. Half a dozen Matlin staffers had gathered at her desk to eat their lunches.

They turned to watch Jude breeze into the office and approach Harry Arnold, her father's new press secretary. Jude unloaded her Georgetown University book bag, poured a cup of coffee—black with sugar, her sixth of the day—and studied the labyrinth of desks and partitions and boxes stacked and unpacked along the wall. Nearly every desk had a computer, and every other desk a television that broadcast live via C-SPAN from the Senate floor, House floor, this committee or that committee, wherever the greatest action, hottest debate, or most significant legislation was being stirred by polemics and cooked into law. Whenever

C-SPAN was dull, staffers turned to the soap operas and sitcoms.

Harry leaned back and watched Jude with obvious pleasure. Having worked for Senator Longstreet, he enjoyed the elevated status placed upon him by the relatively inexperienced Matlin camp, most of whom were Alaskans new to the Washington power game. To them, Harry was a Capitol Hill veteran who had learned his political sagacity one trick at a time, and would, they assumed, by osmosis if not brute force, teach those tricks to them.

"Where's Shannon?" Jude asked.

"At home, sick," Harry answered.

"She's never sick."

"She is today. She called in at four-thirty this morning and left a message."

"Four-thirty?"

Harry nodded with slow, theatrical certainty.

Jude furrowed her brow. She had spent last night at the Ballston townhouse rented by her father and mother, not at the Georgetown apartment she shared with Shannon. Without asking she picked up Harry's phone and called. No answer; the message machine didn't even come on. It just rang and rang. She grabbed her books and dashed out the door.

"Goodbye," Harry said.

"Tell Shannon we hope she's feeling better," Denali called.

Jude ignored them.

~

Shannon removed her pantyhose to feel the cool hardwood floor on her feet. She opened the window, pulled down the collar of her blouse and let the breeze knead her neck. Seated in a high-backed chair, she tilted back and set her feet on the windowsill. The wind billowed her skirt up her thighs as she opened her legs by delicate degrees. She rolled her head and closed her eyes and took a deep breath, held it, let it out slowly. She placed one hand palm-down on the seat of the chair, braced her shoulders behind her and arched upwards. With the other hand she reached up her skirt and in one swift motion pulled off her panties. She took another deep breath. In, out… in, out.

The cool breeze played with her hair.

Jude always kept the apartment too warm.

Shannon grabbed a pint of mango sorbet from the table behind her and spooned down a dollop. She surveyed the gabled rooftops out the window, the traffic on cobblestoned streets, the trendy boutiques and grand estates along the C&O Canal, the people in their eastern finery always in a hurry, always pressed beneath a gray insipid sky that seemed incapable, perhaps unwilling, to snow. She considered the choices before her on this new day, made clear in too many ways.

She pulled her hair forward and let it fall across her chest. Her mother would braid it for hours when she was young. That's good enough, Shannon would say, twitching, squirming. But it was never good enough for her mother and her wasted perfectionism. *Sit still, girl. I can't do anything with you, for crying out loud. I don't know why you fight me so. You have such beautiful hair. Buoyoootiful hair.*

Shannon cursed every lock and curl.

—I don't want to do this, Shannon.

—Just cut it, Dad, please. If you don't, I will.

Black locks fall onto the autumn tundra; autumn being mid-August this far north. She sits stone-still. He finishes, hands her the scissors and walks to the river. She adds some finishing touches and examines herself in the small mirror. Not bad. Not good either. The Treblinka look. She tucks the mess under her baseball cap and joins him. They skip stones. It would be easier on a lake. Everything is easier on a lake. Lakes reside, rivers travel. Lakes are a destination, a beginning, an end. Rivers are a journey.

Tomorrow they go home. Eddie arrives in his Cessna and takes them to Fairbanks. From there it's fifty minutes by Alaska Airlines to Anchorage. Mom and Travis at the airport, guarded.

—If you can grow a beard, I can cut my hair.

100

—You think so?

She gets eight skips. Beat that.

He gets nine. Says nothing.

The next morning they break camp. Her cut hair has blown away in the wind. Before the plane arrives, Charles finds some strands caught in the nearby willows, interlaced with yellow leaves and caribou fur. He collects some and puts it in his pocket.

When at last they hear the plane, they look at each other. She knows he is different, and she accepts him for those differences. But what about her? Beyond him, who will accept her?

"Good morning," Mark said, rising onto one elbow on the sofa.

Shannon turned. "Good afternoon."

"Afternoon. It's that late?" Mark rubbed his brow.

"How's the head?"

"Uh..." He felt the bandage at his hairline. "Okay, I think." He got to his feet, wobbled a bit and walked to her.

She pulled over another chair and chuckled.

"What?" he said.

"You're a mess. Your hair, your clothes, I wish your editors could see you now."

He bowed like an urchin— "Thank you, your grace" —and sat down beside her.

"Did you sleep okay?"

"I think so."

She offered him some sorbet. He indulged and said, "That's good." He studied the pint container with bleary eyes. "What's the difference between sherbet and sorbet?"

"Sherbet is for friends. Sorbet is for lovers."

"Oh?" He stared at her, glanced down at her exposed thighs, the panties on her lap. "Are you drunk?"

"No, I'm not drunk."

He arched his eyebrows to regard her with pleasant suspicion.

"I was never a sorority girl in college. You know what I always wanted to do?"

"No. What?"

She stretched her elastic panties from one hand to the other and shot them out the window. "That."

Mark stared at her, a smirk curling the corners of his mouth. They got to their feet and peeked out the window; saw the panties on the sidewalk below. They watched an elderly woman walk by and stiffen as she pretended she didn't see them. They ducked back inside and laughed. It took them a minute to calm down. "Where's Rollie?" Mark asked.

"In Jude's room, asleep on her bed. Imagine that."

Mark shook his head, trying to clear his thoughts. "I thought you'd be upset after last night."

"Right now, I don't know what I am. I can't bring back my father or my brother, and I'm not going to dwell on it. But I think you're onto something with your research."

"You've been reading it?"

"All night."

Mark had printed a synopsis before going to sleep on Shannon's sofa, using her home computer and printer.

"You haven't slept?" he asked her.

"Not yet." She picked up some papers off the floor. "I only recognize a couple names on the list. The guy who died in the plane crash was a friend of my Dad."

Mark nodded. "I think he was the only State of Alaska employee who knew that test result. He was a good pilot. He had more than ten thousand hours of cockpit time, and he crashed in perfect weather right after a one-hundred-hour checkup."

"You think it was carbon monoxide poisoning?"

"I do. It could have been rigged. Carbon monoxide has a much higher affinity for hemoglobin than oxygen. It doesn't take much. A slow leak at high elevations can be undetectable and fatal."

"But pilots have CO early-warning patches on their instrument panels."

"This guy didn't. The mechanic who did the maintenance quit his job and disappeared that same day. The plane went down in rugged terrain, scattered along a cliff. The pilot's body wasn't recovered for a week. His family declined to have him autopsied."

They discussed the other accidents, which Shannon admitted seemed less and less accidental the more she studied them. She got to her feet and stretched. Pulling her arms high over her head, she stood on her toes and looked down at Mark with a coquettish smile. She walked into the kitchen to make tea. Mark found some old photographs on the table. "Is this you?" he asked.

"Skinny legs and all, from my first summer in the refuge, ten years ago."

He found one of a young, mischievous Shannon holding caribou antlers atop her father's head, her father laughing away the years. "Who shot the caribou?" Mark asked.

"I did."

This didn't surprise him.

"I knew who I was up there," Shannon added.

"I can see that."

They heard a key slide into the front lock, the timbre of metal on metal. The front door opened and Jude walked in. Though she did this quietly, her entrance seemed abrupt. She stared at Mark and the blanket on the sofa. She said to Shannon, "I heard you were sick."

"I'm fine."

"I tried calling but the phone just rang and rang."

"I unplugged it."

"I don't like it when you do that, Shan."

Heaven forbid we should live unwired, Shannon thought.

"Guess what I saw," Jude said as she plugged in the phone. "A dog walking down the sidewalk with a woman's underwear in its mouth."

Shannon blushed.

Mark grinned. *Lucky dog.*

At that moment Rollie opened the door to Jude's bedroom and stepped out. Hair askew, face swollen, his arm in a cast and his back hunched, he was a comic figure, a gargoyle in Georgetown.

Jude gawked at him and turned to Shannon. "What's going on here?"

"It's not what you think," Shannon said.

Rollie sat on the sofa, trying to shrink under Jude's stare. *If you don't leave me alone, I'll go find someone who will.*

Jude walked to the window and closed it, then went into the kitchen, opened a can of Coors and gulped down half with one long tilt of her head. She leaned against the counter and said, "I come home and find two guys who look like the walking wounded in my apartment, one of them in my bedroom, and what am I supposed to think?"

"It's nothing, Jude," Shannon said.

"This is my apartment, Shan. I got you this apartment. I deserve to know what's going on."

Mark gathered up his research.

Jude said to Shannon, "Did Mr. Meadows here tell you that he was on a forced leave of absence from the *Post?*"

Mark appeared ready to let the comment go, but her provocation was too great. "Is that what you think?" he asked.

"That's what I know."

Mark shook his head. "My editors told me to take a break. I've been back on staff since January first."

"They told you to take a break because your stories were unsubstantiated, that's what I heard." She knocked back another gulp of Coors. "So, you must be plotting your next scheme, no doubt something big. Let's see...I'll bet you're planning the next Age of Enlightenment, is that it?"

"That's it," Mark said, playing along. "The President himself has commissioned me. The next enlightenment will be a time of no fears or desires or rationalizations."

"And I suppose no possessions or growth or wealth or freedom," Jude countered.

"Growth and wealth will be everywhere," Mark replied, "but they'll be spiritual growth and wealth. And possessions will marry with altruism, which won't be easy, since the Gandhian doctrine of nonpossession isn't popular with Big Oil or Libertarians or spoiled children."

Jude laughed.

"Life will be a metaphor for existence," Mark added.

Jude looked at Rollie, who averted his eyes. *Please put her out of my misery.*

"You know," Jude said to Mark, "only a fool would argue with Congressmen Worley the way you did, or sneak into that party using a fake name and a fake signature."

"That's me," Mark said, "a fool."

Jude finished her Coors and tossed the can aside. "You and your crazy environmentalism. It's just a fashion, that's all. You're a journalist who's supposed to be neutral, but you're as green as clover. No wonder you lost your job." She walked into her bedroom and closed the door.

After a moment of uncomfortable silence, Shannon said to Mark, "You should probably leave."

Rollie stumbled out the door and was gone.

"Is what Jude said true?" Shannon asked

Mark lifted his heavy head. "Yes. I was let go from the *Post* for a year. I'm on probation now."

Shannon took a deep breath.

"I'm sorry. I should have told you myself."

"You expect me to trust you now?"

"No."

"Do you still plan to go to New York?"

Mark nodded as he finished packing.

"You don't mind moving around?"

"Not really. My life is interrupted by routine."

"Like a nomad?"

"Or a fugitive."

"Help Rollie get his arm fixed."

"Yes, ma'am."

She kissed him on the cheek, and he stared at her, astonished.

"Don't worry," she said. "I think your theory has merit."

"You do? Can I interview your father and ask him about the test result?"

Shannon drew back. "I told you, Mark. He can't talk. Parts of his brain are scar tissue."

"But you said that he can sometimes nod or blink in response to questions."

"Sometimes yes. Usually no. Mom did say that he's more alert now. She put him in that care center where they've got him on light therapy and a special high-protein diet."

"That's good news. If he can understand and respond, his testimony will work in court."

"In court?"

Mark grabbed her hand. "There's a difference between incompetence and incapacitation. Your father is incapable of walking and talking. He's physically incapacitated but he may not be incompetent. His mind—at least part of it—might be fully aware of everything around him. He could have one hundred percent recall of important events. He could be the key to unlocking what ANZA is hiding."

She chewed her lip.

"Are you going to the Wise Use convention during Fur Rondy next month?" Mark asked her.

"I think so. Sam Matlin's going. I could see Dad again."

"I'll be there and could use your help." He brushed her hair off her cheek, a feathered touch, and leaned toward her just as Rollie reappeared in the doorway and said, "Let's go."

Mark's eyes seemed dusted like before, full of things unsaid as he slipped out the door and closed it softly behind him.

Shannon opened the window onto concrete and brick, the traffic in the streets, the constant noise, the gray January day that

106

promised a dreary, foreign rain. For the first time in many years, she cried.

~

"I don't know where Mark is," Mrs. Luther told the stranger as she analyzed him through the crack in her door. He had a disarming smile beneath a prominent nose, and satin eyes, and he must have stood a foot taller than her. "Who are you?" she asked.

"My name's Daniel. I'm a friend of his."

"I've never heard him mention you."

"Probably because he thinks I over-edit him. He works for me at the *Post*, in the newsroom. I haven't seen him lately and I'm wondering if he's okay." That smile again.

Mrs. Luther relaxed her soured face. "Well you know, he travels a lot, that's what he tells me."

"And he's traveling now?"

"Heavens, young man, you're just full of questions. I'm not his secretary. I just peeked out my door at three-thirty this morning and he was carrying boxes down the stairs, going somewhere with that pretty girl. He had a bandage on his head, and I did hear him say he'd be eating bagels in concrete canyons, if that's any help."

"A little. Can you remember anything more?"

"Nothing more than you would at my age."

"Of course, thank you. You've been very kind."

Five minutes later and three blocks away, Daniel was Stephen again as he climbed into the car with Pyro and said, "Meadows has left for New York. He's probably got Dawson with him. Get up there and play his contacts. You've got his file?"

"Yep. What about you?"

Stephen pulled an ivory-toothed comb from his pocket and ran it through his thick hair. "I'm going to find Shannon DeShay."

The letter arrived addressed to Mr. Alan Quail, Chief Executive Officer, ANZA AMERICA, One Noble Plaza, Houston, Texas. At first glance it was nothing unusual, white envelope, laser print, single stamp, Seattle postmark. What caught the secretary's attention was the absence of a return address. She opened it, as she was instructed to do with all non-restricted correspondence to Mr. Quail, knowing that letters with no return were often written by angry, faceless, powerless citizens who aimed to scold ANZA for one petty thing or another. Most she threw away. This letter was unsigned, and as she read it she paled. Mr. Quail would need to be contacted, but he was in Baku where it was midnight. She phoned the office of Deputy CEO John Sires.

Half an hour later Sires finished a conference call and opened the letter, now marked confidential.

"Dear Mr. Quail," it began. "By now you've no doubt convinced yourself that I achieved nothing more than a security and publicity inconvenience last month. You're wrong. Either you come straight with the American people and tell them what you're hiding, or I'll have you and your illegalities on the front page of every major newspaper across this country. We both know what I'm talking about. By the way, I admired the teak trim in room 2820, but thought the Jon Van Zyle wolf print clashed with the screen savers on the Compaqs. And your security system, though inadequate, was entertaining. Disrespectfully yours, Jumar."

February

FOURTEEN

As far as Eddie Tagarook knew, he was the only one-eared, gimpy-legged Eskimo bush pilot and part-time dog musher in arctic Alaska. Born in Barrow and settled in Kaktovik on the frozen shore of the Beaufort Sea, he stood with one foot in the jet age and one in the Ice Age, straddling a chasm of cultural change deeper than any ever faced by his people. Eddie had adapted better than most, as he owned two small planes, a Cessna 185 and a Piper Super Cub, each in disrepair and of questionable aeronautical ability. Aircraft maintenance for Eddie was a matter of borrowing parts from one plane to make functional another, a common if not praiseworthy practice among bush pilots in Alaska. Both planes were out of service for the winter, parked next to the airstrip about half a mile away.

This dark February morning found Eddie behind his house, harnessing up nine howling huskies at twenty-five degrees below zero. While his good ear good could discern a change in the wind, his other ear lay at the bottom of the Gulf of Alaska, sliced off on a longliner while fishing for black cod twenty years ago. And despite a bum leg that was shattered at the knee when he crashed a plane after engine failure in the Brooks Range, he worked with the viscosity of a man pre-adapted to the north, blending one motion into the next. He loaded his toboggan birchwood sled with a shovel, axe, sleeping bag, tent, headlamp, flashlight, snowshoes, batteries, two weeks of food for himself and his dogs, cooking supplies, a high-powered rifle and box of ammunition, an alcohol stove and an emergency location transmitter. His wife and two young sons helped, though they would not accompany him on this journey. His destination was Prudhoe Bay, one hundred miles to the west. He aimed to be there in a week, in time for the summit between the KANAK Native Corporation and ANZA. An ANZA Lear would arrive in Kaktovik in six days to transport villagers by quick flight, but Eddie wanted to make the journey his own way. He pulled on his parka, its hood with a wolverine ruff to protect his face from the wind. He waved goodbye to his wife and sons, and they waved back.

"Hup," he yelled in the frigid air, and his dogs bolted, silent now, the energy of their barking and howling converted by canine chemistry into forward motion, tight in their harnesses, tails high. They passed the health clinic and school, the nicest buildings in town, built with oil money.

An hour later they were alone, one man and nine dogs swallowed by the immense nothing that to Eddie was everything.

"Whoa," he commanded his team as he stepped on his sled brake and pushed it into the wind-scoured snow. "Everybody okay?" he asked. The huskies looked at him as if to say they were doing just fine, thank you; this was their place too.

The stars winked away as daylight spilled over the summits of the Brooks Range to the south. Eddie tossed a frozen whitefish to each husky, a slightly larger portion going to Innoko, his lead dog. He opened his sled bag, removed the stove, fired it up and melted snow for drinking water. Dehydration was a serious debilitator of sled dogs. If they didn't drink they didn't eat, and if they didn't eat they didn't pull. Besides, Eddie hankered for some hot tea.

Sunrise came in pink pastels, painting the ice in half-light, half-shade, brilliant, alive, suffusing musher and dogs with the radiance of a star, throwing their shadows over the sculpted artwork of ice and snow. Eddie felt suspended, more above the earth than upon it.

Trotting on, the dogs made good time as they moved inland from the coast. Five months from now this white land would sing in a chorus of nesting birds, calving caribou, wildflowers, willows, mosses, lichens, grasses and sedges. And the sun as conductor would stay up twenty-four hours a day. But winter reigned now. Eddie stopped his team to read the isolated tracks of arctic fox, ptarmigan and polar bear.

Ah yes, Eddie thought, *Nanook, the ice bear.*

These particular tracks were large, more than a foot long, adult-sized, probably a male. Eddie knew a female's tracks would be slightly pigeon-toed and lacking the peripheral markings of long hairs. In summer Nanook usually hunted seals far out to sea along the edges of ice floes. In winter he might move on shore to den on north-facing slopes of the Brooks Range. An unpredictable hibernator, Nanook in fact did not hibernate at all—not in the strictest sense—for any month he could emerge from semi-sleep to patrol his domain, as this male had done. The tracks were new, uncompromised by wind, probably no more than a day old. "Well fellas," Eddie said to his dogs as he scanned the horizon, "we've got company."

Known to stalk prey with snow on its black nose to improve camouflage, Nanook was a clever hunter. It seldom attacked men. But every winter several sled dogs fell victim. Last year in Kaktovik a polar bear had crushed the skull of a husky with one swipe of its paw. This bear was not near, otherwise the dogs would have barked up a storm. But it was not far either. Eddie touched his rifle and spoke aloud in Inupiaq: "Ice bear, find your way. Your spirit is strong. Your skill is great. Find your way, ice bear, and I will find mine."

Halfway around the world in Baku, the capital city of Azerbaijan, on the western shore of the Caspian Sea, Alan Quail and his ANZA entourage had in mind the same destination as Eddie Tagarook. Prudhoe Bay, Alaska. It seemed light years away.

"Jesus Christ, how long does it take to get fuel around here?" Quail asked with exasperation.

He drummed his fingers in the forward lounge of his corporate Gulfstream V, more spacious than a Learjet, and waited for Mustafa, a longhaired Arab with a drooping moustache who once an hour emerged from the tiny airport office to tell them the fuel truck would arrive any minute. While at his desk, Mustafa fingered prayer beads from the Taza-Pir Mosque and ogled miniskirted women in contraband magazines from his Shiite Muslim buddies on Tolstoy Street, downtown.

Violence had erupted with neighboring Armenia, and everybody—Russia, Turkey, Iran—wanted a piece of the pipeline that would transport the oil when the fields were developed. Worse yet, Russian hardliners had convinced the Azeris to annul the Contract of the Century, and promised leaders of six former Soviet republics greater prosperity under a new cooperative workers' union that would develop the Caspian without any help from foreign parasites such as ANZA. All profits would stay in the region. Quail was sick with disappointment as he watched ten years of delicate negotiations begin to crumble. Three days earlier officials had confiscated every cellular phone and notebook computer belonging to the ANZA team, plus their Gulfstream fax machine. All other requests had been refused. Quail needed to fly to Novosibirsk, where pro-Western Russians would help him contact John Sires.

Maya deplaned, walked to the tiny airport office and banged on the door. Mustafa appeared and spoke in Arabic outbursts. He waved his arms wildly, and Maya waved hers. Mustafa screamed, and Maya screamed back. He crossed his arms and she crossed hers. More screaming and finger pointing, until finally he invited her inside where she stayed for an hour, unseen.

"You think she's okay?" somebody asked on the Gulfstream.

Ten minutes later Maya returned, and two minutes after that the fuel truck arrived.

"What'd you say to him?" Quail asked her.

"What all Arab men want to hear, that he has a penis to rival any camel on the Caspian, and he is a great man whose wives will give him many sons. He offered to marry me."

Members of the ANZA team looked at each other, their eyes wide.

"Actually," Maya added with a cryptic smile, "all he talked about was the movie, *Titanic*. It's Kate Winslet he wants to marry, not me."

Everybody laughed.

"Let's go," Quail said once the fuel tanks were full and they had paid Mustafa.

Maya declined to say that while in his office she had bribed Mustafa into allowing her to make one phone call to Washington.

~

Harry Arnold hung up the phone, considered the news, and dialed Anchorage. "Darryl, I just spoke with Maya in Baku. Things are screwed up for ANZA."

"I know. The Caspian is a mess. It's on CNN."

"The night of the ANZA party, when that guard threw you out of the lobby, did you see Susan and Shannon DeShay arrive?"

"No. But I know that Zarki saw them upstairs, in the penthouse. Why, what's up?"

"I think there was more in room 2820 than we bargained for."

~

Darkness fell and Eddie Tagarook made camp. The next day dawned clear and windless. Perfect mushing again, followed by another quiet camp. Wearing only polypropylene long under-wear and vapor barrier boots, he rustled from his sleeping bag at 3:00 a.m. to relieve himself. Northern lights danced through the Big Dipper.

"Look at that," he said to the dogs. "That's a sight."

They lay curled together, tails over their noses.

Every day, every mile, musher, dog team and ice bear moved closer to the greatest industrial complex in Alaska, Prudhoe Bay, that rose phantasmagorically above everything around it. Musher and bear moved closer to each other as well, on paths that by design or coincidence seemed destined to meet. Eddie made good time until a storm pinned him down for three days and the wind chill fell to minus seventy. His objective was no longer Prudhoe Bay, but mere survival, as he made camp and fed his dogs hot high-protein, high-carbohydrate meals. Snowdrifts covered them and insulated them from the cold, with only their wet noses vis-ible for breathing.

Nanook moved northwest.

The storm died on the fourth morning and Eddie harnessed his team. He crossed the frozen Canning River and departed the Arctic National Wildlife Refuge. In so doing, he entered the "Alaska of Tomorrow," an ANZA image strategist's term for the growing grid of seismic survey sites and exploration wells that reached east more than forty miles from Prudhoe Bay. Places with names like Klondike Strike, Nine Lives Cat, Admiralty One and Black Gold Ten. Eddie saw their alien profiles stab the horizon, and he steered a wide berth. This was not his Alaska. Not any-more.

That night an ANZA jet hissed overhead, filled with Eskimos who would dine on Prudhoe Bay prime rib. Eddie pulled his sleep-ing bag over his head and tried to sleep. Morning came reluc-tantly, weighed down by winter. The wind had doubled back on itself to blow from the east, putting Eddie and his team at a disadvantage, upwind of Nanook.

With the huskies harnessed and moving before sunrise, Eddie hoped to make Prudhoe Bay by late afternoon. Two hours later he saw the great oil facility before it was visible, as a winter temperature inversion created a *fata morgana*, a mirage that enabled him to see over the horizon. Steel spires impaled the sky. Bright lights blazed atop netherworld drill pads. Primary colors adorned the metal buildings. Hot gases vented from flare pads, licking the sky with red and yellow-blue flames. "There it is," Eddie said to his dogs, "New Jersey North."

He was late and knew friends from Kaktovik would be wondering about him; they might even come looking for him. He also knew the ice bear was near.

Then it happened. Ten miles from Prudhoe Bay as he stopped to feed his team, Eddie saw the horizon move, a subtle shift to the southwest, white against white, a mile away or more, something approaching. Black nose. *Nanook, at last.*

It walked as ice bears do, rounded shoulders, fluid legs, paws flicking down with each step, head low and swinging back and forth, sinuous neck, broad hips, bone-crushing jaws. Eddie reached for his rifle.

The wind stopped and Innoko lifted his head. The other dogs too. Before they could bark Eddie commanded them to be quiet. They obeyed, grudgingly emitting low growls. The bear moved into the sinking sun where it stopped to throw its long shadow over musher and dogs. Eddie squinted at the halloed silhouette, the bear's amber breath rising in backlit clouds. *Was this a hunting technique? A stalking strategy? A Nanook trick to blind its intended victim?* In all his years in the arctic Eddie had never heard of an ice bear doing this.

They stood in a prism of time and light: bear, man and dogs. Eddie chambered a round in his bolt-action .30-06, hoping the bear would leave, but it did not. Eddie spoke: "Ice bear, find your way. Your spirit is strong. Your skill is great. Find your way, ice bear, and I will find mine."

Then he heard a strange whop, whop, whopping that came from the direction of Prudhoe. He turned to watch a helicopter fly in a wide arc, kicking up snow in a powdered mist, rotors cutting the sky, the engine shredding the silence. Eddie saw a rifle barrel emerge from the helicopter door, aimed at the running bear. He opened his mouth to protest, "Nooooo..."

~

Two hundred Eskimos waited in the cavernous Prudhoe Bay central cafeteria while John Sires sat on stage and read an e-mail printout from Alan Quail: "John, trust you made it to Prudhoe. 1002 Area now high priority with new developments in Baku. Chaos worse than before. Will join you by 8 p.m. No additional contact means I'm on schedule. Alan."

Sires folded the e-mail as a junior ANZA executive introduced him, "...one of the most distinguished industrialists in America, please welcome the deputy CEO of ANZA, John Sires."

Wearing a new Eddie Bauer shirt and fur-lined boots, Sires crossed the stage to a tepid applause, "Thank you, thank you," he said. "It's good to be here. Most visitors to this great facility are impressed with three things: how clean it is, how good the food is, and how many caribou inhabit the area. Of course there are no caribou here now, since they all migrate south for the winter. But I don't need to tell you that, do I?"

A sea of dark faces studied him, the eyes distant amid the florescent lights and linoleum floor and stainless steel fixtures. The Eskimos wore Carhartts and mukluks, but also the passive postures of a people out of time and place, caught between then and now, artifacts from another world to be bought and sold by a more aggressive, dominant race.

"We at ANZA are very proud of Prudhoe Bay and know you are, too," Sires continued. "We believe it's in your best interests to support the energy bills that were introduced last month in Washington by Senator Longstreet and Congressmen Worley.

You'll find synopses of these bills in your information packets."

Papers rustled through the room as Sires explained the bills, the ANWR drilling provisions, how they will advance through Senate and House subcommittees and committees, and ultimately into conference committee. "By the way," he asked, "did y'all enjoy your dinner and the movie last night?"

A few nods.

"Good. We have a turkey dinner planned for tonight that y'all should enjoy as much as last night's prime rib. The cranberries and stuffin' are excellent. My aunt Ella makes the best turkey stuffin' in Texas and it's not as good as what we make here. Now that's saying somethin'."

No response.

Sires elaborated on the importance of the Alaska Native Alliance and their support of the energy bills. "Equally important will be your testimony against the Janstadt Wilderness bill, since it aims to lock up Anwahr and put you on welfare. Is that what you want?"

Some heads shook desultorily. Others nodded.

Sires scanned the room with insincere warmth. An old Eskimo raised his wrinkled hand.

"Yes, you in the back."

"My name is Walter Kiviikanak. I am—"

"You'll have to speak louder," Sires squelched into the microphone.

A young, hard-featured woman stood up next to the old man and shouted, "My name is Elsie Kiviikanak. My grandfather wants to know why the press wasn't invited to this?"

"This is a private matter between ANZA and you good people," Sires said. "Remember, it was the press who started rumors of oil leases in bowhead whaling waters in the Beaufort Sea, and exaggerated post-spill salmon and herring crashes in Prince William Sound, all of it untrue. We don't deal in rumors or lies. We deal in facts. We need to move forward, not backward."

Elsie appeared unsatisfied, but sat down under the glare of

stares from elders around her.

Sires asked for more questions and received none. "Don't forget," he added, "that those of you who want to testify in favor of the energy bills can sign up for free transportation to Washington. Dinner will be served in thirty minutes. After that we'll call our meeting of village and corporate leaders. Meanwhile, I invite you to play pool and watch television. This is the cleanest, most efficient and environmentally safe oil facility in the world. Y'all deserve nothing but the best."

~

More than three thousand miles to the southeast, in Manhattan's Greenwich Village, Mark Meadows slipped into a coffee shop and met Tony Carzoli, a fellow *Washington Post* reporter. They sat in a booth in the back, with Tony facing away from the door, and Mark toward it. Tony looked his typical confident self; Mark did not. "How's it going?" Tony asked him.

"Fine."

"How's it going, really?"

Mark sipped his coffee. "I'm being hunted."

Tony's terse expression didn't change. "By those same guys you told me about? The ones who roughed you up in your apartment?"

"One of them, the one with the broken finger. I didn't recognize the other guy. I saw them a couple blocks from here yesterday, showing my picture around. They're not very discreet." Mark forced a grin. "I think I'll hire my cousin's wife. She's an unemployed off-Broadway make-up artist. Maybe she can make me look like Arnold Schwarzenegger."

"I doubt it," Tony said as he poured sugar into his coffee. He and Mark had been friends since their first day together at the *Post* seven years ago. "So if these guys aren't with Parkendale or ANZA, who are they?"

Mark shrugged. "I don't know, the Gestapo maybe. Is Hutch

losing patience with me?" Lowell Hutchinson was Mark's editor.

"Probably. I know he's talked to Gil about this ANZA thing. They like Rollie's photos and want to run them, but they need something to carry it. They can't pay you for speculation. You need to get to that geologist, Charles DeShay."

"I'm leaving for Anchorage tomorrow."

"The *Post* got an anonymous tip that Alan Quail and John Sires are in Prudhoe Bay talking with the Eskimos."

Mark shook his head. It was easy to connect the dots. With trouble in Baku, ANZA would aim for the Arctic Refuge with renewed vigor. "Can you do a little research for me?" he asked Tony.

"Sure. What?"

Mark handed him a thin paper file. "See what you can find out about this guy, Richard Leavitt. He died in the car crash with Shannon's brother."

"She called for you the other day."

"Shannon? What'd she say?"

"Whoa, Marco, do I see love in those monastic blue eyes?"

"I'll tell you, Tony, she's something." Mark told him about the panties out the window, the kiss on his cheek.

"Did you kiss her back?" Tony asked.

"Uh...no, I was going to but—"

"You're a fool, my friend. A fool."

FIFTEEN

Alan Quail and his courtiers landed at Prudhoe Bay with the wind chill at sixty below. As he stood in the central foyer and removed his vapor barrier boots, hooded parka and thick gloves, he received a celebrity's reception from scientists, technicians, administrators, even the cooks from the kitchen. This was the first time an ANZA CEO had visited Prudhoe Bay in the dead of winter. A plateful of hot chocolate chip cookies made the rounds. Sires maneuvered toward Maya Donjek, but Quail preempted him and walked him down the hall and asked in a tight voice, "Anything I need to know about?"

Sires thought Alan looked ten years older, his eyes deep in their sockets, the lines creasing his face. He briefed him on the Eskimos. Quail pulled a toothpick from his pocket and began to chew it. "Who've they got here for legal counsel?"

Sires listed the Stanford and Harvard attorneys hired by KANAK and other arctic village corporations. The toothpick bobbed up and down between Quail's teeth. Sires could see canker sores in the corners of his mouth, brought on by stress. He wondered if Alan's strain was from the Baku debacle, or from his daughter's failing health. Probably both. Quail spoke about Baku, then asked, "What's the latest on the Jumar letter?"

"Johnny Parkendale says it's a hoax. He says the inner vault in room 2820 wasn't penetrated. He's got a short list of suspects and says he'll crack the case soon."

Quail chewed the toothpick but made no comment. He looked at the ceiling and attempted to take a deep breath. Down the hall, two bodyguards—one for him, one for Sires—watched closely, and beyond them stood a dozen Eskimos. Quail directed the bodyguards to escort the Eskimos into the conference room.

"How's Aliena?" Sires asked about his daughter, thinking talk of her might brighten Alan's spirits.

"She's not well," Quail said. "It's a tumor. I need to get home and be with her."

A tumor? Jesus, Alan. Sires had never had much of a warm spot for Alan. *The Board should have awarded the CEO position to me, not to you.* But now he found himself feeling sorry for Alan, an emotional terrain new to him.

They walked down the hall toward the conference room where fifty Eskimo leaders waited with their corporate attorneys. They spoke about the Parkendale investigation, the possible motive and suspects, the fact that the evidence bag that held the videotape of the intruder had disappeared. Quail shook his head. "This break-in worries me, John. Damn us and our dirty little secret."

"Which one?" Sires asked with mild sarcasm. "Baku or Anwahr?"

Neither man spoke for a moment. The toothpick was pulp. Quail spit it out. Sires thought he was under too much strain to conduct this meeting, but the CEO ducked into a restroom and emerged looking refreshed, his silver hair neatly combed. "Let's do it," he said.

They entered the room, and Quail flowered. He shook hands with every Eskimo and white attorney, putting his right hand firmly into theirs while he performed miracles with his left, touching their forearms and shoulders, clasping them two-handed. He knelt beside an elderly woman who had trouble standing. He called her by name and asked about her son and his recent hunt, the last berry harvest, how many jars of jam she had made. One by one he loosened their resolve with perfect transcultural diplomacy, until he met Elsie Kiviikanak.

"You're late," she said with a scowl.

Quail looked at her with no discernable emotion, then directed everybody to sit down. He smiled at the faces before him, faces less suspicious than five minutes before. "Please begin," he said. "Your concerns are our concerns." His decorum was perfect, his negotiation smooth. He gave nothing without getting something back. He spoke about the energy bill and proposed a sliding royalty for those explorations and easements on Native inholdings. There would be plenty of profit for everybody, he said. He mentioned big numbers. The Eskimos smiled.

"Can you guarantee all of this," Elsie asked from the back row.

"Guarantees don't exist in the oil business," Quail lied decorously. "But we'll do our best."

Elsie brushed a strand of hair from her thin, hard face and asked, "Why haven't you released the 1002 test drill result?"

"When it's in our best interest and in yours, we will."

"You were required by law to release that result two years ago," Elsie countered. A dozen Eskimos shifted in their chairs.

"The disclosure agreement between ANZA and KANAK has been amended," an ANZA attorney said. "ANZA is no longer under any obligation to release that result at any time."

"Why isn't the press here?" Elsie asked.

"They've already written extensively about Anwahr," Sires said.

"You mean the Arctic National Wildlife Refuge."

"Yes, exactly."

Elsie crossed her arms. "They haven't written about covert meetings like this."

"See that door," Quail said as he pointed to the back of the room. All heads turned. "It's open. Anybody is welcome here. This is not a secret meeting."

"I think it is. I think this whole thing is a farce."

"Be quiet, Elsie," a voice admonished her from the other side of the room. It was ninety-seven-year-old Tom Jack, former mayor of the village of Point Wolf. Everybody watched as he pulled himself out of his chair to stand barely five feet tall. A thousand storms had contoured his face and watered his eyes. His toothless mouth moved slowly, like his words. "I see many sufferings for many winters," he said, "and many people die too soon. Many changes, not all good. But my life saved in a health clinic built by oil, my wife, too. My great-grandchildren born there. Not so many young people die now, 'cept from whiskey. Remember that, Elsie." Tom Jack sat down.

Many Eskimos nodded in quiet confirmation as Elsie and her grandfather looked sheepishly at the floor. The ANZA high command sat in sustained, blissful silence.

~

Eddie worked in the darkness without a headlamp. He slipped his .30-06 Remington from his sledbag and emptied a box of armor-piercing ammunition into the pocket of his parka. He watered and fed his dogs, then ate his own quick meal, still brooding on the helicopter incident. He set an ice stake forward of the team and a snowhook in back to hold the dogs in position while he was away. Innoko watched him, aware with a dog's intuition that his master was still angry.

"It's okay, Innoko," Eddie whispered. "Stay here and be quiet." Innoko nuzzled Eddie's neck. Something serious was about to happen. "I'll be right back," Eddie said. Time to avenge the wrongful killing of a polar bear, and other transgressions.

He shined a penlight flashlight onto his compass and took a heading on the Prudhoe Bay ANZA central facility—an island of eerie lights in a sea of darkness—one mile away on the coast, south-southeast. To return to his dog team after finishing his job, Eddie would need to travel on the opposite heading through the black night across the frozen Beaufort Sea. He had seen James Bond do something like this once. *Or was it Mission Impossible?* Eddie figured that north-northwest out on the sea ice would be the last place ANZA would look for him, since they'd last seen him southeast of Prudhoe.

~

On the other side of the continent, Jeff Meola and Denali Sisto ate ice cream and watched a movie in his apartment on Capitol Hill. Somebody knocked on the door, and Jeff looked at Denali with surprise. He walked to the door, peeped through the hole and saw two men distorted in the fisheye glass. "Who is it?"

"Parkendale Investigators, Mr. Meola. We need to talk to you."

"I've spoken to you guys twenty times on the phone."

"We have some papers to serve to you." One of the men held up a manila envelope.

"Mail them to me."

"We need to serve them to you now."

"It's after midnight. Go away or I'll call the cops."

"Open your door and sign these papers, Mr. Meola, or we'll be the ones who call the cops. And they'll arrest you."

"What for? On whose authority?"

"The Municipality of the District of Columbia, the Ninth Circuit Court in San Francisco, and the District Attorney in Anchorage."

Jeff was a graduate of the University of Washington Law School. He knew constitutional law, civil rights and due process. These guys were talking bullshit. Denali sat on the sofa with her pint of Cherry Garcia half-eaten, her otherwise sunny face cloudy with fear.

"Open the door, Jeff."

"No way. Slide the papers under it. If it's a legitimate warrant for search and seizure, I'll open the door. Otherwise, I'm calling the cops."

Jeff waited. When he looked through the peephole again, the two men were gone.

~

"My father," Alan Quail said to his Eskimo audience, "always told me that new problems require new solutions. We will open Anwahr to oil exploration because we can accomplish things together that neither one of us—your great culture or our great industry—can accomplish alone. ANZA will film national television ads about Anwahr and we'd like you to audition for parts. Those of you who are accepted will be flown to the filming locations and receive free passes to Disneyland. Is that acceptable?"

Of course, the Eskimos said.

"Finally, we have a surprise, if you'd please join us down the hall in another room."

The Eskimos walked ahead as Sires and Quail followed. Sires spoke quietly, "I neglected to tell you that Eddie Tagarook was supposed to be here."

"The Kaktovik pilot?"

"He's Elsie Kiviikanak's cousin. He was traveling by dog sled and ran into a polar bear a few miles southeast of here. We sent out a chopper and found the bear practically on top of him. Our boys shot the bear and Eddie got upset. We offered to fly him here, but he refused."

"Where is he now?"

"We don't know. There's no sign of him. He must be running his dogs with his headlamp off."

"Could he make trouble?"

"Here? Now? I can't imagine how."

"Then screw him."

~

Eddie knelt next to a gas compressor building, aimed and fired. The shot crackled through the cold air as sparks danced off a metal utility box sixty feet away. He fired again. More sparks.

Somebody yelled in the distance.

Eddie chambered another round, fired again and missed. He had removed his large mittens, and now his fingers, protected only by thin polypro gloves, stiffened in the cold. He chambered another round, took careful aim, and fired again.

The lights went out.

Hostile voices came closer, searching voices. "You go left, you go right. Shoot the bastard if you have to."

The lights came back on with auxiliary power. Eddie knew this would happen. He moved behind a smaller dehydrator building, held his breath, listened, heard feet crunching on snow, moving away, then nothing. He crossed a parking lot and spotted the metal encased auxiliary cable near a water processing facility.

"Randy, is that you?" a voice came nearer.

Eddie ducked between a large vertical exhaust and a metal grating. He quietly chambered another round and took aim at the auxiliary line eighty feet away. It would be his last shot.

~

The junior executive opened the curtains to reveal a waist-high, three-dimensional ANWR 1002 Exploration Display tilted five degrees for optimum viewing. The Eskimos walked toward it. Suddenly the lights went out and everybody froze. "It's okay," Quail said. "I'm sure things like this happen now and then, don't they, John?"

"That's right," Sires stammered. "No need for alarm." He held his hand to his face and saw only blackness.

"We have power outages in our village all the time," an Eskimo said.

"That's right," Quail added. "This is nothing serious. I grew up on a farm in Idaho and learned to read by a candle. The modern world has come a long way since then. This is a state-of-the-art facility with auxiliary power that will kick-in any minute. Everybody stay where you are and—"

The lights came on.

"Well," Quail said, "what did I tell you? A fully modern facility. Now, everybody, please step this way."

The Eskimos circled the display and pointed to topographic features they recognized, places they knew well, places that defined them and their history. Quail let their intrigue build for a minute. "Now for the future," he said. "I would like everybody to pay careful attention as a new day dawns for us all in the 1002 Area."

He rotated a dial that dimmed the overhead track lights. In ten seconds he would flip a switch to illuminate a grid across the display, announcing the arrival of ANZA in the Arctic National Wildlife Refuge. The Eskimos would gasp in wonder. Everybody leaned forward with anticipation.

Quail smiled smugly at Sires, and Sires back at him. He flipped the switch. "Behold," he said as Eddie Tagarook fired his last shot, "the future of the…what the hell? Goddammit, who's monkeying with the lights around here?"

Elsie Kiviikanak laughed in the darkness. "Anybody got a candle?"

Sixteen

Shannon found her window seat on the Boeing 727 and made herself comfortable. The flight from Washington's Ronald Reagan National Airport to Seattle's SeaTac would take five hours, and to Anchorage another three, where her mother would be at the gate, wearing some silly hat pinned to her head, her eyes wounded, her voice like a lariat. Shannon could hear it already, the same voice Mom used to snare her feral daughter and husband when they returned from their first summer in the arctic.

—*Oh, Shannon, your hair. She pulls off Shannon's ball cap. Stands there, aghast, hand at her mouth. Fingernails painted pink. No hugs or kisses. Oh, que feo! What have you done?*

—*I cut it, Mom. It'll grow back. Hair does that.*

Charles pulls Susan aside, walks her down to baggage claim, tries to calm her. Shannon and Travis follow.

—*You work to upset her, don't you? Travis says.*

—*Leave me alone, Travis.*

Problems that winter come in black and white, like the season. Edges abrupt and hurtful. The dying light takes all buoyancy with it. Shannon dreams of the drumming of hooves on the tundra. She joins a junior hockey league. Comes home cut and bruised.

—I don't know how you got so wild, Mom says, meaning how you got so out of control.

Papa Hector dies three days before Christmas. Mom and Travis go to Mexico City for the funeral. Shannon refuses. She detests the suffocating smog and traditions of death down there. She and Dad play cribbage and shovel snow. On nights when she cannot sleep, he tells her stories about the arctic. His words strum her sternum and send her into visceral dreams.

Three young men come calling. They stand in the kitchen, the snow on their boots melting onto the hardwood floor. They have finished their math exercises and need to give them to Travis, their tutor. Dad's at work. Shannon is alone. She takes the papers; regards the boys with mild interest, as they do her. The quiet one is named William Alt. He has burdened eyes that will not forget this lithe girl in her baseball cap and hockey jersey. He gives her a deferential nod, and leaves with his friends.

When Mom and Travis return, Shannon spends more time alone in her bedroom, reading. They fight one night about something, anything, nothing. Shannon refuses to eat dinner. Later, Dad knocks on the door, softly, in that way of his. He brings her a plate of food, sits on her bed, doesn't say anything for awhile.

—Be careful in your loneliness game, Shannon.

—It's just a game.

—Yes, it's just a game. But it's a game you can lose.

Shannon caught a smile from a familiar man taking his seat two rows forward of her.

"Hello," he said without hesitation.

"Hello." She remembered him as any warm-blooded woman would. Faded jeans, bolo tie, dark features, tall and handsome.

"Didn't I see you yesterday in the Dirksen Building?" he asked. "At the hearing on mining law revisions?"

"Oh, yes." She felt her temperature rise. "You left early."

"I had to. I wish I could have stayed. How was it?" His tenor voice floated from a finely sculpted mouth beneath an aquiline nose. His persuasive, satin eyes reminded Shannon of old photographs of the mystic Russian monk, Rasputin; eyes the color of semi-sweet chocolate, her weakness.

She composed herself and said, "Senator Drummund ended up pounding his fist on the table and turning beet red. I thought he was going to have a heart attack."

Rasputin Eyes laughed. "It'd serve him right for all those years of smoking cigars and financing the tobacco industry."

Shannon didn't usually make men laugh.

He leaned over his seat. "I saw you taking notes. Are you with the press?"

"No. I work for Senator Matlin."

"The new senator from Alaska. Good for you."

A stolid woman prepared to sit next to Shannon when Rasputin Eyes asked her, "Excuse me, ma'am. Do you mind trading seats with me so I can sit next to my friend?"

My friend? Shannon swallowed.

"You'll have a better view of the movie," he added with a wink. The woman consented, and Rasputin Eyes slid in next to Shannon. "I hope you don't mind."

"Not at all," Shannon said, wondering if she did.

"Are you on Senator Matlin's private staff or a committee staff?" he asked.

"Private staff. I mostly answer constituent mail. But sometimes I get to write the senator's talking points, or proof bills to match their House versions. They have to be word for word or else they won't go through the computer." *Stop jabbering. Avoid his eyes. A five hour flight next to this man. Somebody give me oxygen.* The plane backed away from the gate and approached the runway. "What about you?" she asked him.

"I'm a geologist."

"Oh?"

"I used to be in private practice in California, advising insurance companies on earthquake probabilities. Five years of that was enough. I'm with the U.S. Geological Service now."

Geological Survey, not Service. Strange that he would say it that way. "I co-majored in geology in college. My father was a geologist."

He extended his hand. "I should introduce myself. I'm Stephen York." His hand was strong but gentle, fingers long, nails square. No wedding ring. She told him her name and he said, "That must mean your father is Charles DeShay."

"That's right." *How come everybody knows my father?*

"He authored some peer-reviewed papers on metamorphic petrology. Didn't he get his Ph.D. at the Colorado School of Mines?"

"Yes." *Because Mom wanted him to. Papa Hector had studied there. A pipeline school into the oil industry and good money.*

The 727 climbed skyward over Washington and banked west. Stephen York ran an ivory-toothed comb through his thick dark hair and said, "Well, Shannon, it's a pleasure to meet you."

~

Three thousand feet below, Tyler Kyle placed a printout of the *Anchorage Daily News Online* on Senator Longstreet's Sitka spruce desk and pointed to the headline. KAKTOVIK MAN ARRESTED IN PRUDHOE BAY SHOOTING.

Longstreet read it while he rolled up the sleeves of his Ralph Lauren shirt.

Kyle only had a minute. He had been up since four-thirty, read five newspapers, drank six cups of hot water, and had urgent business in his office next door.

"Eddie Tagarook," Longstreet said. "I've heard of him. This Elsie Kiviikanak sounds like a pistol."

"She's Eddie's cousin. She broke the story."

"Sounds to me like ANZA did Tagarook a favor, shooting that bear."

Kyle waited for the senator to grasp the important elements in the story. Longstreet pinched the bridge between his nose and closed his eyes. "This changes things doesn't it?"

"I thought you'd greet it as good news."

"I do."

"Quail and Sires were in that facility when the lights went out, probably sweet-talking the Eskimos with venture capitalism and sliding royalties and..."

Longstreet's mind cascaded back to the 1002 test result and Maya's caveat. *You know, senator, I wouldn't put too much faith in that... that the result is what you think it is.*

"...Quail's always had an appetite for Anwahr," Kyle was saying, "and now with trouble in Baku..."

Longstreet seemed far, far away.

"...Senator?"

"Yes?"

Kyle locked his elbows and leaned onto the desk. "Quail will recruit pro-drilling Eskimos to testify on the Hill. If we can come to terms with him on a leasing arrangement, I believe he'll release the 1002 test result."

"I think you could be right."

Kyle nodded. "I've been working with the Foreign Affairs Committee. For a couple earmarkings in Appropriations, Chairman Balznic will postpone his trip to Baku, which would discourage the Majority Leader, and if he doesn't go, neither will the Secretary of Energy, who wants the mission to be bipartisan. The delay will prolong Azeri and Armenian destabilizations, and increase ANZA's desire for Anwahr oil." Kyle surrendered a modest grin.

"What earmarkings?"

"Pentagon mostly, and a new military museum in San Antonio."

Longstreet peered over his bifocals.

"I also spoke with Senator Romper's office. He'll be phoning you soon. He needs your help."

"Let me guess. Nelson Romper's got problems with the Securities and Exchange Commission, and he wants to talk turkey with somebody who can get his butt out of a sling?"

"I wouldn't know."

"No, but let's say you did know. I don't suppose it would be possible to document how the honorable senator from California, a cosponsor on Bruce Janstadt's Wilderness bill, suddenly ran into difficulty with the SEC and needs a favor from me, the author of the opposing energy bill and an old Army buddy of Bill Corey, who chairs Banking and Finance."

Kyle moved only his mouth. "Certainly not."

"Perhaps I worry too much."

"Perhaps."

"Senator Romper is a wealthy and resourceful man."

"More wealthy than resourceful."

"Ah yes, there are others in Washington more resourceful..."

"A few."

Longstreet eased back in his chair. Seconds passed as neither man spoke and no accounting was requested in this silent benediction between a senator and his chief of staff. How Kyle did what he did was beyond Longstreet's reckoning. Political payoffs, black magic, forbidden dances on the edge of right and wrong. The senator refused to ask and in return was never told. Nelson Romper had engineered a small coalition of pro-Wilderness Republicans that needed to be broken, whatever the cost, and Kyle had done what he needed to do. The truth doesn't matter when you have an agenda.

Kyle moved toward the door and said, "Your Wise Use keynote address is scheduled for nine o'clock tomorrow morning. Today's lunch is at twelve-thirty at the Red Sage with senators Balznic and Corey. We need to be at Dulles at three."

Longstreet stood and opened the curtains as Kyle exited and the secretary rang over the intercom, "Senator Romper on line two for you, senator."

Longstreet sat in his sumptuous chair and pressed a button. "Nelson, how the hell are you?"

"Could be better, Oliver. How are you?"

"Good, good. How are Janet and the kids?"

"Janice, you mean."

"Yes, Janice."

"She's fine. I'll tell you what, Oliver, I work the market, you know that?"

"Yes, I've heard—"

"Well here I am ass deep in computer-generated derivatives and commodity futures and interest rate swaps and synthetic securities and equity-linked bank deposits and yield curve notes, all of it legal, of course."

"Of course."

"Unless this retroactive portfolio insurance bill sails through Bill Corey's committee. I'll tell you what, if you could have a word with Bill..." Nelson Romper was the richest man in the Senate, his fortune estimated at six hundred million dollars. Like most rich men and gamblers gilded as statesmen, he regarded his wealth as an organism unto itself to be pampered and groomed, to grow as large as possible.

Longstreet breathed audibly over the phone so his colleague would understand the supreme weight of his request, then he said, "I suppose you know that Bill and I fought together in the same battalion in Korea."

"Is that right?"

"You ever had the sirloin at the Red Sage?"

"Can't say as I have. My stomach's been actin' up. Janice has got me eatin' yogurt, if you can believe that." Romper laughed nervously.

Longstreet grinned. "I'll tell you what, I'll talk with Bill. How about you and me get together next week to discuss this market business and my energy bill? Have our secretaries set it up."

"That'd be fine, Oliver, mighty fine. Thank you."

Next door in his dim office, Tyler Kyle recorded every word spoken by Longstreet and Romper. He removed the tape, made a copy and placed both copies in his briefcase, one for his files, one for a safe deposit box in the Bitterroot Mountains of Idaho.

An hour later a FedEx letter arrived from a fictitious Florida backwater, where a Merlin apprentice had infiltrated Parkendale Investigative Services. As with every piece of FedEx and UPS mail addressed to him, Kyle had instructed that the secretary sign for it and hand it to him unopened. Inside was the guest list from the ANZA Christmas party, four hundred and twenty names on eight pages, with each page stamped CONFIDENNIAL across the top.

~

The tall man who called himself Stephen watched his prey, Shannon DeShay, exit the plane at SeaTac Airport. She was smarter than he had anticipated, and not as forthcoming about her father, the man he had crippled and now needed to kill. He watched her stride through the concourse and glance back to search for him once, twice, three times in less than a minute.

Sitting at her gate, Shannon scanned the crowd for Stephen York. She knew wild animals that could disappear: martens in a spruce forest, moose in a willow thicket, foxes in beach grass, ravens in the night. *But a man in an airport? Whose plane was about to depart?* She felt uneasy that his connecting flight was the same as hers. She boarded early and found her window seat and watched for him. He had been polite on the last flight, yet too practiced and strangely calculating. Feeling him entrap her, she had buried herself in magazines and books.

Then she saw Harry Arnold standing in the aisle, his beady eyes and smarmy smile. "Is that your seat, Eleven F?" he asked. "Unbelievable. I'm in Eleven E." He shoved his mammoth carry-on bag into the overhead bin and plopped down next to her, displacing her elbow with his on the armrest between them. Shannon's seat was suddenly small.

Harry kicked off his shoes and said, "They got any sports magazines on this plane?" He had just been at the timber summit in Portland, and he proceeded to tell Shannon all the details. "I'll tell you what, those Oregon loggers, what a breed, or should I say inbreed?" He chuckled.

Shannon considered the barf bag. How many kinds of air-sickness were there?

A flight attendant offered newspapers, and Shannon took a copy of the *Anchorage Daily News*. She stared at the headline across her lap.

"You okay?" Harry asked her.

"I know this man." Shannon pointed to the article. "Eddie Tagarook. He's a friend of mine. He was my dad's pilot in the Arctic Refuge. He's been arrested for a shooting in Prudhoe Bay."

"Sounds like a crazy Eskimo to me."

Shannon read the story with dread. Eddie was in an Anchorage jail. A creature of far horizons and open tundra, he would wither in a small cell of concrete and bars. Suddenly overcome with sadness and fatigue, she reclined her seat and closed her eyes and fell into a dreamless sleep.

When she awoke it was dark.

"Good morning," Harry said, looking up from his crossword puzzle.

"Where are we?" she asked.

"Somewhere over Prince William Sound, about twenty minutes out of Anchorage." He returned to his puzzle. "What's a five-letter word for a wolf or a lesion? Starts with an L."

"Lupus," Shannon said instantly.

"Very good." Harry filled it in. "How about a six-letter word for Plato's conundrum that begins with an E and ends with an A?"

The lights came on in the cabin as the captain announced their imminent landing in Anchorage. Stephen York walked up the aisle past Shannon and Harry. She watched him, fascinated. *Where had he been sitting? How did he board without me seeing him?* He returned a magazine to an attractive flight attendant who appeared anything but inconvenienced by him. He walked back with his eyes on Shannon. She crossed her legs as he stopped and towered over Harry, who craned his neck to look up.

"I enjoyed meeting you," Stephen said to Shannon.

"I enjoyed meeting you, too." *Don't say what you don't mean.*

"Perhaps we could get together sometime, have dinner?"

"Perhaps." She hardly knew him. *But that's why people go out, isn't it? Loneliness is just a game, but it's a game you can lose.*

Harry's mouth hung open, his eyes blinking in the kind of assimilation most people reserve for things vaguely familiar. Stephen glanced at him, then walked back to his row as the captain called for passengers to take their seats.

"Do you know that man?" Shannon asked Harry.

"No." But Harry said this too abruptly, she thought.

The lights of Anchorage twinkled out Shannon's window. She recognized rivulets of traffic on the Seward Highway, running along the blackness of Turnagain Arm, *the same highway that took away my father and brother. Get over it.* She closed her eyes and saw Dad on the tundra, his face aglow with something she could not define. A word swelled up inside her. "Enigma."

"What?" Harry said.

Shannon looked at him. "A conundrum that begins with E and ends with A. The answer to your puzzle. Enigma."

SEVENTEEN

In its first forty years of statehood covering the twilight of the second great Christian millennium, Alaska had become more than part of a global superpower, a mere white star stitched onto a field of blue with forty-nine others. It had become a power in itself, a subcontinent more than twice as big as Texas, harnessed and put to work by American determination. It had survived one catastrophic earthquake and thousands of smaller ones, one catastrophic oil spill and thousands of smaller ones, and dire words from every naysayer, doomsdayer, deerslayer, bricklayer, taxpayer and city mayor who portended difficult times.

Alaskans had seen and heard it all, but nowhere as acutely as they would this Saturday morning in mid-February in downtown Anchorage. For the first time in its short but incendiary history the Wise Use movement and its annual back-slapping, boot-stomping, greenie-bashing conference had come to the last frontier. The crowd of mostly Anglo-European white males that filled Anchorage's Sullivan Arena made the annual hook-and-bullet Alaska Sportsman's Show look like a Star Trek convention. Who said John Wayne was dead and the kegger was over? The parking lot outside bulged with four-wheel drive pick-up trucks sporting Easy Rider Rifle Racks and Foxy Lady Mud Flaps. Ten uniformed police officers stood guard inside and out. A SWAT team waited in two disguised vans at the front and rear entrances. A huge banner hung from the concrete rooftop, illuminated by ground-based floodlights in the winter morning twilight.

EN-VIRAL-MENTALISTS ARE COSTING YOU JOBS

A steady stream of traffic flowed off Gambell Street into the parking area where two dozen protesters held pro-Wilderness placards. The mercury ballasted a few degrees below zero as a pink sunrise silhouetted the Chugach Mountains to the southeast. A truck roared past a woman protestor and a Coors bottle sailed out the window and hit her in the head. Police hurried to her aid, and removed other protesters for their own safety. It happened so fast, nobody got a good look at the truck.

"Christ, Jerry, great shot," Lynx Hirschik exclaimed as he parked the truck at the far end of the lot and began to laugh. "That's the funniest damn thing I've seen in years."

"Anybody after us?" Jerry Levy asked as he looked out the back window. Nobody seemed to be. "Man, I didn't think I'd hit the stupid bitch. I think I mighta killed her."

"Serves her right," Lynx said with another laugh.

William Alt sat between his two hee-hawing friends and said, "Let's go. This thing is gonna start in a couple minutes."

"Hold on, buddy," Lynx said, his laughter subsiding. "You punching a clock or something? Loosen up. Have a beer." Lynx and Jerry had already had two apiece and it was not yet 9:00 a.m. Lynx got his name from his slightly pointed ears. Everybody used to call him Spock, as in the logical Vulcan, but Lynx hated that name. In fact, he hated logic. So his friends came up with Lynx, the only wild cat in Alaska.

Jerry handed William a cold Coors, but William refused as he reached across Jerry's lap and opened the passenger door.

"Killjoy," Lynx grumbled. He was a boxcar of a man, built like William but already hobbled by old football injuries.

"You need a lobotomy," William berated him as he walked toward the Sullivan Arena.

"I'd rather have a bottle-in-front-of-me than a fron-tal-lo-bot-omy," Lynx roared. Jerry roared back. Each opened his third beer, chugged it and laughed until his sides hurt. Damn, everything was funny after three pre-breakfast beers.

Their laughter died in his ears as William walked toward his rendezvous with patriotism and twenty thousand dollars.

This year's Wise Use Conference coincided with Anchorage's annual Fur Rendezvous Celebration, the largest winter carnival in Alaska. Many conferees wore the rendezvous trappers' traditional fur hats, red fox being most popular. The hats contained not just the fur of the dead animals but the heads, tails and dangling paws; the eyes glazed and unblinking. A dozen Humane Society members protested outside with bloodstained placards. "Down with Deadheads." "Stop the Road-Kill Look."

These "humaniacs," as Alaskans called them, were removed with other protestors after the flying Coors bottle incident.

Inside the arena, the air was thick with don't-tread-on-me secessionism and anti-intellectualism, the voices of concerned if not angry men, and a few women, chugging their coffee and donuts and sharing terse convictions that green organizations weren't worried about the environment so much as they invented dooms-day threats to recruit members and raise money. Environmentalists were new pagans who worshiped trees and destroyed people.

Each attendee received the Wise Use Agenda, a land-use manifesto that listed twenty-five major goals of the movement. At the very top, above abolishing national parks and the Endangered Species Act, was immediate oil development in the Arctic National Wildlife Refuge. The conferees pored over it as if it were holy writ. Another banner was unfurled above the stage:

EARTH FIRST! WE'LL MINE THE OTHER PLANETS LATER

"Conservation is the WISE USE of Natural Resources."

"The first duty of the human race
is to control the earth it lives upon."
—Gifford Pinchot, Chief Forester,
US Forest Service, 1910

A wave of applause rolled through the crowd of five thousand cowboys, trappers, ranchers, loggers, miners, mill workers, off-roaders, on-timers and shucks y'all, just downtrodden populists and commie-conspiracy theorists—ordinary people, really—who filled the arena.

Shannon had never been to the circus. She stood amid the unmuzzled Wise Users but didn't shout an I-me-mine sentiment or anti-environmental slogan. She didn't have one. Having stayed up most the night with her father, and reading to him, she now felt dazed with fatigue. She had wanted to take him from his sickly antiseptic world, break him free and return him to the arctic. But the nursing home had been good for him, as reluctant as she was to admit it. His eyes had cleared. His fingers moved. He had even managed a weak smile—his first in months —when his daughter walked into the room. Mom cried when she reminisced about Travis, and each tear reminded Shannon of a thousand open wounds.

William did not feel the stranger's hand slip into his pocket. He and Jerry and Lynx were too euphoric with the energy around them, thrusting their arms into the air, shouting like crazy men and pounding chairs. Braveheart, beer, donuts, anarchy, everybody being different in the same way. What a way to start a day.

A large white-bearded man walked to the podium. He wore silver-rimmed glasses and a checkered shirt buttoned tightly to his fleshy neck. He lifted his arms, and the applause intensified.

He motioned the crowd to take their seats. Everybody jostled into deep rows of metal chairs on the main floor and balcony. Shannon found her chair stage left of the podium, in the last of three rows reserved for scheduled speakers, their families and staff. Across the stage Shannon spotted the ANZA delegation seated at a long white table, all men except the woman with golden hair and green eyes, looking directly at her.

Seated next to Alan Quail, Maya pointed out grassroots organizations, sportsmen councils and political action committees. He spoke back to her with genteel detachment, visibly uncomfortable with the rodeo atmosphere. The opera was more his style. He turned to John Sires and said, "Baku was a bust, and Eddie Tagarook screwed up Prudhoe Bay. I'm tired of disappointment. I don't want anything to go wrong here."

Shannon unpacked her laptop and prepared to do her job, as assigned by Kelly Calvert, a rail-thin, officious woman who was Senator Matlin's chief of staff. Jeff Meola and Denali Sisto sat to Shannon's right, while Jude sat directly in front, with Harry Arnold next to her.

The speakers occupied the forward row, with Kelly Calvert directly behind Senator Matlin. Tyler Kyle was nowhere in view until Shannon saw him approach from an angle, a slight man who appeared to quarter against a wind, his sails reefed, coming her way. She figured he would sit behind Senator Longstreet, as Kelly had behind Senator Matlin. But he walked down the back row and planted himself next to Shannon. He crossed his legs, wrapped one tightly behind the other, and hunched forward, elbows on his knee.

"Tyler Kyle," she said. "My name is—"

"Shannon DeShay. You're on Sam Matlin's staff. You've spent a lot of time in the Arctic Refuge." He spoke without looking at her or offering his hand, his voice a whisper.

"Yes, I have. And you've spent a lot of time in Washington."

He tendered a small smile and adjusted his glasses with thin white fingers. "I'm afraid I have. Not many caribou there."

"It used to be a marsh, didn't it?" Shannon had read a book on the history of Washington.

"A wetland," Kyle said. "I doubt the Founding Fathers ever got a permit to fill it in. Maybe we should prosecute them."

"Statute of limitations. We're too late."

"Ah yes, how good of you to remind me."

"Besides," Shannon said, "they're all dead." She thought this was funny, and in her fatigue she nearly laughed. But he looked at her with eyes that were mirrored or masked somehow behind tinted glasses, and for an instant she thought it was her own face she saw, superimposed on his. A shudder ran through her and she looked away. Something about him was not right. There was a hole where the soul was supposed to be. He reminded her of exfoliating granite, an intrusive igneous rock formed under great pressure but now exposed, the layers peeling away as he executed some strange calculus.

"Attention fellow westerners," announced the white-bearded man at the podium. "We are fortunate to have Pastor Joshua Rainey of Anchorage to lead us in prayer this fine morning."

The conferees stood in solemn silence as the pastor approached the podium. Shannon looked about and wondered, *Where's Mark?*

"Let us pray," Rainey intoned.

EIGHTEEN

"Amen," the crowd recited as they sat down, a congregation now.

White Beard seized the microphone, thanked Pastor Rainey and said, "Did you hear the story about the hunter and the environmentalist who went hiking together and came upon some fresh moose droppings? The environmentalist had never seen moose droppings before, so he asked the hunter what they were. 'They're called smart pills,' the hunter said. 'Eat one and you'll see why.' The environmentalist ate one, and it tasted like shit. But after considerable chewing he managed to swallow it down. 'Now will you tell me why they're called smart pills?' he asked as his face turned green. 'Because once you eat one,' the hunter said, 'you're smart enough to never eat another.'"

Laughter rippled through the audience.

"I'm glad you enjoyed that," White Beard said, " 'cause that's about as funny as I'm going to get. We're here to destroy the environmental movement before it destroys us. That's why we've come to this resource colony called Alaska, to sharpen our guillotines and save a free way of life and protect the principles that made America strong."

He introduced the keynote speaker as "a lifetime member of the NRA and a friend of the common man, a great patriot, Senator Oliver Harding Longstreet."

People applauded as Longstreet took center stage. "Thank you fellow guardians of the public trust. I must confess that I was disappointed last year when my colleague, Jack Worley, Alaska's lone member in the House of Representatives, received *Sierra Magazine's* Eco-Thug Award, and I did not."

The crowd howled as Worley jumped to his feet and waved.

What a bozo, thought Shannon.

Longstreet adjusted his glasses and looked over the crowd like a Caesar addressing his legions. "You and I know that anyone can write history. College liberals do it all the time. It's become very popular to rewrite history; just make it up however you like. History is rewritten so often in Russia these days, they say it's impossible to predict the past."

Mild laughter.

"The real goal of environmentalists is to control what is yours, to regulate your life and take it away..." For another twenty minutes he dissertated on left-winged "tundra tyrants" who aimed to steal Alaska. He exhorted the crowd to take back what was theirs: "This land is your land!"

People shouted, whistled, stomped, applauded, chanted, whooped, hollered.

"Great speech," Jude crowed.

Denali mumbled something, and Jude turned on her. "Did you say Senator Longstreet made a testicle of himself?"

"I said he made a spectacle of himself."

"You're always in denial."

"No, I'm not. You didn't hear me properly, that's all."

"I hear fine," Jude said.

You hear, Shannon thought, *you just don't listen.*

Shannon looked at Tyler Kyle, who was folded over his laptop, typing as if engrossed not by events around him but by some abstract time and place.

Congressman Worley took center stage and ranted for an hour. Sam Matlin spoke next, more pacific yet still disappointing to Shannon who had hoped he wouldn't lie down with confederate dogs and get up with fleas. The Republican governor offered his harvest-minded appraisal of the natural world, and the morning ended with an announcement that events would continue that afternoon at the Hotel LaPerouse, downtown.

Shannon darted for the door.

Two men followed, each having watched her closely the last three hours.

Outside, she found the cold air a tonic as she lifted her face to the sun and let it warm her. Other conferees hurried past as she basked in the disparity of cold and warm, her breath climbing in small vaporous clouds against the cobalt sky. She turned and hurried on to her car.

Stephen York pulled a fur hat low to his brow and waited from the arena doors, careful not to shadow her too closely.

As Shannon approached her car in the back of the lot, she spotted a man on an intercept path, his scruffy black goatee protruding from the collar of his parka. "Excuse me," he said.

She ignored him and unlocked the door and climbed in.

"Shannon?" he said, his voice familiar. "It's me, Mark."

She appraised him: Filson hat, Carhartt pants, an oversized wool shirt, a black moustache and crooked goatee that crowded a serious mouth. His eyes were brown, not blue. But his voice?

"What is truth?" she asked him.

"The enemy of power."

"It really is you?"

"We need to talk."

"I didn't recognize you."

"Good."

"I've been wondering about you. Are you okay?"

"I'm fine."

Shannon started to climb out of her car.

"Stay where you are." Mark glanced around, nervous. "Meet me tonight at the Mount Susitna Care Center, at eleven, okay?"

Shannon sunk back into her seat.

"To interview your father."

"He's close to dying, Mark."

"That's why I have to see him. He's my only hope."

"He's my only father."

"Then give him back his voice."

"I never took it from him."

Mark knelt next to her. "It's nice to see you again."

"You too. Why haven't you called?"

"I was afraid your phone might be bugged." He told her about the men hunting him in New York, his meeting with Tony Carzoli, his continuing research. He touched her shoulder. "Did you ever think that your father has a secret he wants to tell, one that could let him die in peace?"

"Not until I met you."

Mark glanced about. People walked to their cars. Others boarded a dozen idling buses for transportation downtown.

It's Meadows, Stephen told himself. *Has to be. He's wearing a disguise and talking to her about—what? ANZA? Her father?* He felt a surge of adrenalin as he approached.

"I have to go," Mark said to Shannon. "Meet me at the care center. I'll have Rollie and a couple other guys with me."

"I have to go too," Shannon said.

"Where?"

"Jail."

Stephen targeted Meadows, seventy yards away. Moving cars, vans, trucks and buses turned the lot into a maze as he struggled to keep his target in view. He walked in front of a car that skid-

ded to a stop and honked. Undistracted, he moved forward, stalking, a lion on a hunt.

Meadows was at fifty yards, moving away. Forty yards. Just
then a big silver bus rumbled in front of Stephen and stopped. A
second bus passed the first. Stephen moved to his right, but a
third bus intervened. He darted between them and was nearly hit
by a truck, glancing off its hood.

"Hey, watch where you're going," somebody yelled.

Stephen gained his balance, looked for Meadows. No sign of
him. He ran to where he had seen him last. Nothing. He scanned
the parking lot and searched car to car. He combed a nearby
stand of birch and opened a dumpster but neglected to rummage
through the trash. He ran back into the lot, searched more ve-
hicles, began to panic. "Damn." He kicked the back tire of a truck.

A big man jumped out, his hands pulled into fists. "Hey
asshole, what's your problem?"

Part of Stephen wanted to kill him, but he backed off and
said, "It's been a rough day."

"Then go kick your own damn truck."

~

The ANZA bodyguards cut through the rowdy crowd to bring
Alan Quail and John Sires on stage where eager admirers en-
circled Oliver Longstreet. Sires raised his hand. "Oliver, great
speech."

Longstreet waved back. He looked at Quail just as a Caltex
man—an ANZA competitor—stepped forward and engaged the
senator in animated chatter.

This is nonsense. Quail turned to leave as Longstreet broke company with the Caltex man and said, "Alan, John, bad news in
Baku, 'eh?"

Quail turned back but said nothing. He didn't like Longstreet
and his cowboy diplomacy and his appropriations blackmail, and
it irked him to play these games.

"Pretty rowdy bunch here," Longstreet said.

"Pretty rowdy," Quail agreed. He loathed this uncontrolled situation.

"You feeling okay?" Longstreet asked, thinking, *You sure don't look okay, Alan. You look like dog shit.*

"I'm fine. We need to talk."

"Come see me in Washington."

"We need to talk here, now."

Longstreet looked inconvenienced, an expression he had perfected among unsavory lobbyists. "I have no time now, Alan. But I agree, we need to talk. Come see me on the Hill."

Groveling was not part of Quail's repertoire. He would not comply with this man, yet. He held grudges like a bank account, tight-fisted and interest-bearing, yet he also knew something more was happening here. Longstreet was reluctant to work with ANZA in the Arctic Refuge. Why?

John Sires stood next to the two men but heard nothing as he scanned the arena for Maya.

~

William Alt departed in a sullen mood, thinking he had been duped. *Did I do something wrong? Should I have come alone? The man on the phone didn't tell me to come alone, did he?* William could not remember. *Damn.*

"Those cowboys really know how to party," Lynx said as he fumbled for his truck keys.

"Hurry up," Jerry said. "I'm freezin' my butt out here."

William stuck his hands into his coat pockets, where his numb fingers felt a small envelope folded in half. He pulled it out.

Jerry and Lynx looked at him.

William opened the envelope and found twenty crisp one hundred-dollar bills wrapped in a single sheet of paper.

"Holy shit, William," Jerry said.

Lynx ogled the money. "Well, rich boy, you're buying lunch."

~

Tyler Kyle huddled in a phone booth in the Fifth Avenue Mall and described to Merlin what he had seen between Longstreet and Quail on stage in the Sullivan Arena.

"You worry too much, Tyler," Merlin responded. "Your senator wants to humble Quail without losing him. That's not an easy job and I suspect he'll tire of it quickly. What about Meadows?"

"Stephen is following a woman we think Meadows will contact here in Anchorage. I've been in touch with Minneapolis, by the way. We're about to make Bruce Janstadt a national disgrace."

"He already is."

"Can we afford a quarter million in allegiance money?"

Merlin hesitated. "It depends."

Kyle explained the Janstadt scandal.

Merlin asked, "Are these men married with children?"

"Every one. They're all former Boy Scouts and registered Republicans who run their own businesses. And they all cheat the IRS."

"Okay. Start with one man, then have the others come forward with compatible testimony."

~

Mark lifted the lid of the dumpster half an inch and surveyed the Sullivan Arena parking lot. All quiet. He had shivered inside the big metal box for an hour, reluctant to leave, buried in garbage, his coat and pants smeared with sundry mysterious condiments and lubricants, ketchup, relish, motor oil, mustard. Grey Poupon no less. *Classy dumpster.*

He jumped out and fell on cold, stiff legs. He picked himself up and walked as fast as he could to his Rent-A-Wreck Buick half a mile away. He glanced over his shoulder and saw no sign of the man who had angled toward him in the parking lot. He reached the Buick, climbed inside and locked the door. It started reluctantly and rumbled in protest as he pumped the accelerator and sputtered down A Street.

~

Shannon stepped through a secure door—no handles or knob on the inside—that closed behind her. She sat at a counter that fronted thick glass, with a chair on the other side. She fingered the phone and waited. The room smelled faintly of sweat and smoke. An opposite door opened and Eddie Tagarook came in. He smiled and the room changed. He sat opposite her, ponytail down his back, the lines in his face deeper than Shannon remembered. He moved in his same fibrous way, reed-like, still with a limp. He wore a canvas blue shirt and pants, with CIPT above the left pocket. Cook Inlet PreTrial Facility. His shoes, also blue, had the big toes worn out.

He picked up his phone. "Hello beautiful," he said.

"Hello handsome."

"Whaddya doin' here?"

"Seeing you. When do you get out?"

"Tomorrow morning, when they hang me."

"What?"

"I jokes. I thought you were doin' the political thing with Mayor Matlin, whatever."

"He's a senator now."

"Yeah, too bad."

"I'm just here for the weekend."

"You come to rescue me?" His dark face crinkled into a grin.

"I brought you some muktuq but they confiscated it."

"What kind?"

"Bowhead."

"Ohhh, my favorite."

"I read about you in the paper."

"Yeah, I'm famous. Those ANZA guys shoot a polar bear and get a rug. I shoot a power box and go to jail. They violated the

Marine Mammal Protection Act, ya know."

"Defense of life and property," Shannon said.

Eddie shook his head. "That bear never charged me. It was running away when they shot it." His voice faded as he studied the backs of his hands and said nothing. He didn't have to.

Shannon knew. *We all have our winters, but only some of us see how much remains after everything is gone.* She looked at her own hands and saw her own distant arctic map in the veins and bones; in the absence of calluses that said they were city hands now, too soft for her own good.

Eddie smiled and said, "It's nice to see you again."

"It's nice to see you too, Eddie."

They placed their hands on the glass, palms facing, one map given to another to make the world round.

NINETEEN

Charles DeShay moved his lower jaw as if he wanted to speak but could not. His eyes blinked slowly; eyes that seemed tired more from lack of living than lack of sleep. His bed was raised into a sitting position so a shunt could drain water from his brain. An intravenous tube fed and hydrated him. Every couple hours a petite nurse named Cynthia arrived to salve his lips, which dried constantly from his labored breathing.

Seated next to him, Shannon pulled a tattered, hand-bound journal from her purse, the one from her second summer in the Arctic Refuge when she turned sixteen. She leafed through pages heavy with ink and memory, and read to him. "I don't think I ever shared this with you, did I? Remember that bear we saw, the one with the cream-colored ears?"

He blinked.

The lone grizzly crosses the tundra as only a bear can, full of jurisdiction. Father and daughter watch from a distance. They see fur ripple over its back, a hump at the shoulder. It breaks into a run, stops, digs for awhile. Continues upslope.

—Isn't it something, he says, how a single bear can fill up this place as much as ten thousand caribou?

—We should call him Party Hat, with ears like that, Shannon says.

—No, let's not call him anything. Let's leave him unnamed, like maps and horizons used to be.

Shannon says nothing. The stillness has its own eloquence. No names. . . It has never occurred to her. No names, no dimensions. Even mythology fails at that.

~

From his rented, idling Toyota near the back of the Mount Susitna Care Center parking lot, Stephen watched the front doors and waited. No Shannon. He assumed she was still inside, but was careful not to bank too much on assumptions. He remembered Kyle's instructions. *Get Meadows, get his research, and get rid of him.* But Meadows posed a challenge. Stephen could not just kill him. He had to get his computer password, then dump the body. *But where?* All the lakes and rivers were frozen in this stupid state. Stephen pulled a syringe from his pocket and studied the yellow toxin inside. Once injected it would be impossible to detect, and death would be immediate.

He pressed on the accelerator, turned the heat to maximum, rubbed his hands together and checked his watch. Ten-fifty. Visiting hours would end at midnight and Shannon would have to leave by then. But what if she did not? What if Meadows were in there right now?

Make sure he keeps his mouth shut, Kyle had said about Charles DeShay. *He knows too much. Nobody, least of all Mark Meadows, should speak with Charles DeShay.*

Stephen shut off the Toyota and walked to the front entrance. He slipped past reception as two other visitors exited. Nobody paid attention as he walked down the hall. All was quiet except for two old men in wheelchairs who played checkers and berated each other, and a crazy woman in a nearby room who moaned,

"My bed's on fire, my bed's on fire." An orderly collected food trays on a small metal cart.

Stephen turned down a wing hall and entered an empty restroom. He studied himself in the mirror: binocular vision, high nose, sleek frame, the face and physique of a predator. *But we are actually poor predators, aren't we? We have no sharp teeth or talons or claws, no powerful vision or great speed. Yet here we are on top of the fucking mountain, using tools to kill each other and everything else. We got here by being clever, and that's how we'll stay.* He fondled the syringe in his pocket. He never carried a gun. They were too loud and easy; they made your mind go soft. *Better to use your head and hands.*

Suddenly the door opened and an overweight cabbage of a man came in, his purple jacket wrinkled, his jeans twisted, his arm in a sling. He glanced at Stephen as he stepped to the urinal and sang, "Oh baby, when the hangover's over, your memory's still hanging on."

Stephen exited and checked his watch: five after eleven. He heard Shannon's voice in the main hall, and crept down the wing to listen from around the corner. "...okay Mark," she was saying. "Do your interview. But if I think it's upsetting my dad at any time, I'll stop you."

"So will I," added Cynthia, the nurse.

Stephen froze as their voices drifted down the hall. From behind him the cabbage man breezed by, turned the corner and disappeared in the same direction.

"Where's Rollie?" Mark asked as they began to set up video recorders around Charles DeShay, who appeared to be asleep.

Rollie came in and offered Shannon a bovine grin, thinking again of all the ways she reminded him of Angie. Dang wimmen. *I've got tears in my ears from lying on my back crying over you.*

Two other men assisted Mark and Rollie.

Charles opened his eyes, and Shannon said, "It's okay, Dad. I want you to meet a friend of mine, Mark Meadows. He wants to ask you some questions."

Charles stared vacantly at Mark. "Hello Charles. Shannon's told me all about you. You raised a wonderful daughter."

Charles blinked.

Mark looked at Shannon expectantly. "Does he always communicate with his eyes, blinking like that?"

"He used to more often in the past, but he hasn't in long time. This is a good day. He's surprisingly alert. The nurses think it might be a new high-protein diet they've been feeding him."

Mark said, "Charles, I'm a journalist with the *Washington Post*, and I'd like to ask you some questions about ANZA and the 1002 Area of the Arctic National Wildlife Refuge. Is that okay?"

Another blink.

Mark introduced his assistants to Shannon as Bill and Bob. Nice guys, Shannon thought. Well dressed, short hair, clean-shaven, just like Bills and Bobs are supposed to look. Bill was a lawyer from New York, Bob a brain trauma specialist from Seattle.

Out in the hall, Stephen inched toward the open doorway as he strained to hear the conversation inside. Somebody said that the clamp was broken on the tray next to Charles' bed. Shannon grabbed a roll of duct tape from her purse and repaired it, and Stephen heard her say, "Duct tape, there is no substitute."

Bill then asked Shannon and Cynthia to step aside. They walked to the door, just around the corner from Stephen, where Bill said, "What we'll begin with is a test called Oriented Times Three. Are you familiar with this?"

Shannon shook her head.

"Person, place and time," Cynthia said. "It's a simple mental health exam to determine competency."

"That's right," Bill said.

"Is it stressful?" Shannon asked him.

"No."

"How can you be certain?"

Bill arched his eyebrows. "I can't, not with my limited apparatus. But for this interview to be admissible in a court of law your father can't be coerced in any way. If at any time you or the nurse object to Mark's questions, tell me and we'll redirect the interview."

"Okay," Shannon said. "Let's get started."

TWENTY

Video camera on. Tape recorders on. Bob checked Charles' vital signs and found them strong.

Mark spoke in a slow, clear voice. "Charles, I am going to ask you some questions that you will answer with a simple yes or no. For each question you will signal yes by blinking your eyes once, or raising a finger once. You will signal no by blinking your eyes twice, or raising a finger twice. Do you understand?"

Charles blinked once.

"Is your name Charles Chandalar?"

Charles did not respond.

Mark took a deep breath. "Is your name Charles Chandalar?"

Charles blinked once, then, slowly, a second time.

"Is your name Charles Galloway?"

Charles blinked twice.

"Is your name Charles DeShay?"

Charles blinked once. Mark looked at Shannon, Cynthia and Bob, and all three motioned for him to continue.

Stephen retreated down the hall. He had to stop what was

happening. Time to be bold, creative, clever.

"Are you now in your own home?" Mark asked Charles.
Charles blinked twice, slowly.
"Are you in Anchorage, Alaska?"
One blink.
"Do you have a wife named Susan?"
One blink.
"Do you have a daughter named Karen?"
Two blinks.
"Do you have a daughter named Shannon?"
One blink. And a raised finger. Yes.
Shannon bit her lip.

"My bed's on fire, my bed's on fire," the woman moaned as
Stephen slipped into her dark room. She was neither hysterical
nor loud, just rhythmic. So rhythmic that the nursing staff had
stopped paying close attention to her. She had a roommate, an
ancient woman who slept in a bed near the window.

Neither woman saw Stephen enter, nor reach into his shirt
pocket and pull out a cigarette lighter and flick it on. But the
pyrophobic woman had a keen sense of smell. Her worst nightmare was about to come true. She picked up her head, anchored
on her withered neck, and saw Stephen's ghostly face illuminated
by the little flame in his hand. He held the flame under the curtains, under the roommate's blanket, under the bed sheets, but
none would alight. He grabbed a box of Kleenex, set it on the
woman's bed and lit it. She looked at him, rigid with terror, and
opened her mouth to scream. But nothing came out as the flames
climbed toward her.

"Charles," Mark asked, "Did ANZA drill a single test well in a
KANAK inholding in the 1002 Area of the Arctic National Wild-
life Refuge?"
One blink, yes.

"Do you know the result of that test?"

One blink.

"Do you believe your knowledge of that result placed you in danger in any way?"

Charles' eyes opened wide. His lips moved against his teeth but accompanied no voice. His respiration rate increased. Mark repeated the question and Charles blinked once, yes.

"Do you believe the car wreck in which you were injured was an accident?"

Shannon raised her hand to stop the interview, but not before her father answered Mark with two rapid blinks.

"Charles, do you believe the car wreck in which you were injured was attempted murder?"

One blink, yes.

"Do you know who tried to kill you?"

Two blinks, no.

"Do you believe your attempted murder has to do with ANZA and the 1002 Area test drill result?"

One blink, a second, a third. Three distinct blinks. Then a forefinger lifted three times.

Mark looked at the others and received confused expressions. He asked, "Charles, did you—"

The fire alarm erupted in a shrill, high-pitched wail.

Cynthia darted for the door and said to the others as she went out, "This doesn't happen very often. You'll have to exit the building immediately."

"What about my father?" Shannon asked.

"He'll be fine. We have a full fire sprinkler system here." Cynthia ran down the hall.

Shannon could hear people yelling. A dinner tray clattered on the hall floor. Fear washed over Charles' face. "It's okay, Dad," Shannon told him, though her own words left her unconvinced.

"I need to ask him a couple more questions," Mark pleaded.

"No," Shannon said. "It's time to go."

"But I think I've given him the chance to say something he's wanted to say for years."

Charles blinked.

"Is that right, Dad? Do you want this interview to continue?"
One blink, yes.

Cynthia poked her head back into the room. "Let's go. This isn't a drill. Time to leave. Now."

The sprinklers came on and everybody jumped clear. Mark and Rollie draped their coats over the equipment and began to pack while Shannon shielded her father. The alarm stopped and the sprinklers shut off after less than a minute, but the confusion persisted amid wet floors and smoke. An old woman had fallen. A man had cut his head. The two curmudgeons in wheelchairs played checkers unabated. Cynthia told Shannon, Mark, Rollie, Bill and Bob to use the fire exit in the back.

Outside, Shannon waited, undeterred by the cold as sprinkler water froze on her coat and in her hair. She was not about to walk away from a burning nursing home with her father inside. She wanted confirmation that everybody was fine. Two fire trucks arrived, and soon a policeman assured her that the small blaze was contained, and all the patients were safe.

Not good enough. Shannon waited another half an hour until the nursing home staff allowed her to revisit her dad. She found him awake but calm. His eyes flickered when he saw her.

"You okay, Dad?"

One slow blink.

She stayed for an hour and soothed him by reading aloud from his favorite books. At 2:00 a.m. she kissed his forehead and said, "You be good. I'll see you in the morning."

~

Stephen waited in the bottom of a large laundry basket for more than four hours, covered by dirty towels and bedsheets. Again and again he told himself to be patient, to avoid flamboyance. His act of arson would be obvious. Cops would arrive and investigate and leave.

When at last he peeked out from the room, he found the hall returned to normal, dimly lit, with only one nurse at reception at the far end. He slipped down to DeShay's room, listened for voices, and entered. The old man was alone, sleeping. Stephen pulled the syringe from his pocket.

Charles opened his eyes.

"Good evening, Dr. DeShay," Stephen whispered as he held the syringe up and squirted a couple drops of toxin out the needle. "How are we feeling tonight?"

No response.

"Difficult to sleep? I have just the thing for you."

Charles didn't move or blink. His expression suggested something more distant than death itself. His chest rose and fell at a quickened pace.

"You see this?" Stephen held the syringe over him. "It's your ticket out of here, no charge. Give my regards to your son."

Charles blinked twice.

Stephen stabbed the toxin-filled syringe into the intravenous line. A minute later, as he slipped out the door, he looked back to see Charles DeShay go into his first and final convulsion.

~

Four days later Tyler Kyle caught the last Metro to Rockville and called Stephen from the station phone booth. "I've just heard there's going to be an autopsy on Charles DeShay."

"So?" Stephen replied.

"Fewer than ten percent of people who die in nursing homes are autopsied. I want you out of town by daybreak."

"Why?"

"We can't be sure what a pathologist will find, or what any nurses might have seen. Meadows is loose and neither of us knows what he learned from DeShay before you killed him."

"Shouldn't I follow DeShay's daughter in case she leads me back to Meadows?"

"I'm putting Tank on her."

"Tank?" Stephen sputtered. "He's not—"

"You can have the DeShay girl someday. Right now I want you to disappear." Kyle hung up and told himself it might not be so bad. Charles DeShay, the last of the ANZA troublemakers, was dead. The toxin would be impossible to detect. Political mayhem was deepening in Baku, and the Senate Foreign Affairs trip there had been cancelled. ANZA appeared eager to discuss ANWR, and Senator Romper, the yogurt-sucking Californian, had dropped his support of the Wilderness bill. Highest priority now was the demise of Senator Bruce Janstadt. Kyle dialed Minnesota.

~

Books were her blanket.

Shannon could be anonymous here, a nameless traveler in her favorite bookstore, at her favorite table, having smoked turkey on sourdough, and a cold Corona with a twist of lemon. A longhaired guitarist in the corner played a steel-stringed Martin, hitting the inflections with crispness and power. He tuned the bass E string down to D, a technique Travis had often used.

She never figures him for a coffee shop musician. But late one night in Anchorage she and two friends happen upon him doing a solo gig in an elegant midtown restaurant. He wears a Moroccan fez and a Mexican fiesta shirt, and sits alone on a four-legged stool. Says nothing. Just plays, head back, eyes off the frets. Shannon and her friends slip into a booth in the back.

—I'd like to dedicate this next song to my kid sister, he says.

He's seen her.

It's Gaelic, this song of his, something endemic to sadness and estrangement. He says it's a voiceless ballad of the Woodkerns, an ancient people who lived in the forests of Ireland and communicated with musical notes, like birds, but were extirpated by the British who cut down all the trees to build ships.

She thinks of her brother differently that night. He does have a landscape inside of him, latent, but alive. He agrees to accompany her and Dad on their next trip to the refuge, after she graduates from high school. He says he'll bring his old guitar and play on the riverbank. But the lights go out. Two weeks later he is dead.

She reminds herself that the angel of death is still an angel; that death itself is not as bad as dying. A son is not supposed to die before his father dies, but in that spirit world they might find the peace that eluded them in this one.

Twelve days ago Shannon uncurled her mother's tight fingers from her own, seated next to her in the small Catholic church, and walked to the pulpit to say something about her father. How peculiar the pained faces appeared to her, old family friends, ANZA colleagues and distant acquaintances who seemed to require tragedy in their traditions. Sam Matlin was there, and Jude. Cynthia, the nurse, grieved in the back, filled with guilt that she had told Shannon her father would be fine that night. Eddie Tagarook and Elsie Kiviikanak sat in the back as well, their northern faces on the other side of some internal river that separated them from the rest of the world. Alan Quail had announced that ANZA would open a geology scholarship in Charles DeShay's name. John Sires sent a fax.

All Shannon could think to say was what Dad had told her once: *The rest of your tender years, that's your gift. The best you can do in this life is to bring out the best in others.*

And what brings out the best in me?

Rivers. Rivers and chocolate. No, rivers of chocolate. She took another gulp of beer. Okay, rivers, chocolate and Corona. And caribou. Better put caribou before chocolate. She took another swallow and suddenly had the urge to cry, to let the whole deep reservoir spill out in a flood of tears. But she fought it back, biting her lip. She always fought it back.

The bookstore stood on Independence Avenue, a few blocks east of the Hill. From her pocket, she removed the condolence note from Mark, written in a neat hand that contradicted the weight of his words. It spoke in metaphor and rhyme and gained gravity with each reading.

She picked up a discarded section of the *Washington Post*. The front page carried yet another story on the breaking Bruce Janstadt scandal. A man in his mid-thirties had accused the Minnesota senator of sexually molesting him eighteen years ago when he was a Boy Scout, and Janstadt his scoutmaster. Now two other men had come forward with the same story. Janstadt's office had issued a denial, saying the charges were ludicrous and false. But the Republican-controlled Senate Ethics Committee was already considering an investigation.

A man bumped into her table and knocked two new books onto the floor, one a biography of Wallace Stegner, the other a collection of Gary Snyder poems. He picked them up, straightened their dust jackets and handed them to her. "I'm sorry," he said. He was clean-shaven with sandy, thinning hair, dressed like an accountant with too many pens in his pocket. Mid-fifties. Big ears and an intelligent face, soupy eyes, but a serious mouth. He walked out of the store and didn't look back.

Twenty minutes later, when she opened the Stegner biography, a business card fell onto her table, face down, with a handprinted note on the back: YOU ARE BEING FOLLOWED. CALL ME, BUT NOT FROM YOUR APARTMENT –L.C. Shannon turned it over: *Lincoln Crozier, Special Agent, FBI, U.S. Department of Justice.*

Spring

March

TWENTY-ONE

J eff Meola?" Alan Quail asked. "Who's he?"

"An aide for Oliver Longstreet," Johnny Parkendale answered.

Quail pulled a hand to his forehead and buried his brow. Johnny was afraid this would happen. Twenty minutes earlier, when he had arrived at Quail's Arapaho-motif condominium in Aspen, Colorado, Alan didn't look well. The luster had left his eyes, and his posture suggested a great burden, as if he were Sisyphus rolling that rock up a hill only to have it roll down again.

"But as I said before," Johnny added, "Meola accessed nothing in the inner vault."

Ned Camis frowned. Johnny looked at him with mild irritation. He had hoped to have this meeting with Alan alone, but here was this Camis-guy, a lawyer, that's how Alan had introduced him, as a "legal linebacker," leaving Johnny to incorrectly assumed that he was an ANZA corporate attorney.

"What?" Johnny asked defensively, looking at Camis.

Camis had a large square head made more distorted by small ears and eyes. He projected a fierce intelligence, and said, "I'm wondering about your methods, how you determined it was Jeff Meola who broke into room 2820. Was your reasoning inductive or deductive?"

"Deductive." Johnny handed each man a dossier that contained an eight-page list of four hundred and twenty names. He ignored Camis and spoke to Quail. "This is every guest who attended your Anchorage party, in the order they arrived. Those you asked us not to interview—Sam Matlin, Jack Worley, Joshua Rainey, people like that—are highlighted in blue. The twenty-five consecutive names highlighted in red on page five are the ones who were signed in by the young parking attendant, Tom. They're the ones we concentrated on. Meola's name is near the bottom."

Quail looked at the list and said nothing.

Johnny said, "We know Jeff Meola left the building with everybody else, dressed as if he'd been there the whole evening, which he'd not. The drunk in the lobby was a decoy who distracted the guard while Meola scaled the outside corner."

"He must have had an accomplice," Camis said, "somebody who signed for him at the desk."

"Harry Arnold. His name's just below Meola's. He forged Meola's signature, then did his own."

"Harry Arnold?" Quail asked as he grabbed a toothpick. "Oliver Longstreet's press secretary?"

"He's Sam Matlin's press secretary now."

The blood began to drain from Quail's salon-tanned face.

"This Tom," Camis said, "the one who checked everybody past security, he didn't see Arnold sign two names?"

"He's just a high school kid," Johnny explained. "He was nervous and distracted watching William Alt toss the decoy out of the lobby. Arnold could have easily fooled him."

"Why Meola and Arnold?" Quail asked.

Johnny shrugged. "I don't know, Alan. You wanted the intruder, not the motive."

"I want both."

"Okay, I'll get both."

Quail chewed the toothpick.

Johnny said, "Jeff Meola's a champion wrestler and a martial arts expert. That's how he pummeled your security man. He rides a bike all over Capitol Hill. He's soft-spoken, nice-looking and deceiving. He dates a Matlin aide named Denali Sisto. He keeps a clean image and a low profile. People remember seeing him at the ANZA party toward the end, but not early on."

"What's Harry Arnold say?" Camis asked.

"All the right things, that he and Meola arrived separately but left together in Arnold's car. He says Meola was sick and in the men's room most of the night. Meola says the same thing."

"And the Jumar letters?" Quail asked. Last week ANZA had received a second one nearly identical to the first.

Johnny shook his head. "They're bogus. Anybody who does a little research could write those letters."

"What about Mark Meadows?" Quail asked.

"We only get voice mail at the *Post* and his apartment. People say he hasn't been there for a couple months."

"He had nothing to do with the break-in?"

"No. He's a lone wolf who's gotten in trouble at the *Post* for sloppy reporting. Still, he's dangerous. He and a photographer, Rollie Dawson, were with Charles DeShay the night he died last month."

"What?" Quail's toothpick froze between his artificially whitened teeth.

"DeShay's daughter was there too. It's all in the Mount Susitna Care Center report in your dossier." Johnny explained the details and added, "The witnessing nurse said the interview involved a competency test and questions about ANZA. But Meadows didn't finish. You know why?" He paused while the two men raised mute stares from the dossiers. "Because somebody started a fire in another patient's room. DeShay died four hours later."

Camis flipped through his dossier. "He died almost a month ago. Why'd it take so long to acquire this information?"

"The Mount Susitna report only came out last week. We asked for an advanced copy, an interview, anything, but the nursing staff wouldn't cooperate, or I should say"—Johnny elevated his voice at Camis— "their lawyers wouldn't cooperate."

Alan Quail stared out the window at something only he could see. Camis said, "It says here that DeShay died of apparent heart failure."

"Yes. The autopsy and pathology reports are secret."

"Secret?" Quail asked without moving his head. "Why?"

"Mount Susitna won't say."

Quail looked out the window and saw it again, not the lights of Aspen or the starry sky, but his own tired reflection, the face of a man fifty-nine going on ninety-five who failed to mask his aching heart. Next month his daughter, Aliena, only twenty-four, would marry her fiancé, and nothing else mattered, as she was dying from a malignant brain tumor. Her wedding had been moved to April, because by June, the original date, she could be gone. Her parents had taken her to the finest specialists around the country and received a unanimous diagnosis. Her condition was inoperable and irreversible. She had one to six months to live. Her mother had gone into shock while her father—a man who ruled an empire ranked number one on the Fortune 500, that employed one hundred thousand people in ninety countries and grossed revenues greater than the economies of some nations—broke down and sobbed.

"From the looks of this," Camis said as he flipped through the dossier, "your case is built on eyewitness accounts and hearsay. You have no hard evidence on this Jeff Meola, and the videotape is still missing."

"The Anchorage Police demoted the detective who lost the tape," Johnny said. He glared at Camis.

Quail said, "I want to know what Mark Meadows knows. Is Shannon DeShay still with him?"

"We don't know," Johnny said.

"Then find her, follow her, and find Jeff Meola too. I want to know who he contacts, where he goes, everything."

"I'll need to add more agents."

Quail waved a hand.

Johnny climbed to his feet and thanked Alan Quail. He wanted to pat Ned Camis on the head, good dog. They shook hands with the warmth of wolverines, and Johnny departed.

~

One floor above, John Sires and Maya Donjek hosted an ANZA gathering of six Eskimos, four congressmen, and ten Aspen developers. While Jack Worley regaled the developers with hunting stories, Maya sat with the Eskimos on a large sofa and watched the end of a Knicks-Celtics game. They talked about tomorrow's schedule, when they would fly by helicopter to Glenwood Springs to film ANZA advocacy commercials. Glenwood Springs didn't look anything like the arctic, the Eskimos said, but Maya assured them that most Americans wouldn't know the difference.

Laughter erupted from the crowd clustered around Worley. Maya returned to the wet bar, where Sires sidled up and caressed her. "Are the natives restless?" he asked.

"They're just tired. They've had a busy schedule."

"Shit," Sires said in a raspy whisper. "They stay in the finest hotels, eat the best foods, drink the best booze and get fall-down drunk. They want us to respect the best of their culture while they imitate the worst of ours. We shouldn't need their cooperation to drill in that refuge, if you ask me."

"I didn't ask you, John."

His hand moved onto her hip. "How about you and me find some time for ourselves?"

Laughter exploded from the other end of the bar, and Worley yelled at Sires between guffaws, "Did you hear that one, John?"

"No, what?" Sires quickly removed his hand from Maya.

She slipped away while Worley cornered Sires to repeat a joke, then to educate him and several others on the destructive nature of the Endangered Species Act. "First the spotted owl," Worley griped, "then the mottled murrelet...marbled mudlet...mangled muppet...whatever the hell it is, and now the Alexander Archipelago gray wolf. What are they going to do next, enshrine the cockroach?"

Sires ducked away, but couldn't find Maya. He rushed down the hall to her room, fantasizing her in a peach-colored negligee, waiting for him atop her firm bed. He reached her door and knocked quietly. "Maya? It's me babe. Maya, are you there?" He turned the knob, but the door was deadbolted and a small plastic sign hung on a latch: PLEASE DO NOT DISTURB.

~

Ned Camis mixed a vodka tonic for Quail and a double martini for himself. The CEO slumped into his chair and stared out the window. "Tell me, Ned," he finally said, "if whatever Mark Meadows is researching somehow catches fire and ANZA ends up getting burned, I mean something really big, a major story in the national press, what are my options?"

Camis took a long drink. "My value to you is commensurate with the information you give me, Alan. Unless you tell me about every skeleton in ANZA's closet, and your part in putting them there, I can't help you that much. I suspect this has something to do with that test well drilled in Alaska ten years ago, right?"

"Do you know that of the ten people who knew that result, five are dead?"

Camis furrowed his brow. "How'd they die?"

"Simon Rylesbach, the former CEO, had a heart attack on a putting green. I think you knew that."

"He smoked himself to death. And the others?"

"Three in accidents, and now Charles DeShay. He was crippled in a car accident six years ago, and I'd convinced myself it really was an accident. But now he dies in a nursing home under questionable circumstances. I don't know..." Quail chugged his vodka.

Camis sat across from him, elbows on his knees. "You think these accidents were murders?"

"Yes."

"The Anwahr test drill is that outrageous? It makes people kill each other?"

Quail turned again and looked out the window. This time the darkness soothed him. How ironic that sometimes black was white, and white black. Camis wisely remained quiet until the aging man spoke. When he finally did, his words seemed pelagic, as if washed out to sea. "This whole thing...well, I'm not personally responsible. It wasn't my idea. Simon Rylesbach and John Sires cooked it up ten years ago, before I was CEO, and now it could explode."

"What 'whole thing?' Stealing? Cheating? Fraud?"

"Fabrications."

Camis set his double martini on the Florentine marble table and loosened his safari silk tie. "Fabrications of the test result?"

Quail nodded.

"You have multiple results, but only one that's true?"

Another nod.

"Okay," Camis said evenly, "if we can prove that Rylesbach and Sires authored the fabrications, then you're clean. Let's begin with the ramifications for ANZA. They're not bad. If or when the scandal breaks you'll express immediate, public and total shock that anybody in ANZA could have done such a thing. You'll volunteer with authorities to apprehend the wrongdoer, in this case Sires, who will need to be isolated. There's no other way. It's a small price to pay. One scandal, one man. For now you should distance yourself from him. The press will feed on the ANZA carcass for awhile before you pay a large settlement to the SEC and plead *nolo contendere*. That'll be your resurrection. You'll send a letter of explanation to shareholders that will appear in newspapers across the country as a full-page ad."

"Like we did with Prince William Sound?"

"Exactly. In the letter, you'll refer to a company renegade who made serious mistakes, who coerced and duped others and has been fired. It's the old the-butler-did-it routine. He'll be gone, and you'll assure the American people that such behavior will never tarnish ANZA again."

"John Sires isn't exactly a butler."

"In this case he is."

Quail chewed his toothpick.

"Remember, Alan, corporate *nolo contendere* allows you to maintain solvency for settlement payments. Never plead guilty, unless you want ANZA to sink under lawsuits piled up from here to the moon. You want to win in a court of law, and in the court of public opinion. You want to win on Wall Street, and at every gas station across America."

Quail's face seemed to focus on some fourth dimension.

Camis crossed his hands behind his cubic head. "I wouldn't worry about Mark Meadows."

"Have you ever heard of Ida Tarbell?" Quail asked.

Camis squinted. "Who?"

"Ida Minerva Tarbell, the woman who torpedoed John D. Rockefeller."

Camis offered a blank look.

"There he was," Quail said, "the wealthiest man in America, the world's first billionaire, a friend of presidents, senators and kings. Untouchable. Along comes this woman journalist almost twenty years his junior who writes a series of magazine articles and shoots him down like the Red Baron. She couldn't even vote. But her investigations were so influential that a few years later the Supreme Court dissolved the Standard Oil Trust, the most powerful industrial monopoly in the history of the United States."

"So?" Camis asked.

"So ants can slay elephants. Mark Meadows worries me. Four spurious accidental deaths worry me. The fabrications, the letters signed Jumar, Bruce Janstadt and his Wilderness bill. Eddie

Tagarook, Oliver Longstreet, Caltex, Russian hardliners, Armenian idiots, tariffs and taxes, my board of directors, they all worry me, Ned. I worry a lot. It's my specialty. My hair was gray at thirty, my insomnia constant at forty, my blood pressure high at fifty." Quail stood up, exhausted. He hadn't even mentioned his other ANZA secret, the one about Iran and Baku, where *he* was the butler. "I appreciate your advice, Ned. But right now I'm tired. We'll talk later."

That same day Alan Quail phoned Wall Street and sold two percent of his ANZA stock for six hundred thousand dollars. That night his precious daughter, Aliena, flew into Aspen. She was too ill to ski, so the foursome—Aliena, her fiancé and mother and father—spent a quiet evening watching movies.

The home office called the next day to arrange a board of directors meeting for the first week of April. "One more thing," Quail's secretary added. "Mr. Sires has asked to speak with you again. Shall I patch him through?"

"No. I'll speak with him when I get to Houston."

"We're all thinking about you and Mrs. Quail and your daughter," the secretary added.

"Thank you." Quail turned off the remote phone and looked across the spacious condominium at Aliena who played a board game with her fiancé and mother. How fragile and lovely she was.

"Come join us, Dad," she said, wrinkling her nose in that special way of hers.

"In a minute," he answered.

For now he turned his lusterless eyes out the window and did what he did best. He worried.

TWENTY-TWO

Shannon found Mark alone in the back of an Irish pub near Dupont Circle. He stood to greet her, to reach for her, and in that reaching to bridge so many things that neither of them could define. They had spoken by phone but not seen each other for weeks. He had written her letters and poems as cool waters for her fevered mind, and now she hungered for his touch. She thought he might kiss her, but he hesitated, and in that hesitation the moment was lost when a man appeared at their table.

"Mark Meadows, I'm Special Agent Lincoln Crozier, FBI."

They sat down and positioned themselves at polar ends of the table. Mark asked to see his identification, and Crozier obliged.

"Are there any live tape recorders at this table?" Mark asked.

"None on my part," Crozier said. "And you?"

"None."

"This is going to require some trust on the part of each of us," Crozier added. He looked at Shannon, who nodded. She had arranged this meeting at Crozier's request. Crozier grabbed a peanut from a bowl and shelled it with his large fingers. Shannon thought he still possessed a vestige of the Iowa farmboy, something no city could breed out of him, but that his hounddog eyes masked a calculating mind.

"So," Mark asked, "how many cards do we put on the table here?"

"How about one at a time?" Crozier said.

Shannon nodded. "That's fair."

~

Ten miles away, Tyler Kyle scoured the ANZA December guest list for the hundredth time and decided something about it wasn't right. He phoned the operative in Florida, the man who had infiltrated Parkendale Investigative Services and sent him the list. No answer. He phoned William Alt in Anchorage. No answer. Kyle slammed down the phone. The impudence of these people being out of touch when he wanted them. He exited the booth and hurried through the night.

~

The waiter arrived and Crozier ordered Coca-Cola with no ice. Mark ordered a Guinness, Shannon a Corona. Crozier gave the man a hundred-dollar bill and said, "This is to reserve these two tables next to us. Keep them empty."

"You betcha." The waiter turned and left.

"Did you come here through the Capitol Building?" Crozier asked Shannon.

"Yes."

"Good. Keep mixing the times and routes you use going to and from work."

"Is she in danger?" Mark asked.

"She could be."

"She could be? Is that how we're going to conduct this meeting, in innuendo?"

Crozier folded his arms on the table and leaned forward. "The FBI knows you're researching ANZA and the mysterious deaths of some key people. We also know it's much bigger than you realize. We've got patterned homicides and high-risk assessments involving several development-versus-preservation issues across the country. It's the work of extremists, and what you've found is just the tip of the iceberg."

"Who are they?" Mark asked.

"We're not certain. That's why we need your help."

"You're not certain, but you have theories?"

"We always have theories."

"And you want my ANZA files?"

"We want your voluntary compliance. When we break the case, we give you the scoop before anybody else. It'll be big."

"It's big now. It's my story."

"Only the ANZA chapter is yours. There are others. It can all be yours if you cooperate. If not, the whole thing could collapse. You're an intelligent man, Mark. Don't lose the shark for the fish. A superficial newspaper story on ANZA now would only send these people into hiding."

"A couple days ago I e-mailed a summary of my story to my editor, Lowell Hutchinson. I'm meeting with him and Gil Trebideaux tomorrow." Trebideaux was editor-in-chief of the *Post*.

"Do they want to run it?"

"I'm not sure."

Crozier puffed his cheeks and ran a hand through his thinning hair.

Shannon was elsewhere, far away, riverbound, thinking.

Mark asked, "If ANZA is only one chapter, how do I know the FBI hasn't cut similar deals with other journalists investigating other chapters?"

"You don't. You have to trust us."

"I have to trust the FBI?"

"Frightening, isn't it?"

"I could give you my ANZA files and keep a copy myself. I'd give you one week. If you didn't break your case by then, the Post would run my story."

"No deal. You work on deadlines. We don't."

"Time is important for reasons other than catching the extremists," Shannon said. She looked at Crozier. "You're aware of the energy and Wilderness bills moving through Congress?"

"Yes. One of them is Bruce Janstadt's. It's been headlines with his scandal."

"That's no scandal," Mark said. "That's a frame. Somebody's paying those guys to say those things."

"Is that right?" Crozier asked facetiously. "And you know who it is?"

"No." But Mark had Tony Carzoli, his friend and fellow reporter, working on a connection in Minnesota.

"You need evidence," Crozier said to Mark.

"Absence of evidence isn't evidence of absence."

"Maybe not among journalists, but it is in our judicial system."

"Let's stay on target," Shannon said.

Mark looked into her eyes and a wave of amnesty washed over him.

"We can subpoena your files," Crozier told him.

Mark shook his head. "That won't work and we both know it. The FBI tried it with Watergate and the Pentagon Papers, and the Post's attorneys tied up the subpoenas for weeks."

"You're playing a dangerous game," Crozier said. "It's not only yourself you're endangering, it's Shannon too." He looked at her with cold authority, no trace of the farmboy. He reached into his pocket and handed her a folded sheet of paper.

She opened it and drew a sharp breath. It was a sketch of Rasputin eyes, Stephen York.

"You recognize him, don't you?" Crozier asked.

"Yes."

"Is it accurate?"

"Yes." And no.

"He killed your father, and probably your brother."

Shannon dug her fingers into the palm of Mark's hand and felt her mouth go dry. She didn't hear Crozier's exact words after that, something about the sketch being an "e-fit," a computer-generated composite created from the eyewitness accounts of many people, including Mrs. Luther, who said the man came calling for Mark at his apartment. And Rollie Dawson, who remembered seeing the man in the nursing home restroom the night Shannon's father died.

In a hollow voice Shannon heard herself say, "He sat next to me on the flight from Washington to SeaTac, and I told him that my father was in a care center near Providence Hospital, in Anchorage."

"You should know," Crozier told her, "that Harry Arnold says he's never seen a man of this description."

"He's lying. He saw him on the flight from Seattle to Anchorage."

Mark looked at the e-fit sketch and asked, "What's his name?"

"He's not Stephen York and he's not a geologist," Shannon said.

"His true identity?" Crozier said. "We don't know."

"Do you know who he works for?"

"No." Crozier looked at Shannon. "He killed your father with a pumiliotoxin from the skin of a Panamanian jungle frog, lethal and undetectable, except that he made the mistake of squirting some onto the floor before injecting it into the intravenous line. That's where we found it."

"On the floor?"

Crozier nodded. "The organization he works for has no name and exists nowhere on paper or on any silicon chip. It's a phantom. Not even the Wise Use movement knows about them." He looked at Mark. "Your turn."

Mark thought for a moment. "Have you heard of the Contract of the Century?"

"ANZA in Baku?"

"Right. Did you ever wonder how ANZA signed that deal and no other oil company got a piece of it? How OPEC was shut out? How the pipeline was arranged to run from the Caspian Sea through Iran instead of Armenia, all while Ayatollah Khomeini was in power?"

"That's for the CIA to figure out."

"Not when it affects billion dollar deals in Alaska."

"You've found a connection?"

Mark smiled. "Your turn."

Crozier didn't smile. "We estimate that this so-called Stephen York has killed two dozen people. He's daring, he likes role-playing, and he knows when to hide. His buddies are not as sophisticated, but they're vicious. They've come after you once, and they will again. Am I making myself clear?"

Neither Mark nor Shannon said a thing.

Shannon was thinking. *A toxin from a jungle frog? How will I ever tell Mom about this?*

Mark told Crozier, "I interviewed Shannon's father the night he died. When I asked him if he thought his attempted murder had something to do with the Anwahr 1002 Area test drill result, he blinked three times, and raised his finger three times."

"Meaning?"

"I don't know. The number three must have significance beyond yes and no. I need to meet with Hutch and Gil before I say anything more. I'll tell them about your offer."

"Time is critical, Mark. We need to apprehend those guys who were after you in New York. You need to put us onto them; they probably work with this Stephen York."

"Okay."

"Another thing. I'm out on a limb with this investigation. If I don't get your research or some other breakthrough soon, the director could scrap this whole thing."

Mark said nothing. The Irish pub had become crowded with patrons playing darts, laughing and cheering. Shannon had pushed her chair away—and her mind as well—while still holding the sketch in her hand. She must have detected them looking at her, as she turned her dark eyes to them and said, "I have an idea."

"To catch Stephen?" Crozier asked.

"No, to save a refuge."

TWENTY-THREE

Early the next morning ten senators faced off on the hardwood half-length basketball court beneath the Rayburn House Office Building. Five Democrats versus five Republicans, all friends; *esteemed* friends, to use the parlance of floor debate, wherein gentlemen agreed to disagree in the fluctuating fraternities and temporary allegiances that defined their legislative machinery. Never wound a foe too deeply, was the unwritten Senate rule, because today's adversary could be tomorrow's ally. Thus evolved the functional if not sincere Washington political subculture rich with rituals and symbols of status.

Bruce Janstadt played for the Democrats, Sam Matlin for the Republicans. Each typically scored half the points for his team.

The game accelerated into a spirited battle complete with body checks and uncalled fouls. Janstadt controlled the backcourt, and Matlin the forecourt. Soon Janstadt was hobbling, Matlin was fighting for breath, and they lost track of the score and said it didn't matter.

Janstadt dressed quickly in the locker room. Exiting, he limped down Rayburn Hall, suddenly aware that somebody was next to him, a woman with black hair pulled into a braid, wearing a twill skirt that billowed around her lean legs. No makeup. Her only jewelry was a striking pendant made of caribou antler. Her dark eyes flickered with anticipation. "Senator Janstadt, my name is Shannon DeShay. I'm an aide for Senator Matlin."

He studied her without slowing. He had a palpable vigor even when in pain, and he stood nearly a foot taller than her. Bushy eyebrows rested above his serious eyes.

"What can I do for you?" he asked.

"Keep Big Oil out of the Arctic Refuge."

He stopped and stared at her. "You said you work for Sam Matlin?"

"Yes. I think I'm his only staffer who supports your Wilderness bill."

"I'll bet you are."

"I have an idea." She had to hurry. The other senators, including Matlin, would come down the hall any minute. "Take a handful of undecided senators whose votes could make or break the Wilderness bill, and invite them on a rafting trip down a river through the refuge."

Janstadt narrowed his eyes.

"Take four rafts," Shannon continued, "four guides and no oil men. Let the river do the talking. Begin in the Brooks Range and end on the Coastal Plain of the 1002 Area. Travel unhurriedly. Float a day, hike a day, ten days total, maybe twelve."

"When?"

"Late June, when there are few mosquitoes but lots of caribou."

"Let the river do the talking. I like that," Janstadt said. "Reminds me of James Baker and Eduard Shevardnadze on the Snake."

"Or Huck Finn and Jim on the Mississippi."

"Or David Brower and Floyd Dominy on the Colorado."

"*Encounters with the Archdruid*, you've read it?" Shannon asked.

"One of my favorites." Janstadt tendered a small smile.

Shannon was thinking, *I like this guy*.

Husky laughter. Hoopmen coming down the hall, rounding a corner into view. Janstadt turned as Sam Matlin called to him. "Hey Bruce, you lost?" The others chuckled.

When Janstadt turned back to address Shannon, she was gone.

TWENTY-FOUR

All eyes focused on Gil Trebideaux and the framed edict on his office wall: NEWSPAPERS ARE THE FIRST ROUGH DRAFT OF HISTORY. He ran a bony hand through his zinc-gray hair and pulled his lips tight across his teeth. "I still see too much conjecture here, Mark. Not enough substance."

Mark had explained it all. The 1002 test drill and its secret result, the deaths made to look like accidents, the thugs in New York, Stephen York, the FBI, Baku, Shannon and her father. He spread a map of arctic Alaska on the table, surrounded by the editorial board and Tony Carzoli, there at his request.

"I'm sure the FBI promised no timeline," Trebideaux said, "at which time we get the exclusive story."

"You've seen this sort of thing before?" Mark asked.

"Oh yes." The feisty editor pushed an intercom button, "Jim, get FBI Deputy Director Liam Bristol on the line for me." He released the button and picked up his tennis racquet, fingering the strings. History was a big responsibility, and Trebideaux wasn't in the business of printing fiction. He twirled the racquet and said, "I've got a friend who's retired from the CIA. He analyzed conspiracy dynamics for twenty years. One I remember is if you take the number of people who know a secret and square that number, that's the increased likelihood the secret will be leaked. A secret among four people will be sixteen times more difficult to contain than one held by just one person. Among ten people, one hundred times more difficult."

"Like Kepler's law of physics," Mark said.

"Exactly. What astounds me about this ANZA thing is how ten people could keep this test result quiet for so long."

"Money," one of the editors said.

"Has to be more than that," another responded.

"A lot of money."

"Remember what happened in major league baseball in the late 1980s?" said Lowell 'Hutch' Hutchinson, the managing editor. "The owners and managers on all twenty-six teams secretly agreed not to hire any player on free agent status. They got away with it for several years before somebody caught on. If that many people can commit collusion in major league baseball, they can pull it off in the oil industry."

"All because of money."

"Not always," Mark said. "Fanatics work for causes, not money. They blow up abortion clinics and federal buildings and kill people and get paid nothing."

The intercom signaled, "Mr. Trebideaux, there's a Shannon DeShay on line three for Mark."

Trebideaux arched his eyebrows. "Go ahead, Jim, put her through."

"Hello, Mark?" A searching voice.

"Hi, Shannon."

"Am I on a speaker phone?"

"Shannon, this is Gil Trebideaux. I'm here with senior members of my staff. If you wish to speak with Mark in private you can, but I assure you that we maintain strict confidentiality here."

After a measured pause, Shannon said, "Mark, I just confronted

Harry Arnold in the office about him telling the FBI that he's never seen the man who called himself Stephen York."

"And?"

"He lied again, and denied it all. And, well, I lost it..."

"You lost it?"

"I got pissed and told him that my father had been murdered, and that I'm sick of his bullshit games, and now the whole office is talking."

Mark leaned heavily on the table.

"Are you still there?" Shannon asked.

"Yes, I'm still here. I'm just thinking." Mark looked at the somber faces around him

Shannon said, "I have to go. I'm late."

"No, wait, Shan—"

She hung up.

The editors sat in silence while Mark rubbed his brow. Before anyone could say anything the intercom signaled again, "Mr. Trebideaux, Mr. Bristol with the FBI is on line two."

"Put him through." Trebideaux shooed the others out of his office as he switched the call person to person. "Liam, you rascal, how's your net game?"

"He'll be on that call for half an hour," Hutch said in the newsroom. "He and Liam Bristol went to Penn State together." The other editors excused themselves. They had deadlines. Hutch invited Mark and Tony into his office.

~

Kelly Calvert, Sam Matlin's chief of staff, towered over Shannon, adjusted the padded shoulders in her silk ensemble and said, "The senator wants to see you."

Shannon walked behind her as if being taken to the woodshed. Outside Sam's door, Kelly turned and said, "You need to remember something, Shannon. You're not in Alaska anymore. You can't be an earth mama here. Reconsider how you dress. Start using makeup. Lose the bone pendant. And curb your opinions." She opened the door without knocking.

Sam Matlin was on the phone. He motioned the two women to come inside. He ended the conversation, made a note on a legal pad and said, "Now, Shannon, what's this nonsense about your father? I've never heard of such a thing." He invited her to sit down.

She did, and after a deep breath she said, "I can't elaborate."

Sam looked at Kelly, who remained standing, arms crossed over her chest. Sam looked back at Shannon. "Why not?"

"I just can't. Is this what you wanted to talk to me about?"

"Yes, and other things. We're worried about you. We're disappointed in your efforts on my subcommittee talking points on the energy bill. We think you could have done better."

"Oh?"

"You see, if your beliefs weaken the ability of this office to represent the voters who put me here, then we have a problem."

Shannon made no response.

He spoke paternally. "Remember, you're not a common citizen anymore. You represent this office and the people of Alaska, sixty percent of whom support oil drilling in that refuge of yours."

"But sixty percent of Americans oppose it."

Sam scowled, "I don't represent America. I represent Alaska."

"Then let Oliver Longstreet and Jack Worley represent the sixty percent of Alaskans who support drilling, and you represent the forty percent who don't."

"Don't be ridiculous," Kelly said.

"What do you think your father was doing up there all those years?" Sam asked. "Writing poetry? He was looking for oil-bearing substrate."

"Actually, he did write some poetry."

"Yes, well," —Sam waved his arm— "but why did he go up there?"

"Because he loved the place. He loved the wildness."

"Sort of ironic, don't you think?" Sam smiled in a stinging

way that Shannon hadn't seen when he was mayor. Washington had changed him somehow. *Has it done the same to me?*

"I need to get back to my work," she said, standing.

"How's your mother?" Sam asked.

"Fine."

"Does she know about this murder?" He said *murder* with a sarcastic drawl, as if it were some Savannah fiction.

"No."

Sam nodded. "If your father loved the wildness so much, why'd he go to the arctic as a point man for ANZA?"

"Because he loved my mother, and she wanted him up there, out of the way, so she could have time with Travis. She wanted a husband who would make three times more money working for Big Oil than he would being a professor, which was his real dream."

"For crying out loud, Shannon. Your mother cared for Charles for six years after his accident. She did—"

"I know what she did. She loved him more when he was half a man than when he was a whole man."

Sam stared at her. "What's gotten into you?"

"The truth, and it hurts. Do you have any more questions?"

"No." He shifted in his chair and looked at Kelly. "Do you?"

Kelly said, "I think it would be best if Shannon answered more constituent mail and did less legislative work for awhile."

"I agree," Sam said. He looked at Shannon. "You're a valuable member of this staff, and we don't want to lose you. Just watch what you say and where you say it. Come talk with Kelly or me at any time. We're a team, remember?"

Shannon walked to the door and paused. Sam and Kelly caught her imploring eyes. Did she have something to say? They stared across the wide gulf of their experiences: a young aide who had blossomed in the Arctic Refuge, a senator who had never set foot there, and a chief of staff who devoted more time thinking about her hair than any ecosystem on earth. The door closed.

"I thought she was going to apologize," Sam said.

Kelly nodded. "So did I."

Oliver Longstreet pulled out his Verminator slingshot and a box of birdshot, aimed at the gray pigeon that crapped on the ledge, and fired. The pigeon died on the wing and fell like a leaf, wings out, spiraling down, hitting the pavement just as the senator, grinning, closed the window and his secretary announced over the intercom that the APA had arrived.

"Show them in," he said.

The door opened and six smartly dressed men from the Alaska Petroleum Association entered. After greetings and pleasantries, the APA men reiterated their commitment to the energy bill and opening ANWR; to minimizing the gas tax and arranging a fair ANWR royalty for the State of Alaska and, oh yes, they wished to make a sizeable donation to the Republican National Committee, all soft money of course. The senator thanked them yet remained deftly noncommittal on ANZA and the 1002 Area.

The APA president said, "The Arctic Slope and Fairbanks North Star Borough want the State of Alaska to get a ninety-ten split with the federal government from Anwahr oil, not a fifty-fifty split. They say the Alaska Statehood Act guarantees—"

"I'm aware of the Statehood Act," Longstreet said. "I helped to write it. Tell them the provision will survive in the energy bill only if it promises the Federal Treasury a fifty-fifty split."

The APA president mentioned something about the soft money being unavailable under conditions of a fifty-fifty split.

Longstreet said, "We've known each other a long time. Support the fifty-fifty split now so I can get the bill passed. The State of Alaska can then sue the federal government for its ninety-percent rightful share. The bill has an Achilles heel written into it. I know every constitutional statute and case law that will enable you to win. Just keep your arrows sharp."

"Idiot," Kyle mumbled in his dark office next door. He listened by hidden microphone to Longstreet cut the deal. "I'm surrounded by idiots."

~

The phone rang in the middle of a Bruce Willis mayhem movie, with everything exploding and burning. William Alt, unemployed yet hopeful for a new and brighter future, muted the movie and answered the phone.

"William?" The soft voice said.

"Yes, hello." William killed the movie and sat up straight.

"You got the money?"

"Yes. But I—?"

"In a few days you'll receive an envelope containing a key for a box at the Russian Jack Post Office. In the box you'll find a large envelope with a list of names and eight thousand dollars."

"Jesus, How can I—"

"William?"

"Yeah?"

"You'll know everything soon."

~

Hutch, Mark and Tony were in Hutch's office watching the videotape of the interview of Charles DeShay when Trebideaux blew in like a gust of wind. His tennis racquet in hand, he said to Mark, "The FBI wants to apprehend those guys who roughed you up, the ones who've been following you in New York. You'll need to go up there with them. You up for that?"

"I guess."

"Good. Get to Jeff Meola and Harry Arnold and find out what's going on there. Then get some reliable named sources who'll go on record about ANZA."

"So you're not going to run the story?" Mark asked.

"Not yet. I need facts, not conjecture. Not anonymous sources or third-person hearsay or unsubstantiated charges or innuendo.

This is a newspaper, not a damn tabloid."

An uncomfortable silence—rare in a newspaper—filled the office. Hutch chewed on his glasses. Mark hung his head.

"I have an idea," Tony said. All morning he had quietly studied Mark's abstract without saying a word. They looked at him expectantly. Tony's sad, sleepy eyes cloaked a fierce intelligence reserved for times like this. "Have Mark write a profile of Oliver Longstreet for the Sunday magazine," he said. "Use Rollie's photo of him deplaning the ANZA Lear for fireworks. Longstreet's the most powerful political figure Alaska has ever produced. He chairs Appropriations and rolls pork by the billions into a state that has only one-fifth of one percent of the U.S. population. He's pro-oil, but from reading this" —Tony held up the abstract— "he's got a strained relationship with ANZA. Why? Flesh it out. Make it biography, not an investigation of murders masked as accidents. That way the FBI will still work with us."

"I like it," Hutch said.

"So do I." Trebideaux picked up the phone to call the editor of the Sunday magazine.

Hutch walked to the window and said, "Look at that. I haven't seen it snow like that in Washington in years." Mark and Tony joined him, mesmerized by the white cascades.

Trebideaux hung up the phone. "Okay Mark. No conjecture, just a clean, solid profile. Five thousand words in two weeks. Can you do it?"

Mark grinned. "You bet."

~

The minute Shannon saw the snow, she got up and walked out.

"Where are you going?" a co-worker asked.

"Skiing."

She rode the congressional subway to the Capitol Building and emerged to see platinum light on the beckoning Mall below, the Washington Memorial veiled in snow, the Lincoln Memorial not even visible, the traffic moving at a crawl. *A southern city? Not today.*

Jude wasn't home. Shannon found her skis and within an hour was kicking and gliding through the George Washington Memorial Parkway along the Potomac River. With no solid base and only four inches of wet snow, the skiing was marginal, but Shannon reveled in it. On the remote backside of her third loop, with daylight dying, she came upon a large branch fallen across the trail. *Odd, it wasn't there half an hour ago.* Without removing her skis, she bent over to move it and was slammed from behind. Her body crumpled to the ground. A knee dug into her back, a hand pushed her face into the snow as another pinned her arms behind her. She opened her mouth to yell but only swallowed snow, locked in a powerful human vise, unable to move or breathe. *My God, I'm going to die.*

Her legs and feet twisted against her skis. A man's voice whispered hoarsely into her ear, "Scream for help and I'll kill you, I swear I will. Where's Mark Meadows?"

He lifted her head and she gasped for breath and he slammed her down, hitting her nose on the ground.

He lifted her head again. "Where is he?"

She gasped. He pushed her back down and grabbed her in a two-arm twist lock. "Tell me, or I'll break your neck."

She closed her eyes and saw a vision of her brother, Travis, his arms outstretched for her, his face so young, tears in his eyes.

Her attacker wrenched something hard against her throat, preparing to crush it. Then gone. He was suddenly gone, the weight, the vise—gone. Shannon lifted herself, coughing, bleeding, sick with pain, her neck, back, shoulders and arms stiff and wet and cold. She never saw him, not even a glimpse. The snow beneath her was red with blood. Staring at her from the trail forty feet away was a young mother pulling a child on a sled, their faces filled with alarm, and next to them a large mongrel dog with no bark yet very sharp teeth. In a raspy voice Shannon asked the mother if she had seen the attacker. But the woman hurried away with her child and dog.

Shannon left her skis and walked to the Metro and rode to a hotel in Ballston. Using a credit card from her coat pocket, she got a room and took a long hot shower. She called Carzoli's to speak with Mark, got the answering machine and hung up without leaving a message. She called Agent Crozier at his home and told him everything. An hour later he met her at the hotel and asked many questions. He gave her extra clothes, a cell phone, a four-wheel drive rental car with five days of groceries and a route map to a rustic cabin in the Shenandoah Valley, a secret place where she would be safe.

~

Wrapped in blankets, Shannon watched the snowfall through smoke-stained windows. She traced her fingers over candle wax that had spilled and hardened onto the rough wood. She tended the wood-burning stove and thought of too many things, running images like refracted light through the prism of her experiences, searching for rainbows. She wrote in a small book and tried to express the inexpressible. Sparrows and finches came to a feeder she filled with seeds found in a jar. The wind died and the storm ended, leaving the trees filigreed with snow, their branches rising in white supplication to the sky.

She considered calling her mother.

—Shannon, come down from there, Susan yells. You're going to fall and hurt yourself.

—She's fine, dear. Let her go.

—She falls on her head, Charles, it's your fault. I'm keeping Travis inside. I don't want him up there with her. Susan walks into the house and slams the door.

He looks up at her. You a monkey?

—Yeah. Shannon, only eight, climbs a couple more branches in the big

birch. I don't want Travis up here, Dad.

—Neither does your mother.

—Why is she like that?

—Oh, it's complicated. Some people can only love other people when they have them in a cage.

—I can see the top of the house from here.

—Five minutes, Shannon, then I want you to come down. No excuses.

—Mom is always mad at me.

—She worries about you, that's all.

Up another branch, Shannon asks, Do parents have favorites?

—Favorites? What do you mean?

—You know, favorite things, like kids?

—You mother loves you very much.

—She does?

—Of course she does. You know that.

—I do?

~

On the last day of March, Susan DeShay answered the phone in her home in Anchorage. It was Shannon. They spoke in ellipses for awhile, then Shannon said, "Mom, I have something to tell you about Dad and Travis, something you need to hear from me before you hear it from anybody else. You might want to sit down."

April

TWENTY-FIVE

The great storm ended. Temperatures climbed and flooding threatened vast areas of Washington. Shannon took long walks in the Shenandoah, and spoke with Mark and Crozier daily by phone. Mark wanted to come see her, but she said no, she needed time alone. "The man who attacked me was looking for you," she told him. "Be careful, Mark."

Mark stayed in Tony Carzoli's home near Rock Creek Park in northwest Washington. The FBI insisted that he accompany them to New York, but he delayed, wanting to finish his profile on Senator Longstreet. Five thousand words in two weeks, with one week gone to research. "I'll make it," Mark told Tony. "Jack London and Edgar Allan Poe each wrote a thousand words a day."

"And both were dead at forty," Tony replied.

"Thanks for the confidence."

"Anytime."

Mark phoned Longstreet's office, introduced himself and his project, and asked to speak to the senator. A woman put him on hold.

A new voice came on the line, deeper yet softer. "Mr. Meadows, this is Tyler Kyle, Senator Longstreet's chief of staff. We're
pleased you want to profile the senator. Are you on the Hill?"

"At the moment, no."

"When's your deadline?" *Bait the hook.*

"One week."

"Not much time. Let's see…the senator is very busy these
days with committee re-scheduling. If you give me a number
where you can be reached, I'll phone you as soon as I speak with
him."

Mark gave Kyle his voice mail number in the newsroom.

"The senator works late and I'll probably need to reach you
on a spur of the moment when a scheduling window opens. Do
you have an evening number?" *Lower the hook, slowly.*

No response. Mark was thinking.

"Mr. Meadows. If I can't contact you directly then I'm afraid a
last minute interview will be impossible." *Jiggle the line.*

Mark had told nobody other than Shannon where he was
staying.

"Are you there?" *Gently, gently.*

"Yes."

The fish approaches. "Do you have an evening number?"

Mark gave him Carzoli's number.

The fish bites. "Very good," Kyle said. "I'll be in touch. I look
forward to meeting you."

~

In his hideout in Idaho, Stephen picked up the phone on the
first ring.

"Get back here," Kyle said. "Meadows is in Washington."

~

Eddie Tagarook and Elsie and Walter Kiviikanak arrived in

Washington's Dulles International Airport as proud and power-less as three Celtic warriors before the Roman legions of Vespasian. A tide of strangers swept them through the gate to-ward baggage claim. None of the three had been East before, and in his eighty-two years Walter had been out of Alaska only once, long ago, for heart surgery in Seattle. So many tall build-ings there, he remembered, it was a wonder that Seattle didn't sink into the sea. Now he and his granddaughter and her cousin had arrived in Washington to testify before a Senate subcommit-tee on the Arctic Refuge. They moved with the crowd, caught in mid-stream, eyes glazed.

Somebody called to Eddie in a familiar voice. He raised his head and saw Shannon wave from the wall thirty feet away. He freed himself, and Elsie did the same. But poor Walter—bow-legged and half-blind—did not. Eddie dived back into the throng and fished him out. They descended to baggage claim, then drove to Georgetown in the rental car on loan from Agent Crozier.

Shannon had arrived at Dulles from the Shenandoah; this was her first time back in Washington since the attack.

Elsie sat up front with her. Eddie sat in back with Walter, who promptly fell asleep. Eddie looked out the window and said, "All these cars and highways and office buildings and shopping malls, you know, I think the whole world's gonna be just metal and money and concrete someday, ya know? Nothin' else. Just metal and money and concrete."

Elsie asked about the energy and Wilderness bills, and Shan-non briefed her. Longstreet's energy bill had sailed through a Senate subcommittee with the Arctic Refuge drilling rider un-touched, and now awaited action in full committee.

Eddie watched the traffic. "Don't all these people get tired of each other? I mean, how many people live here? A zillion?"

Shannon told them about Janstadt's Wilderness bill. Because Republicans controlled the Senate fifty-two to forty-eight, they chaired every committee and subcommittee and wielded tremen-dous power. If a Democrat introduced a bill they didn't like, they simply ignored the bothersome thing and let it die. But Janstadt was a ranking minority member who had displayed enough sagacity over the years to win bipartisan respect. He was diplomatic, likable and a sports star. He debated that the Arctic Refuge was a national refuge, not a state refuge, and that all Americans, not just Alaskans, should determine its future. He threatened to filibuster Longstreet's energy bill unless the chairman of the Public Lands Subcommittee showed him the courtesy of at least scheduling his Wilderness bill for a hearing.

Shannon drove over the Key Bridge and Eddie looked down at the Potomac. "Hey, is that the river that's so polluted it caught on fire?"

"That was a river in Ohio," Shannon said.

"Thirty years ago," added Elsie.

"Look at that," Eddie said. "Is that the Washington Monument? Man, would I love to fly my Cessna around that."

At midnight Shannon unlocked the door with the three Eskimos shuffling behind her. She found Jude seated on the sofa, a glass of bourbon in her hand, and Harry Arnold next to her, the Orwellian blue glow of the television on their faces, the sound of CNN chanting bad news. Harry got to his feet and said, "I'd better go."

"You don't have to go," Jude said.

"Yes, I do." Harry pulled on his coat.

Shannon appraised him, and he gave her a hard look. After ten days in the tonic of the forests and mountains of the Shenandoah, Shannon was back in Washington and already it seemed like a snake pit. Harry slithered out the door.

Jude said to Shannon, "You have a lot of explaining to do. Where have you been? Have you been listening to the news? Look at this." She motioned Shannon over to a small television.

"The Caspian is on fire," said the breathless reporter. "Here, in this landlocked sea, where ten percent of the world's oil lies waiting to be plundered, unidentified war planes have struck oil fields near Turkmenbashi, and Shiite Muslims are shooting each other from their armor-plated Mercedes in downtown Baku. Unconfirmed sources say Iranian forces have positioned themselves along the southern boundaries of Azerbaijan and Turkmenistan, apparently in a bid to secure a pipeline route for Caspian oil through Iran and Turkey, rather than a route through Azerbaijan and Georgia."

The picture flashed back to the home desk in Atlanta, where the woman anchor said, "In Moscow, Russian hardliners have announced suspension of all contract law and land titles in Baku. We take you there now..."

A new reporter appeared. Then a mean-faced man came on the screen—Shannon missed his name—and in thick, broken English he said, "No more Nike or Mickey Mouse or Big Mac cheeseburgers. No more western imperialism. Remember the words of Lenin: 'When it comes time to hang the capitalists, they will argue with each other to sell us the rope.' I say let them argue and let them hang. Foreign imperialists have two days to get out."

The picture flashed back to an aerial view of black smoke rising from the Caspian Sea.

Jude chugged her bourbon. "Can you believe that?"

"Just like that river in Ohio," Eddie said. "Burnt water."

~

Oliver Longstreet, Sam Matlin and Jack Worley watched CNN in Longstreet's hideaway office in the basement of the Senate wing of the Capitol Building. Longstreet tromboned his glasses up and down his nose to catch every detail, then shook his head over the threat of another Cold War.

Worley said the good fortune of Russia was the bad execution of bad laws. "At least this will make it easier to get into Anwahr. I'll bet Alan Quail is having a heart attack right now."

~

"Two days," John Sires sputtered as he kicked the table. "We've got three thousand people over there and they have to be out in two goddamn days? That's impossible. Somebody should shoot that Russian and dump him in the Volga."

Nobody spoke.

Sires surveyed the dour faces around him in the executive suite of the Andrew Jackson Hotel.

Maya said, "You don't want anybody to shoot the Russian, John."

"No? Why not?"

"Because one murdered martyr is worth a hundred posturing politicians."

"I'm not so sure."

"I am. I lived in Israel."

Alan Quail emerged from the adjacent room, his face drawn. He'd been on the phone for hours. It was 1:00 A.M. and everybody sensed he wanted to speak privately with Sires. They bid their solemn good nights and departed for their rooms. Quail sat down and said, "I just finished a conference call with the board. They want to release the 1002 test drill result."

"Really?" Sires said. "Which one?"

~

"Hello, Carzoli's residence."

The delicate voice of a little girl lingered in Tyler Kyle's mind, a voice from earlier when he had called the number Mark Meadows gave him, and realized with tingling excitement, *of course, he's staying with his fellow Post reporter, Tony Carzoli.*

Finding the Carzoli address was easy. Now, departing the last Metro, Kyle entered another booth and made a final call, this one to William Alt in Anchorage. It was the seventeenth time they had spoken in little more than two months, with the bond deepening each time as William told his mysterious benefactor things he never told anyone else. "Ten thousand bucks is a lot of money," he said. "When do we get down to business?"

For a brief moment Kyle bathed in his astuteness. He'd chosen William well. Beneath the bravado was a young man who understood honor and wanted to *get down to business*. A young man indebted, who had killed and would kill again for the right reason at the right time; a young man who had suffered a less than honorable discharge, and a firing from ANZA, and was ripe for the respect that Merlin and Kyle and others would give him.

Kyle told him to pull out his list from the ANZA party, four hundred and twenty names on eight pages. Kyle asked if there was anything about the list that struck William as odd.

"No," William said with military crispness. He was grateful to help this caller who had shared so many hours of philosophy with him, the best philosophy he had ever heard. They discussed the twenty-five names highlighted on page five, those people who had signed past security while William booted the drunk from the lobby. Kyle described Jeff Meola and Harry Arnold, and while William said he remembered Arnold, he drew a blank on Meola.

"Anybody else who struck you as strange or out of the ordinary that night?"

"Not really. There were lots of rich people and beautiful women."

"Did you see anybody leave the party that you didn't remember from when they arrived?"

"A few. They probably signed in while I threw the drunk outta the lobby."

"This drunk. What was your impression of him?"

"I thought he was just another drunk at first. But then he didn't seem right. He didn't seem drunk."

Kyle leafed through the papers and said nothing.

"I knew most of the ANZA employees," William elaborated. "It was the first time I'd ever seen Mr. Quail. He's like a god at ANZA. He was sure pissed when he had to evacuate everybody. Captain Zarki was giving orders and—"

"Captain Zarki, who's he? Anchorage Police?"

"No, ANZA Security, my boss, Captain Carl Zarki. He fired me."

"He was called to the building when the alarms went off?"

"No. It's weird, he attended the party."

"What's weird about that?"

"Zarki never goes to crap like that, fancy parties, at least none that Jerry and me knew of. He was all duded up like some fancy executive."

"Zarki, Zarki." Kyle leafed through the list.

"Captain Carl Zarki, retired Army," William said. "He arrived early with some people I didn't recognize. Had a woman on his arm, not his old lady. She's dead."

Kyle found Carl Zarki, the top name on page two.

"That's right," William said. He came in and asked me for the previous shift report, and I got it for him while he signed in. The others signed in after him."

"They weren't ANZA employees?"

"No. Not in Alaska anyway. I know every ANZA person who works in that building, all fourteen hundred of them. I'd never seen these people before."

"You know fourteen hundred faces?"

"Yes, sir. I usually worked day shift or graveyard. I learned them all on day shift."

"If you usually worked day shift or graveyard, why were you working swing shift that night?"

"I don't know. Jerry and me liked swing shift best, and Zarki just gave it to us."

"For one night? The night of the biggest party of the year?"

"Kinda weird, isn't it? The two youngest guys on the ANZA security team getting that shift that night. We couldn't believe it."

Neither could Kyle.

TWENTY-SIX

Shannon awoke early on the floor of her Georgetown apartment with her sleeping bag curled around her. Dressed in her nightgown, she quietly opened the window and climbed onto the gabled roof. In the hour of birds she allowed their songs to comfort her, like a prayer, so many melodies, each singular and different and yet no two discordant, weaving their histories in the pale vestibule of day before people would rise and start their engines, and take it all away.

She showered and dressed in traveling clothes and fixed a light breakfast.

Eddie sprawled atop a sleeping mat wearing nothing but ridiculous purple jockey shorts. Elsie stirred awake on the sofa. Both sat up and looked at Shannon. "What'cha doin'?" Eddie asked.

"I'm catching a plane out of Dulles at seven-thirty."

Eddie scratched his head. "You were just there. You must like that place."

"Where you going?" Elsie asked.

"Minneapolis."

Jude opened her bedroom door with her hair in a mop. "Min-

207

neapolis? What for?"

"It's a long story," Shannon said.

Jude scowled. "You need to go back to work. You haven't been in the office in more than a week. Daddy's been wondering about you, and Kelly's pissed that you've been gone so long."

Shannon swallowed her orange juice. "I'll be there tomorrow."

"In time for the hearing?" Elsie asked.

"That's the plan."

"The plan," Jude said. "What plan?"

Somebody knocked on the door. Jude raised her eyebrows at Shannon. "That's Mark and Tony," Shannon said. "I've gotta run."

Jude opened the door, and there stood Mark Meadows and Tony Carzoli. "Good morning, Jude," Mark said. "We're off to Bolivia to rob banks, and we're taking Shannon with us."

Shannon's heart skipped a beat. She had spoken to Mark by phone many times but hadn't seen him in ten days. *This trip to Minneapolis is important,* Mark had told her. *It could turn the tide on Janstadt's Wilderness bill. We need you along.* He had spoken as he often did, with the infectious passion of an against-all-odds insurrectionist. She had grown to enjoy his feral nature and bright intuition, which by comparison made the Washington political elite and their practiced courtiers seem like stockyard cattle fattening on green pastures of money.

Shannon joined them at the door. Mark kissed her on the cheek, which Tony acknowledged with a smile. In every way Mark was light, Tony was dark, his hair, skin and demeanor, not in a moody way, but rather contemplative, as if to ascertain what people really meant to say. Where Mark talked, Tony listened, and this, Mark would admit, is what made Tony the better journalist.

Shannon grabbed her travel bag. Mark and Tony ushered her out the door. Shannon caught Jude's bewildered stare and said, "Thanks for letting my friends stay here."

Jude waved her off with a cigarette.

Shannon, Mark and Tony crossed the foyer and were about

to exit the front doors when Lincoln Crozier stepped from behind a corner and stopped Mark with a hand to his shoulder.

"Whoa, Agent Crozier, Federal Bureau of Intimidation. What's up?"

"You agreed to accompany me to New York, remember?"

"I've got other commitments right now. I'll get back to you in a couple days." Mark started walking toward the foyer door.

"I wouldn't go out there if I were you," Crozier said. "There are two Parkendale agents out there. They just arrived."

"They know we're here?" Mark asked.

"No. They're persistent but not very smart. They're probably looking for Shannon to find you."

Shannon said, "We can exit down the fire ladder from the other end of the hall."

"What about Tony's car?" Mark asked. "It's parked out front."

Crozier had a solution. Ten minutes later the foursome was en route to Dulles in his old Pontiac. "Why Minneapolis?" he asked Mark. "Something to do with Senator Janstadt?"

"Yes." Mark didn't elaborate as he watched Shannon stare out the window and rub her neck, still sore from the attack.

Crozier watched her as well, with eyes not hounddoggish like before, but flint-edged. He liked this young woman but couldn't afford the luxury of feeling sorry for her. The world was simply a dangerous place for a person of conscience. Shannon caught them looking at her and said in a hollow voice, "Part of me doesn't want to believe any of this. None of the conspiracy, none of murders. Why is that?"

"Because you don't have a devious mind," Mark said. "You see the good in people, not the bad."

"I never saw the good in my brother," she said quietly.

Nobody spoke for awhile as morning claimed the eastern sky.

"Any more cards you want to put on the table?" Crozier finally asked Mark, eyeing him in the rear-view mirror.

Mark shook his head and declined to say he was writing a profile on Senator Longstreet. He looked at Tony, who spoke to

Crozier for the first time. "You say these killings aren't the work of ANZA?"

"I doubt it," Crozier said.

"Then how do the killers know who to kill?"

"We're not certain."

"Somebody inside has to be targeting the victims," Tony said. "Somebody who knows everybody who knew that test result, and probably knows it himself, and wants the murders to look like accidents. That would be an ANZA person."

"Why?"

"Because odds are that six of the ten people who knew the result were with ANZA," Mark said. "And three of them are still alive."

"Let's say this person perceives the others as a threat," Crozier asked. "What's the threat?"

"The truth," Mark said. "Nothing threatens the rich and powerful more than the truth."

"And what's the truth?"

"Charles DeShay blinking three times."

Crozier stopped the car in front of the terminal and Mark asked, "How do we find the guy who killed Charles?"

Crozier said, "I'm more afraid that he'll find you."

Shannon had already slipped out and walked to the terminal. She stood alone at the entrance, forty feet away, watching something. Crozier saw it too, a solitary little bird, a finch, perched on a metal rail near the automatic doors. Face to face with the end of nature, it darted into the traffic and disappeared.

~

A man of many gifts and masks, Tyler Kyle greeted the ANZA team—John Sires, Maya Donjek, and an attorney—as they entered Longstreet's office. Maya surveyed the familiar turf and asked, "Where's the senator?"

"The bipartisan meeting on entitlement reform is running late,"

Kyle lied. "He sends his apologies and asks that I meet with you on his behalf. I'm aware of the magnitude of what we're about to discuss, and its impacts on tomorrow's hearing."

Sires said ANZA was willing to release its 1002 test result under certain conditions.

"Excellent," Kyle said.

Sires explained the conditions: ANZA receives first-rights-of-refusal on all Department of Interior leases, and cancelled retroactive federal taxes on revenues from Prudhoe Bay; a reduced gas tax in the energy bill, and a promise that the export ban on North Slope crude will not be reinstated with instabilities spreading throughout Russia and the Middle East.

"Is that all?" Kyle asked.

"That's all."

"The 1002 result, I assume it's good?"

"Very," Sires said. "Alan Quail is en route back to Houston. He'll announce it there tomorrow after meeting with the board."

Kyle planted his elbows on the armrests and tented his gypsum fingers under his nose. "Why not announce it here?"

Sires blinked. "Here? In Washington?"

"At tomorrow's subcommittee hearing on the Wilderness bill. It'll steal Janstadt's thunder and make a big splash in the press."

Sires drummed his fingers and said, "Alan and the board could watch it on C-SPAN."

"We'll need to get Alan's permission," Maya cautioned.

"Yes, yes," Sires nodded. "That shouldn't be a problem."

"As soon as you clear it with him I'll call the subcommittee chairman and have his staff schedule you for testimony," Kyle said.

The attorney cleared his throat. "We'll need a promissory letter that says the senator will secure what ANZA needs."

"My word is good enough for now," Kyle said. "The senator will draft a letter later."

"I'm afraid that won't do. Mr. Quail will need it for his meeting with the board, to get their approval when they meet in two hours."

"Two hours?"

The ANZA team nodded, every one of them.

"I'll e-mail it to him," Kyle said.

"It has to be a fax, so it's on official letterhead," the attorney responded. "It would go from this office to Mr. Quail's office and remain in strictest confidence."

Maya smiled, and moonlight seemed to spill from her eyes. For a sexless man like Kyle, the effect was profound. He shifted in his chair. The others looked at her, none with greater hunger than John Sires. "Just think, Tyler," she said excitedly. "Tomorrow the biggest secret in the American petroleum industry will be public knowledge, the fervor to open Anwahr will be ten times stronger than it is now, and Bruce Janstadt's stupid Wilderness bill will be dead."

"I'll dictate something to the secretary," Kyle said.

It was done in an hour, one page, concise, on U.S. Senate letterhead, proofed and approved by the ANZA team.

"What about a signature?" the attorney asked.

Kyle pulled out an inkpad and stamp, and affixed the signature of Oliver Harding Longstreet.

Sires laughed. "Well, look at that. An actual rubber stamp."

~

Shannon stared out the window of the jet at manicured Indiana thirty thousand feet below. Mark slept beside her, and Tony across the aisle. Both had been up all night, Mark working on his profile, Tony on research. She studied Mark. Even when sleeping he appeared to know something no one else did. She reached over to lower his seat and make him more comfortable. He opened his powder blue eyes, only inches from hers. "I've been thinking," he whispered.

"About what?"

"You."

She blushed. "You were smiling in your sleep."

He touched her face and she thought he might kiss her. He tenderly brushed back her hair, his fingers light on her face. His forearm touched her breast and she gasped with pleasure.

"You okay?" he asked.

"I'm fine. I got up too early. I feel a little dopey."

"It's better than feeling grumpy, or sneezy."

Shannon wrinkled her brow at him.

"You don't know the Seven Dwarfs theory?" he asked.

"The what?"

"The Seven Dwarfs theory, as in Snow White. You haven't heard this theory?"

"No."

Mark took her hand in his and said, "This is one of the most important theories in the study of human sleep. Each hour of the seven that you sleep is occupied by a dwarf. If you wake up during that hour, that's who you become. An hour too early and you're Grumpy. Two hours too early and you're Dopey."

"And three hours too early?" Shannon asked.

Mark thought for a moment. "Sneezy."

"I'd sneeze all day?"

"Yep."

"What about Happy, or Doc?"

"Doc? There's no dwarf named Doc."

"Sure there is. If you wake up during that hour, what are you, a physician?"

"I don't know. Maybe you're a doctor of philosophy."

"Or political science." She grinned.

"I can see this theory needs some work."

"I like it." She snuggled into him.

"Shannon, about your dad, I'm sorry—"

She put her fingers to his lips.

He kissed them and said, "I've hurt you. I didn't mean to."

"There's still time to save my dad. If we can save the refuge, we can save a part of him."

"You really believe that?"

She turned away and looked out the window, and commented wistfully on the endless farmland thirty thousand feet below.

Mark asked, "Do you think it's wise to compare every landscape with Alaska, and every man with your father?"

They held hands in silence as the jet descended into Chicago.

Tony awoke on the flight to Minneapolis and told Shannon a story about an old friend who had earned an Ivy League MBA and been recruited on the corporate fast track. But before embarking on his new career, this friend took a short vacation to Europe. Five years later he was still over there, tromping sandal-footed on the physical and spiritual paths of St. Francis of Assisi, the gentle Italian monk who eight hundred years earlier founded a new religious order and was today considered the patron saint of birds and animals. Tony's friend finally came home as Father Carroll, a member of the Franciscan Order, and settled in Minneapolis. He stayed in touch to discuss political events. Tony asked him for a favor, and two days ago Father Carroll phoned with a remarkable development.

They landed at the Minneapolis-St. Paul International Airport and drove into the heart of Minneapolis with sunlight slanting through oaks that lined the boulevards. They stopped at a soup kitchen next to a friary in the shadow of a basilica. Entering, they found the destitute and the hungry, and amid them Father Carroll, unmistakable to Shannon though she had never met him. He looked up with a peaceful face, saw Tony and his friends and walked toward them. He wore the Franciscan habit, a brown robe made of coarse wool with the capuche, or hood, and a white cord around his waist tied in three knots to represent his vows of poverty, chastity and obedience.

He embraced Tony and shook Mark's hand. His eyes were the kindest she had ever seen. She liked him before he addressed her. "You must be Shannon." He put her hand into his. "It's a pleasure. I've heard a lot about you and your father. I look forward to meeting him."

Shannon said, "He's deceased."

"Ah well, I suppose I'll have to wait my turn then, won't I?"

"I believe that to honor him I need to save the 1002 Area of the Arctic Refuge. Is that crazy?"

"No. That's why you're here, to right a wrong. I have somebody I want you to meet."

They followed Father Carroll through the kitchen to where a man in his early thirties, nice-looking, sat at a wooden table reading the Bible. He wore a double-breasted pinstripe suit, jet-black shoes and a downturned mouth. His name was Frank Beasley. Father Carroll asked Shannon to tell Frank about her father, and her time with him in the Refuge. When she finished, Frank asked her no questions, but instead told his own story, one of deceit and regret.

"Are you willing to come back to Washington with us and testify?" Mark asked him.

"Will Senator Janstadt be there?" Frank asked.

"Definitely."

"Then I'll testify."

TWENTY-SEVEN

S hannon took a deep breath as the chairman gaveled the hearing to order. The subcommittee members sat behind a mahogany rostrum with the chairman at its apex, and Bruce Janstadt, the ranking minority member, next to him. Other senators occupied the rostrum's dihedral wings, ten Republicans down the right wing, nine Democrats down the left, their numbers reflective of their party's ratio in the Senate. Aides stood along the paneled wall, ready to whisper researched facts into the senators' hungry ears. A standing-room only crowd spilled out the door and into the hall.

Shannon and twenty other aides gathered in a conference alcove behind the hearing room. Kelly Calvert shot her a disapproving stare for skipping off to Minneapolis after missing a week of work. Jeff Meola and Harry Arnold huddled conspiratorially at the far end of the alcove while everybody else watched a television that carried the hearing on C-SPAN. Shannon watched Harry walk to a table of Janstadt aides and engage them in lively banter.

Then she saw that woman, Maya, sitting in a soundproof

phone booth near the entrance to the alcove, one hand at her brow, thumb at her temple, the other hand scribbling notes. Long golden hair. *She's a lobbyist; she's not supposed to be here.* Then to Shannon's amazement the woman raised her head and stared right at her with eyes that looked—*what? Furtive? Frightened? No, expectant.* While everybody but Shannon watched the television, the woman exited with some cream-colored folders in her hand. She glanced at Shannon, darted her eyes back at the booth, then slipped out of the alcove. Shannon entered the booth. Near the floor, wedged between the glass wall and the metal frame, was a cream-colored folder labeled SENATOR JANSTADT, FYI. She pulled it out, opened and read it.

Five minutes later, her hand shaking, Shannon slipped the folder onto the table occupied by the Janstadt aides, placing it behind them as they watched the television. When she backed away, she saw Harry Arnold staring at her, his face like something out of Dorian Gray, ashen and aging before her. He turned and exited as Shannon stood in stunned silence.

Senator Janstadt was speaking about his bill and the importance of wilderness in America. "I'm not talking about simple scenery," he said, "In scenery you see more than you can absorb. In wilderness you absorb more than you can see..."

~

"Oh, Christ," grumbled the ANZA chief financial officer, one of thirteen board members watching Janstadt on C-SPAN from atop corporate headquarters in Houston. "I can't believe the people of Minnesota elected this guy."

"Uff da! Uff da!" said another board member.

Everybody laughed. A third round of drinks was ordered. Alan Quail said that John Sires would testify soon and announce the long-awaited test result. They all agreed that the conditions secured by Sires from Longstreet's office were excellent. ANZA's stock—and each of their private fortunes—would jump like a

Mexican bean after the announcement. Mesquite-smoked ribs arrived as they watched the first testifier step to the microphone, a dark-skinned man with a ponytail, who limped.

"Who'd they say this guy was?" somebody asked.

"Eddie Tagarook," Quail said with a frown.

~

Sequestered in his office with the curtains closed and the lights off, the small television playing on his tinted glasses and pallid face, Tyler Kyle grimaced at the sight of the limping Eskimo. He phoned Kelly Calvert's pager, left his number and hung up. Kelly was smart, but more important, obedient. Ninety-eight seconds later—Kyle counted them—she called back. "What's up, Tyler? I'm in the middle of the Wilderness hearing."

"You know that Eskimo, Eddie Tagarook, who's about to testify?"

"Yes."

"He can be stopped."

"Really? How?"

~

"My culture is dying," Eddie began after stating his name and place of residence. "Sure, big industry always brings jobs and nice schools and health clinics and stuff like that, you know. We got lots of money, the corporation, KANAK, I mean. But what about ancient customs and identity and pride?" He stopped reading from his written testimony and looked at each senator. "Television and mail order catalogs don't make wild Inupiat dreams. Money don't make us hunt or fish or pick berries together. We don't make new stories no more. Stories of hunting, fishing and whaling, they're our books, ya know. Used to be, anyway. Now it's *Wheel of Fortune* and *The Young and the Restless*. We can buy all sorts of things now, but they don't give us stories…"

Kelly Calvert inched along the wall to Sam Matlin, and whispered into his ear. He nodded, leaned into his microphone and interrupted Eddie. "Excuse me, Mr. Chairman."

"The Chair acknowledges the senator from Alaska."

"I apologize for the interruption, but word has come to me that I believe has important bearing on the testimony of this particular individual. He has been charged by the State of Alaska with two counts of criminal mischief, and is currently out on bail, and by the rules of this and other congressional subcommittees he must forfeit all rights to testify."

The chairman looked at Eddie. "Is this true, Mr. Tagarook?"

"No," Eddie said.

"That's a lie," somebody yelled from the back of the room.

The chairman slammed down the gavel. "Quiet. There will be no misconduct during this hearing." He asked Eddie, "You deny this allegation?"

"Yeah, sure."

The chairman looked at Matlin for an explanation.

"He's out on bail for a shooting in Prudhoe Bay," Matlin said.

"Good for him," somebody else shouted.

Again the gavel slammed down. The chairman looked at Eddie. "Mr. Tagarook, I have to ask you to step away. Your testimony will be stricken from the record."

"It was three counts of criminal mischief, you honor," Eddie said, "not two."

"Fine. Now, please step away."

"Just wanted to set the record straight, judge."

"I'm not a judge. I'm a chairman. Now, you must—"

"You act like a judge."

"Mr. Tagarook, please step away from the microphone or I'll have you removed by force."

Those seated next to him scooted away to give Eddie room, but he did not move.

"Sergeant-at-Arms, remove that man."

A large uniformed officer walked over and grabbed Eddie's

arm, lifted him to his feet and escorted him out the room. Kodiak
Jack Worley and the Wise Users grinned. John Sires tapped his
briefcase that held the 1002 result. It was going to be a great day
for ANZA.

Suddenly Elsie Kiviikanak jumped to her feet and shouted,
"Fuck this hearing and these grinning rapists who buy and sell
people and their homelands like commodities. Fuck all—"

"Contain that woman!" The chairman pounded the gavel.

"Fuck you, fat cat. Contain ANZA. They're the ones who fuck
up the tundra and the coastlines of Alaska. They're the ones—"

A security guard grabbed her, yet Elsie managed to swing a
fist and hit him on the chin and knock him backward. People
gasped, some cheered.

"Order, order," the chairman yelled. "I will tolerate none of
this."

The red-faced officer grabbed Elsie while another cuffed her
hands and dragged her away.

Nobody seemed to notice old Walter Kiviikanak, Elsie's grandfather, stand on a chair and wobble for an instant, then lift his
face to a sky only he could see. He began to sing in Inupiaq, his
words melting like a snowfield in the mountains; words cold on
ears that didn't recognized them, but warm to Shannon. The creek
became a river as Walter's voice flowed with hope and pride, not
a deep voice, but clear and ancient as it pervaded the room with
the power of a heartbeat. Nobody moved. The chairman raised
his gavel but did not slam it down, as Walter seemed to tran-
scend into water itself, the maker of landscape and life. He finished on a suspended note, his voice cracking. He climbed off
the chair and walked out of the room unaccompanied. Pro-oil
leaders of the Alaska Native Alliance stared ahead without looking at him. Shannon realized that they knew the song just as they
knew the land, but in refusing to sing along they had created in
Walter an allegory of their own lives, a river without tributaries.

~

"Jesus, Alan," a board member said, "you didn't tell us these

Senate hearings were a talent show. Who does that old guy think he is, Frank Sinatra?"

Quail chewed a toothpick.

~

One by one the testifiers sat before the subcommittee and expressed their heartfelt beliefs for and against wilderness. In the wake of Elsie's earthquake the after-shocks were small, no raised voices or theatrics. A Wise User described Wilderness as the anathema of American freedom. Western ranchers and loggers lamented the ends of their ways of life, the destruction of homes and families and communities. One cowboy recited an altered refrain of Hank Williams' *Your Cheatin' Heart* that portrayed environmentalists as doing all the cheatin'. The president of the Alaska Native Alliance, a handsome man wearing a snowy owl necklace and a Nordstrom suit, told the senators that his organization, the largest Native organization in Alaska, supported oil drilling in ANWR.

Shannon could feel her nerves fraying. She saw Mark, Tony, Father Carroll and Frank Beasley seated together in the back row. She watched Senator Janstadt and thought of the cream-colored folder from Maya. Then it occurred to her: *Was the folder a trick? Have I been duped?*

A regional director of The Wilderness Society spoke about bioregionalism and ecosystem decay, which elicited smirks from the Wise Users.

Then came John Sires, who placed a briefcase on the table, and next to it a chocolate-colored rock the size of his fist. He introduced himself and ANZA. "This rock," he said, "comes from an upthrusted and exposed outcrop on the Coastal Plain of Alaska's North Slope." He held it aloft to capture everyone's attention. "It's sandstone, but not the conventional buffish-tan color you'd expect of sandstone. I invite you to inspect it."

He handed it to an aide who handed it to Sam Matlin.

"Smell it," Sires suggested.

Matlin pulled it to his nose. "Smells like oil."

"Exactly, senator. Pass it along to your colleagues. This rock, together with other carbon-rich source rocks, are what lie below the 1002 Area of Anwahr. Beneath and adjacent to these are vast expanses of porous reservoir rocks filled with the fossil carbon remains of Paleozoic organisms. And above this entire oil rich complex is an impermeable barrier of cap rock..."

The entire room was still.

"...as most of you know, preliminary estimates from seismic tests were promising but inexact. Ten years ago, ANZA sank a single test well to determine a clearer prognosis. That result has never been made public, until now. I'm pleased to report that the 1002 Area has a seventy-one percent chance of holding ten billion barrels of recoverable crude, and a fifty-two percent chance of fifteen billion barrels. In plain English, senators, the odds are significant that the 1002 Area of Anwahr is another super giant, another Prudhoe Bay."

~

"Attaboy Johnny," shouted an ANZA board member.

"Get that in quotes and mail it to every shareholder," said another.

"Send Janstadt to Antarctica if he wants wilderness."

"Or the moon. Uff da, Uff da!"

They all laughed, including Alan Quail.

~

John Sires answered a few questions, and his exciting testimony was finished.

Next came a Gwich'in woman—an Athabascan Indian—who spoke softly about how drilling in the refuge would destroy the caribou calving grounds and her people's way of life.

The chairman nodded: yes, thank you, your time is up. Next.

The last to testify was none other that Oliver Longstreet, who wasted no time. "Gentlemen, distinguished colleagues and friends, thank you for the opportunity to speak here today..."

An aide approached Janstadt and whispered into his ear. Janstadt rose from his seat and departed the room into the alcove, not an uncommon practice among senators during testimony. But it caused Longstreet to stutter.

Shannon's heart pounded.

Janstadt returned with a cream-colored folder in hand.

"...all because of oil," Longstreet was saying with great authority. "Wars are won by oil. The Germans invented the jet fighter, but they needed farm animals to tow it to the airfield. Japan's kamikaze pilots flew their planes into our ships because they didn't have enough fuel for their return trip. Is that any way to run a nation or win a war? Or sustain a peace? Or promise prosperity? Oil has made America strong, and will continue to, but only if our most promising fields are explored, not locked up. We fought the Gulf War to protect oil interests in the Middle East. Young Americans died in that war. Today, we import more than half the oil used in this country. That reliance on foreign production, and the likelihood of another war, will only increase unless we develop our fields at home and reduce our imports. It would be unconscionable to turn away from a fifteen-billion-barrel super giant one hundred miles east of Prudhoe Bay, where the infrastructure is in place and is environmentally safe. I urge you to kill this bill. The 1002 Area of Anwahr must be developed. It's the right thing to do. It's the American thing to do."

He thanked the subcommittee and began to leave.

"Not so fast," Janstadt said. "I'm the ranking minority member on this subcommittee, and with the chairman's permission I have some questions for the distinguished senior senator from Alaska who's honored us with his esteemed presence here today."

TWENTY-EIGHT

Oliver Longstreet, halfway up from his chair, sat back down, his hands tightening around the armrests.

"Tell me, senator," Janstadt said, "if this refuge is developed for oil, will there be a fifty-fifty split between the federal government and the State of Alaska on royalties?"

"That's right."

"Not ninety percent to the state and ten percent to the feds?"

"That's right. It's in my energy bill."

"Do Alaskan borough governments accept this?"

"Yes."

"I'm sure you've spoken to them about it."

"I speak with everybody about everything in my state."

Janstadt stroked his chin with an easy folksiness. "But didn't you once argue vehemently against building an oil pipeline across the Coastal Plain of the Arctic Refuge?"

"I always argue vehemently," Longstreet said.

"Yes, I'm aware. Didn't you once say that to build a pipeline across the 1002 Area would be comparable to slashing a knife across the face of Marilyn Monroe?"

"That's absurd. I remember no such thing."

"Let me jog your memory. I have here a copy of a 1972 caucus that discusses how Prudhoe Bay crude oil should be transported to U.S. markets. You supported the construction of an all-Alaska Pipeline to Valdez, in Prince William Sound, where the oil would be shipped south in single-hull supertankers. Many people questioned the safety of those supertankers in Prince William Sound, but you assured them—"

"Yes, yes," Longstreet interrupted, "what's your point?" His eyelid twitched.

"In arguing for your all-Alaska pipeline to Valdez, you defeated a proposed overland pipeline east from Prudhoe Bay through what is now the 1002 Area of the Arctic National Wildlife Refuge, into Canada's Yukon Territory and down to Alberta. You said that to build a pipeline across that refuge would be, and I quote, 'comparable to slashing a knife across the face of Marilyn Monroe.'"

"For crying out loud," Longstreet yelled, "that was thirty years ago. I was a freshman senator then. Do you deny that we need all the domestic oil we can get?"

"It depends. Do you?"

"No, never."

"Then why ship Alaskan oil overseas?"

"What?"

"Why do you support shipping Alaskan oil to Asian markets? Five years ago you pushed through legislation to drop the North Slope crude export ban. Remember?"

Longstreet clenched his fists. Veins bulged in his neck. His nose turned crimson.

Janstadt held up another piece of paper. "Can you explain this promissory letter on your letterhead, signed by you, that says ANZA will have first right of refusal of Department of Interior leases in the Arctic Refuge? And will be assessed no retroactive taxes. And can be certain, that's what it says, 'can be certain,' that efforts to reinstate the North Slope crude export ban will be thwarted despite an unfavorable political climate."

"That's a damn lie," Longstreet screamed.

Down came the gavel. "Enough of this," the chairman said. "It's time for the senator from Alaska to—"

"No," Longstreet thundered. "I ask the chair to let me defend my honor, and the honor of Alaska. Let me finish."

"Then make your point."

"I want to warn the senator from Minnesota that if he's going to kill a grizzly bear he'd better make sure he finishes the job, because there's nothing more dangerous when it's wounded."

Janstadt shook his head.

Longstreet pointed a long accusatory finger at him. "Let the record show that for reasons of national security and fiscal responsibility I do not support the frivolous exportation of Alaskan oil."

"Fiscal responsibility?" Janstadt exclaimed. "I'm pleased to discover that the Chairman of Appropriations, who sends more pork per capita to his state than anyone else in this room, is suddenly interested in fiscal responsibility."

"That's a bold accusation," Longstreet hissed, "coming from a child molester."

The room fell silent. The subcommittee members sat in shock.

"Mr. Chairman," a ranking Republican finally said, "I recommend that the previous exchange be stricken from the record, and that this hearing be adjourned."

The stunned chairman appeared not to hear him.

A commotion arose in the back of the room as a man stood on his chair and held up a small piece of paper. "This is a check for forty-five thousand dollars," he said loudly. All heads turned toward him. "I've written it to the Boy Scouts of America and I offer it with my sincerest apologies to—"

"Gavel down that intruder," Longstreet yelled. "I'm not finished."

The chairman leaned into his microphone and said, "Be quiet, Oliver, please." He nodded to the man in the back. "Continue."

"I offer it with my apologies to my former scoutmaster, Senator Janstadt, for all the pain I've caused him and his family. The allegations against him are false. I know. I made some of them." Frank Beasley's voice began to break. "I made them because I was paid forty-five thousand dollars to make them. I needed the money. Forgive me, God. I'm sorry." Frank covered his face with his hands.

The room erupted into mayhem. The chairman adjourned the hearing as Shannon struggled to reach Mark, and Mark to reach her. People and voices stirred everywhere in a boiling pot, and above it all shrieked the lone hysterical voice of Senator Longstreet, "Point of order. Point of order, Mr. Chairman. I'm not finished, goddammit. Shut up, all of you. Point of order."

Nobody acknowledged him.

~

Tyler Kyle ripped through the pages of the ANZA December guest list, scanned the names and found her. His heart sank with dread. He felt a tightness in his throat. How had he missed her before? *I'm slipping. I can't afford this.*

He put on his coat and hat and flew out of his office, surrounded by confusion. "Tyler," the secretary said, "we're getting a zillion calls and e-mail messages about the hearing. Did the senator really say that about Marilyn Monroe?"

Kyle ignored her.

Half an hour later he called Anchorage from a phone booth in L'Enfant Plaza and to his relief got William Alt. He told him to fetch his copy of the ANZA guest list. "See the last name on the bottom of page one?" Kyle asked him.

"Maya Donjek?"

"She would have signed in just before Carl Zarki, who's at the top of page two. You said you remembered a lot of beautiful women from that night. You should remember Maya, eastern European, Jewish, small build, green eyes, blonde hair in a widow's peak."

"Wow, I don't remember anybody like that."

"Did you see her leave?"

"Maybe, that was a crazy time."

Kyle took a breath. *So Zarki distracted this kid. He asked for the previous shift report, and signed another name—Maya Donjek —before he signed his own.*

He asked William, "Have you spoken to your friend, Lynx?"

"Yes, sir. He's checking the alarm system now. He's got a buddy who installs them."

"Good. Be careful, William. You're a valuable member of our team."

Kyle hung up and called Merlin.

"Not good, Tyler. I just watched the whole thing on C-SPAN. Your senator made an ass of himself."

"The FBI is questioning Frank Beasley."

"Who got to him?"

"I don't know."

Merlin grumbled. "Well, find out. The other former Scouts all have families. Do what you have to do."

The third and final call was to the Carzoli residence. In an uncharacteristically robust voice Kyle left a message with Tony's wife saying that Senator Longstreet could meet with Mark Meadows at four o'clock tomorrow afternoon in his office in the Hart Senate Office Building. He hung up, exhausted. Once upon a time he could manipulate one hundred people on two hours' sleep and never feel it. Not anymore.

~

Oliver Longstreet stormed into his office, ruddy-faced from too many whiskey sours. "Where's Tyler?" he demanded.

"He stepped out," the secretary said. "We're getting lots of calls and—"

"Notify me when he gets here. Tell everybody I'm not available. And turn off that damn fax machine."

He swept into his office and slammed the door. He needed to talk to the majority leader, the chairman, his wife, everybody and nobody. He pulled out his Verminator and ten minutes later three pigeons were dead on the sidewalk below. Another wobbled on the windowsill, wounded.

Tyler Kyle entered without knocking.

"We've got problems, Tyler," Longstreet said as he slipped the slingshot into the desk drawer. "Did you see Janstadt treat me like that? What's all this bullshit about priority leases and retroactive taxes and the export ban? Somebody's leaking absolute bullshit around here."

"That would be me," Kyle said with reptilian coolness. He sat down and explained what was said yesterday between himself and ANZA, the signed promissory letter, the agreement to announce the test result during the hearing. "I stamped your name. I've done it many times. You know that."

"So what went wrong?"

"I don't know," Kyle lied. He knew what went wrong, but he couldn't tell the senator.

Half drunk, Longstreet seemed to drift away as he spent an absurd minute straightening family portraits on his desk. "What are we going to do about the Marilyn Monroe thing? I mean, Christ, that was a long time ago." His voice was almost pathetic.

Kyle handed him a list of names. "Here's everybody you need to call and speak to immediately for damage control..." He reminded Longstreet of the cardinal rule of Washington scandal management. Dispose of the damaging information early and don't look as if you have something to hide. "It's too late for any of this to appear on tonight's nightly news. I got you a remote camera interview tomorrow on *Good Morning America*. Remember, it's important to be mildly contrite without making a direct apology. Never give up the high ground. You've always protected the interests of Alaska first. You did it in 1972 by pushing for the Trans-Alaska Oil Pipeline, and you're doing it today by opening Anwahr.

Times have changed. It's the new millennium. Marilyn Monroe needs a face lift."

"I should say that?"

"No, imply it."

"Oh, right."

"Mark Meadows will be here tomorrow afternoon to interview you for a feature story in the *Washington Post Sunday Magazine*."

"Mark Meadows?"

"We can handle him."

"You'll be here?"

"Yes." Kyle had to leave. He had a million things to do. He walked to the door, paused and turned. "One more thing, senator. Stop shooting pigeons. Janitorial has found them dead and wounded on the sidewalk below. There's one dying on your windowsill right now. It won't be long before security traces it to you, unless you stop. If the press ever found out, you'd be in every cartoon and late night punchline in America."

He closed the door.

~

John Sires hung up the phone in his hotel suite, uncertain if he should be elated or concerned. Each ANZA board member had congratulated him on his testimony, a job well done, yet twice he had asked to speak with Alan Quail, and twice been told he was unavailable. *If every other board member could speak with me, why not Alan?*

He remembered Maya.

He grabbed a bottle of Chardonnay and bounded down the hall like a dog in heat. Her door was propped open by a wet bathroom towel. His heart jumped. Was this an invitation? "Hello Maya. You here babe? Maya?" He searched the room and found nothing, and called the front desk.

"I'm sorry, Mr. Sires. Miss Donjek checked out an hour ago."

~

Stephen York, Pyro, and Tank Wallace, the man who had attacked Rollie Dawson on the Clymmer tarmac and Shannon on the ski trail, made a mean, streetwise trio, not the kind of guys who would attend a Senate hearing—too many cameras. But when they arrived at Stephen's apartment in southeast Washington at 3:00 a.m., they found a phone message waiting from Tyler Kyle: "Good morning, gentlemen. Today is your lucky day."

~

Of the few things that Lynx Hirschik did better than William Alt, burglary was one. He had fleeced a dozen wealthy Anchorage homes the past five years and not been caught. "So what are we after?" He asked William as they skulked through wet snow and leafless alders outside the Hillside home of Carl Zarki.

"Files," William answered.

"Secret government type stuff?"

"ANZA files, that's all."

"So this guy, the one you've been talkin' to on the phone, he's cool?"

"Yeah." William parroted Kyle's rhetoric on patriotism, freedom, law and justice. He quoted John Locke and Alexis de Tocqueville, as Kyle had to him.

Lynx wiped his nose on his jacket sleeve and seemed to hear none of it. "You sure you don't want me to steal nothing from this guy? Shit, William, he fired you."

"I'm sure. Just the files. Be careful, he's not very big, and he's kinda old, but he's tough as nails."

"Yeah, yeah."

They moved closer in familiar terrain. Lynx had poisoned a neighbor's dog two nights earlier to ensure quiet tonight. He moved from door to door, window to window, confirming the inside floor design with a penlight flashlight. Both men wore ski masks, gloves and neoprene XTRATUF boots two sizes too big. Lynx pulled out the tools of his trade. He sliced through a sliding glass door, opened the lock and stepped inside. They removed their boots and put on slippers. Lynx moved from the kitchen to the living room, then down a hall to a study and two bedrooms, one empty, the other full of exercise equipment. Zarki was asleep in the bedroom at the end.

Lynx motioned William into the study with his penlight. William closed the door behind him and flipped on his own small flashlight. A two-drawer metal file cabinet stood in the corner, both drawers locked. William found the keys taped behind the file cabinet, same place where Zarki kept his office keys at ANZA. William opened the bottom drawer first: taxes, finances, insurance. A large file marked "U.S. Army, 101st Airborne." A paratrooper? William didn't know Zarki had been a paratrooper. He pulled the file, and another labeled "Correspondence," and a third marked "ANZA." Lynx was in the living room, quiet but busy. Neither man heard Zarki, who was equally quiet, rise from his bed, walk to his closet, grab a loaded shotgun, open his door and move down the hall past the study.

The shotgun blasted like a cannon. Glass shattered. William ran for the door, flung it open and collided with Zarki in the darkness, knocking him backwards in the hall. The shotgun fell and Zarki reached for it, but William got it first and shoved the barrel into his chest. Neither man moved; then with lightning speed William snapped the shotgun one hundred and eighty degrees—a trick he learned in combat training—and cracked the heavy stock over Zarki's head.

William slipped back into the study, grabbed the files and ran from the house, carrying the shotgun. He found Lynx in the truck half a mile away. "Are you okay?" he asked breathlessly.

Lynx laughed like a maniac. "Hell yes, I'm okay. That stupid fart just shot his television and his VCR."

They drove away chortling, but ten minutes later it was not

funny when William realized to his horror that he was wearing slippers. He had left his boots at Zarki's.

TWENTY-NINE

Where am I? What time is it? Shannon lifted herself off a futon. *Has to be early morning.*

She could see Mark writing at a desk, his back to her, a candle throwing his shadow onto a wooden floor. She smelled the sweetness of pine, and heard the insomniac sounds of the city leaking through an open window. She was under a quilt, dressed in a soft robe with the initials *BJH* on the sleeve. *BJH?* She saw her clothes folded neatly over the back of a chair, her shoes underneath. Her pendant and earrings rested on an end table, next to her purse. Her eyes adjusted to see another futon against the wall, and somebody asleep on it.

The open window brought tendrils of fresh air, the timpani of rain, a hope from years past that a bruised sky would prevent helicopters from flying into camp and ruining the day.

—*You like that one, don't you?*

—*Yes. What is it?*

—*An arctic poppy. He kneels on the tundra beside her, then gets on his belly for a better look. She joins him, careful not to crush other flowers around them.*

He holds the stalk between thumb and forefinger. See the blossom, he says. It's a little parabolic dish that tracks the sun and acts like a solar collector to create its own microclimate. That way it stays warmer by a couple degrees.

—A couple degrees make a difference?

—In the arctic, every degree makes a difference. You're a lot like this little flower, Shannon, always turning toward the sun, which is good and bad.

—Bad? How?

—Because there are false suns that create false light and promises. Be careful who you follow.

—Maybe I shouldn't follow anybody. Maybe I should lead. That's how caribou cross a river, isn't it? The females go first.

Her father smiles, thinking, We are most brave when we are most vulnerable.

Then they hear it, the metal archaeopteryx, throbbing from afar, growing nearer, coarse and demanding even before it comes into view. It sets down next to camp, its foreign wind scattering anything that is loose. Shannon runs after a bandana, some coffee filters. It's always like this when the red ANZA helicopter arrives.

It's him again, Mr. John Sires. He steps away with her father to have another chat. Last time he did this he stood on the only arnica within a large radius. This time he stands on the only arctic poppy. A man at two with nature.

They argue, arms gesticulating. Shannon strains to hear, but the humming helicopter drowns their angry words. She looks at the pilot, who in his dark goggles and helmet strikes her more as an insect than a human, the dutiful ant from T. H. White's The Once and Future King *who operates on the dictum that "Everything Not Forbidden Is Compulsory."*

She can see that her father is distressed. Mr. Sires hands him a roll of maps, then jabs a finger into his chest. That's it. Shannon walks over to them. Sires looks at her as if he has never seen her before.

—What is it, Shannon? her father asks.

Shannon addresses Mr. Sires. You're standing on a flower.

—What? he says.

—There's only one arctic poppy in this area and you're standing on it.

He looks down at his feet, steps to the side. The yellow blossom is crushed into the tundra. He rolls his eyes at Charles and says, We don't have time for this.

"Mark?" she called quietly.

He turned from his typing, walked over and sat on the futon next to her, the wooden floor squeaking under his feet. "Good morning," he whispered.

"Where am I?"

"The Brother John House, on New Hampshire Avenue."

Yes, it was coming back now. Father Carroll had brought them here after pizza and too much beer, and Agent Crozier telling Shannon not to return to her apartment. "Have you been up all night?" she asked Mark.

"I slept for two hours."

"You didn't go home with Tony?"

"No." He stroked her hair as she reached over to touch his tawny beard. He took her hand and kissed her fingers. She traced the wrinkles around his eyes, then arched up and drew his hand under her back. He lifted her and kissed her on her lips, a breathless dream. Her heart raced.

The person sleeping on the other futon rolled over.

"Who's that?" Shannon asked.

"I don't know. Some guy Father Carroll rescued off the street." Mark leaned into Shannon for another kiss.

"Mark, we're in a Catholic mission."

"Exciting isn't it?"

She grinned. "Who folded my clothes on the chair?"

"I did, after you fell asleep. You took them off, though."

"That's good." Part of her wanted to hear him say that he undressed her last night, to have him do it now, pull the soft robe off her shoulders, the poet lover devouring her in one ecstatic breath.

"You took off your earrings, too," he said. "One at a time."

"That's how I put them on, I suppose that's how I should take them off."

"I was admiring them. What are they made of?"

"Porcupine quills."

"Porcupine quills? There's a significance to that?"

"They protect me."

"From?"

"Life in Washington. Things I can't control." She rolled her head slowly and let her black hair fall over her face. "You're not going to New York with the FBI?"

"Not until I finish this profile. I've got a four o'clock interview with Oliver Longstreet, and a deadline tomorrow."

Shannon sat upright. "Do you know that woman who used to work on Longstreet's staff but is an ANZA lobbyist now, Maya Donjek?"

"No."

Shannon told him what she saw yesterday. Mark asked, "You think Bruce Janstadt used information in that folder to challenge Oliver Longstreet?"

"I do. Every time I see that woman she looks at me like we have a shared history, like I should know more about her than I do."

"Because you get the feeling she knows more about you?"

"Exactly. And the ANZA man who testified yesterday, John Sires. My last summer in the Refuge, he would fly into our camp in a helicopter and argue with my dad..." Shannon recounted what she could remember.

"You think they argued over the 1002 test result?"

"I think it's a strong possibility."

Spokes of sunlight spilled through the clearing rain, and cherry blossoms graced the Mall. Dogwoods lingered in bloom, and warblers and chickadees sang from a hundred blushing trees. Yet Shannon felt no lightness in her spirit as she walked from the Brother John House to Capitol Hill, and arrived at the offices of Samuel F. Matlin, U.S. Senator, for the first time in nearly two weeks. She went straight to Harry Arnold's desk and without preamble said, "We need to talk."

"I'm busy."

"I want to know what's going on between you and Jeff Meola."
No response.

"What are you hiding, Harry?"

He stood up and brought his face to hers, everything about him suddenly ominous. "I hide lots of things. It's my job. Where have you been the last couple weeks? What are *you* hiding?"

"I don't—"

"You don't know shit." His face flushed red and his mouth hardened. She had never seen him like this. "You put the FBI onto me."

She opened her mouth to speak, but he jabbed a finger into her chest. "Watch yourself, Shannon. You're in way over your head."

She pulled his hand off her. "Don't touch me. And keep your hands off Jude."

She walked to her cubicle and found her desk buried beneath stacks of boring constituent mail, the slagheap of legislative work. She had told nobody about the attack on her, only that she had gone away for personal reasons.

Denali Sisto came by. "Shannon, hi, you're back."

Others offered tepid welcomes; some ignored her. By midday when nobody invited her to lunch, Shannon knew she was a pariah. She had disappeared for no good reason, gone to Minneapolis with two *Post* reporters—which Jude no doubt told everybody—and she opposed oil development in the Arctic Refuge. She did not belong. She did not *want* to belong.

~

At exactly four o'clock Oliver Longstreet reached over his Sitka spruce desk to shake Mark's hand. "I'm pleased you want to do a story on me."

"The pleasure is mine, senator. Thank you for your time."

For five minutes they discussed acquaintances in Washington and the snowstorm last month, how the weather seemed to be more erratic these days. Mark mentioned a General Longstreet who had served with distinction in the Civil War, and asked the senator if he was any relation. "A distant one, yes," the senator replied. "General Longstreet was Robert E. Lee's right hand man in the Confederate Army. He would have saved Lee from his stinging defeat at Gettysburg if Lee had taken his advice."

"Not to go through with Pickett's Charge?"

"That's right."

Mark sensed a clouded energy in Longstreet. He suspected that the senator desperately wanted to ask him about the argument he had with Jack Worley last December in Anchorage.

"So, Mark—May I call you Mark? —what is it about me you would like to know?"

Mark had researched Longstreet's early life, family, political record, ideologies. No need to engage him in debates that existed in the *Congressional Record*. Ninety-five percent of the profile was written. What he needed was a new illumination. "What three books have had the strongest influence on you?" he asked.

Longstreet answered without hesitation, "The Old Testament and New Testament of the Bible, I consider those two books. And *The Grapes of Wrath*."

Mark arched his eyebrows to elicit an explanation.

"I believe that good can come from suffering," Longstreet said. "The human spirit is indomable."

"Indomitable," Mark corrected him.

"Exactly. A man without food, clothing or shelter is in a bad environment. It's my job to protect his basic freedoms and keep big government off his back. I have to give him the best opportunity to make the most of himself."

"What do you consider to be your greatest political achievement?"

"Easy. The Trans-Alaska Oil Pipeline. We won that by one vote, you know. A tie-breaker by Richard Nixon's Vice President,

Spiro Agnew."

Mark wrote in a little yellow notebook. "And your greatest political failure?"

Longstreet leaned back in his chair. "My greatest failure, let me see...I don't really think I have one."

"Let's go back to the Civil War and the Confederacy for a moment, as an analogy. Are you aware that some historians and columnists refer to Alaska today as the New South?"

Longstreet stiffened. "I've heard the term. I think it's silly."

"How do you feel about the accusation that while many Alaskans see themselves as tough and independent, and want nothing to do with the federal government, they never turn down federal assistance or a subsidy check?"

"It's an exaggeration. Alaskans deserve fair compensation. Alaska is remote and expensive, and most of the resources are locked up in federal control."

Mark wrote this down and was about to ask another question when the senator asked, "This 'New South' theory, just what is that supposed to mean?"

Mark finished writing and said, "I believe it means that Alaskans are as provincial in their ways of thinking, and as arrogant in their self-appointed stewardship of the land and sea, as southerners were toward African-Americans one hundred and fifty years ago."

Longstreet leaned forward until his collar pinched his neck. "Has anybody told these pointy-headed liberals that Alaskans don't own slaves and don't have a slave-based economy?"

"It's not slavery they criticize. It's a dominion-minded attitude toward the non-human world."

Longstreet waved a hand. "It's ridiculous, that's what it is."

"What do you think about Machiavelli's conundrum?"

Longstreet gave him a puzzled look.

"Machiavelli's conundrum," Mark repeated. "Can any government remain in power that practices the same morality it preaches to its people?"

As the senator digested this, a soft voice answered from behind, "No."

Mark turned in his chair to see Tyler Kyle leaning against the
wall next to the door. He had slipped in unseen and unheard.
Kyle brandished a counterfeit smile and said, "Machiavelli saw
politics as combat among men in search of power, nothing more,
nothing less. He regarded the successful ruler as both a lion and
a fox who deceived his subjects."

"That was then," Mark said. "What about now?"

"The same," Kyle said.

"But we buy our politicians."

"No, they buy the system, and the people pay into it."

"Ahem," Longstreet cleared his throat. "Gentlemen, this interview is about me, not about some dead Italian."

"Consider this time generous, Mr. Meadows," Kyle said. "Law
clerks for Supreme Court Justices lose their jobs if they're seen
talking with journalists for more than ninety seconds."

"Is that right?" Mark said.

Kyle nodded. "I trust this isn't an ambush interview."

"Not at all."

"Then I look forward to reviewing your manuscript."

"I'll have it to you by six tonight."

"Six tonight?" Longstreet stammered. "Two hours from now?"

"Yes, I'm almost finished. I just wanted this interview to fill in
a few blanks."

"A few blanks, how can that be? You just met me?"

"I don't need to meet the person I'm profiling, senator. Some
of the best biographers in the world never met their subjects. It's
research and synthesis that matter, not interviewing. But it's nice
of you to accommodate me. Would you like me to e-mail the
manuscript to you, or bring it by on paper copy?"

"Paper copy," Kyle said. He excused himself, closed the door
behind him and thought, *You didactic, smart-mouthed grammarian, by
this time tomorrow you'll be dead.*

Mark thanked the senator and left. He moved down the balcony above the atrium to the reception room of Senator Matlin, where he paged Shannon. Kyle watched from the balcony, then phoned Kelly Calvert.

"How'd it go?" Shannon asked with wide-eyed interest.

"Great," Mark said. "Can I use your desk and printer?"

"You bet." Shannon fetched a chair. He pulled out his laptop and began splicing new material into old, cutting and pasting.

"How'd it go with Harry Arnold?" he asked Shannon.

"I'll tell you later. Here comes Denali Sisto."

"Is this who I think it is?" Denali said cheerfully.

Mark stood up to greet her. He knew that Denali was a favorite of Shannon's. "I confess that I haven't read any of your articles," Denali said, "but I'd like to." Freckles filled her round face.

"Your parents named you after the mountain?" Mark asked her.

"No, they named me after a sled dog that was named after the mountain. Actually, they named me after a distant cousin, who was named after a sled dog that was named after the mountain."

Shannon asked Denali if she had seen Jude today.

"Not yet. I know she's going to dinner tonight with Harry, at some Mexican restaurant in Georgetown."

"How's Jeff?" Shannon asked.

Denali hung her head. "He went back to Anchorage to see his parents. That's what he told me, anyway. I have to go. Kelly would kill me if she saw me here with you. It's nice meeting you, Mark." Denali turned to leave and there stood Kelly Calvert, thin, officious, stern. "Oh, hi, Kelly. I was just leaving."

"What's going on here?" Kelly asked, her jaw set.

"My friend is borrowing my printer," Shannon explained as Mark connected the printer to his laptop.

Kelly scowled at Mark. "Are you a resident of Alaska?"

"I am," Shannon said. "And he's my guest." She looked at Mark and said, "Go ahead, print it."

"Not if he's a non-resident," Kelly said. "We have strict rules about this."

"Print it," Shannon repeated defiantly.

"You'll pay for this, Shannon," Kelly said. "I promise, you'll pay."

At 5:55 P.M. Mark returned to Longstreet's office and handed the receptionist a 9"x12" envelope marked, SEN. LONGSTREET, CONFIDENTIAL, URGENT. He departed a second time for Matlin's office, walking the balcony above the atrium. Watching him, Tyler Kyle signaled Tank Wallace.

THIRTY

"Dear Senator Longstreet," the cover letter began. "The enclosed manuscript is a draft. The annotations refer to source material not included in this package for obvious reasons of convenience. Please direct your comments promptly to Lowell Hutchinson or me at the *Post*. This story is scheduled to appear nine days from now. Regards, Mark Meadows."

"What kind of horseshit is this?" Longstreet said. The twenty-page manuscript shook like aspen leaves in his hands.

THE MOST DANGEROUS MAN IN ALASKA
by Mark Meadows

By page five Longstreet was sweating, at ten he was livid, at fifteen he swallowed his heart medicine. Kyle read it and said, "Call the *Post* and tell Gil Trebideaux this is inaccurate."

"I'll tell him I want it cancelled."

"No. That's his decision. Don't step on his authority. Step on Meadows' lack of accuracy and objectivity." Kyle elaborated, then added, "Find out if Meadows has e-mailed it to the *Post* yet."

Longstreet made the call. Trebideaux wasn't in, but Hutch was. The senator voiced his extreme displeasure, and Hutch offered no apologies, only to say that he had not yet received the story.

Good news, Kyle thought. *Meadows still has it. When he disappears, so will the story and his ANZA files.*

Mark phoned Hutch less than a minute after Longstreet hung up, and Hutch told him about the conversation. "What'd he say?" Mark asked.

"All nondenial denials. He's angry and says you're hunting without a permit."

"I also search without a warrant and practice without a license. The Constitution says I can. Even if this story were complimentary, he'd say I failed to capture his genius."

"E-mail it in."

"I'd like one more night to read it over."

"One night, Mark. Have it in here tomorrow morning."

Mark and Shannon left half an hour too late to ride the congressional underground subway.

"You think this is okay?" Shannon asked as they stepped outside. It was the first time in six weeks she had departed a Senate building above ground.

"The subway is closed," Mark said. "What else can we do?"

She looked around and saw nothing suspicious, but seeing in the city required different eyes than seeing on tundra. She tilted her face to the sky and took a deep breath. The attack last month had shaken her badly, but now somehow with Mark and the longer days, danger seemed as distant as winter.

Pyro followed on foot, Tank on a bicycle, Stephen in a Ford Escort. Each man had a two-way radio and a handgun. It irritated Stephen to see Shannon with Meadows, arm in arm. They walked west for miles, all the way to Georgetown, and entered a Mexican restaurant, Zapata's. "There they are," Mark said.

Jude and Harry looked up from their margaritas. Harry frowned. Already half drunk, Jude wore a décolleté dress and a florid face, and suggested that they share a table for four. But Harry was on his feet in seconds, reaching for his coat.

Still seated, Jude turned to Mark. "I suppose your trip to Minneapolis had something to do with that Boy Scout making a scene at the subcommittee hearing?"

"I suppose."

"Let's go, Jude," Harry said.

Shannon watched him. "Denali says that Jeff has gone home. Is he okay?"

Harry put on his coat and punched his arms through the sleeves. "How would I know?"

"He's your friend."

"Is that right? Since when are my friendships defined by you or by anybody else?"

Shannon did not take her eyes off him. An awkward silence elbowed between them.

"So Mark," Jude said to lessen the heat on Harry, "how's your silly presidential commission on the Age of Enlightenment?"

"Fine."

"That's all you can say, 'fine'?" Jude dusted down her margarita as Harry helped her into her coat and she played the provocateur. "It must be a big job, this Enlightenment. You have any idea where to begin?"

"I'd end the poverty of consumerism."

"The poverty of consumerism, meaning what?"

"Never having enough. It's our new poverty these days. Haven't you noticed? The more we have the more we want. We are a nation of overfed starving people, starved for meaning in our lives. We are thirsty in the rain."

"Thirsty in the rain," Jude repeated. "You know what, I think you're a nut, that's what I think. But you must be a nice nut for Shannon to like you." She adjusted her dress.

"That's me. Mr. Nice Nut."

"I'm outta here," Harry said as threw a twenty onto the table and exited Zapata's. Jude followed him in a hurry.

Shannon said, "I'm going after them. I don't trust him with her."

"I'll come with you," Mark suggested.

"No. Get back to Tony's, proofread your story and e-mail it in. I'll be fine." Shannon kissed him on his cheek. "I love your soft beard, Mr. Nice Nut. Call me from Tony's."

She was fifty feet down the sidewalk, her long stride fluid and swift, when Mark called, "Shannon?"

She turned. A wisp of black hair swept over her eye. A smile curled the corner of her mouth. Her lips were sensuous even from a distance, her head tilted just right. He raised his hand and appeared to want to say something, a thousand things, every desire he felt for her, but he only waved.

She waved back, and hurried on.

"Showtime," Stephen radioed Pyro and Tank. Stephen was now on foot, Pyro on the bike, Tank in the Escort. They followed Mark south. The night had turned cool as musicians in straw hats played mandolins in the Georgetown streets.

"What if he hails a cab?" Pyro asked over the radio.

"He won't," Stephen answered. "He's headed for Foggy Bottom, to take the Metro to Tenley Town, the nearest Metro station to the Carzoli residence." Sure enough, Mark exited at Tenley Town and walked east toward Rock Creek Park, each step taking him deeper into the darkness, no longer a grid of streets but a maze of lanes, loops and cul de sacs. Perfect ambush territory.

Yet an ambush was far from his mind, as Shannon occupied his thoughts. What joy he found in touching her, smelling her and hearing her voice, how everything about her was music and fragrance. He remembered his Thoreau: "There is no remedy for love but to love more."

Two blocks from Carzoli's, he rounded a corner and walked into Stephen.

Unable to comprehend the dark threat before him, Mark sidestepped the stranger but Tank pinioned his arms from behind and Stephen struck a fist to his stomach. Mark buckled, the nausea rising in his throat. He dropped his briefcase with the laptop inside. Stephen grabbed it and told Tank, "Tie and gag him."

Suddenly a voice said from the darkness, "Let him go."

"Who the hell—?" Tank said.

"Let him go and back away," the voice commanded.

Mark heard a loud popping— "pop, pop, pop...pop, pop"— and drew a sharp breath. *My god, somebody's shooting a gun.* A body fell next to him, running footsteps, a dog barking. A searing pain ripped through him as he fell to his knees, burning in the ribs. The headlights of a car suddenly vanquished the night; Mark heard the guttural complaints of a man taking flight. The car stopped and somebody stepped out and a woman's voice said, "Honey no, don't get out. Let's leave, now."

Mark reached across the rough pavement and found his briefcase. A man lay nearby, shot through the chest, gurgling his final breaths, drowning in his own blood. "Who...who are you?" Mark asked.

No answer.

The driver of the idling car knelt next to him. "Hey buddy, you okay?"

The pain ripped into him, worse than knives and needles as he heaved for breath through a dry mouth. One hand felt paralyzed. With his other hand he reached to his lower back and felt his moist, warm blood.

"Try not to move," said the man from the car. He dialed three numbers on a cell phone, and Mark heard him say something about an emergency.

I've been shot. I don't believe this. This can't be happening to me. Shannon, are you okay...Shannon?

~

Not until a week after the shooting were the two dead men reported as Parkendale agents. Tank had killed one, Stephen the other, but not without taking a slug in his forearm that caused him to drop Mark's briefcase. Tank lost the end of his nose, where a bullet had clipped it off and compounded his ugliness from the profound to the preposterous. Pyro had missed the attack while he waited as backup at the Tenley Town Metro station. In her farmhouse in eastern Maryland, Winniemae used her old nursing skills and contraband medicines to patch up Stephen and Tank as best she could. She tended to them with a mother's care, and fed them hot meals while they awaited new orders from her brooding nephew, Tyler Kyle.

~

Mark lost one kidney, two liters of blood and any lingering doubts he had about the threatening nature of his ANZA research. From his hospital bed he told Lincoln Crozier his story a dozen times. Friends came to visit and see his wound and tease him. Jude brought a box of chocolates with a card signed to "Mr. Nice Nut." Mark thanked her, and Shannon ate the chocolates. Together with Gil, Hutch, Tony and Shannon, Mark decided to give his three years of ANZA research to the FBI.

Shannon shuttled him off to the Shenandoah after his ten days in the hospital, and cared for him in the rustic cabin where she had stayed before. He slept day and night, and shivered with nightmares. She curled her body around his and held him. She put her hand on his sternum, and his on hers, and whispered to him of rivers—of saints that care for the lost and wounded. The cabin had a wood-burning stove where she built crackling fires morning and night, and made delicious soups. There was no shower, only a creek nearby where she bathed every day, standing barefoot on the wet rocks and drying her black hair, veiled by a willow. From the porch Mark could complete her contours in dream-like ways he believed not far from the truth.

"I don't want to go back to the city," he told her on the same night he said he loved her.

"Let me take you to my refuge, Mark. Let me show you who I am."

The next day she phoned the office and Kelly Calvert began to scold her. Shannon told her to save her breath. She had decided to resign.

~

The Longstreet profile hit the American conscience like a tsunami, undetectable at its origin but devastating on the distant shores of Alaska. It contained moments of flattery, a glowing accolade from the majority leader, and victories as a young attorney in Anchorage. But as readers progressed they discovered a political candyman who had financed mining dredges, missile silos, military bases, timber clearcuts, fish hatcheries, dams, pipelines and oil patches, any development by anybody who, while deaf to the songs of birds, could hear a dollar bill fall on the tundra. Gil and Hutch said that Mark's writing was clean, accurate and yeasty, his best ever, and they stood by him one hundred percent. He offered no impenetrable style, no left wing sympathies, no ivory tower abstractions. Just the facts. All conjecture about ANZA was avoided, but Rollie Dawson's photo was not. It ran across two pages and showed Senator Longstreet deplaning an ANZA Lear and carrying an ANZA tote bag and a teddy bear.

Longstreet responded the following Monday on CNN, "It was just a small gift for my granddaughter, for crying out loud."

~

The Anchorage detectives arrived at Vic's Motor Shop looking for William Alt. Vic told them to get a warrant or get out. William heard the commotion and sauntered forward. "Hey, I got nothing to hide. I'll talk to you guys."

The detectives asked about his relationship with Carl Zarki, his firing last December, his whereabouts one night last week.

"I was right here watching a Mariners game, ain't that right, guys?" William said.

"That's right," the gang at the motor shop said.

The detectives departed.

In his apartment late that night, William opened the back of his stereo speaker and removed Zarki's Army Airborne file. Something about it intrigued him, perhaps because Zarki had never mentioned being a paratrooper. It contained transfer, promotion and discharge papers, and many photos. One, the only black and white, showed a large group of people wearing swim suits on a beach, their arms around each other. From the back row a small face peered out and hit William like a hammer. Why had he not seen it before? It was the drunk, the same guy who had stumbled into the ANZA lobby and run away on winged feet when William threw him out. He was dressed differently in the photo, clean-shaven and younger. But it was him. And standing next to him, smiling, was Captain Carl Zarki.

~

The following Saturday young Aliena Quail, unable to speak or walk, married the man of her dreams in a lavish ceremony in Houston, Texas. Her father pushed her down the aisle in a wheelchair, and gave her away.

Twelve days later she died.

On the last day of April Alan and Alexis Quail departed Galveston on a two-week sailing getaway aboard their 42-foot ketch, *Aliena*. They would never return.

May

THIRTY-ONE

J ohn Sires, acting CEO of ANZA AMERICA, sat atop his king-
dom at One Noble Plaza and fingered the US Coast Guard
report that concluded a massive explosion had destroyed the
Aliena. No sign of Alan or Alexis Quail, or their bodyguard. Just
boat fragments in the Gulf of Mexico. He cradled a phone to his
ear as Johnny Parkendale blathered on about how his men had
been following Mark Meadows last month when something went
wrong.

Obviously, Sires thought. "What's the status with Jeff Meola?"

"He still says he's not the intruder. He's got—"

"Have you seen the Coast Guard report on the *Aliena?*"

"Yeah, poor Alan. The last time I saw him he looked real tired,
you know, real worn down."

"That was here, in Houston?"

"No, Aspen. He was with one of your lawyers, Ned Camis."

Sires felt a pit in his stomach. "Ned Camis, you're sure?"

"Sure I'm sure. Guy's got a head like a cube, right?"

Camis isn't an ANZA attorney. He's one of Alan's personal lawyers. What was Alan doing with Camis in Aspen? Shit. Sires asked Johnny to recount everything he could remember from that night. Later, Sires left a message at the law firm where Ned Camis was a partner.

Camis waited four hours to return his call. "John, Ned Camis here. Just got your message. What's up?"

"Have you seen the Coast Guard report on the *Aliena?*"

"Got a copy right here." This was not true. The nearest copy was in a vault across his spacious office. What Camis held instead was a manila folder with a heavy bond business envelope inside, wax sealed and stamped with the Quail family crest. He tapped it casually on his leg.

Sires expressed concern about Alan's and Alexis' missing bodies, and Alan selling nineteen percent of his ANZA stock when shares were at their optimum, after the 1002 result was announced but before the Longstreet profile and ANZA Lear photograph landed in the *Washington Post Sunday Magazine.* "Brilliant timing, don't you think?"

"Luck," Camis said.

"Alan didn't believe in luck."

"He sure did. He turned a profit betting on the Celtics and the Red Sox for thirty years. That takes plenty of luck."

Celtics and Red Sox? Since when was Alan a Boston fan? And a betting man? Suddenly it occurred to Sires that although he liked and respected Alan Quail, he in fact never really knew him. He never *attempted* to know him. Not once in twenty-five years had they had a heart-to-heart talk. Not once had they watched a Celtics or Red Sox game, or discussed sports, or family, or spirituality, or any values beyond money and oil.

Sires' palms were sweating.

"...You know Alan," Camis was saying. "He never did forgive the Red Sox for selling Babe Ruth to the Yankees."

"Uh, right," Sires said, forgetting to ask about Aspen.

~

The photograph said nothing and everything.

Tyler Kyle studied it with a four-power magnifying loupe. It was an eight-by-ten black and white, tattered with age, that showed thirty people in swimsuits on a beach, all fit, mostly men, about five women, some with their arms around each other's shoulders, some with Hebraic inscriptions on their suits. No names, date or location on the back, though Kyle suspected Israel. On the front William Alt had circled two faces with a black marker and written "Captain Zarki" above one, "the drunk" above the other.

Something caught Kyle's eye. The black circle around the drunk covered half of the face of a woman who stood next to him, opposite Zarki, her arm around his waist. Built like a ballerina, she was slight yet muscular. Kyle found a bottle of mild solvent and applied it gently with a Q-Tip. In less than a minute he removed the black circle and unveiled Maya Donjek, younger by ten or fifteen years, shorter hair, the only person in the photo not smiling.

William had said he never forgot a face.

No wonder he covered her with the black marker. To him she was insignificant, a face he did not recognize because she never checked through security that night in Anchorage five months ago.

~

"Okay," Gil Trebideaux said, "make the call."

Mark looked around Trebideaux's office and received agreeing nods from Lowell Hutchinson and the two FBI men, Lincoln Crozier and Deputy Director Liam Bristol. Each listened on his own line as Mark dialed Senator Longstreet's office.

"Tyler Kyle here," came the breathless reply, as if already exasperated with the caller.

"Mr. Kyle, this is Mark Meadows at the *Washington Post.*"

A slight pause. "Researching another character assassination?"

"Not exactly. But I am recording this conversation."

Kyle hung up.

Mark dialed again, and Kyle answered. "The tape recorders are off, Mr. Kyle. Can we talk?"

No response.

"You've heard about Alan Quail?"

"Yes. A tragedy."

"Will it have any bearing on Senator Longstreet's energy bill?"

"Not at all. The energy bill is fine."

"Then why has it received so little attention in committee?"

"Other bills have higher priority right now, that's all."

"You're not worried about the recent strength of Bruce Janstadt's Wilderness bill?"

"Not at all."

"And neither is Senator Longstreet?"

"Not at all. I'm a busy man, Mr. Meadows. Is there a purpose for this call?" His voice was not so much a whisper as it was contained contempt.

"I've been trying to reach Jeff Meola. Your office said he went home to Anchorage. I called there, but his parents told me they spoke with him just two nights ago here in Washington."

"And this is my problem?"

"He's suspected of breaking into the ANZA Building in Anchorage."

"Is that right? I heard that you were suspected of doing that, or at least that you acted as an accomplice."

"Rumors."

"Terrible, aren't they?"

"Something else intrigues me," Mark said. "Why would Harry Arnold leave your office and join Senator Matlin's?"

"He wanted a change, simple as that. Ask him."

"Did you know that of the ten men who knew the result of the 1002 Area test well, six are dead?"

"No, I didn't."

"Five of them reportedly died in accidents. But the *Post* has reason to believe they were not accidents. We believe that some of these men were murdered. Do you care to comment?"

"That deserves no comment."

"We have proof that one of the men, Charles DeShay, an ANZA geologist, was fatally poisoned in a nursing home in Anchorage in February."

"What makes you think Charles DeShay knew the result?"

"A preponderance of evidence."

"A preponderance of evidence? Not beyond a reasonable doubt? Mr. Meadows, you sound like a freshman law student who thinks he's legal counsel in a small town civil trial. Call me back when you're no longer writing rumors for the fiction page." Kyle hung up.

Mark smiled.

"He's smooth," Hutch said.

"Too smooth," Crozier added.

"His smoothness implicates him in nothing," Bristol said.

"Where's my tennis racquet?" Trebideaux asked. "I think better with my tennis racquet."

"I wasn't finished with him," Mark said. "I wonder if having just one kidney diminishes my interviewing abilities?"

Crozier asked Mark, "Besides Shannon, you told only one person you were staying at Tony Carzoli's while writing the Longstreet profile, and that one person was Tyler Kyle?"

Mark nodded.

Trebideaux fingered his racquet. "I'm willing to go to print with this and define the pattern and see what happens, but suggest no ramifications."

"Or consistencies with cases outside this one," Liam Bristol said to his old college friend. "If Kyle is involved, he'll be cautious, and caution has its own set of signals. The Attorney General has given us more latitude on wire tapping and phone traps since the Oklahoma City bombing." He looked at Crozier. "Run another background check and rotate teams on him."

Crozier made a note.

Trebideaux told Mark to call Sires. Each man picked up his

phone. Thirty seconds later John Sires answered in his Houston office and said brusquely, "Mark Meadows, I didn't appreciate your slandering ANZA in that Longstreet story."

Mark said, "I was sorry to hear about Alan Quail and his wife and daughter."

"Get to the point. This isn't a condolence call."

"Does the name Richard Leavitt ring a bell?"

"Yes, vaguely..."

"Before you elaborate, you need to know that I'm taping this conversation."

"What for?"

"I'm preparing a story on your 1002 test drill result, the murder of Charles DeShay and the possible murder of several others who knew that result, including Alan Quail and—"

"Jesus Christ, are you insane? What are you talking about?"

"Do you deny that Charles DeShay was murdered?"

"I don't deny or confirm anything. Charles was a good friend. So was Alan. Christ, I don't believe this."

"Charles DeShay was your good friend?"

"Damn right he was."

"Did you ever argue with him in the Arctic Refuge?"

No reply.

"The tape is rolling, Mr. Sires."

"Fine, let it roll. We'll play it at your libel trial."

"I'd like to confirm these names with you..." Mark read them, finishing with Sires himself. "These are the ten people who knew the 1002 Area test result, is that right?"

Silence.

"May I take your silence as a confirmation?"

"You may not. Christ Almighty. In your simple mind you see ANZA is some sort of comic book Evil Empire, don't you? Do you realize what contributions we make to scholarship and fellowship funds around the world? To the March of Dimes and the Anchorage Imaginarium and the Juneau Folk Festival and The Nature Conservancy? Do you?"

"Any comment about Richard Leavitt? He died in an automobile accident with Charles DeShay's son, Travis. We've found that the more we investigate him, the less he exists."

"Richard Leavitt was a consulting engineer who worked for us in Alaska and the Middle East."

"My colleague here at the *Post*, Tony Carzoli, discovered that he's a graduate of the CIA."

"The CIA? I don't believe this. This is absurd."

"The Culinary Institute of America."

"The what?"

"He was a pastry chef for the Shah of Iran, then he ended up in Baku when Alan Quail signed the Contract of the Century. Sort of odd, don't you think?"

No response.

"What about Jumar?" Mark asked.

"Jumar?"

"Yes, Jumar. Any comment?"

A nervous laugh, then a grunt. "I'll tell you what, Meadows, go ahead and write your cockamamie story and watch your career sink like a rock. Do you hear me? Is Gil Trebideaux listening to this? ANZA is the most powerful corporation in the world. We have a billion shareholders. Do you realize that?"

"That's a lot of zeros."

"You smart ass. Remember the golden rule: He with the gold, rules. We'll own the *Post*. Wouldn't that make a great headline? ANZA buys the *Washington Post*. One word of your libelous, defamatory bullshit and you'll be on the street selling pencils."

"Jumar, Mr. Sires. Any comment?"

Sires slammed down the phone.

"Whoa," Hutch said, "that guy needs a distemper shot."

Trebideaux looked at Mark. "One kidney is all you need. Write your story."

An hour later Shannon found Mark at his desk in the newsroom. They updated each other. She pulled a gift from her daypack and presented it to him: an Emily Dickinson poem, matted and framed. "I wanted you to have it before you wrote your ANZA story."

Mark read it aloud.

Tell all the Truth but tell it slant—
Success in Circuit lies
Too bright for our infirm Delight
the Truth's superb surprise
As Lightning to the Children eased
With explanation kind
the Truth must dazzle gradually
or every man be blind—

~

Tyler Kyle exited the Rockville Metro Station a few minutes before midnight, his shoulders tight with frustration. His men had shot two Parkendale agents and let Meadows slip away. Frank Beasley had ratted, and would soon pay. Senator Longstreet was too full of hot rhetoric and empty results. And making matters worse, Janstadt's bill, transfused by his exoneration in the Boy Scout scandal, had gained momentum and rolled into full committee. A clever tactician, Janstadt had brokered a deal with the majority leader to swing a dozen Democratic senators into the GOP camp on a defense spending bill, in return for support of his Wilderness bill. Rumor had it the majority leader was furious with Longstreet and other Senate chairmen for refusing to apologize or even appear contrite after the public learned about their January ANZA junket to Houston.

Kyle knelt near the phone booth and retied his shoes. *Anybody watching me?* He had never felt so paranoid. Three people walked by from the midnight Metro. Kyle waited until they got into their cars and drove away. A minute later he entered the phone booth.

Two FBI agents watched him with binoculars from inside their Toyota at the far end of the lot. After Kyle hung up and walked away, they wiretapped the phone.

~

News of Frank Beasley's accident did not surprise Agent Crozier, but it did Shannon and Mark. He called them at The Brother John House. "What happened?" Shannon asked.

"He drove off a highway north of Minneapolis to avoid a head-on collision. Sounds familiar, doesn't it?"

"Is he okay?"

"He's stable. His car had airbags. Father Carroll is with him in the hospital. It's time for both of you to get out of Washington and stay out."

~

Four days later Tyler Kyle sat alone in Winniemae's farmhouse kitchen and read Mark Meadows' article in the *Washington Post*.

MYSTERIOUS DEATHS SURROUND ANZA ALASKA TEST WELL

It was the newspaper story he dreaded. It began with the disappearance of Alan Quail and the poisoning of Charles DeShay, then detailed the history of the ANZA 1002 Area test drill, its delayed public release and the political implications of the delay. It was surgical, well restrained, and clever for what it did not say as much as for what it did say. Kyle hated it.

Next he scoured a Senate memo and considered the strengths and weaknesses of his plan. The memo detailed next month's petroleum summit in Anchorage, and the one day "fact-finding" trip to Prudhoe Bay, followed by a nine-day raft trip down the Kitvik River in the Arctic Refuge. Five senators would take the trip with a few aides, family members, guides, one reporter, one photographer and two Alaska State Troopers. Sixteen people total. Janstadt and Matlin would go, one pro-Wilderness, one pro-oil. The other three senators were undecided. Janstadt aimed to persuade them to his side, Matlin to his.

Kyle studied reports and maps and found that every June the north-flowing rivers of arctic Alaska cut canyons through layers of overflow ice—called *aufeis*—as much as fifteen feet deep. Cold blue vertical walls. Inescapable vaults. Ice tunnels that formed and collapsed everywhere as rivers shifted channels. One guidebook called it "a dynamic, thrilling and dangerous place."

Perfect, Kyle thought.

All five senators hailed from states with conservative Republican governors. Should they die on the Kitvik, not only would America see the folly of ANWR as a place for recreation, but also the governors would choose their replacements. The widows could intervene, but here again providence prevailed, for all three Democrats were divorced, and the two Republicans, Matlin and Romper, had wives of steadfast party loyalty who would not object to a new pro-oil appointee. Five votes from five new senators would kill the Wilderness bill.

Kyle wondered how to unveil the plan to Merlin. Then came another idea. He would not tell him. For years he had explored the possibility of graduating beyond Merlin's strict tutelage. In Kyle's estimation the big man had grown timid and weak in his failing health, and he too often played a cautious hand precisely when every countermeasure against the environmentalists required boldness and iron resolve. If his apprenticeship should ever end, Kyle reasoned, let it be now. The bird in a nest must break its shell before it can fly. Kyle had done this. He had grown and flown and attained a key position on Capitol Hill, a position so important he believed that Merlin would never sacrifice its disclosure over a minor dereliction of duty. If his plan worked, Kyle would take responsibility and share his genius with Merlin. If it did not, he would tuck his wings into the storm and see where he landed. William Alt would be the key, for unlike Stephen, Pyro and Tank, he did not know Kyle's identity. He could lay no accusations on him, not even a suspicion, if he was the only one left alive on the Kitvik River. Pickett's Charge had failed because it was the third day of the Battle of Gettysburg. Johnny Reb was tired; BillyYank had the high ground. Brothers killing brothers. *This will be different*, Kyle told himself. On the Kitvik River, four men will have the high ground and overwhelm a party of sixteen rafters like falcons on ducks. Sitting ducks.

Kyle pulled the curtains, turned off the lights and fell asleep to Beethoven's *Moonlight Sonata*. He felt at peace for the first time in months. But the progression of notes worked on his mind like a kinship dirge that brought the flying face straight at him, broken from the rocks below.

"No," Kyle screamed as he jolted awake.

~

By the end of May the FBI had fifty agents quietly working on the ANZA case in Washington, Texas, Idaho, Minnesota and Alaska, but none in Panama.

The surgeries were completed in the same clinic on the same night by the same plastic surgeon, one of Panama's best, recently retired but always available for the right price. Both patients received a face-lift and a restructured nose. They dyed their own hair. Once healed, they looked twenty years younger. Securing Chilean passports and identification was easy, again, for a price. They caught a plane to Santiago, then another to Mount Pleasant Military Airport in the Falkland Islands. From there they traveled by freighter to Tristan de Cunha, in the middle of the South Atlantic, one of the most remote islands in the world, and bought a potato farm. The man painted watercolors and the woman sculpted, and in this way Alan and Alexis Quail found their new lives.

Summer

June

THIRTY-TWO

For ten thousand years caribou have pulsed over the tundra of arctic Alaska, crossing rivers and mountains with an ebb and flow as determined as the tides, incessant as the wind. The easternmost of three great arctic herds, the Porcupine Herd, takes its name from the Porcupine River of Canada's northern Yukon Territory, where the caribou spend their winters in the boreal forest. Come spring, the herd—some one hundred and thirty thousand animals—moves west-northwest through the Brooks Range and onto the Coastal Plain of Alaska's Arctic National Wildlife Refuge, where all the pregnant females give birth to their calves in the same place, the 1002 Area.

On this particular sunny mid-June day a Cessna 185 roared above the foothills ten miles south of a large aggregation of the herd. "You fellows wanna see some caribou?" the young freckle-faced pilot asked his three passengers.

"No thanks," said the handsome man next to him.

The pilot looked at the two men in the back seats. They shook their heads. Nope, no caribou. Not important. Not today.

"You sure?" the pilot asked. "Part of the herd is just over those hills. We can be there in a few minutes. It's an awesome sight. I won't charge you for the time."

"No thanks," the handsome man repeated tersely.

They flew west over the Jago, Kitvik, Hulahula and Sadlerochit Rivers, west to the Sadlerochit Mountains that rose like a Devonian castle above the Coastal Plain. The pilot circled a makeshift airstrip below—nothing more than wheel ruts across a level stretch of dry tundra—and checked a piece of orange survey flagging tied to a tall stake. Light wind from the east. He banked steeply.

Seated behind him, Pyro turned green. A minute later the plane landed and jostled to a stop.

"Here we are," the pilot said cheerfully. "So, you guys are geologists, huh?"

"Yep," the handsome man said. He wore sunglasses and a ball cap and a short-cropped beard flecked with gray.

"Lookin' for oil?" The pilot asked.

"Nope. Doing gravimetric studies to determine tectonic shifts."

They unloaded supplies, including several large boxes marked FRAGILE INSTRUMENTS. The party's fourth man was still in Kaktovik with most of the camping gear. The pilot climbed back into the Cessna and took off to get him.

The propwash blew off Pyro's hat. "I hate this fuckin' place," he said, squinting into the sun.

A long-tailed jaeger hovered over Tank, and he threw a rock at it. "Stupid hawk."

"I don't know much about this new guy," Stephen said. "I want at least one of us watching him at all times."

Three hours later, at nine in the evening with the sun still high in the northwest sky, the Cessna returned and landed next to the three waiting men. The pilot climbed out. Behind him came the new guy, William Alt, who called himself Fritz, as instructed by the mystery caller, Tyler Kyle.

They unloaded gear.

"That's it," the pilot said. "You guys got a VHF radio?"

Stephen said they did. He asked for the frequencies used by bush pilots flying around the refuge. It would be important to monitor their whereabouts. He confirmed the pick-up time.

"You got food for several extra days?" the pilot asked. "I might not be able to get you out when you want. Thick fog rolls in from the coast and sometimes grounds us."

"We'll be fine." Stephen thanked him.

He climbed into his plane and took off.

Minutes later the four men were alone in the silence of the arctic. The jaeger returned, hovering. Tank took a .44 Mag Colt Anaconda from his pack and with one shot blasted the bird's head off. The men laughed, though Stephen thought William's laugh a little contrived.

~

"See anybody suspicious?" Crozier asked Mark and Rollie as they stood in a dark corner of the conference room in the Hotel LaPerouse, downtown Anchorage, watching the petroleum summit through a narrow opening in the curtains.

"No," Mark said. He had received four death threats since publication of the Longstreet profile and the ANZA expose. Rollie shook his head as well: nobody familiar or suspicious.

John Sires stood on stage and praised those U.S. senators and representatives who had come north to learn the "real story" of oil in the arctic.

Oliver Longstreet, Sam Matlin and Jack Worley each gave a short speech. Sure was good to be back in Alaska, they said. Worley told the audience to not believe the fairy tales printed in the press these days, especially those in "the Washington ComPost and the New York Crimes."

Oliver Longstreet announced that from this time forward all Alaskans would be encouraged to refer to the 1002 Area of the Arctic National Wildlife Refuge by its new, unofficial yet more appropriate name: the Arctic Oil Reserve.

"Skip Prudhoe Bay," Crozier told Mark and Rollie outside the hotel. "Fly straight to Kaktovik and join the other rafters there. It's all remote country after that. You'll be safe on the river."

~

The four men erected their tents and slept fitfully that night. "It's too damn bright up here," Pyro complained the next morning. "It don't even get dark at night."

William befriended the men slowly, speaking only when spoken to. He told a few stories, and Stephen dissected every word. Tank shot three ptarmigan for target practice while Pyro sharpened his serrated knife. They napped that afternoon, awoke in the evening, and at midnight began an arduous thirty-mile hike over tundra and ankle-twisting tussocks to the Kitvik River. Each man carried an eighty-pound pack with a full-immersion dry suit tied to the top, a three-foot-long metal pipe tied to the side, and a knife in a sheath on his belt. They left behind two tents, a rudimentary kitchen and sundry supplies to make the Sadlerochit site appear like an occupied camp.

~

The arctic, the arctic, the arctic.

Shannon's heart raced as she flew north over sunrise on the Alaska Range, north beyond Fairbanks and the Yukon River, into the weathered bones of the Brooks Range, over valleys without names, over rivers that would ransom and redeem her. While other passengers on the Boeing jet chatted and ate, she looked out the window at the generosity of space, the clarity of light. This was her geography, the farther north the better, into syncline and anticline, batholith and basalt, the furrowed brow of a tumultuous earth, wilderness as far as the eye could see.

Then Prudhoe Bay appeared, the Haul Road, the insatiable

pipeline and drill pads and vented gases and gleaming red and silver buildings, a world straightjacketed into flowlines and causeways, sacrificed to the hydrocarbon age. Other passengers pointed with interest.

Shannon pulled down her window shade.

That afternoon perfectly mannered ANZA Prudhoe guides ushered the guests through sumptuous lobbies and a vast cafeteria, past tropical potted plants and into a state-of-the-art fitness center where off-duty workers pumped iron and listened to Credence Clearwater Revival and greeted the senators and representatives with choreographed courtesy. Then on to the heated swimming pool, volleyball gym and movie theater.

The politicians nodded approvingly. What a place.

The Great Indoors, Shannon mused. While the politicians went on a pipeline tour, she watched birds through a chain-linked fence.

The next morning the rafting party flew to Kaktovik, one hundred miles east of Prudhoe Bay. Ice covered the Beaufort Sea, and snow profiled the town. A cold fog threatened to roll in from the north, descending everything into muted gray.

Waiting on the tarmac was Eddie Tagarook in jeans and a cotton shirt, and next to him Mark and Rollie, Mark with his hair disheveled but finally appropriate in the arctic wind, and Rollie reinvented, twenty pounds lighter and sporting a bandana tied to his head, like a pirate. He said he had a new girlfriend. *She'll love me to pieces, but will she put me back together again?*

Shannon greeted them and said, "Did you hear about Oliver Longstreet? Somebody delivered a package bomb to his office in Anchorage last night."

"Is he okay?" Mark asked.

"Yes." But it changed things. Two Alaska State Troopers had been pulled off the rafting trip and put on his protection. An Anchorage FBI agent would come instead. Bruce Janstadt had also decided that the sixteen-person-trip should be reduced to twelve, with just three rafts.

Shannon turned to Eddie. "How are you, old friend?"

"I'm good, maybe, you know. Come over to the house and I'll get out the chainsaw and cut up some frozen caribou steaks."

"I can't, Eddie. We're on the hop here."

All day long the expedition transferred into the headwaters of the Kitvik. First, two Cessna 185s flew people and their gear south to the foothills of the Brooks Range, requiring eight round trips, four per plane. Then two fabric-winged Piper Super Cubs ferried everything deep into the mountains, the pilots following the Kitvik River until the steep, rocky slopes closed around them in the heart of the Brooks Range—*terra borealis incognita*—land of wolf and bear, caribou and fox, eagle and jaeger.

The weather deteriorated but the Super Cubs kept flying, each trip carrying supplies and one white-knuckled passenger who sat directly behind the pilot. Shannon liked her pilot, a freckle-faced kid who already had three thousand hours in single-engine tail-draggers. He admired the landscape with her, admired her too. "Ya gotta love this country," he said. "Where the road ends the real Alaska begins. By the way, you married?"

Back and forth the pilots flew until everyone and everything was safely delivered to the upper Kitvik. The sky threatened snow. Visibility dropped. The pilots double-checked pick-up times and locations with the guides. Jude looked at her Tiffany watch and asked, "When's dinner?"

The older pilot, a gnomic man, asked to see her watch. Jude removed it and handed it to him, and he climbed into his plane and flew away with it.

Jude's mouth fell open.

"He'll give it back to you when your trip's over," the freckle-faced pilot told the flabbergasted redhead. "No need for watches up here. You're on arctic time now." He gave Shannon his tattered business card—said it was his last—and told her to look him up in Fairbanks. He yelled, "Prop" to clear the area, then fired up his plane. He taxied down a gravel bar, turned and took off into the wind, dipping a wing as he roared overhead. Everybody waved. How frail the little plane looked in the rock-ribbed vault of the Brooks Range, the fin-backed ridges of argillite and schist rising into bruised clouds, the scree slopes at their angles of repose. As it flew away it seemed to take all of civilization with it, leaving only the land and silence, and a little island of humankind.

Shannon walked down to the river to hear what it had to say.

THIRTY-THREE

Hello old friend." She sat cross-legged at the river's edge, forearms on her knees, letting the wind carry her upstream, the waters down. She traced a wolf track in the mud with a willow stick; asked forgiveness for being away so long. She removed her boots and socks and gripped the cold rocks with her toes. The distant prattle of her campmates seemed remotely profane. She wondered, *If some people are born awake and others asleep, what am I?*

She closed her eyes.

—You weren't born until you came here, her father tells her.

She says she feels bad about that.

—Don't. Most people stumble through their entire lives and never find themselves. They get old and lie down and discover they're at the end of somebody else's life, somebody else's dreams.

—That's sad.

—Yes, well, there are no guarantees.

She skips a stone eight times.

He skips one seven; looks at her, sees that rueful smile. Don't get cocky, he tells her.

—So you really think Travis will come up here with us in July?

—I do.

—And he'll bring his guitar? The old one?

—I suppose. Might be nice to have a little music in camp at night, don't you think?

—I guess. Isn't there music enough already, just being here?

—Hey. He wrote you a song.

—Yeah.

—You two could use a little more time together.

—I guess.

—Shannon, what's up? Why the sour face?

—Nothing. She throws another stone across the river, sidearm. Nine skips.

Soft footsteps from behind. She turned to see Mark as he asked, "Are you molting?"

"I guess I am." She patted the ground next to her.

He sat down. "I wanted to join you earlier, but I could see you needed time alone. Being here is a private process, isn't it?" He held her hand, interlocking his fingers with hers.

She looked across the river. "Six years, Mark. I haven't been back here in six years."

"How's it feel?"

"Like a dream."

"Has it changed?"

"No. It's timeless. I've changed, but it hasn't."

Mark took a deep breath of the cool air. "The whole rest of the world is being shaped by people, but not this place—yet."

She lowered her head.

"Did I say something wrong?"

"It's just that the last time I was here with Dad, we planned to go back to Anchorage and return in a week with Travis. I was jealous that I would have to share him with my brother, like he was my father and nobody else's. I had always had him to myself up here. This was our place."

Mark pulled her to him. "But you never did come back, did

you?" He held her for a minute while the river tumbled over ancient rocks.

"I always thought it was Travis' fault that we didn't get along, and Mom's too. But now I wonder if it was me all that time. I never really knew him. He was my own brother, my only brother, and I never really let him in."

After a moment Mark said, "Listen. Do you hear that?"

"What?" Shannon perked up. "Hear what?"

"The river. The water on the rocks. It's saying something like... 'Iphorgiiiiiveuuuu, Iphorgiiiiiveuuuu...'"

"You think this river is my absolution?"

"No. Only you can think that."

Dinner time. The husband-wife guides, Burly and Lisa, helped anybody in need set up a tent. Beyond his duties as photographer, Rollie served as the third guide to reprise his previous life when he worked as an oarsman on the Colorado River. He created a kitchen by tipping two inflated rafts onto their sides and supporting them with paddles. He spread a tarp over their leeward sides, pulled it taut with corner braces, and staked guy lines into the hard ground. Shannon watched him with amazement. Rollie smiled at her as he tied knots. *The only thing I can count on now is my fingers.*

Two large pots contained hot lentil stew that everybody agreed was spiced to perfection. They sat and ate on overturned plastic buckets. The five senators huddled over the hot meal, wearing stiff boots and creased parkas fresh from mail order catalogs. Among them, only Janstadt seemed at ease in the wilderness. Shannon, Burly and Lisa possessed the casual grace of people rooted in the arctic, while Mark and Rollie and the FBI agent, Ben Leighton, each rotated in his own elliptical orbit. And finally came Jude, more of a moon than a planet or a star, her light and path determined by those around her.

Bruce Janstadt said, "We're going to be on this river awhile, I think we can dispense with titles. My name is Bruce. I'd like you to call me that. Not senator. I'm sure my colleagues agree."

They nodded.

"Okay Bruce," Lisa said, "have some dessert." She opened a Dutch oven with a baked cake inside. "Twelve hot charcoal briquettes on the top and six on the bottom. Works every time."

Mark brought Shannon a cup of hot chocolate while Sam Matlin and Bruce Janstadt talked basketball. Agent Leighton talked firearms with Burly and senators Romper and Ulrich. Rollie heated dishwater as the wind kicked up and snowflakes swirled about. Walking back to their tent, Jude lamented to Shannon, "I didn't think it would be so cold in June. What am I doing here?"

"Living," Shannon muttered.

They climbed into their tent, stripped down to their long underwear and snuggled into their sleeping bags. Shannon wanted to make amends with Jude, as times had been rough between them since she resigned from Sam's staff. "Remember when we were kids," she said softly, "and we went on vacations together and played those crazy games?"

"Yeah," Jude said. "Remember the time..."

They talked and laughed for an hour before falling asleep.

The next day brought a vicious wind, and everybody lingered in their warm bags. Finally Shannon heard rustling in the kitchen, pots and pans, people laughing, then Burly's voice, "Outta your bags, campers. It's pancakes and hashbrowns now, or cold cereal later."

Three inches of wet snow covered the ground beneath a gray skullcap sky. Storm clouds raked the summits as all day long everybody ate and slept to snub the cold, waiting for the storm to break. Warm in her bag, Shannon imagined Mark's hands on her, so understanding of her desires. Shocked by her lasciviousness, she would scold herself with good Catholic guilt until she fell asleep and awakened again to sensual imaginings. She hungered to share her tent with him, her sleeping bag, her everything. But Jude had asked to share a tent with her. Perhaps she, too, wanted to make peace.

That night around a dinner of Jambalaya—a spicy mix of beans and sausage—Sam spread out a topographic map of the refuge and said, "Look at this place. Twenty million acres. It's huge. We're here in the mountains and the 1002 Area"—he swept his hand across the map—"is way out there on the Coastal Plain. ANZA could be drilling there right now and we wouldn't hear a thing."

Lisa offered everybody cheesecake, and Rollie passed around a Thermos of hot chocolate and a bottle of Bailey's Irish Cream.

"I just don't see the conflict," Sam said.

"Obviously," Bruce replied.

"When does it all end?" Mark asked nobody in particular.

"When does what end?" Senator Soucie asked him.

"The human juggernaut. The growth machine. When does it end?"

"Economies have to grow," Senator Nelson Romper said as he filled a cup with Bailey's.

"If we stay on this path," Burly said as he cleaned the shotgun, "in fifty centuries the entire world will be automated by genetically engineered people who'll live antiseptic lives."

"That's only half right," Mark said. "The other half will pay the price and live in abject poverty and utter chaos."

"But they'll have an atavistic robustness that the wealthy Utopians will not," Burly said, grinning. "They'll make love like animals. Monogamy will be a thing of the distant past. They'll live and die like comets, bright and brief."

"And each half will threaten to destroy the other," Mark added.

Senator Ulrich squinted with skepticism. Ben Leighton listened without expression, sipping his Earl Grey tea. Jude pulled a small mirror from her pocket to check her face.

"There comes a time when certain types of growth make us poorer, not richer," Bruce said. "I think we're there."

"Capitalism and democracy cannot survive without each other," Sam said after finishing his hot chocolate.

"Too bad," Shannon said.

The wind whipped the tarp overhead. Lisa and Rollie tightened the guy lines.

"We're an inventive and innovative people," Bruce said. "We can create electric cars and gravity-free pharmaceuticals and new paradigms for economic stability. But only if we want to. It's not just the threat to this refuge that's serious. It's the end of nature, the loss of genetic diversity and habitats everywhere, all the backyard creeks and wildflower meadows that are gone. The songbirds and frogs around the world that don't sing anymore."

"By the year 2100 we'll be able to manufacture genetic diversity," Senator Soucie said. "The average human lifespan will be double what it is now."

"God help us," muttered Ulrich.

"In another thousand years people won't even die," Mark said. "That's the ultimate objective of our technology, to remove us so far from nature that we no longer die."

"There'll be organ replacement shops," Rollie added, "like today's auto parts stores. Need a spleen? We're having a blue-light special on them, marked down to forty-nine ninety-five."

"There'll be no more diseases," Soucie observed.

"Sounds boring," Burly said.

"Wilderness will be a thousand times more valuable than oil or gold," Shannon added.

"Will it?" Sam said, fixing his eyes on her, still disappointed that she had resigned from his staff.

"What's the big deal with wilderness?" Jude asked. "I've never needed to come here before. It's interesting and all that, but I can't imagine ever coming back."

"The destruction of the natural world all comes down to money," Lisa said quietly. "Money talks."

"In Washington it does more than talk," Bruce said. "It keeps up a running conversation."

Sam shifted. "It's unfair when the rest of America foists its environmental guilt on Alaska, and puts Alaskans out of work."

"It's not environmental guilt," Shannon replied. "It's a new awareness, a new vision."

"The curve of binding energy," Burly said.

"Don't build your sainthood on the sins of others," Sam warned Shannon.

"She's not," Mark responded.

"You're a fine one to talk," Sam persisted. "What you wrote about Oliver Longstreet was a cheap shot. I think you owe him an apology."

"Whoa doggies," Burly said in his deep voice. "This is a refuge, an honest place. I don't want it desecrated with arguing. Let's get along, okay?" He held the shotgun across his lap, buffing it with an oiled rag.

Agent Ben Leighton smiled.

After a moment Sam said, "An honest place...I understand honesty in people. But what's an honest place?"

Burly looked at him with wise eyes. "You have eight days and one river to figure it out, senator."

Shannon awoke in the middle of the night and knew something had changed. She unzipped the tent and rainfly to see the storm breaking, swords of amber light slicing up the valley, cutting high peaks dusted with new snow. She pulled on her clothes and boots, grabbed her binoculars and scurried outside. Stillness everywhere. Melting and newness, like the first day of creation. She ran over the tundra and smelled the freshness of Lapland rosebay, dryas and saxifrages, colorful blossoms rising through the snow. She raided the food stash of raisins and chocolate, then headed upslope on winged feet.

She reached the summit—three thousand feet above camp—in two hours, then worked her way down the northeast ridge into the rising sun. An hour later and only a thousand feet above camp, she could see Burly, Lisa and Rollie in the kitchen making breakfast. Today the float trip would begin.

Ben Leighton watched Shannon from below as Mark hiked up to meet her. She sat in the sun on a large flat rock, her trim athletic frame at ease, belonging.

"Good morning," Mark said, a little out of breath.

"Good morning. How's your kidney?"

"Lonely and overworked. Did I tell you, now that I have only one kidney, my friends at the *Post* call me Kid Ney?"

"I like Mr. Nice Nut better." A cloud crossed her face.

"What's wrong?"

"I wish we hadn't argued last night. Burly's right, it doesn't belong here."

"It wasn't an argument. It was a discussion."

She looked across the Kitvik Valley and made no response.

"Have you ever seen the Alaska State Constitution?" Mark asked. "It reads like an Elizabethan charter to vanquish the wilderness and tame the land. No wonder most Alaskans don't want outsiders telling them what they can't do. They'd rather repeat history than learn from it."

"They see it as tyranny," Shannon said as she found a soaring raptor. "Rough-legged hawk."

Mark found it too. "You sure it's not an immature golden eagle?"

"Yep. It's a rough-legged, a dark phase male. See the white under the wings, and the banded tail?"

They watched it for unaccounted minutes. Mark finally said, "If anybody is selfish enough, everything to them is tyranny."

"True. But you need to see how people in Alaska see their liberties dying."

"Liberty in Alaska is enjoyed by the loud at the expense of the quiet, and by the aggressive at the expense of the passive. These oil people who want to drill in the caribou calving grounds, would they approve of building a gas station in a day care center?" He sat down and sighed. "Why does capitalism have to be so creative and so cruel at the same time?"

"You're a philosopher. You figure it out."

"Did you know that philosophers can be divided into two

classes? Those who believe that philosophers can be divided into two classes, and those who do not."

Shannon laughed and patted the rock on which they sat. "Isn't this a cool rock? A glacier deposited it here thousands of years ago. It's an erratic."

"An erotic?"

She smiled. "With you and me on it right now, it could be."

He leaned into her as she parted her lips to receive him, every inch of her flushed with pleasure. He whispered, "Do you think that FBI guy is watching us down there with his binoculars?"

"I know he is."

"We could embarrass him."

"And ourselves."

Mark looked at her with admiration. He didn't know if he could do this, falling for her this much. He sat up and looked for the hawk.

"You okay?" she asked.

He nodded and pulled her to him and kissed her forehead. They stared across the great expanse of arctic space, the valley like a magic bowl that filled with light. "So they drill and create jobs and oil for a few decades," Mark said wistfully. "Then what? The world will have more people and cars and greenhouse gases and the same economic narcotics and hangovers it has now. And this ten-thousand-year-old place," —he allowed himself to look north— "will be an American Serengeti ruined by rusting oil rigs." He shook his head, more solemn than she imagined he could be. "It's madness, Shannon. How do we stop it?"

"We teach our children."

He stared at her. "*Our* children?"

She stood up and pulled him downslope. "C'mon, Mr. Nice Nut. Let's go eat. I'm hungry."

~

Getting a master key was easy. Anticipating Maya's comings and goings in the Hotel LaPerouse was not. The solution was simple. Tyler Kyle would enter her room and wait. Desperate times required desperate measures.

Maya slipped away from the Anchorage petroleum summit unnoticed—she thought—and returned to her room on the fifth floor. She opened her door with the card key, threw her briefcase on the bed and phoned Washington. "Hey, what's up? No, I've heard that... No, Harry, the Baku thing won't work right yet. Let ANZA cook in that stew for awhile... Okay, call Darryl, but don't do anything before we talk tomorrow... Okay, talk to you soon."

She went into the bathroom and started the shower. She undressed and stepped in and closed the opaque glass door. Hot water streamed down her neck and shoulders. She breathed deeply, facing the water stream, and was beginning to relax when a man's soft voice pierced her, "Hello Maya."

She jumped. The lights went out and a chill ran through her, deeper than the hot water.

"It's me, your old friend." He slapped a metal pipe in the palm of his hand. "Don't move, Maya. Don't do anything stupid."

"Tyler? What are you doing here? Get out of here."

"I've got some questions for you. I know all about you, Maya, if that's your real name."

~

"I'm sorry, Mr. Sires," the front desk clerk said. "I can't give you a key to Miss Donjek's room without her permission."

Sires leaned into the young woman. "Do you know who I am? I'm the acting chief executive officer of ANZA AMERICA. With one stroke of my pen I could kill the largest corporate account on your books. I need to get these papers to Miss Donjek right away. If you don't want to lose this account and your job, I suggest you cooperate."

"I'll phone her room and ask her."

"Not necessary," Sires said.

Not intimidated by this obnoxious man, the desk clerk dialed anyway. It rang several times. "There's no answer," she said.

Sires held out his hand. "Then give me the key so I can drop these papers in her room."

The desk clerk called her supervisor, a pallid-faced, obsequious man with plastered hair who immediately obliged Sires and rebuked the clerk. Sires walked to the elevator with his bodyguard. At the elevator he turned and said, "Take a break. I'm going up to see a friend, nothing more."

He emerged on the fifth floor and walked to Maya's room. *This is it. I'm tired of playing games. There comes a time when a man just takes a woman. They never say it, but it's what they want. Predator and prey.*

~

"You know Carl Zarki don't you?" Kyle asked Maya as steam filled the room.

A pause.

Kyle swung the pipe and hit one panel of the sliding shower door. Maya screamed. The glass crushed but did not shatter.

"Don't you?" Kyle hissed.

"Yes."

"The two of you go back a long way."

"What...what do you mean?"

"You know what I mean. We're a lot alike, you and me. We live double lives that reveal themselves in darkness like this, don't they?"

"I...I guess."

"How do you know Carl Zarki?"

"We're old friends."

Kyle slapped the metal pipe in his hand. "Army Airborne, is that right? I don't remember that on your résumé."

"It wasn't."

"Then how about joint U.S./Israeli operations?"

No response.

"Maya, I don't have to kill you. All I need is your cooperation. The fake drunk in the ANZA lobby on the night of the party last December, who was he?"

"Darryl Goodson."

"A former Army Airborne paratrooper?"

"Yes."

"So while he acted his part you climbed up the outside of the ANZA Building."

No answer.

"You have small bones, Maya. We don't want anything to happen to you. The poor maid would find you in the morning and be sick to her stomach. Answer me. You broke into the ANZA building, didn't you?"

"Yes."

"And when Carl Zarki signed in at security and asked the guard for the previous shift report, he signed your name and then his while the guard wasn't looking, didn't he?"

"I don't know."

Kyle smashed the other glass panel. Maya jumped but didn't scream.

"Of course he did," Kyle said. "The clever man, he was the one who destroyed the evidence bag with the videotape. He assigned William Alt and Jerry Levy to swing shift that night knowing that Levy was impetuous and would be unable to wait for the police when he saw you on the twenty-eighth floor. Why'd you do it? What were you looking for?"

"The Contract of the Century."

"Really? Not Anwahr? And what about Harry? It occurred to me not long ago that he was the only Longstreet staffer hired by you, not by me. How does Harry fit into all of this?"

No response.

"Answer me," Kyle yelled, his voice charged with madness. "I know you leaked sensitive documents to Bruce Janstadt, including the one to ANZA on Longstreet letterhead."

"But written by you," Maya said in the darkness, her eyes adjusting, her mind working through options.

"That's right. Bruce Janstadt will pay for that. So will the others he's with right now."

The steam thickened as Maya asked, "What do you mean, 'they'll pay?'"

"Shut up! I'm asking the questions. Tell me about Baku and the Contract of the Century."

Sires slipped the card key into the door and opened it quietly. He saw her purse and briefcase on the bed, then heard the shower running. He would take her by surprise, like a lion. He stripped off his clothes and tiptoed to the bathroom door.

"I know what you're thinking," Kyle said to Maya. "In martial arts it's best to have your opponent move first, as it shows his weakness and allows you to use his momentum to your advantage. But I have all night and a metal pipe in my hand, and you're wet and naked and in the dark. So tell me about Baku."

The bathroom door suddenly opened and a naked man stood there, silhouetted by bright spokes of light. "Hey. What's going on in here?"

All three people lunged at each other.

THIRTY-FOUR

D own the river. The three rafts pushed away from shore onto the fluid backbone of the Kitvik and began bobbing over vertebral waves. Twelve adventurers accustomed to solid ground now floated in a new dimension, carried by an unbridled current that over the next several days would take them north through the Brooks Range to the Coastal Plain and the 1002 Area.

Burly stood in the first raft to read the riffles ahead. The river occasionally braided into many channels, some too shallow, and these he wanted to avoid. "Back paddle," he commanded as he pulled on the oars. The three paddlers in his raft stroked with uncoordinated enthusiasm, clunking their paddles together and laughing. "You'll improve," Burly said. "At least I hope you do."

They did, slowly.

The miles rolled by, but weren't counted as such. Distance was measured instead by riffles and rapids, bends and bars, a bird here, an animal track there, features common to wild rivers. Under the mid-day sun, the Kitvik was a bright meltwater ribbon fed by glaciers and snowfields. Not especially rough. Most of the time the rafters didn't paddle at all.

Shannon trailed her hand in the water and studied how the river bent her arm. Refraction. She saw in the face of the river her own face, an expression of joy she once thought irretrievable. Reflection. She rested against a pile of gear, looked skyward and watched clouds build. Convection. Everywhere was the interplay of air, water, earth and light. Perfection.

They pulled ashore for lunch, and Lisa spread a checkered tablecloth on the ground.

"Any canyons on this river?" Sam asked.

"Just those formed by aufeis this time of year," Burly replied. "Fifteen-foot-high walls of ice, deep blue, spectacular stuff. The river changes course every hour or so as one channel is dammed by falling ice and another channel forms. We'll portage around it."

"Look!" Jude exclaimed. All eyes turned to where a lone animal trotted upriver along the opposite shore.

"Wolf," Burly said. "Sit still and be quiet."

Head down, ears up, mouth open. Shannon could see the grasping curve of fangs on the lower mandible, the large paws flipping over the sandy shore, the feet and legs of a traveler. It moved with urgency, this gray wolf, bound for the mountains, as perhaps every hunter should be. It stopped only once to assess the twelve strangers and their acrid odors, staring across a thousand years of persecution and myth. The nose wrinkled, the ears twitched. Then it was gone, slipping into the willows as quickly as it had appeared, wolf and time on the move again, unbounded.

Everybody took a breath. "Wow," Jude said, "a real wolf."

Shannon caught a deep smile from Mark.

They covered a fair distance that afternoon and set up camp. The next morning Lisa and Rollie made blueberry pancakes and everybody ate like truckers. Back on the river at noon, Burly sang ribald sea chanteys in his baritone voice, rowing as he did. Soucie joined him with a tenor, and Jude added her soprano. Lisa pulled out a flute and played accompaniment. Later, the rafters grew quiet and watched clear waters carry them over timeless rocks and unfathomed histories. After so many riffles and bends and arcs of the sun, they pulled ashore and pitched camp. At dinner they told stories, some of the best coming from Agent Leighton. Shannon and Burly skipped stones in a contest that ended in a draw, fourteen skips each.

That night, most of the party headed upslope and hiked until three in the morning in primrose light. Sure-footed as a Dall sheep, Shannon could have gone higher but stayed with Mark to show him arctic poppies, Lapland rosebays, yellow cinquefoils, white avens and other flowers. Back in camp, Jude tottered on tired feet but smiled like a child through her fatigue; Sam too, as father and daughter walked with their arms around each other. Bruce said it was the finest wilderness hike he had taken in years. In a private moment Shannon asked Mark which flower he liked best.

"The arctic poppy," he said.

~

Nine miles to the north, William Alt awoke in a willow thicket and checked his watch. Time to set the trap. He, Stephen, Tank and Pyro hiked down to the aufeis, a large plateau of ice more than a hundred yards wide and a quarter mile long. The river entered it in three channels, but only one that was navigable.

The four men stood atop the ice cliff and looked down at the narrow, swift water fifteen feet below. "We'll wait up here on the cliffs, out of view," Stephen said, "then jump into the rafts as they pass below and knock the people into the river. With these ice walls, they'll have no place to escape. They'll be unconscious in three minutes and dead in ten."

"What about knives?" Pyro asked. "Do we cut the rafts?"

"The rafts have at least four separate air compartments," William said. "They're tough to sink."

"Good point," Stephen said. "Knives won't work. The whole thing needs to look like an accident. We'll hit them hard, throw them into the river and let them drown. Send them into that tunnel down there."

Tank pointed. "They might climb out on that tilted slab of ice next to the tunnel entrance."

"They'll be frozen stiff by then and unable to move," Stephen said. "The important thing will be the element of surprise."

"No guns?" Tank asked.

Stephen shook his head. "No guns."

Pyro licked his lips, hungry for the attack.

~

The Crack-of-Noon-Rafting-Club was back on the river for their final full day in the mountains. They floated only five miles and stopped on a broad alluvial terrace between two ridges. Jokes and laughter filled the camp. Burly told limericks to Rollie and Bruce. Senators Soucie and Ulrich walked along the river, unhurried, then sat on the ground and traded stories about their grandchildren. Sam, Jude, Lisa and Agent Leighton played cards and teased each other about cheating. Nelson Romper, the millionaire Californian, found a comfortable rock and planted himself with a book, but rather than read, he looked at the sky and river and land as if drinking a new clarity in his life. Mark sat against a raft and wrote in his notebook, occasionally looking at Shannon.

She watched it all and remembered the words of Norman Maclean in *A River Runs Through It*: "If you don't know the ground, you're probably wrong about everything else."

Nobody saw the lone figure of Tank Wallace two thousand feet up the slope, watching them with binoculars from more than a mile away. He disappeared after an hour, content that the doomed rafters would reach the aufeis on the day Stephen had predicted.

~

Six hundred air miles to the south, Maya opened her eyes. Only one person was in the room with her, a man and a room she did not recognize. "Where am I?" she said hoarsely. "What time is it?"

He came toward her. "Providence Hospital in Anchorage. You've been beaten."

She tried to lift her head but he put his hand on her shoulder. "Don't move. You have a possible concussion."

"I have to get up. I have to go."

"Where? Where do you have to go?"

She searched his face for anything familiar. "Who are you?"

"I'm Special Agent Lincoln Crozier, with the FBI. Can you tell me who did this to you?"

She lifted her head. "I have to go..."

A nurse came into the room followed by an anxious Oliver Longstreet and two aides. "Maya, dear God, what happened?"

"No questions," the nurse said sternly.

Maya's head sank back onto her pillow, her eyes closed.

Longstreet asked Agent Crozier, "Did she tell you anything?"

"No."

"Did she—"

"Gentlemen," the nurse said, "you must leave this room and have your discussion outside."

In the hall, Longstreet breathed in shallow gulps. Somebody had threatened his life. John Sires was in a coma. Alan Quail was apparently dead, and now Maya... "For Christ sake," he said to nobody in particular. "What's going on around here?"

Crozier offered no answers.

Another nurse went into Maya's room, then a doctor who emerged a few minutes later and told Longstreet, "We think she's going to be okay. There's no swelling in the brain, and she's not sleepy. Those are good signs. She's a tough gal, but she'll need plenty of rest and no visitors. Go home, please."

Crozier had already left.

Ten hours later, when she was feeling better and able to sit up, Maya asked the nurse to bring her a phone. It was all she would need to arrange her disappearance.

~

Shannon and Mark hiked upslope, aiming for the ridgetop two thousand feet above. Mark stopped to photograph a flower. An hour later he found her waiting on top with a small wooden box in her hands. The sun had entered its low northward arc over the vast Coastal Plain, now in full view, and it washed her face with ocher light. She took his hand and walked with him to a precipice on the far side of the ridge. From the way she moved he knew she had been up here before. She removed the lid of the box and turned it upside down. A fine stream of ashes drifted on the arctic breeze.

He expected her to say goodbye, or to cry, but she did neither. After a minute she said, "He belongs here."

Mark let the silence grow; there was nothing he could say that the arctic could not say better.

They walked along the ridge to where a delicate fold in the land gave shelter from the breeze. Shannon stopped and removed his daypack, and her own. She pulled him down to his knees, onto the soft tundra, where his head was at her waist.

"Undress me," she said.

He unbuttoned her pants and lifted the tail of her shirt and kissed her firm stomach. She dug her fingers into his hair as he ran his hands up her back, under her arms and onto her breasts. She arched into him as he moved his lips down. "Oh, Mark..."

He was so patient yet commanding and hard; so gentle but bold. He whispered everything she wanted to hear, and when he told her he loved her, she cried and he kissed away her salty tears. How universal were those words—I love you—yet she knew now why they hurt. She had never heard them from her mother. So she gave herself to Mark and rolled him onto his back and mounted him and looked at him and knew then, in the mirror of his eyes, that she was precious.

Afterward, he pulled a bivouac blanket from his daypack and rolled with her inside it to kiss and touch and say nothing. She fell asleep, and when she awoke he was ready and entered her again, slowly, perfectly, taking her down a river of a thousand dreams and desires.

Hours later, they dressed and hiked down the ridge, hand in hand, following its smooth spine to the northwest. They stopped for a snack but took most of their nourishment from each other and the unbroken vista of roadless Coastal Plain. "Not many views like this left in the world," Mark said.

"There's the aufeis," Shannon observed. They could see the Kitvik River fifteen hundred feet below where it flowed north-northeast and made a broad seventy degree turn to the west, then turned north to slice through the aufeis and enter the Coastal Plain.

"Looks like the fog is moving in," Mark said.

Kaktovik was already obscured beneath the great white blanket a thousand feet thick advancing south from the Beaufort Sea over the Coastal Plain, toward the mountains. Shannon pointed to a small drainage valley that ran off the backside of their ridge and joined the Kitvik about five miles downriver. "That's the spot," she said. "That's where I first camped with Dad. I need to do this, Mark. I need to go there." She looked at him with an odd mix of sadness and hope. "I'll meet you and the others this afternoon where the drainage joins the river."

It was their original plan, and had sounded simple and appeared harmless, but now, after making love, it felt excruciating to let her go. Mark knew that Shannon had hiked alone many times and was no fool in the wilderness. She had a compass, map, first-aid kit, water, food, parka and extra clothing in her daypack. "What about the fog?" he asked.

"I'll just stay in the small side valley, see," —she pointed— "it's got low willows in it down where it enters the Kitvik at the aufeis. That's where I'll wait for you and the others, on the aufeis. I need to do this, Mark. Don't ask me why."

He didn't. He already knew. It was part of why he loved her.

They were about to part when Shannon saw something dash into view, then disappear.

"What was that?" Mark asked.

They followed the slope until a fox appeared below, and behind it two more. Shannon knelt to appear less threatening, and Mark emulated her. She was farther downslope and had the better view, and she signaled Mark something he could not understand, her hand off her nose, then flashing a forefinger followed by four other fingers together. The foxes frisked about, turned and bounded out of view.

"What beautiful animals," Shannon said later when she and Mark joined company.

"I saw three," Mark said.

"I saw five. One adult and four kits. The other adult is probably out hunting. They must have a den near here."

"What were you signaling?"

"Oh" —a smile— "it's how Dad and I used to communicate. We had different hand signals for different animals. This" —she formed a cone off her nose— "means fox."

"And the others?"

She made two more signals. "This is adult, this is young."

"Then you raised your fingers to signal how many of each?"

"Exactly."

Mark sat down with a strange heaviness.

"Are you okay?" Shannon asked him.

"I don't know. I just thought of something about your dad."

"What?"

"The hand signals. When I interviewed him I asked him to answer by lifting his finger or blinking his eyes."

"And he blinked his eyes."

"Except on the last question. Remember the last question? 'Do you believe your attempted murder has something to do with

ANZA and the 1002 test drill result?'"

"And he blinked three times."

"And raised his finger three times."

"You think he was signaling that there were three results?"

"Yes. Why else would he signal three times? Look at the parallels. The last word in the question was 'result.' That's what he was trying to tell us. There's more than one result. When the two of you signaled about wildlife you determined the object first, the number second. Foxes, five. Results, three."

Shannon chewed her lip.

"ANZA might have fabricated results," Mark said. "And the ten people who agreed to fabricate them are beginning to die because they're uncomfortable with the secret, and the killers know it."

Fabrications? Would Dad agree to such a thing? Is that why he argued with Mr. Sires? Shannon got to her feet as a bitter flood of uncertainties stirred inside her. "I can't think about this now. I need to go hiking. Just meet me at the aufeis."

"Okay," he said, hurt by her sudden distance. He wanted to say he was sorry for resurrecting old ghosts, but too much had been said already. She moved downslope, heading north.

~

Maya walked out of Providence Hospital at 5:15 A.M. and found Carl Zarki waiting in the parking lot with her change of clothes. An hour and forty-five minutes later she boarded the early-bird Alaska Airlines flight to Fairbanks, and Zarki drove to the Hotel LaPerouse to find Tyler Kyle.

"Be careful," Maya had warned him. "He's crazy."

~

Special Agent Crozier arrived at the hospital at 8:15 A.M. "She's gone?" he asked with disbelief. "What do you mean gone? Where?

When?"

"She was last seen in her room at five o'clock," the nurse said. "She was discovered missing at six."

Crozier followed his intuition and checked the airport. Sure enough, an agent at Alaska Airlines confirmed that a bruised and bandaged Maya Donjek had checked in going to Fairbanks. Her flight had landed forty minutes ago.

"When's the next flight to Fairbanks?" Crozier asked.

~

Shannon followed the drainage downslope as the steep terrain tapered into a moist basin of mosses and equisetum, and thick fog eclipsed the sun. She pulled on her red parka and traced a rivulet of water lined by willows six to eight feet tall. No hurry. She estimated the aufeis at less than two miles away. The rafters would not get there until early afternoon. She stopped to snack, and to watch an upland sandpiper. She heard a twig snap and turned and saw the last thing she expected to see: a man walking toward her.

~

"Any word?" Crozier asked two Alaska State Troopers as he deplaned in Fairbanks.

"She's on her way to Kaktovik with Dowding Flying Service. She left forty-five minutes ago."

"Can we turn the plane around?"

"Not really. It's a Navajo Chieftain, a commuter flight with nine passengers."

"Can we talk to her by radio patch with another aircraft?"

"We tried that already and got nowhere. What's this all about?" The trooper wore his flat hat pulled low over his brow.

"This woman is on her way to Kaktovik. It makes me think it has something to do with the senators on the Kitvik River." Crozier called Dowding Flying Service on his cell phone while the troopers drove him to the other side of the Fairbanks airport. He was still speaking with the manager at Dowding when he walked into his office.

"Hey man," the manager said as he put down the phone to speak with Crozier in person, "I'd like to help you, but I can't turn that plane around. Besides, the fog's so thick in Kaktovik I'm not sure they'll be able to land."

"Then what happens?" Crozier asked.

"They turn around and come back." The manager swiveled in his chair and spit tobacco into a wastebasket.

"What are the odds of that?"

"I dunno, fifty-fifty. This is Alaska, not O'Hare. They fly that plane on instruments and there's good nav aids up there, but if the fog's too thick then the fog's too thick."

"Is anyone else flying there soon?"

"Yeah, Frontier Flying Service this afternoon."

"That's too late. I need to go now."

"Good luck." He rolled his chew with his tongue.

"You got another plane?"

"Yeah, a Chieftain. You'd have to charter it."

"What about a pilot?"

The manager slid open his office window and yelled into the hangar, "Hey Scratch, you got time to charter this FBI guy to Kaktovik?"

A short, greasy man stuck his head out from under a plane engine and asked, "When does he need to go?"

"Now," Crozier said.

~

He came out of the fog like an apparition, a big man with short hair and an ugly nose, walking a city walk. "Hullo," he said.

Shannon stood and glanced around, guarded.

He said his name was Kip or Kit or something like that. Would she like some hot coffee? Before she could answer, another man appeared and said, "Shannon, darling, what a nice coincidence. We're just having breakfast." Stephen York. Rasputin Eyes.

Kip circled behind her.

Shannon furtively looked for options, escapes, anything.

"Who'd have thought we'd run into each other up here?" Stephen said. "Old friends like us—what a small world. Come join us."

"No thanks. I have to be going."

"Don't be rude," Stephen said.

"What are you doing here?" Shannon asked him.

"Gravimetric tests, seismic anomalies. We've been very busy."

She stared at him and he mocked her and said, "You don't believe me? Tsk, tsk, where are your manners?"

She regretted leaving Mark in her lack of tenderness. Would she ever see him again?

Kip shadowed her—she could feel his ominous eyes—as she followed Stephen reluctantly. Then she saw camouflaged sleeping bags in the willows; no kitchen or formal camp, just a small stove set on the tundra with a pot of boiling water that Stephen poured through a filter of coffee grounds.

He served her a cup and said, "Take your pack off and relax."

"No thanks."

"Sit down then."

"No thanks, I'm fine."

"I said sit down. That means, sit down."

She obeyed.

Kip, alias Tank, breathed down her back and asked, "How's the neck?"

A third man emerged from the willows wearing a dirty coat. Pyro, the shrew from the attack in Mark's apartment. Shannon's heart raced. She saw two serrated knives on the ground, and four full-immersion dry suits and metal pipes. *Gravimetric tests my ass.*

Pyro walked toward her with a sardonic twist on his mouth. "Well, well, what have we here?"

"An honored guest," Stephen said.

The three men surrounded her, Tank behind, Pyro to one side, Stephen in front. She set her coffee on the ground. "Too hot?" Stephen asked.

"A little."

A fourth man appeared from the willows. Shannon recognized him as the ANZA security guard from the night of the party. She could tell he was surprised to see her, but in a way different from the others. She picked up her coffee two-handed, at the same time discreetly grabbing a good skipping stone. Tank touched her hair, and she yanked her head away.

"Shannon darling," Stephen said, "your hand's shaking. Don't spill your coffee."

"You killed my father, didn't you?"

"Yes, I'll take credit for that, and for killing your brother too."

"Why?"

He shrugged. "What are you going to do with that rock in your hand?"

"Hit you in the head."

Pyro laughed, but he stopped the instant Shannon threw the hot coffee over her shoulder and hit Tank in the face. Tank screamed as she jumped to her feet and faked a sidearm throw at Stephen. He ducked, now off balance. She threw the rock and hit him hard on the head.

She ran.

"Get her," Stephen yelled as he picked himself up from the ground. "Get her, goddammit."

She ran toward the aufeis and could hear them coming after her. She ran and ran, leaping boulders and cutbanks, and still they followed. A golden plover flew from her path and she envied its flight. She reached the Kitvik and the aufeis and looked back through the fog that made everything surreal. The river rumbled through the ice. She saw two men forty yards away, ghost-like, moving with less agility but equal determination. A third man cleverly angled to cut her off upriver, the direction she wanted to go. The fourth man approached from downriver; he had also circled around. Her only escape was across the aufeis.

She ran with lactic acid burning in her thighs. She jumped a narrow channel, landed and rolled and was back on her feet in seconds. She turned upriver where the thickness of the ice tapered down to a gravel bar. Here she discovered she was on an island, with a large channel blocking her escape and Tank coming at her fast. She faked one way and sent him stumbling into the river.

She picked up a handful of rocks as the other men closed, twenty yards away with the river to her back. She threw one and hit Tank in the chest as he climbed out of the river. Another rock hit him in the ear. She threw at Pyro and missed; threw another and caught him on the chin. Tank grabbed her from behind, but she kicked free and plunged into the river. "You bitch."

Tank grabbed her by the hair and pulled her to shore where Stephen hit her on the head with a large rock. They dragged her across the gravel and onto the aufeis. She bled from her scalp. Stephen slapped her across the face and she looked at him with defiance and he slapped her again.

"Let's fuck her," Pyro said, rubbing the welt on his chin.

"Later," Stephen snapped.

It took them an hour to get her back to their camp. Stephen threw her to the ground and pulled out a large roll of duct tape and bound her wrists behind her back. He crossed her ankles, taped them together, bent her knees, arched her back and taped her wrists to her ankles like a poached animal. He finished with several wraps around her chest and upper arms, and one over her mouth.

She winced with pain and shivered with cold.

Stephen admired his work and said, "Duct tape, there is no substitute."

THIRTY-FIVE

Eddie Tagarook had met many unusual women in his life, but none like this. Bruises all over her face, one eye swollen shut, the other burning with fierce resolve. She said her name was Maya. Stranger still, she was a lobbyist for ANZA. And best of all, she wanted his plane. She had landed in Kaktovik thirty minutes ago on the Dowding flight—the fog had thinned just enough—and now stood before Eddie with her arms akimbo as he tinkered with his Cessna.

"I remember you from the Wilderness bill hearing in Washington," she said. "You're Shannon DeShay's friend."

"Sure am." Eddie wiped engine oil on his pants.

"If you want to save her life you'll help me." She said the rafting party was in danger, and every hour was critical. "If somebody wanted to kill them on the Kitvik River and make it look like an accident, where would be the best place?"

"The overflow."

"The aufeis?"

"Yep, same thing. Overflow ice along the river."

"I agree," a freckle-faced pilot said from across the hangar. "I

301

flew those senators up there five days ago and saw it. It's huge. Big cliffs of ice."

"Did you see any other camps?" Maya asked him.

"On the Kitvik? Nope. There's one float trip on the Jago and two on the Hulahula, and some geologists in the Sadlerochits. That's about it. Nothin' real close."

"When will the Kitvik rafters get to the aufeis?" Maya asked.

"Geez, I dunno." Freckle Face removed his ball cap and scratched his head. "Probably sometime today, I reckon."

Eddie agreed.

"I've got to get there now," this Maya-woman said.

Freckle Face chuckled. "Hey lady, nobody's flying VFR today until this fog burns off."

"When will that be?"

"Hard to say. Could last all day. Besides, we can't just land wherever we want along the Kitvik. It's rough country. There's only a few spots to put down on tundra tires. You might be able to get a 'copter outta Prudhoe."

Maya had called there already. Helicopters were unavailable. She needed to go now. "Have I made myself clear? These people could get killed."

"We could take off in this fog and get above it," Eddie said with a glimmer in his eye, "but we couldn't land."

"We don't need to," Maya said. "All I need is a parachute."

"A parachute?"

"Yes, a parachute. You got any?"

"Yeah, maybe sure," Eddie said. "I think there's some military ones over at the DEW station."

"So whaddya gonna do?" Freckle Face asked Maya. "Jump outta Eddie's plane?"

"Exactly."

"You look beat up already."

"There's another problem," Eddie said. "I've been grounded by the FAA."

"Screw the FAA," Maya said.

Freckle Face laughed. "Yeah Eddie, screw the FAA. It's only your future."

The second Dowding Air Service Navajo Chieftain landed as Eddie finished fueling the Cessna, and Maya sat in the co-pilot seat with the parachute at her feet. Crozier bounded from the Chieftain and ran toward her. She was plainly visible, as Eddie had removed the door on her side of the plane.

"What's going on here?" Crozier asked, winded from the run.

Maya, Eddie and Freckle Face looked at him but didn't speak.

He flashed his badge. "Special Agent Lincoln Crozier, FBI. I want to know what's going on."

Two Alaska State Troopers jogged up behind him from the Chieftain and everybody looked at Maya. "The senators are going to be attacked on the Kitvik River," she said, "probably today in the aufeis. I need to warn them before it's too late."

"We've got a Fish and Game helicopter that could be here in three hours," a trooper said.

"No good," Maya responded. "Let's go, Eddie."

"Wait," Crozier said. "How do you know this?"

"Let's go, Eddie," she repeated.

"Prop," Eddie yelled as everybody stepped back. The plane sputtered and roared to life.

The propwash blew Crozier's hair straight back. "Get out of this plane," he yelled at her, "or I'll detain you."

"On what charge?" she yelled back with fire in her eyes.

"I need to talk with you."

"Get lost."

"This isn't your own private little war."

"Yes it is!"

"Why? What is it you know?"

Maya shook her head, mocking that she couldn't hear him as the engine roared louder. The plane rolled forward and Crozier jogged alongside it, holding onto the wing strut and the open doorframe. "Stop this plane. I need to know what's going on."

Maya motioned Eddie to take off. Eddie cleared all systems go as the Cessna accelerated.

"Do you think you're Superwoman?" Crozier screamed at Maya at a full run. "Are you going to jump out of this plane?"

Maya nodded.

"Dammit, I'm on your side. I can help you."

"Then get in."

He made a desperate leap and pulled himself inside as the Cessna zoomed down the runway and lifted into the arctic sky.

~

"Grab her parka and hat," Stephen said. "We'll need them."

They would be valuable decoys as Shannon's friends came looking for her, rafting to their deaths. Dressed in dry suits and carrying metal pipes, the four men regarded her for a final time. Pyro ran his hands up her thighs and said, "I'm looking forward to our date."

Tank laughed.

"Let's go," Stephen commanded.

William avoided eye contact and departed with the others, leaving her to shiver on the ground.

~

The little Cessna spiraled up and up until it broke above the fog in full sunshine at twelve hundred feet. Eddie banked south toward the Brooks Range. "See those two peaks?" He pointed ahead. "The Kitvik runs between them."

The wind howled through the plane's open door and blasted Crozier in the back. Eddie handed Maya and Crozier each a set of headphones.

"Have you got a gun?" Crozier asked Maya.

Yes. Eddie had given her one, and a VHF radio. She would call as soon as she landed.

"Helicopters are on their way," Crozier said. "They'll be on the Kitvik soon."

"Not if the fog stays like this," Eddie said. "It's stacked up against the foothills." The farther inland they flew, the thicker it became. The plane climbed.

"You've done this sort of thing before?" Crozier asked Maya. "Jump out of airplanes?"

"A little."

"A little?"

Maya shook her head.

"Look, if those people down there are in danger, I want to save them as much as you do."

She stared at him and said, "You forgot your parachute."

~

"Is that a plane?" Stephen asked as he tilted his head to the fog-shrouded sky, straining to hear over the rumbling river.

Tank and Pyro listened but heard nothing. William shook his head and found Stephen staring at him with inquisitional eyes, his face etched with guarded trust.

They inspected the river and found that an icefall had occluded a small channel and redirected its course. But the major channel still flowed strong as it curved into a deepening ice-walled chasm that turned a corner and entered a tunnel that appeared to run for about an eighth of a mile. Anybody sucked into that tunnel would surely die. Stephen gave Shannon's red parka and wool hat to Pyro, and positioned him upriver. He then walked the main channel to replay the attack in his mind. It would happen with madness and genius, as swift as the river—swifter.

~

The rafters slipped into the netherworld of the arctic fog, surprised by its thickness and chill. Mark regretted letting Shannon hike alone. So did Agent Leighton.

The three rafts closed ranks and approached the aufeis, less than a mile ahead. Burly sang another ribald chantey that received good laughs amid the restless riffling river, all too loud for anybody to hear the Cessna high above.

"You know," Jude said reflectively, "I think this trip is the most amazing thing I've ever done in my life."

~

Eddie flew upriver to where the fog dissipated and they could see the Kitvik below.

"There it is." He banked the plane to look down. "I don't see the rafters. I've tried hailing them on VHF. They must not have their radio on. Makes me think they're not in trouble."

"Or they're already dead," Maya said. "Where's the aufeis?"

"Downriver about three miles, in the fog." Eddie turned and headed for it. Maya told him to climb to five thousand feet.

"I hope we're not too late," Crozier said.

"You've been too late for six years," Maya replied as she fastened herself into the parachute harness.

Crozier grabbed her shoulder. "What's that supposed to mean?"

No reply. She pulled on an old pair of Army issue goggles.

"John Sires is in a coma," Crozier said. "Do you know that?" She paused.

"Who beat you? I have to know—"

"No," Maya screamed, turning on him. "You can't help me because you can't promise me that the people I love won't be hurt."

"You mean the murders made to look like accidents?"
She looked away.

"Here we are," Eddie announced. "The aufeis should be right below in forty seconds. Be careful, there's big cliffs just east of the river." He throttled down and nodded to her.

Maya removed her headphones and crawled out onto the wing strut. The wind shrieked and slapped against her pant legs.

Crozier screamed at her, "You don't have to do this."

"Yes I do."

"Why?"

She looked at him, and for the first time he saw fear in her eyes.

"Don't jump. Tell me what you know about ANZA. I need you here."

"They need me down there."

"Why? Why are you doing this?"

"They killed my father," she said, and she let go.

~

Bound and gagged, Shannon shimmied across the tundra toward a rocky outcrop. She guessed the rock was schist, a metamorphic laminate with layers of micaceous minerals, flaky but sharp. Sharp enough to cut duct tape, she hoped. She was wet and cold and lightly hypothermic, yet filled with determination, breathing hard through her nose and wincing with pain as she reached the outcrop. She rotated onto her side, put her back to a knife-edged fin of the schist and began to rub. The tape was so tight she could not feel her hands. After ten minutes the tape binding her wrists to her ankles snapped. She sat up and felt a bolt of pain through her back. She rubbed again, this time between her wrists, careful not to cut her radial artery. She freed her hands in another ten minutes, then ripped the tape off her mouth.

Adrenalin surged through her as she freed her ankles and arms. She stood up to run but fell on cold, stiff legs. Up again, she wobbled, unable to feel her numb feet. Slowly, painfully, the sensations returned. *Go, go, go,* she told herself as she began to run toward the aufeis.

~

The rafters pulled ashore at the entrance to the aufeis so Burly could reconnoiter the safest channel. "This might require some portaging," he said. "There could be tunnels ahead."

"Where's Shannon?" Mark asked. "She should be here."

"There she is," Jude said excitedly.

They saw her waving through the fog in her red parka, about two hundred yards downriver on the aufeis.

Bruce Janstadt and Nelson Romper waved back.

"I wonder why she's way down there?" Mark pondered aloud.

"She's waving us down," Jude said.

Shannon knew rivers and aufeis as well as anybody, and they could see her waving them down. "It must be a good channel," Burly said. "Let's go."

"Wait a minute," Ben Leighton said, "hand me those binoculars." He stood in the raft and glassed downriver as Shannon appeared to sit down, then stand up and wave again. The fog was too thick to make a positive identification, but who else could it be? "Okay," Ben said.

One at a time the three rafts pushed into the channel and quickly gathered speed. Jude stood to wave at Shannon, but lost sight of her as the rafts entered the deepening ice chasm. Everybody fell silent amid the blue canyon walls and stratigraphy of ice, the dynamics of water, the feeling of being swallowed like Jonah in the whale. The five senators—Janstadt, Matlin, Romper, Soucie and Ulrich—craned their necks like children in a fantasia. From his perch on the ice cliff up ahead, Stephen saw them as chickens to the slaughter.

"This is incredible," Jude said.

Indeed. But Burly, Lisa, Rollie and Ben immediately sensed they had made a mistake. There was no place to make safe landfall, no escape. As the river turned a blind corner, Ben Leighton reached into his vest, activated an ELT—an emergency location transmitter—and pulled out a .40 caliber SIG-Sauer.

THIRTY-SIX

D*rink the wind, Shannon. Run hard at those men and use their best weapon against them: surprise them. Give them no warning.*

She heard her father's voice as if in a dream, speaking from everywhere and nowhere, urgent against her own ragged breathing. She found herself strangely detached, thinking about madness, about Shakespeare's lunatic, lover and poet, how madness when explained dissolves away so much mystery, how madmen think the rest of the world is crazy, how some say *that not to be mad is a greater form of madness.* Her head pounded with sickness and rage. At one point she tripped and hit the ground and was back on her feet in an instant, running, running, unaware of her own wounds. *Are we all born mad and only a few remain so?* She heard her labored gasps as she ran over the tundra toward the aufeis. She stopped only once to pick up rocks, not simple skipping stones but hefty, egg-sized rocks to crack a man's skull. *Madness.*

She plunged through the fog and over the aufeis, her entire being propelled by the inertia of fear. She saw the four men through the white veil, crouched atop the ice cliff, facing away from her, each roughly fifty feet from the next, each with a metal pipe in his hand and a wool mask pulled over his head, waiting to jump, unaware of her approach. She knew in that moment that she did not want to stop them, she wanted to *kill* them. And in that wanting she knew that a part of her own self must die, perhaps the best part. *It's in each of us, this wanting to kill, even just a little, is it not?* She received no answer from Heaven or Hell as she ran toward the man who was farthest upriver, the one who wore her parka and would be the first to attack the rafters.

Twenty feet behind him and at full speed, she heard a voice yell. The man turned and raised his pipe—too late. Shannon struck him hard, feet first, flying—the owl hits the shrew. Pyro fell backward onto the aufeis. His momentum carried him over the cliff and into the river below. He flailed his arms in the consuming current, trying to grab the icy walls that offered no purchase.

Stephen charged her. She threw a rock and missed. Threw another that he cleverly ducked. But the third caught him in the mouth and he fell.

The first raft rounded the bend and Shannon waved from the ice cliff. "Get away. Get away."

Tank ran toward the raft and threw himself off the ice cliff, screaming like Johnny Reb. Ben Leighton fired his SIG-Sauer and put one bullet through Tank's hand and another through his shoulder. Tank landed hard on the FBI man and snapped his collarbone. He fell back and knocked Jude into the river. Burly swung at Tank with an oar but Tank shielded the blow and struck back hard with his metal pipe. Burly collapsed. Sam Matlin cracked a paddle over Tank's head and the wounded man staggered. Ben pushed him overboard.

The raft bounced along the ice wall beneath Shannon. She jumped and felt her heart fly into her throat, cold air rushing past her ears. Sam grabbed her. "Where's Jude?" he said as he looked about. "Oh God, where's my girl?"

Shannon saw Stephen crouched atop the ice cliff, bleeding from the mouth, waiting to pounce on a raft. Ben Leighton searched for his weapon but could not find it; it must have fallen into the river when Tank landed on him. He grabbed Burly's shotgun but was too late as Stephen jumped into the third raft and hit Rollie with a metal pipe.

"Where's Jude?" Sam yelled again at Shannon. "Who are these guys?"

"I don't know," Shannon yelled back as she pulled on the oars with all her might, trying to slow their progress downriver. They rounded a second bend and heard the river thundering into the ice tunnel, the top of the tunnel only a couple feet higher than the water.

"Highside," Shannon yelled. She, Sam and Ben lunged toward the high side of the raft as it sloshed up against the tunnel entrance. Water quickly flooded the low side, sweeping away gear and paddles and anything loose. The raft rotated ninety degrees and they scrambled out onto the shallow ice slope next to the tunnel. Ben grabbed Burly with his one good arm and pulled him onto the slope while the river roared in protest, trying to suck the raft into the tunnel.

Nelson Romper floated by with terror on his face, holding out a hand, too cold to speak, too far to reach. Shannon looked into his eyes and knew she would never forget them. She grabbed a coiled polypropylene line to throw to him, but the current accelerated and pulled him into the tunnel. She unclipped from the raft an emergency drybag full of clothes and a first-aid kit. "We've got to get up this ice slope, all of us."

Just then the second raft rammed into the first and sheared over its low side. Lisa, Soucie and Ulrich scrambled from the second raft into the first, now partially submerged, and onto the ice slope with the others. "What the hell's going on?" Ulrich demanded.

"Where's Jude?" Sam yelled. "I have to find Jude."

Everything was happening too fast. Lisa cried as she pulled Burly up the ice slope, his head bleeding.

The third raft rounded the bend in mid-river with Stephen standing in it alone, triumphant, having thrown everybody out save Rollie, who appeared either unconscious or dead. Ben aimed the shotgun at him but Stephen dived into the river as he fired. The recoil knocked Ben off his feet and he hit his head hard on the ice slope. His eyes fluttered shut from the impact. The shotgun slipped into the river, and Ben nearly did too, but a powerful hand reached down and grabbed him. The hand of William Alt. Shannon turned to look at him and saw those same tragic eyes from the night of the ANZA party, the flat mouth, the weightlifter's frame. He had not attacked, but had instead run atop the ice cliff downriver to where it joined this slope and the tunnel.

William said nothing as he lifted Ben and carried him up the slope to the top of the aufeis plateau. He returned to help Lisa carry Burly as the third raft rammed into the second and pushed it farther over the first.

Where's Mark? Shannon scanned the river and to her horror found him in the angry current, one arm holding onto Bruce Janstadt, the other arm stroking against swift water that carried him along the far side of the ice chasm toward the tunnel, a doomed course.

She ran across the top of the tunnel and threw the coiled line, a perfect throw.

Mark grabbed it.

William joined her. Each wrapped the line over a shoulder and down the second arm, holding tight with both hands. The line snapped taut as the river's vortex sucked Mark and Bruce into the tunnel. Shannon inched back across the aufeis and suddenly felt the line slacken. Her heart sank; she was certain Mark was gone, lost forever. But when she stepped to the lip of the tunnel and looked down, she saw him pulling Bruce past the rafts and onto the ice slope. A wave of relief flooded through her.

She and Mark pulled Bruce up the slope to the top of the aufeis while William sat apart from the others and everybody watched him, too stunned and cold and afraid to say or do anything. Lisa helped Burly sit up as he cradled his head between his knees. Sam called for Jude in a hoarse voice. Shivering, Mark stripped off his wet polar fleece jacket and turtleneck shirt and dug into the drybag for a change.

Shannon checked Bruce's vitals and found no breathing and no pulse. He looked more like a cadaver than a living human being. She began cardio-pulmonary resuscitation, and was shocked by the ice-cold touch of his face to her lips. Her mind flashed back to the day she intercepted him in the Rayburn Building and pitched the idea of this rafting trip, how his eyebrows twitched with excitement then. A wave of remorse washed over her to see him like this. She breathed into him with great determination, intermittently pumping his chest to restart his heart. "One one-thousand, two one-thousand, three one-thousand..." Save for her voice and the resentful river, a strange stillness settled over everyone.

At one point William looked about and Soucie asked, "Who the hell are you?"

No answer. And nobody approached him.

"Three one-thousand, four one-thousand, five one-thousand..."

"You're wasting your time," a man said as he appeared from behind and towered over Shannon. "Throw the liberal into the river."

Stephen. Shannon recognized his voice but didn't stop her CPR or look into his eyes. She had seen too much of them already. *Where had he come from? How had he survived?*

"I said, throw him into the river." Stephen reached down to grab her.

"Hold it."

Stephen turned to look at William, who pointed a small pistol at him.

"We both know what needs to be done here, my friend," Stephen said.

"Back off and sit down," William said. He motioned Stephen away.

"You're making a mistake," Stephen said.

"I've made them before. Now, back off."

Stephen backed away two steps.

"Eight one-thousand, nine one-thousand..."

Bruce convulsed and Shannon rolled him onto his side as he coughed up river water, gasping and coughing more. "You're okay, Bruce," Soucie told him. "You're going to be okay."

"No, he's not," Stephen said. He glared at William, who glared back.

William thought of the man with the soft voice on the phone, all the motives and perfection and philosophy that now seemed absurd, the idea that he could shoot people like horses. "Did you kill her brother?" William asked Stephen, motioning toward Shannon.

Stephen shook his head and took a small step forward. "Give me the gun."

"Stay where you are. Did you kill her brother?"

Stephen smiled with Jekyll and Hyde caprice. "Hey, I've never met her brother."

"He killed him," Shannon said. "My father too, and probably lots of other innocent people. The FBI's looking for him." She felt the welt on her face where Stephen had slapped her.

Stephen took a small step toward William.

"Come any closer and I'll put a bullet through your chest." William's voice had an edge now, an anger. "Travis DeShay helped me in school when nobody else would, and you killed him and now you want to kill his sister? What's wrong with you?"

"I'm a warrior, so are you." Stephen took another small step, his hands out, palms up. A prayer. A deceit.

"Hold it, man. I'll shoot you. I really will."

Something caught William's peripheral vision, a phantom caribou, one large bull moving along the edge of the fog with regal grace. Everybody turned while Stephen watched only William. Another bull followed, and another, until dozens emerged from the fog, bulls, cows and calves, an arctic procession as old as the mountains, moving as if in a dream, a Kipling fantasy. They came nearer onto the aufeis plateau, some within thirty feet of the bedraggled, motionless rafters. They walked over the top of the tunnel, their hooves clicking, their antlers in early velvet. Stephen took a step toward William and a nearby bull stopped to regard him, suddenly aware yet oddly serene. Stephen took another step and the caribou snorted. Stephen lunged. William fired a single shot. The caribou froze for an instant, a freeze frame, then stampeded, their hooves like thunder on the aufeis. Antlers and legs everywhere.

"Get away," Shannon yelled.

The tunnel collapsed as Mark grabbed Ben and began pulling him toward the distant edge of the aufeis where it tapered onto a gravel bar and soft tundra. Shannon helped Bruce to his feet. Lisa helped Burly. Mark shouted to Shannon, "What about Rollie? He's in the third raft."

Just then William appeared. He picked up Ben with tremendous strength and said, "I'll carry this guy to safety. Go back and get the other guy."

Shannon regarded him carefully. *You knew my brother?*

"Go," William yelled.

Shannon and Mark ran back to the collapsed tunnel where the river, dammed with ice, was a lake of rising water swirled with a thousand pieces of ice and one frantic caribou swimming in circles. "There," Mark said. He pointed to a raft moving away from them, with Rollie still in it, unconscious. They reached the ice slope, now only half as long as before above the rising water.

Stephen lay where William had shot him, face down in a pool of blue ice water and blood.

Mark ran down the slope and jumped into the second raft. He grabbed the oars and began to row toward Rollie, grimacing with pain from the two-month old gunshot wound to his lower back. "Be ready with the line in case the dam breaks," he yelled to Shannon.

She found it and coiled it. The ice dam groaned as it weakened against the rising water. Mark reached Rollie's raft, jumped into it and began rowing back toward Shannon. Something moved behind her and she jumped. "I've come to help," said Senator Soucie, his chin swollen and his lip cut.

Shannon thought, *And I assumed senators would be helpless in the wilderness. Shame on me.*

Mark rowed with every muscle yet seemed to take forever to return to the ice slope, now only five vertical feet above the water, not fifteen as before. A minute later Shannon and Soucie helped him drag Rollie up the slope. They reached the top just as the dam broke and the river, tired of being a lake, converted into a torrent more powerful and angry than before, sweeping three rafts down the gauntlet. "Hurry," Shannon yelled.

Mark and Soucie each had Rollie by an arm, dragging him across the aufeis, facing forward. Shannon tried to pick up Rollie's feet, but she tripped on the coiled line. Neither Mark nor Soucie heard her fall. She scrambled to her feet but a vise grabbed her— Stephen's hand locked around her ankle. He grinned with blood on his chin, still lying on the ice.

Shannon cried out, but the roar of the river drowned her voice. She kicked at him with her other foot, and slipped and fell. Stephen grabbed her knee and said, "It's you and me, Shannon."

The ice cracked beneath them and tilted steeply into the river. Stephen slipped into oblivion, taking her with him, his hand fastened to her ankle as the river pulled him under, still holding on to her, still grinning. *Rasputin, the crazy zealot.* She looked desperately up the ice slope just as Mark appeared.

"The line," he yelled.

She threw the coiled end and held onto the other as the river swallowed her. She went under, holding her breath, the line, every hope she wished to give and receive if only she could live another day, another moment.

You were named for a river, Shannon. Rivers endure.

The cold water thrashed her and paralyzed her but she did not let go. She kicked and pulled, hand over hand. She surfaced and gasped and saw Mark at the other end, his blue eyes never leaving her. He pulled her onto the ice slope and she looked down at her feet.

Stephen was gone.

He had been right. Nobody survived the tunnel.

Stephen was found with the other dead—Pyro, Tank, Nelson Romper and Jude—washed onto a gravel bar a quarter mile downriver. Sam sat there and held his lifeless daughter in his arms and softly cried. How hard and unmerciful the river seemed to Shannon then; she hated it, and she hated herself for hating it.

Soucie and William, the driest of the survivors, retrieved a stove and more dry clothing and kept the others alive by pouring hot drinks down them. The fog never lifted that day, but it thinned enough for the helicopters to arrive by following Ben Leighton's ELT signal. Lincoln Crozier arrested William and read him his rights. Alaska State Troopers mounted a search for Maya and found her half a mile away on a talus slope. The parachute had only partially deployed. She had landed hard and broken her neck. Inside her shirt they found a letter addressed to John Sires, the acting CEO of ANZA, telling him his game was over. It was dated three days earlier and signed Jumar.

Fall

September

THIRTY-SEVEN

Shatterproof glass and a history of deception separated them. Darryl Goodson picked up his phone; William Alt his.

"Can we talk?" Goodson asked, settling into his chair.

William stared at him with narrow, untrusting eyes. He wiped his nose on the orange collar of his inmate shirt and said, "I have nothing to say to you, nothing I want to hear from you."

In a casual sweater and slacks, Goodson looked nothing like the drunk and destitute war vet he played the night of the ANZA party. "The FBI wants your plea bargain," he told William.

"Yeah, I know."

"They asked me to do this. We talk right here, right now. I tell you my story and you tell me yours. They hear both and we each get a reduced sentence. You'll be out before you're fifty."

Fifty sounded ancient. "I was set up."

"Yep, you were."

"So what can you tell me? I know the FBI is listening on the other side of that dark glass."

Goodson told his story.

"So it was a woman who broke into the building?" William

shook his head slowly. "And this Maya, and Captain Zarki, and this Harry Arnold guy, you all knew each other?"

Goodson nodded. "Have you heard of the Mossad?"

"The Israeli Secret Service? That's you guys?"

"That was Maya's father. Years ago he worked undercover as a chef for a royal family in Tehran, and discovered a covert deal between Iran, Azerbaijan and ANZA to help finance Iran's war with Iraq. In return ANZA got the Contract of the Century."

"The thing in Baku?"

"That's right. Azerbaijan is full of Muslims who want to overthrow Saddam Hussein. They cut the deal so ANZA would get the oil, and Azeri Muslims would get revenge—Muslims are big on revenge—and Iran would get a piece of the pipeline from the Caspian to the Mediterranean."

William digested this and asked, "So this Maya, she wasn't even after Anwahr stuff that night? She wanted Baku stuff?"

"She wanted both, but we didn't know that. Turns out that her dad and Shannon DeShay's dad had contacted each other and planned to go to the feds with what they knew about ANZA. They wanted to cut a deal with the Justice and State departments for family protection."

"Her dad was the guy who died in the car accident with Travis?"

"Yep, Richard Leavitt, that was his alias. Harry Arnold was Special Forces with the rest of us. He offered false testimony to Parkendale to make Jeff Meola look like the intruder. He even put something in Jeff's dinner that night, before the party, so he'd be in the bathroom half the night and look more suspicious."

"So ANZA's in deep shit?"

"You could say that. Their stock is way down. It's been in the papers."

"I don't read the papers."

"No, I guess you don't. So what can you tell me about the man on the phone who gave you instructions and sent you money?"

On the other side of the glass, seated next to Lincoln Crozier, Shannon listened. Crozier expected her to tighten with each revelation, but she did not. Nothing seemed to alarm her anymore. Not that she had habituated herself to guile, or grown a callus on her heart, or found reason itself unreasonable. She merely accepted the fact that most things won in innocence were lost in experience. Her mother blamed her for Jude's death—she had a special gift for assigning blame—and still refused to believe that Charles and Travis had been murdered.

Crozier turned back and refocused on the two men.

"So where's Captain Zarki?" William asked Goodson.

Goodson shook his head. "Nobody knows."

~

Tyler Kyle knew. Carl Zarki was in a burlap bag at the bottom of the Susitna River.

He underestimated me; arrived at my room that morning flushed with revenge but no cunning. I played by different rules and turned his own momentum on himself. 'You have no honor,' he said to me as he died. 'And you, military man, have no imagination.'

The Ninth Symphony ended, and Winniemae's Maryland farmhouse filled with *Für Elise*, a single piano in A minor, aching for the unattainable, as Beethoven had for the young woman, Elise, a music student for whom he wrote the piece. Kyle turned it off and paced the wooden floor for the thousandth time. He remembered the vicious moments, madly swinging the metal pipe at Maya and Sires, hitting them hard but taking a few cuts himself. An odd thought had come to him then. The Third Body Rule in chaos theory states that the orbits of two bodies, each influencing the other with known masses and speeds, can be predicted far into the future. But add a third body—in this case, John Sires—and soon all three enter disorder and unpredictability. Afterward, the phone rang and somebody knocked at the door, and Kyle too quickly assumed that Maya and Sires were dead. Haste and worry plagued him as he tried to staunch his own flow of blood. No matter how well he cleaned the crime scene, he knew forensics would find something. *The Locard Exchange Principle.* The Anchorage Police interviewed him that next morning; they talked with everyone who attended the petroleum summit. Kyle was courteous, and alarmed to hear later that Maya was alive. Then came Carl Zarki the next morning, compounded chaos and another crime scene, this one in Kyle's own room in the Hotel LaPerouse. *If Maya told Zarki I attacked her, who else had she told?*

The only life left for Kyle after that was one of exile and reinvention.

He dumped Zarki's body and drove south to Seward, where he hopped a fishing boat to Kodiak, and two weeks later another boat to Puget Sound. From there, avoiding all boundaries, airports, cameras and security system, he traveled by Greyhound to eastern Maryland where he rested and waited at Aunt Winniemae's. She brought him hot meals at the kitchen table and stood beside him and ran her arthritic fingers through his hair. He put his head against her hip and she said, "You're all alone in this now, aren't you?"

"Yes."

"Those senators in Alaska, the attack, you did that?"

"Yes. Do you think I'm evil?"

"Dear God, no, child." She knelt before him. "I think you're beautiful, you know why? Because you were born to do what you have to do, and you're doing it. You've been chosen."

He asked about his mother, and Winniemae spoke of her sister with great affection. "You're a lot like her," she said, "especially as you get older."

Kyle nodded; he somehow already knew this. "What about my brother, was he like her too?"

"No, he was like your father. He was the evil one, in a way, now that I think about it. But still" —she shook her head— "what a tragedy that he fell off that cliff."

Kyle lost his appetite after that.

Later in his room he assembled a plastic barrel, grip, clip and firing pin. Nonmetal bullets remained a problem that would require shopping on the Internet. He reset Beethoven's Ninth Symphony, written when the composer was deaf, and told himself again and again that nothing is impossible. Winniemae brought him a glass of milk and a plate of cookies—fresh-baked oatmeal, his favorite—as he opened his laptop and scanned the world.

~

The flight from England to Ascension Island in the mid-Atlantic took ten hours. Merlin deplaned there and boarded a freighter to Tristan de Cunha, one of the most remote islands in the world, where Alan Quail met him several days later. They had not seen each other in ten years, yet Merlin looked no different, his large head askew on rounded shoulders, his torso like an uncooked biscuit on a cold skillet.

Alan by contrast looked years younger.

Merlin stayed one week and ate more food than Alan and Alexis did in a month. He sprawled across the sofa, spoke loudly and managed to insult every servant in the house. Alexis tried to avoid him, which was impossible. Not until their last night together, after Alexis had gone to bed, did the two men stay up late, drinking brandy and talking. "A potato farm on an island in the middle of nowhere," Merlin said with a laugh. "That's pretty damn funny, Alan."

Quail just looked at him.

"John Sires died, you heard that?" Merlin said.

"Yes."

"Well hell, at least he didn't have to live through being the ANZA scapegoat. Your board is disavowing the Baku deal and the Anwahr fabrications, you know?"

"I don't care."

Merlin snorted. "Sure you do."

"So what went wrong?" Quail asked.

"My man on Capitol Hill operated independent of my orders. He lost his head."

"Who was he?"

"You know I can't tell you that."

Quail looked away. "I never asked you to do it. I never asked you to do any of it."

"Not in so many words you didn't, but you asked me in your own special way."

"I said I had a problem."

"Charles DeShay, and we took care of him."

"I thought every man had his price."

"DeShay was a fool."

"John threatened to fire him. He even helicoptered into his camp in the refuge." Quail slumped into his chair, his old fatigue beginning to show. "I should have never told you about all this. I should have never given you those ten names."

Merlin threw his head back and swallowed his brandy, his Adam's apple pitching up and down in his fleshy neck. "You said they could destroy every chance you had of drilling in that caribou-infested refuge. What'd you expect me to do, with our blood oath and all?"

Quail tossed up his hands. "We were school kids back then, for crying out loud. That wasn't a blood oath, it was a silly ritual between two social losers in the eleventh grade."

Merlin's face flushed red. "You've forgotten, haven't you? Everybody teasing us and calling us names? We needed each other back then. Don't tell me about your regrets when I have my own. I'll fight tyranny and environmentalism 'til the day I die."

"They're not the same," Quail shouted.

"Like hell they aren't," Merlin yelled back. "They both destroy a free way of life."

Alexis called from upstairs, "Alan, please come to bed."

Merlin poured another brandy, gulped it and said, "Remember that damn Eskimo, the one at the subcommittee hearing

326

with the ponytail and the limp? They should never have gaveled him down. You gotta let those stupid people talk and hang themselves. They always do. All that crap about living off the caribou and telling stories is bullshit. They live off food stamps and Tyson frozen chicken and watch every soap opera under the sun."

Quail chewed a toothpick.

Merlin burped and said, "Next time I need to get professionals. This business requires world-class European assassins."

Quail stared at him, the toothpick motionless in his mouth. All those years ago two high school boys had found each other as social outcasts often do, in despair, and together sworn they would accomplish great things. That was the beauty and the tragedy of their friendship, for in summitting their own metaphorical mountains each had inflicted more pain than he would ever suffer himself.

"So tell me, my gelding friend," Merlin asked, "what was the real Anwahr test result?"

"Haven't you heard?" Quail said with a wry twist on his mouth. "It's still a secret."

Merlin laughed. "Well you almost pulled it off. Another Congress and another bill and ANZA will get into Anwahr."

"Not ANZA, I'm afraid." Quail looked out the window and saw his troubled reflection.

"You know what, Alan? You've always been afraid of your weaknesses. All these years, that's been your biggest problem."

"You're wrong. It wasn't my weaknesses that frightened me. It was my power."

November

THIRTY-EIGHT

The Wilderness bill arrived on the floor of the U.S. Senate on the Friday before Veterans Day. After six months of amendments and debate, one failed filibuster and no unanimous consents, the bill's Senate and House versions had progressed into conference committee where members from both chambers reached a compromise. Kodiak Jack Worley had attempted to get the ANZA 1002 Exploration Display on the House floor, and failed. He then tried to remove the 1002 Area from the bill and screamed to no avail, "This is absurd. Anwahr doesn't have an environment."

Three days later the Wilderness bill passed the Democrat-controlled House by twenty votes. Now in the Senate, it promised to be close. At least eight senators remained uncommitted. Two or three on each side threatened to switch. And knotted at the center were the ANZA fabrications, the tightly braided rope of corporate lies beginning to unravel. The energy bill had died months ago in House and Senate subcommittees.

With the President scheduled to deliver a speech at Arlington, C-SPAN offered no coverage of this morning's Senate activities. Anybody who wanted to watch the Wilderness vote would need to be seated quietly in the gallery above the chamber.

Shannon arrived early and sat in the fourth row aisle seat, fingering her caribou pendant and holding Mark's hand. The future of her refuge, sunless and frozen thousands of miles away, was about to be decided in this regal chamber on a warm autumn day. To the other side of Mark sat Tony and Rollie, with only Rollie appearing unrested. He had just returned from Atlantic City to finalize his divorce with Angie. *If practice makes perfect, I'm leaving you perfect this time.*

Shannon felt a familiar radiance in the aisle next to her and looked up. "Father Carroll," she said, "what are you doing here?"

He sat in the seat behind her and put his hands on her shoulders. "I'm very sorry about Jude, and Senator Romper. I know this vote means a lot to you. I thought I should be here." The gentle Franciscan shook hands with Tony and Mark, and introduced himself to Rollie. He addressed Mark. "Tony tells me you've turned down a lot of book deals?"

"A dozen," Mark said. The Kitvik Attack had been national headlines for months, with Mark's syndicated newspaper features appearing everywhere. Tabloids and talk shows called daily. Everybody had a deal, an offer, an angle, and Mark was tired of it. All he wanted was time alone with Shannon. They talked about moving to Alaska.

The White House had called the attack "deeply disturbing," and said the architects of the crime would be "found, prosecuted and punished." The FBI had ninety agents on the case, all reporting to Special Agent in Charge Lincoln Crozier.

"How's Frank Beasley?" Mark asked Father Carroll.

"He's fine. You heard that the other three former scouts confessed? It's all connected, isn't it? The Kitvik Attack, Frank and the others, the ANZA fabrications. And your father, Shannon?"

"And Tyler Kyle," Tony added.

Father Carroll asked, "Who's he?"

Mark explained what he and Tony and Shannon knew, which

wasn't much. He added, "The FBI isn't saying a thing."

"So nobody knows where he is?"

"Nope," Tony said. "He disappeared the same day as Carl Zarki."

~

Over his shaved head Kyle wore a white hairpiece; beneath that, a pair of tinted Trumanesque glasses; below that, a thin white moustache that dropped below the corners of his mouth. Skin cream mixed with grit rendered his face, neck and hands into rough sienna, the aged but distinguished sunbelt businessman look. His beige three-piece business suit was lightly padded at the shoulders. His shoes were elevated one inch. He approached the Capitol Building metal detector with a practiced infirmity, back slightly bent, shoulders hunched, head bobbing. His expression showed no fraction of the tension within him, nothing commensurate to his intentions. In one hand he held a briefcase, in the other a cane. At the detector he opened his briefcase, pulled out his laptop computer and set it on the inspection table with the powercord. Inside the computer was a photograph of two little girls, one dressed in peach, the other in pink.

"Grand-daughters?" asked the woman security guard, her rigid demeanor relaxing as she admired the photo.

"Great grand-daughters," the old man answered in a soft voice, his head bobbing up and down. "They bring me luck."

"I'm sure they do. I'm afraid I have to ask you turn on your computer if you want me to hand-inspect it."

"My battery is low. May I plug it in?"

"Fine, please hurry."

He plugged it in, the screen lit up, and she motioned him through. One minute later, while en route to the Senate gallery, Kyle walked past Denali Sisto and looked right at her. She didn't flinch or blink. He was nobody to her, a face of no significance. *Perfect.*

Ringing bells and a series of lights signaled the beginning of the Senate day. The chamber and gallery grew quiet as the senators sat at their small wooden desks. The vice president of the United States was not in attendance, so the majority leader, serving as president pro tempore, accompanied the senate chaplain to the rostrum for opening prayer. At a long marble desk in front of the presiding officer sat the Senate clerks: the journal clerk to record minutes, the parliamentarian to advise members on rules and procedures, and the legislative clerk to call roll and receive bills, resolutions and amendments. On one side of the chamber sat the Republicans, on the other side the Democrats, with the senior members of each party toward the front and center.

Over the chamber door was the inscription:
ANNUIT COEPTIS—GOD HAS FAVORED OUR UNDERTAKINGS.

The majority and minority leaders each gave a ten-minute speech. Morning business then began with senators introducing resolutions and speaking briefly on subjects of their choice. Shannon noticed that many senators were absent, and that others drifted in and out, chatting with colleagues on the same side of the aisle. At 10:50 a.m. the majority leader reminded his colleagues that he wanted to adjourn the body by noon, and they had yet to vote on the Wilderness bill. He departed the chamber, and the majority whip took his position.

Shannon tapped Mark's arm and said, "I don't see Bruce Janstadt or Oliver Longstreet. Where could they be?"

~

Longstreet felt like he might vomit. He put his head into his hands and said, "This can't be true...it can't be."

The fasciculation sent his eye into such twitching that the upper lid fluttered. His left hand covered his face for a moment, hoping perhaps to shut out all light and truth. He took several slow, deep breaths. He was past anger and denial now, slipping into mild shock, his face ashen in contrast to the burgundy bucket seats of the Chevy Suburban. The somber expressions around him offered no reprieve. He lifted his head and studied them: FBI Director Dugald Toll, Deputy Director Liam Bristol and Special Agent Lincoln Crozier. Another FBI man drove the Suburban around Capitol Hill while they talked. Longstreet asked Crozier, "You're sure about all this?"

Crozier nodded. "We hit half a dozen places early this morning in Idaho and Minnesota, and a farmhouse in eastern Maryland where he was staying until two days ago. The Canadian Mounties hit Alberta, where some of the operations were based. We've suspected him for months. Forensics at two crime scenes at the Hotel LaPerouse in Anchorage was pretty conclusive. That's why he disappeared."

"Why didn't you tell me this earlier?"

"We wanted you and everybody else to go about business as usual, hoping it would entice him back into the public. We've made no mention of him being a suspect."

"Tyler Kyle killed John Sires..." Longstreet whispered to nobody in particular, as if the gravity of each word was too great to say aloud. "What do you want from me?"

FBI Director Toll signaled the driver to stop at the Capitol Building. He handed Longstreet a piece of paper and said, "Yesterday eight senators received this e-mail."

Longstreet put on his glasses, hands shaking, and read aloud. "Kill this bill or join this list..." The list was Nelson Romper and Jude Matlin, the two people who were killed on the Kitvik River. He looked at Director Toll. "This is a joke?"

"It's not. Each message ended with some dirty laundry the sender promised to air out on the senator if he didn't obey."

"Dirty laundry?" Longstreet asked.

"Only one man knows this much about all these men," Crozier explained. "We found stolen paper and computer files in his Rockville apartment, including the ones taken from Carl Zarki's home in Anchorage, and traces of plastic explosives. We suspect that he mailed the package bomb to your office in Anchorage in June."

"Tyler Kyle...wanted to kill me?" Longstreet stammered.

"No, he wanted to pull the Alaska State Troopers off the Kitvik rafters and onto you. Did you know that he bugged your office in the Hart Building?"

"Bugged my office? How?"

"With a small voice-activated device under your desk."

Longstreet shook his head and said, "I have to get into the chamber. There's a vote going on."

"The majority leader is waiting for you in his office," Director Toll said.

"The majority leader?"

Toll nodded solemnly. "Special Agent Crozier will accompany you. We'll be in touch, senator. Thank you for your cooperation."

The driver exited, walked around the vehicle and opened the door for Longstreet.

The senator popped down a heart pill. Deputy Director Bristol offered him bottled water but Longstreet waved it off, feeling feisty, a new wave of denial. *Goddamn FBI, the same bastards who ruined innocent lives at Waco and Ruby Ridge and now they want to ruin mine.* He climbed to his feet and began to ascend the white steps of the Capitol Building. Crozier walked abreast of him. Longstreet became quickly winded and said something about not getting much exercise in his line of work.

"Maybe you should find another line of work," Crozier said.

Longstreet turned on him and put a finger to his chest. "Don't you mock me, mister. I'm a United States senator. I chair Appropriations. I've given forty-five years to the service of my country. I was fighting in the ice and mud in Korea when you were on your mama's floor in diapers. Back off and give me the respect I deserve."

For a brief moment Crozier considered handcuffing him, then

thought better of it.

Ten minutes later Longstreet received his second upbraiding, this one in the majority leader's office, as Crozier knew he would. He listened from just outside the door and enjoyed every minute of it.

"We have a potential crisis in the Senate, don't we, Oliver?" the majority leader asked.

"You've spoken to the FBI?"

"Oh yes. We've been—"

"I didn't know a damn thing about Tyler Kyle and his secret agenda."

"Didn't you? Not a thing?"

"I didn't—"

"Save your breath, Oliver. You might regret anything you say about this until you have legal counsel."

"So what do you want from me?"

"No Appropriations blackmail," Bruce Janstadt said from behind him. Longstreet turned to see the lanky Minnesotan leaning against the wall, his arms across his chest, his face grim.

Longstreet sat down.

The vice president of the United States stood with Janstadt. He opened a door and seven senators entered the room, all of whom, until this morning, were undecided votes on the Wilderness bill, and had received the threatening e-mail from a mystery source the FBI believed to be Tyler Kyle.

Longstreet asked, "What's going on?"

"We have a sympathy vote here, Oliver," Janstadt said as he swept his arm toward the seven senators. "We want to pass this bill and name the 1002 Area the Nelson Romper Wilderness, but not if other legislation in this Congress is held hostage in Appropriations. We thought you could put our fears to rest."

Longstreet stared at them, the eye twitching, the fingers jittering up and down.

The majority leader knelt at his side. "Oliver, listen, if the FBI and senate ethics finds you innocent of criminal complicity, then each senator here will testify that to the best of his knowledge you were unaware of any secret illegalities by any member of your staff."

"It's true." Longstreet grabbed him by the lapel of his suit. "I didn't know a thing. I really didn't."

"Well, there you go," Janstadt said. "Do we have a deal?" He looked at the majority leader, who looked at the vice president, who looked at Longstreet, a desperate man.

For the first time in months, after dozens of stakeouts and hundreds of late nights, Lincoln Crozier smiled. His friend Shannon DeShay just might get her arctic wilderness.

~

The majority leader and the vice president took their positions in the chamber. Senator Janstadt had requested a silent roll call vote, so the legislative clerk began calling names alphabetically as each senator gave thumbs up to support the Wilderness bill, or thumbs down to oppose it. Shannon squeezed Mark's hand.

"Ambridge?" the clerk announced.

Thumbs up.

"Atchison?"

Thumbs down.

"Aude?"

Thumbs up.

"Balznic?"

Thumbs down.

Shannon shifted in her seat. If the vote tied, the vice president would break it and pass the bill with thumbs up.

"Bennett?"

Senator Bennett was not in the chamber. The clerk moved on. Senators who did not respond the first time would be called in a second round. Tony kept score with pen and paper.

Ten rows behind, an elderly man stepped through the door

from the hallway. A security guard stopped him and whispered, "I'm sorry, sir. The gallery is full. You'll have to wait outside until somebody leaves."

Kyle noticed the back of Kelly Calvert's head in the front row of the gallery. He stepped back into the hall and dialed her, leaving his number for a return call. He knew the dutiful woman would not let a minute pass without checking her pager, and when she saw it was Tyler Kyle, whom nobody had heard from in months, she would dial him immediately, wild with curiosity. To do so she would have to leave the gallery. Sure enough, within a minute she walked out in mid-vote, right past Kyle, her phone in her hand, frantically pushing numbers on the keypad.

The guard motioned Kyle through. "There you go, sir. First row. You need help down those steps?"

"Ah no, I'm fine." Kyle walked down the steps, lightly tapping his cane, and sat in the first row, three ahead of Shannon on the other side of the aisle. He pulled a small computer from his briefcase, put it on his lap and lifted the screen.

The first round ended with thirty-seven yeas and forty nays.

Shannon noticed that none of the undecided senators were present for the first round. Neither was Janstadt, Longstreet or Matlin. The elderly man wrapped one leg tightly around the other as the second round of voting began.

"Bennett?"

Thumbs up.

"Drummund?"

Thumbs down, emphatically.

Half a dozen senators entered the chamber to cast their votes, but still no Janstadt or Longstreet. The yeas pulled to within one vote as the elderly man opened his computer battery pack. The screen, still upright on his lap, remained off. Shannon could see on the dark surface the ghosted reflection of a face that was distant yet familiar.

"Matlin?"

Sam Matlin stood. Everybody knew that he had suffered a

terrible loss on the Kitvik River. They also knew parliamentary procedure prohibited him from speaking in the middle of a vote. He took a deep breath. "I've been told that the Arctic National Wildlife Refuge is an honest place..."

Oh, shut up, Kyle thought as he discreetly removed the homemade pistol from the computer battery pack, shielding his hands with his upper body, pushing the clip into the grip.

"...I think my Jude found that honesty. Go up there and sleep on the ground and you will too. You might think—"

The gavel came down and the vice president said, "Senator, we sympathize with you and appreciate what you want to share with us here today, but this is not the right time or place. I have to ask you to cast your vote and relinquish your time."

Matlin gave thumbs up and sat down.

Shannon bit her lip. Mark squeezed her hand.

"McDowell?"

Thumbs down.

"Mirosnikov?"

Thumbs down.

Ten more votes and the nays were ahead by two. Shannon felt herself on the tundra again, the drumming of running caribou, the arctic heartbeat and heartbreak.

The strange man four rows ahead caught her eye as he set his computer on the floor and leaned forward onto the gallery rail, his back tight, like an archer's bow. The drumming deepened, not on tundra but on rock, intrusive igneous crystals of feldspar and diorite, a man of guile and façade. *Who? Why...?*

The third and final round of voting would involve only two senators. Janstadt retained the right to go last, since it was his bill. The clerk called, "Longstreet?"

Murmurs rippled through the chamber and gallery as Longstreet, looking ill, stood and stabilized himself with a hand on his desk. Certainly he would give thumbs down.

The man in the gallery leaned over the rail and focused on Bruce Janstadt thirty feet below.

Shannon froze with fear. *Exfoliating granite, layers peeling away as he executed his careful calculus.* A gasp was heard as Longstreet gave thumbs up. Shannon shook Mark's arm and said, "That man in the first row, on the aisle where Kelly Calvert was sitting, I think he's Tyler Kyle."

"What?" Mark answered, distracted by Longstreet's vote.

"That old guy, there. That's Tyler Kyle." Her own words seemed sluggish to her. She looked up the aisle for a security guard just as Lincoln Crozier entered the gallery. His face changed the instant his eyes met hers.

The clerk called, "Janstadt?"

"It's Tyler Kyle," Shannon said loudly, pointing.

Kyle heard his name as he pulled out the pistol and aimed. But it was not Janstadt he saw below. It was a face flying up from the black Idaho basalt, dreamlike, carried on the broken body of his brother. The eyes hollow. The smell of wet sage. The voice, *Why did you push me?*

Kyle hesitated.

A woman screamed, "He's got a gun."

Crozier took two leaps down the aisle steps and threw himself at Kyle as he turned and fired. The plastic bullet entered Crozier's shoulder and passed one inch from his heart. But his size and momentum slammed Kyle into the gallery rail and knocked the gun from his hand. Shannon and Mark rushed him and kicked the gun away as a nearby spectator hit Kyle hard on the head with a briefcase. Suddenly five people were on him, restraining him. Two security guards handcuffed him.

On the chamber floor below, the vice president and ninety-six senators stared into the gallery with mute disbelief. Bruce Janstadt did thumbs up, tying the vote. The vice president gave thumbs up and called for immediate evacuation of the chamber and gallery.

The guards jerked Kyle to his feet and up the aisle steps. He skidded to a stop opposite Shannon and looked at her with eyes like shark's eyes. She picked up his broken glasses, folded them and slipped them into his coat pocket. He said, "You really think you can save the earth, don't you?"

"When caribou cross a river," she replied, "they never give up."

EPILOGUE

(two years later)

Two hundred people attended Lincoln Crozier's retirement party, most of them FBI. Among the exceptions were Shannon and Mark, who flew to Washington from Alaska, where they now lived in a cabin thirty miles north of Juneau. When Crozier offered Shannon a handshake, she responded with a hug and was surprised how long he held onto her. He told her that with twenty-eight years of service behind him, and his daughters finished with college, it was time for a change.

Shannon and Mark declined invitations from friends and stayed instead in a hotel where they could order room service, take a double bath and watch a movie. That night, her first back in Washington in a long time, Shannon fell into a dream.

Travis laughs and she laughs with him, a silly sibling laugh. The harder they try to stop, like kids in church, the funnier it becomes. He rolls on the tundra and seems so at home, so rooted, perennial. That night in camp he plays his old guitar, A Song for Shannon. Gaelic beat. The notes riffle and braid. She lies on her back and clasps her hands behind her head and watches mid-

night fill the valley with gold and vermilion light.

Dad returns like a wolf, one moment nowhere in view, the next close by. The music weaves river and sky, the air grows cool, but Travis plays on, his fingers cold. When he stops, he says nothing. He looks at his father for approval, then at the mountains and beyond. Dad says, That's fine music, Trav.

They share dinner. Dad talks about arctic time, how for him it is measured in the presence and absence of things, freezing and thawing, living and dying, things circular and whole.

—Life is linear for most people, says Travis.

—So is time, Dad says. But up here, for me, it's circular. The end becomes the beginning. All we have is the rest of our tender years.

Later, Shannon and Travis walk along the river and he asks her, What was Dad saying back there? That he isn't afraid to die?

—I don't know, Trav.

They skip stones, and after awhile he asks, Is this who you always wanted me to be, Shan? Am I a good brother now?

She jolted awake. Mark held her close, as the hotel room offered nothing familiar beyond his embrace. "It was Travis in the refuge," she said. *The Travis who never was.*

Mark said, "On the way home, maybe we should make that visit we talked about."

~

Shannon stood in the visiting room of the minimum-security internment facility, reluctant to sit down. She trusted herself and everything else more on her feet now. William Alt entered through a door on the far side and didn't recognize her at first, but when he did, a faint brightness filled his face. He tried to mask it as he approached her. "Hello," he said.

Each was uncertain what to say. The guard told them they had an hour, and Shannon thought, *An hour? What will we do with an hour?*

No shatterproof glass or phones. Just tables and chairs, four bare walls and this tragic man. Shannon began to second-guess her coming here. Still standing, William averted his eyes.

She asked how he was. Fine, he said. He asked the same of her. Fine. She put her hands on the backrest of a chair. He noticed the ring. "You got married?"

"Yes, in Alaska, six months ago."

He nodded beneath a bent posture older than his years.

"Sam Matlin gave me away at the wedding, since he...well, he lost his own daughter."

William looked at his feet. "I'm sorry about that...on the river...those people."

Forgive him, Shannon told herself. She shifted her weight and said, "William..." —she's never called him by his name; she never knew his name— "I was wondering if you would tell me about my brother."

He lifted his heavy head. "Me? I didn't know him that well."

"Neither did I."

He reached over and offered her a chair, and she sat down. "How much time do we have?" he asked.

"One hour," Shannon said. *And the rest of my tender years.*

ACKNOWLEDGMENTS

Many people read drafts of this story, or isolated scenes, and offered important criticisms. A heartfelt thanks to my writer's group-in-the-rain: Abigail Calkin, Judith Challoner-Wood, Carol Dejka, Lynne Morrow and Sally Lesh who made me laugh and bribed me with sweets. Other proofreaders gave valuable assistance in their related fields: Greg Streveler, the best naturalist I know; Paul Barnes, a tireless hiker of the Brooks Range and a sensitive fisherman of Icy Strait halibut; Jack and Hank Lentfer, father and son deer hunters and defenders of all that is good and wild in Alaska, Anya Maier, a dedicated Juneau family physician and a picker of berries and maker of jams, juices and pies; John Toppenberg, a retired Colorado detective who reinvented himself as an Alaska wildlife photographer; Carolyn Elder, who moved to Oregon and took her lyrical ways with her; Susan Ruddy, former Alaska Regional Director of The Nature Conservancy; Doug Pfeiffer, publisher and editor who has always believed in me; Ross Eberman, who told me that first novels are impossible and to never give up; and Lynn Schooler, Dean Littlepage and Mark Schlenz, good friends and writers who deserve every success.

A special bow of gratitude to writers Hilary Hilscher and Nick Jans who treated my manuscript like a master's thesis. "You must work harder," Nick told me. "You just don't want to be published, you want to be good. After all the work you've already done, what's a few dozen or hundred hours more?" Whatever weaknesses or shortcomings remain are mine alone.

Along the way several literary agents showed interest and faith in this project: Perry Knowlton, Peter Matson, Andrew Pope, Nicole Aragi, Liza Dawson (who at the time was an editor at Putnam), Aaron Priest and Jenny Bent. Special thanks to Perry and Jenny.

Few parents today would take their young children camping in the Arctic. I know of two families who broke that rule and so inspired me: Roy and Kim Corral with their daughter Hannah and son Ben, and Dennis and Debbie Miller with their daughters Robin and Casey.

Bob Dittrick and Lisa Moorehead of Wilderness Birding Adventures introduced me to the rivers of the Arctic National Wildlife Refuge, and perhaps, like Shannon DeShay, I've never been the same since. If whatever liberties I've taken with the cultural and/or natural histories of the refuge offend anyone, my apologies.

I found several non-fiction books of great value during my research, most notably: *Women Who Run With The Wolves* by Clarissa Pinkola Estes, *A Necessary Evil* by Garry Wills, *Make Prayers to the Raven* by Richard K. Nelson, *The Power Game* by Hedrick Smith, *The Gift of Fear* by Gavin De Becker, *Arctic Dreams* by Barry Lopez, *The Prize* by Daniel Yergin, and *The Tibetan Book of Living and Dying* by Sogyal Rinpoche.

I would also like to make note of Ken Follett's novels and how they inspired me to create a young woman protagonist who, when faced with a severe challenge, must reach deep inside herself and find a strength she didn't know was there. I think specifically of Aliena in *The Pillars of the Earth*, and Charlotte in *The Man From St. Petersburg*.

Thanks to Edward Bovy at Greatland Graphics in Anchorage for his help and sponsorship over the years.

Every writer should be blessed with a publisher who writes to him or her, as Jane Freeburg wrote to me, "Thanks again for your vision, inspiration, and for trusting me with your heart's work."

And to Melanie, my loving wife, who has more integrity than anyone I know, this is for you and your deep regard for Alaska.

KIM HEACOX

AUTHOR'S NOTE

I began this story in September 1992 and finished the first draft in April 1995, an 810-page manuscript I called *An Honest Place*. The ending concerned me. I thought it might be too extreme. But that same day news broke of the tragic bombing of the federal building in Oklahoma City, and later that Americans, not Islamic terrorists, were responsible. I researched the psychology of zealotry and found that the unprecedented, horrible act is precisely what terrorists do. They live overseas, but also next door.

Over five more years and many more drafts I cut the manuscript down to 360 pages, and renamed it *Caribou River*. During this time the Republicans swept into power in the U.S. House and Senate, and Alaska's Congressional Delegation gained three powerful committee chairmanships. The U.S. Geological Survey raised its estimates for the amount of oil in the Arctic National Wildlife Refuge, and the delegation introduced bills and riders to open the Refuge to drilling. Grassroots environmentalism, national campaigns, and the Clinton Administration stopped them.

As I write this, the Clinton Presidency closes after the United States' wildest election of the Twentieth Century. The Senate stands split 50-50. A new century opens as George W. Bush takes the White House under a cloud of illegitimacy. Having lost the popular vote to Al Gore, Bush was handed the electoral vote by a U. S. Supreme Court decision of 5 to 4. "Although we may never know with complete certainty the identity of the winner in this year's Presidential election," wrote Justice John Paul Stevens in his dissent, "the loser is perfectly clear. It is the Nation's confidence in the judge as an impartial guardian of the rule of the law."

While President Bush calls for opening the Arctic National Wildlife Refuge to oil drilling amid a U. S. "energy crisis," Americans sail on a sea of prosperity, bumper to bumper (usually one person per vehicle), as the climate warms and gasline prices rise.

What then becomes of the Arctic National Wildlife Refuge? Is the issue about oil, energy, security, jobs, and power? Or is it about the limits of our respect for the larger-than-human world?

Critics say that fiction should not be ideology, at least not somebody else's ideology. "Fiction is like a spider's web," said Virginia Woolf, "attached ever so slightly perhaps, but still attached to life at all four corners."

Some spiders catch more than they bargained for. Some catch nothing at all.

–Kim Heacox
January, 2001